ALL THE SECRETS WITHIN US

JADE LE BRIS

JADE LE BRIS
ALL THE SECRETS WITHIN US

This is a work of fiction. Names, characters, places, and incidents are products of the author's imagination or are used factiously and are not to be construed as real. Any resemblance to actual events, organizations, and persons, whether living or dead, is entirely coincidental.

First published in 2024 by Jade Le Bris.

Copyright © 2024 Jade Le Bris

All rights reserved. No part of this publication may be reproduced or used without the author's approval.

Paperback IBSN: 979-8-9884041-4-9
eBook ISBN: 979-8-9884041-5-6

Content Warnings

'All the Secrets Within Us' is a New Adult fantasy book about two young women who are trying to figure out how to live after winning a deadly tournament on Mount Olympus. While fun, this story also contains elements that might not be suited to some readers. Swearing, hate speech, fighting, and violence are present on-page in the book. Death is mentioned but happens off-page. Readers who may be sensitive to these elements, please take note.

Previous works by the author

Claiming Olympus duology:
All the Gold Between Us (book 1)

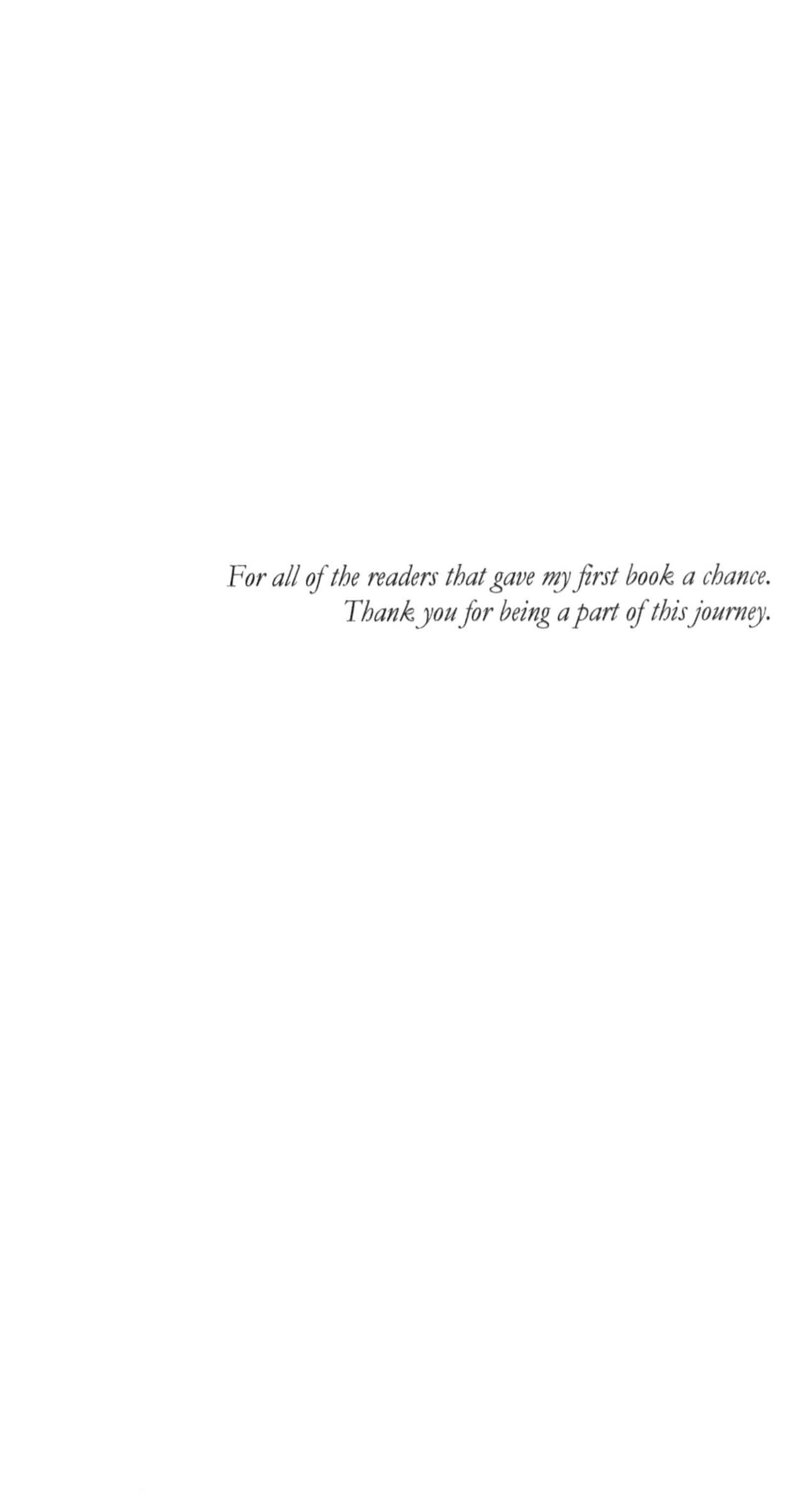

For all of the readers that gave my first book a chance.
Thank you for being a part of this journey.

Chapter One

Kalani

Life on Olympus was very different from what I'd imagined. The version of myself from three months ago would have laughed if someone had told her I would end up living among the Greek gods and goddesses on Mount Olympus. To be fair, if one of the Hunters on Zeus's payroll hadn't mistaken me for a Copper – one of the gods' grandchildren – then I would still be living with my mom and little brother on Earth, juggling classes with my jobs, still blissfully ignorant of the existence of magic.

Unfortunately, because of someone's terrible mistake, I had been magicked onto Mount Olympus and forced to fight against forty other deities' grandchildren in a Tournament, all to win my spot on the sacred mountain and be allowed to live. And, against all odds, I had managed to survive deadly trials and gods trying to prove that humans had nothing to do on their turf. To be honest, I never would have survived without the help of my newly-found friends – Archer, Sadie, and Søren. And Mei too.

Mei who hadn't survived the last trial. Her death had shattered our friend group to the point that even the Aska twins didn't talk to each other anymore.

I could have gone back to Earth after I'd won that last trial. Hecate, the goddess of magic, had offered to try and remove the memory-erasing spell that had been put on my family and friends. Gods knew I missed Makaio, my little brother. However, she couldn't be certain there wouldn't be any side effects, such as scrambling their minds. And, after seeing them together, happy without me… I couldn't do this to them. I couldn't risk their happiness.

Now here I was, back in a land that wasn't particularly welcoming to humans, desperately trying to find my place. Who would have thought that I would end up photographing a fashion model with magical powers as if this was normal, as if I'd always been a part of this magical world?

"Honey, can you turn a little more to the left?" Priya Vasilias's voice was soft but firm, gentle but uncompromising. The model did not hesitate before turning to please her boss. Wanting to please Priya Vasilias was like an unshakable force, driving everyone to follow her orders.

"See there, Kalani? How the shape of the dress flatters her curves and gives her an ethereal feel? The open back is just enough to be flattering without revealing too much. And the texture of the material is the perfect combination of light and silky." Priya moved around the model, her eyes assessing in a clinical and professional manner. "I might have to fix the stitching on the sides, but it should be good enough for a few pictures right now."

Nodding quickly, I wiped my sweaty palms on my jeans — I was blaming it on the heat, not the stress from this internship with my boyfriend's mother — and grabbed the camera. Could it even be called a camera? I wasn't sure. The machine could generate hologram pictures and wasn't anything like my old vintage — not the expensive kind — camera.

You might wonder how I ended up interning as a photographer for Aphrodite's fashion company. Thing was, not many of the skills I'd learned over my twenty-one years of life could be easily transferred to a life on Olympus. There were almost no kids on the mountain, and the few that did live here preferred to learn to fight rather than practice gymnastics. My bartending skills wouldn't help me much seeing as every party was pretty much manned by Dionysus and his Golden children. And the decent biological knowledge I had on marine biology from my college degree was not going to take me far on a mountain surrounded by a sea of clouds.

Thus, the only thing that was somewhat useful was my little side hobby of photographing memories. Priya, being the amazing woman that she was, immediately offered to take me under her wing, and as lead fashion designer for Colors of Beauty, Aphrodite's clothing brand, she was officially offering me an internship three hours later.

Trying to ignore the fact that the magical camera felt like the most expensive and futuristic gadget ever, I tried my best to pretend like I knew what I was doing. After squatting down a little until I reached the perfect angle, I adjusted the camera and then pressed the knob to take the picture. Thus, ensued an awkward half-minute when I slowly walked, half-crouched, around the model to capture her image under every angle. By the time I finally got back to my initial position, my thighs were on fire and I was well on my way to despising those hologram pictures more than I used to hate panoramic pictures on phones on Earth – you know, the ones that would look like shit if your hand so much as slightly shook.

By the time I was done, Priya was already focused on a new garment, this one a fancy toga that looked like it would melt any second. She had decided earlier today that it didn't look perfect and was probably going to spend the next few hours working on making it the most stunning piece of clothing ever.

"Thank you for your work today, Kalani," she exclaimed as I stood up and my back cracked. The Golden with the power of innovation gave me a soft smile and I was caught in this weird place, half relieved that she was letting me go after the long day, and half worried because I wanted to impress her. And I didn't just want to impress her because she was Archer's mom – no, this lady was strong, independent, loving, and had an amazing career. I wanted to be like her when I grew up.

Five minutes later, I was striding out of the museum-looking building that housed Aphrodite's luxury brand. The sun, perfectly warm without burning my eyes, and the usual nice breeze were refreshing after the long day indoors.

"How was your day?"

Unsurprisingly, Archer was there, leaning against the wall, arms crossed over his chest, looking hot as hell. To be fair, though, I hadn't ever seen Archer looking anything less than inhumanely handsome.

"Are you planning on babysitting me every day, Sunshine?" I raised an eyebrow in mock annoyance but still rose on my tiptoes to press a kiss to his lips. One of his hands snaked around my neck, the other gripped my hip, and he brought me closer until our bodies were flushed together. What was meant as a welcoming peck was turning into a lot more. Suddenly, I wasn't annoyed about his overprotective act anymore, and all I wanted was to get more of his passionate kisses.

That man was addictive.

And even though we'd been doing this whole dating thing for three weeks now, every kiss was like the first time – addicting and new and mind-blowing.

I knew he was playing with me and trying to make me forget my earlier question. Archer knew damn well I was weak when it came to him.

Ripping myself away from his lips was harder than it should have been. "Stop that. I see what you're doing."

"Mayfield, come on," he complained, then kissed the side of my neck, and I was *this close* to yielding. "I missed you today. I should have insisted you came to work with me."

He continued to kiss the column of my neck and my brain was working very hard to not drown in him. It took every bit of self-control I had to put a hand on his chest and push myself away. Cheeks flushed and breathing a little harder than I liked, I did my best to look stern as I glared at him.

"Fine," he sighed and rolled his eyes. Then he became a lot more serious. "You know we have to be careful. I can't let something happen to you."

Again. I could hear that word loud and clear, even though he hadn't said it out loud. And now I couldn't be mad at him for his overprotective act because I knew he still beat himself up over what had happened three weeks ago, at the end of the fourth trial. A shudder ran through me at the thought of how close I'd come to dying that day.

"You know it wasn't your fault. We've talked about that."

Archer's jaw ticked and his arms tensed around me. We both knew it had been Elena who had stabbed me after I'd won fair and square, but he still blamed himself for not being there to prevent it. And no matter how often I reminded him that he'd been the one to bargain with his dad, Zeus, to save me, he couldn't rid himself of the guilt.

"We both know some people have been watching you, and I don't want to give anyone the opportunity to do anything they would regret." Without another word, Archer took my hand and started walking.

I thought about arguing, but he was right. Life had been abnormally calm these past three weeks since we had both won the Tournament, but I knew damn well that many people on Mount Olympus weren't happy that a human was now living among them. That included many Gods and Goddesses, such as Artemis who had tried her hardest to make sure I died during the trials. And while no one had attempted anything since the Tournament had ended, I was sure that the dissent and hate were still there, hidden away until people started to feel safe enough to let it out.

I had gone too far, sacrificed too much, to stop making smart decisions now. So, as much as I wanted to be independent and walk home alone, I could see Archer's point.

Deciding to drop the issue, I intertwined my fingers with Archer's and chose to tackle another issue. "Have you talked to the twins today?"

"Søren, in passing. He's still acting like we're friendly acquaintances and finding excuses to leave every time I try to breach serious topics. And Sadie…" Archer swallowed hard, staring straight ahead. "She still hasn't shown up to work."

I could feel a weight on my chest at his words. Sadie had quickly become my best friend over the eight weeks we had trained together. Eight weeks might have seemed short, but near-death experiences had a way of bringing people together. Her disappearance and choice to isolate herself after the way everything had ended… it hurt me, so I couldn't even imagine how Archer felt after having been friends with her for years.

I knew she was hurting. I didn't need to talk to her to know that. Mei's death had been unfair and had broken all of us up like a hammer breaking glass. But I knew what had truly broken her was Søren's reaction – the way he'd refused to look at her after Mei had yielded. Losing her twin had been too much for her. And I wished I could take her in my arms and reassure her that everything would be fine. Because it would. Eventually. It had to be.

"Have you heard where she might be staying?" I wasn't even sure why I asked, I already knew the answer.

"No. It's like she disappeared. And Søren keeps pretending like he doesn't care. I want to shake him, so he wakes up. He knows damn well this was an impossible situation."

I understood the frustration in his voice. There was absolutely no way the fourth trial could have ended up fine for Søren. Sadie and Mei had been paired together, which meant one of them had to die. Mei had decided to yield on her own, and now he was mad at Sadie for letting it happen. But if the situation had been reversed, I couldn't imagine him being okay with that either. There was no winning this.

And Archer was stuck in the middle, especially since Zeus had allowed the twins' dad, Thanatos, to save me. Søren had begged the gods to save Mei. And he hadn't succeeded.

Now, everything had shattered – our friendship, our family, our trust in each other.

And I wasn't sure how we would ever be able to mend the shards of our lives together.

Chapter Two

Sadie

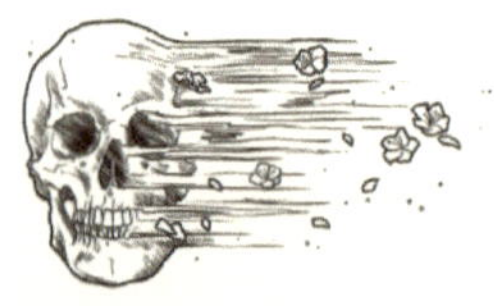

Getting drunk with ambrosia did not make me reach the level of shitty I was aiming for. See, ambrosia tasted like a dream, and all I wanted was to drown deeper into my nightmare. That was what my life had gotten to lately – a living nightmare.

I wished I still had some of that terrible vodka from the last time the guys and I had bribed one of Hermes' sons to take us to Earth for a day. That thought made my heart clench. Stars, I missed my friends.

Refusing to let my nostalgic thoughts win, I gulped another long sip of ambrosia. The liquid was sweet, delicious, and was taking a little too long to drown my thoughts.

"Are you going to drink yourself into a stupor again?"

I scoffed and took another drink. "As if you haven't joined me almost every night."

Nafula didn't deny it and simply took a seat next to me. She had changed a lot since the first time we had met, during the

Tournament. The Copper had been one of the six *lucky winners*, and she now carried the weight of her actions in the Pit like a veil of pain over her eyes. She smiled and she joked around, but there was a heaviness to her soul.

Just like the Tournament had weighed down my soul and that of my friends.

We hadn't talked about it, but I could tell that Nafula was still haunted by the last trial of the Tournament, when she'd drowned her opponent on dry land. It was written on her face the same way my role in Mei's death was tattooed on my heart.

Both of us stared at the sea of clouds that surrounded Olympus, admiring the beauty of our world and just how isolated we were. The view was so beautiful it often brought tears to my eyes. But the endless emptiness on the horizon was a constant reminder that there was no escaping Olympus.

Ever.

The thought was depressing. Especially in my current situation. I would sacrifice a lot to be able to leave this forsaken place. Not *anything* – I still loved my friends and family, there was no stopping that, – but I would be willing to go to extreme lengths to leave the mountain.

And I guessed I had gone to pretty long lengths, hadn't I?

"Are you going to talk about it?"

I heard Nafula's words but didn't turn her way. She was going to try to change my mind. I knew that. And watching her would only make this conversation harder.

"There isn't much to say anymore, is there?"

Nafula scoffed and I could easily imagine her eyes rolling so far that she'd almost blind herself. Who would have thought that Nafula, granddaughter of Poseidon, and I, daughter of Thanatos, would become friends? Waking up one day alone in the world with blood on our hands might have had a role in bringing us together.

"Are you going to play it that way then? Stubborn woman." Nafula sounded annoyed but I knew she was grumbling because she cared. It felt good to have someone who cared and stood by me – it just wasn't enough anymore.

"It's done, I signed the papers earlier today." I couldn't suppress a cynical laugh and moved my arms out in a sign for the sea of clouds. "I present you the newest Huntress on Olympus!"

I finally shifted to look to my left and Nafula was staring at me, dumbfounded. Her ambrosia bottle was hanging limply at her side and I seemed to have finally rendered her speechless. That would have been a first. The woman was a spitfire – her emotions were as wild as the most dangerous river. It was beautiful, really, the way she imbodied her power, her element, so well. She was as beautiful as the stillest lake water, as strong as a tsunami, and as gentle as a spring rain. Maybe her complexities were what had drawn me to her. She was as intoxicating as a cool drink in the middle of the desert.

In another world, another life, she and I might have been more. We had tried it a couple of weeks back. We hooked up. We fooled around. It was more than great. But Nafula wanted a stable life. She wanted a girlfriend who was there once she came back from her lifeguarding shifts every night. She wanted someone who would build a life with her.

I wanted to escape my life.

It was easier for both of us to remain friends. And Nafula was a great friend. She did her best to fill the void that loosing Søren, Archer, Kalani, and Mei had opened in my chest.

The issue was that I wasn't sure there was a way to heal that hole.

"I thought you said that you were thinking about it." Nafula's voice was shaky, causing my heart to twist in my chest.

I wasn't sure how to explain my decision to Nafula. It wasn't that I wanted to go and gather up young Coppers to bring them to the training compound and force them to fight to their death for a right to live on Olympus. No, I hated everything this job stood for and I had never thought that I'd ever become a Huntress. But becoming one would allow me to leave Olympus. And the need I had to leave this place was so big that it was a living, breathing thing in my chest. It clawed at my ribcage and prevented me from breathing.

"I need to leave. I—" I stopped short and took another sip of ambrosia, hoping the alcohol would drown the shame rising in my chest. "I *have* to leave this place."

There was no other choice, really. If I stayed here, on Olympus, I would wither and die under the mountain of shame, guilt, and self-hatred that kept on growing. I had to go. As fast and as far as I could. Even if it went against everything the old me – the *before* me – believed in.

"I know. I hate it, but I know." Nafula let a beat go past before continuing. "I can't see you as a Huntress. All of that undying loyalty to the thrones…" she trailed off and mimed throwing up. I couldn't suppress a laugh at her words.

"I'll practice my kiss-the-godly-asses face in front of my mirror tonight."

"You might need more than one practice session. Defiance is written all over your face."

I couldn't deny it. Society on Olympus had always seemed wrong to me. But after the past few months? Stars, there weren't enough words to express how much I despised this world.

Silence stretched between us. It was comfortable. Nafula and I clicked that way. It reminded me of Kalani and I – two great friends who could talk about anything while still enjoying each other's silent presence. Stars knew I missed her.

"I am going to miss you."

The pain in her voice was a knife to the heart. Yet another one. Somehow, I couldn't stop disappointing the people I cared for.

I turned her direction and watched the way the pink and orange lights reflected off of her face. She was stunning, and for a second, I had the urge to kiss her. The urge to stay with her, if only for a little bit more. But I knew deep in my soul that going to Earth was the best thing I could do for myself.

"I'll be back. And in the meantime, I know you'll be fine. No one can resist your smile."

"Usually when someone says, 'I'll miss you,' it's polite to say it back."

"Stop being a pain in my ass."

"Oh, trust me, I am going to be *such* a pain in your ass, you'll feel me all the way on Earth."

I scoffed and shook my head at her words. Fair enough.

The next morning, I was fighting a headache while standing at attention in front of my superior. The leather armor I now had to wear as uniform wasn't as squeaky as I had expected, but it was much tighter than my usual clothes – it was uncomfortable, especially as the hangover made my skin hypersensitive.

"Huntress Aska, your first mission has been moved up on the planning. You're leaving tomorrow."

I couldn't suppress a surprised sound. My first mission? Already? I had literally signed up the day before.

"Sir, I thought new Hunters and Huntresses had to undergo specialized training before being allowed on Earth."

Kellan, the Golden who was my new boss, was one of Hermes's sons. The guy looked more like one of Ares's though – all muscles and dark aura. Most of all though, Kellan looked annoyed. Hopefully, he was annoyed at the situation and not at me.

"Yes," he sighed. "Training is usually required. However, special circumstances have made it so that you were chosen to go on mission early. As you might know, few Golden decide to join, it's usually mostly Coppers. Someone high in the chain of command decided a Golden might help solve an… issue we've had with one of our targets."

"An issue," I prodded, my eyebrows raising in question. I had hoped for an easy enough job, not to be put on the toughest missions right away.

"Yes. One Copper has evaded three Hunters so far. None of them have been able to remain close to him for long enough to use their transportation devices successfully."

Kellan's words made me pause. Either the Hunters were supremely undertrained, or the Copper was extremely powerful. None of this made me want to go and follow in the footsteps of my colleagues.

"What happened?"

Ensued a long silence during which Kellan looked both mortified and angry, clearly still strung up on why three of his employees had failed.

"The Copper is a grandson of Melinoë. You know each other, right?"

I shrugged because sure, I had met the daughter of Hades and Persephone multiple times. After all, dad worked in the Underworld with her parents. However, the goddess of madness and nightmares was not the kind of person you could get to know easily. She was slightly paranoid and had some of the worst mood swings I'd seen on Olympus.

"Well, he has inherited an interesting combination of powers from Melinoë and Persephone. He can grow plants that are both carnivorous and venomous, causing their infected preys to become mad. So far, one Hunter was killed and the other two were infected – they are both still restrained at the infirmary, so they don't attempt to kill themselves or others in their madness."

What a shitshow.

"And you expect me to go in and save the day?"

"We expect you to step up and do the job you signed up for," Kellan snapped, crossing his arms over his broad chest. "And the guy won't be able to kill your zombies now, will he?"

Fair enough.

"You don't have a choice, Huntress. If it's any consolation, Asclepius is working on the antivenom and doesn't believe the madness caused by the Copper's powers will remain permanent."

Sure, that made me feel *so* much better. I had no desire whatsoever to go after this rogue Copper but, to be fair, that was the job I had agreed upon. Plus, a tough mission would mean more time on Earth – more time away from here.

"Alright. Where am I going?"

"France."

Chapter Three

Sadie

The first time I'd used my powers, I'd been twelve. Before that, I had known I'd been different – not all kids were able to see ghosts or had a dad who could control death. I had always had that link with death itself. Interacting with the dead had brought me and dad closer together. But I hadn't used my powers over dead bodies until that day, in the middle of summer.

Søren and I lived with our mom on Earth, in a small town in Denmark. Dad would visit every so often, but he wasn't able to stay with us. I had begged my mom for months to have a pet – a few of my friends at school had one and I was so jealous. On the first day of that summer, she had finally given up and bought me a guinea pig. I'd called him Ben.

I had loved him so much. I had played with him and fed him and watched him run on his little wheel. Søren hated the sounds he made every night, but I enjoyed knowing that there was a little being that counted on me in this world.

He'd died after two months. None of us knew why. One night I'd gone to bed after playing with him, and the next morning, he wasn't breathing anymore.

I'd been heartbroken.

I wasn't sure how it actually happened. Somehow, in between my tears, I'd used magic. And Ben's little body had moved.

At first, I'd been ecstatic because my sweet little Ben was back. But then I had remembered – using godly powers meant having to leave Earth. I didn't want to leave my mom and I didn't want to go to Olympus without Søren, who hadn't shown any signs of magic yet.

So, I hid. I hid my magic and buried it so far down that, by the time I was fifteen, everyone thought I was a dud. The daughter of a Primordial God who couldn't do anything more than see ghosts. How disappointing.

I could have gone on like this for years, hiding my powers from everyone. I didn't mind the heaviness of my unused powers, or even how antsy I sometimes became when the urge to release some of my magic was too strong. I didn't mind because it allowed me to remain at home.

Then Søren almost burned down the ice cream place downtown because of a girl.

Everything fell apart.

Suddenly, dad had no choice but to bring Søren to Olympus and I hadn't been able to let him go without me. I loved my mom with all of my heart. But Søren was my twin, the second half of my soul.

I still remembered the morning before we left. Mom had woken me up early with my favorite breakfast in bed. We never ate food in our beds – she was strict in that way – and I had known then that it was a truly special day.

I could still see the way her face softened as she sat on the side of my bed and put a gentle hand on my cheek. I could still feel the love pouring from her.

"Sadie, my sweet girl," her smile was sad as she murmured the words. "I want you to know it is okay to not be sweet and kind sometimes. I know that you care a lot about people – I love that about you – but, where you are going, people will not always be kind in return. It is okay for you to be selfish and do whatever is necessary to be happy. Live for yourself. You don't have to be the perfect daughter, sister, or friend. You just have to be yourself, okay?"

"Mom, I—"

"Let me finish, alright?"

Throat too tight for words, I had nodded and leaned farther into her touch.

"I want you to continue to dream. You have such a pure soul, so don't let the gods taint it or dim your light." She had blinked back tears while mine were falling down my cheeks in silence. "You are not responsible for your brother's actions, but if you can keep an eye on him for me every so often, I'd appreciate it. And remind your dad that education is important. I don't care if people on Olympus spend their whole lives partying and having fun. Educating yourself is a right and it will enable you to form your own educated opinions. Do not let others dictate what you should think. Ever."

Mom had waited until I nodded before continuing.

"Please be careful with yourself. When you go to parties, always keep your glass with you. Do not ever drink from someone else's glass or from a drink you have left unattended. Ever. And if someone ever attempts to take advantage of you, remember to fight with all that you have. You are also not responsible for other people's behavior – the way you dress or act cannot be reason for someone else to assault you. And don't let anyone tell you otherwise."

One more stroke of her hand on my cheek.

"One day you will fall in love. Remember that love goes both ways. No matter how hard you fall for someone, you cannot love them enough for the both of you. Do not let yourself settle for someone who cannot or will not love you just as fiercely as you love yourself. You deserve someone who will cherish you and love you with every beat of their heart."

I had nodded then but I couldn't yet comprehend exactly what she meant. I was barely fifteen and true love was a foreign concept, something for when I'd be older. And I was confused because, while I knew I was leaving for Olympus, I didn't think that meant I wouldn't see my mom ever again.

"I love you so much, Sadie. You and your brother are the best things that have ever happened to me. You will forever live in my heart, min elskede."

Min elskede. My love.

No one had ever called me that beside my mom. Just thinking of the words made my chest squeeze in pain.

I missed her.

This had been the last conversation we had had together. Then dad had taken us away to Olympus and I had learned that our mom would never remember us. Søren and I had been wiped from the surface of the Earth.

Now, as I stood before the small restaurant with its yellow front, characteristic of the northern city of Skagen, I felt nostalgia at all the memories we used to have here. Søren and I would come here after school and sit in a corner of the restaurant until mom was done working. We'd get snacks and do homework, and this place had always felt like our second home.

The snow was falling in a heavy blanket over the whole city and it was late in the evening, but a light was still on in the kitchen. I knew right away that it was mom. She loved this place like a third child.

Or fifth, actually.

She got married and had two sons a few years after Søren and I left. It had hurt, but she didn't remember we existed.

Søren and I had come over a few times over the years to check on her. The trips weren't exactly allowed but Archer was friends with Hermes, and he gave us a few translocators to use. So, we came over a few times to have lunch at the restaurant and watch from afar how mom was doing.

It broke my heart every time, but I couldn't just forget about her.

So, here I was again. Standing in the snow and watching through the kitchen's window like a freak. And here she was, working on what looked like a new dessert. She was decorating with chocolate fudge and looked hyper focused on her work.

I could have recognized her anywhere.

She was almost thirty-five years older than that day we left – time went much faster on Earth than Olympus. Her hair was gray and not blond anymore. Her skin was wrinkled around her eyes and mouth, and she looked more tired than she'd been before. Years were tough on human bodies.

But even though her body was aged and tired, she still had the same passion for cooking and creating new things. I had loved being her test subject when I was a child – I'd try out all of her new recipes and, nine times out of ten, they were amazing.

Stars, how I wished I could come in and hug her. After everything that had happened these past few weeks, a hug from my mom would be a dream. I longed for her warmth and love.

Except she did not remember I was her daughter. There would be no love coming from her ever again.

Stop it. Don't go there.

Instead of wallowing in self-pity, I looked at the new phone I'd been given for this mission. Earth technology was pretty much foreign to me, seeing as I'd left this world over thirty-five years ago, but Kellan had shown me how to use it before I left, and it would be a convenient way to follow my target's whereabouts.

Mom always lost track of time when she worked on new recipes, so I wasn't surprised when I saw that it was almost midnight.

I knew I had to go. I had made a detour coming here to see mom, but I was supposed to be in Paris to catch my target. If my boss knew where I was, he would probably talk my ear off about duty and time management.

However, watching my mom take a bite of her dessert and sigh in contentment, I couldn't find it in myself to leave.

Five more minutes, I promised myself.

Five more minutes.

Chapter Four

Kalani

Archer knew I was hiding something.

I knew that because he kept looking at me with a suspicious frown whenever he thought I was focused on something else. I didn't think he knew exactly what I was hiding, though. I hadn't let anything slipped, and I trusted him not to use his powers to go through my mind like a public library.

To be fair, I had been hiding something from him and the guilt had been so strong that I had almost told him everything multiple times over the past two weeks.

My conversation with Thanatos was still weighing on my mind like a three-ton boulder. It all seemed so surreal – how could I not be fully human? I had never been anything but human, never shown any capacity for magic or heightened abilities. I bled, cried, and got hurt like a human.

I couldn't be anything else.

Somehow though, I couldn't bring myself to talk about the conversation I'd had with the god of Death to Archer. It wasn't that I didn't trust him – I did. I trusted him with my life and my heart.

Still. Something was preventing me from saying anything.

I felt terrible hiding it from him but I just— I couldn't.

I promised myself I'd tell Archer if something happened and I suddenly started using magic. It hadn't happened yet and that made me hope that Thanatos had been wrong.

There was nothing to say, anyways, right?

"How is the fish, sweetheart?" Priya Vasilias's voice brought me out of my thoughts.

"It's amazing," I exclaimed after swallowing.

The Golden smiled and cut another piece of her own dish. I was still somewhat uncomfortable around her – she was the kind of woman whose mere presence was intimidating. Working with her had helped a little, and she was always so nice that there was no way to do anything but like her. Still, I didn't want to do or say something dumb in front of my boyfriend's beloved mother.

"How's your last collection, mom?"

I could have kissed Archer for the distraction he provided. Priya's gaze, while kind, was very intense. I was glad that it was suddenly focused on his son and not on me anymore.

"The collection is great. I think the theme we came up with is powerful and innovative. The fabrics we chose are simply gorgeous. Some of the pieces we designed for this season are actually favorites of mine, even compared to the collection we released twelve years ago – the one inspired by the snow. Aphrodite is more than satisfied, and I honestly cannot wait for the show."

"I can't wait to see it all come together either!" Archer smiled at his mom, and it warmed my heart. Gotta love a man who loves his mom. "You always manage to create more stunning pieces every time."

Priya graciously accepted the compliment by putting her hand on her son's. The sight of their relationship – the love, the care they felt for one another – made my chest hurt.

I had been running away from any thoughts related to my mom and brother. Seeing them together at the skatepark, witnessing how they fit together without me—

No. Don't think about it.

I forcefully shoved a piece of fish into my mouth, hoping the delicious meal would help me focus on something other than the family I missed with every breath.

Archer and his mom were still talking about the new collection that Priya had designed. I listened but focused my gaze on the view – the sea of clouds surrounding Mount Olympus never failed to take my breath away. Tonight though, it couldn't quite take my mind off of thoughts of my brother.

A hand landed on my thigh. Archer. One look and I saw that he was still focused on his mother, even as his thumb traced gentle circles on my skin. I wasn't sure how he always knew when my mind went to dark places. I sure hoped it wasn't because of his handy magic. It might have been the special connection we had – something that had developed during the Tournament when we learned to trust and love each other.

"It will be a great learning experience for you, Kalani. You'll see, Olympian fashion shows are very different from those you might have seen on Earth. The magic adds a touch of dream and passion. It truly enhances the experience."

I didn't have the heart to tell her that I had never been to a fashion show before. There hadn't quite been an opportunity between my jobs, college classes, and taking care of Makaio. Plus, there was the issue of us not having enough money to even buy brand new clothes. Instead, I nodded and smiled.

"I am excited to see it."

And I was. Interning for the Golden had been full of new knowledge and experiences. I had worked with models, stylists, other photographers, and event planners. Seeing the show and knowing I had been a part – albeit a tiny one – of its planning would be an awesome experience.

"Archie, honey, I am going to ask you to not wear your leather armor for the event. I'd like to see you in nice clothes *for once*," the Golden said with a strong emphasis on the last two words.

As Archer started arguing with his mother that suits were too impractical and togas too flowy, I had the bittersweet thought that Mei would have sided with Priya. The Copper had hated those leather armors that Søren and Archer insisted on wearing to every official event. She had loved fashion and finding new ways to pair clothing items together.

She would have loved working with Priya.

Suddenly, the fish tasted like ash. I felt sick to my stomach.

The past few days had been better for my mental health – I had been able to enjoy life a little more without feeling guilty about everything I had been forced to do and witness in the Tournament. But, every so often, I still had those moments when a conversation, sight, or smell brought me back to some of my worst memories from the past few months. And here I was again, on the brink of falling into a dark, dark hole.

I fought, though. I had decided that I would not be letting myself wither and die. I would not give up.

So, instead of letting myself fall into that dark place in my mind where all of my worst memories resided, I took a couple of deep breaths and forced myself to be present once again.

Priya and Archer were not arguing about the leather armor anymore. Instead, they were talking about the different guests that were coming to the show. As an intern, I hadn't been privy to the VIP guest list, but I wasn't surprised to hear that all twelve of the main Olympian gods would be present.

The thought of having to face Artemis again after she had done everything in her power to make my trials more deadly was slightly terrifying. I had played it tough at the end of the second trial, taunting her, but the goddess was one scary lady. And I wasn't sure whether she still hated everything I represented or not.

"I have added both of you to the guest list for the after party," the Golden announced casually before taking a sip of her wine.

Immediately, Archer stiffened next to me. His hand stopped the slow movements on my thigh, and I frowned, unsure what this was about. An after party?

"We're not going."

I had never heard Archer speak in this way to his mom. His tone was harsh and cold. Unyielding.

"Archie," Priya sighed. "I talked to him. He won't be a problem."

"He is always a problem."

Who was the *he* that they were talking about?

"He won't be this time."

"I won't risk it. The last time I came to one of these events, he cornered me, and I ended up in the Tournament. I don't want a repeat of that, especially not with Mayfield there for him to use against me."

Oh. Zeus. It was rare to see Archer so angry, but I could feel the rage coming off of him in waves. It was a reminder that even Archer – always strong, competent, unafraid – had been hurt by the people on this mountain.

This time, it was me taking his hand and squeezing it gently, hoping to offer some comfort. Archer's hand relaxed in mine, but he remained tense otherwise, the conversation bringing back memories he didn't want to relive.

"I know, Archie. And I am so, so sorry that I couldn't do anything to help you then. But I can promise you that it won't happen again. Not under my watch."

The simmering rage was visible in Priya's eyes, and I could almost feel the way the air became colder around us. It was so unlike the warm and kind Priya Vasilias that it made her reaction all the more frightening. I could only imagine what the

Golden could do with her powers over innovation to exact revenge on Zeus.

Even with her mom's reassurances that nothing would happen, Archer remained silent. The muscles in his jaw ticked, and I could read the pain mixed with hate and rage on his face. I wished I could do something – anything – to help him, but Archer and Zeus' feud had started years ago, long before I'd come into his life.

"I think it would be good for your image," Priya added with a serious expression. "It would show that you are not afraid and that you came back stronger from the Tournament. It would also be a great occasion to show that Kalani is a part of the family. You need to ensure that *everyone* knows that you are not to be played with, son. The after party can be the start of that."

I could see Priya's point. Archer had been glued to my side every moment he and I weren't working, always insisting that we spend our free time in places that were safe – pretty much only his apartment.

I knew that the last trial during the Tournament had been tough for him. Watching me die, losing both of his best friends, having to plead to his abusive dad… yeah, it left some scars behind. I could understand that Archer wanted to stay away from his father and stepmother, as well as ensure I remained as far away from any threat as possible, but this bubble wrap life we'd been living for the past few weeks was not sustainable. I was on Olympus to stay and I would not spend the rest of my life hiding away.

"Sunshine," I murmured and tugged on his bicep to grab his attention. "I agree with your mom. We can't continue on like this."

Archer stared into my eyes for long seconds, his jaw ticking in time with my rapid heartbeat. It always amazed me how quickly I lost myself in his ocean blue eyes. One look and I was lost in him, the world falling apart around us. It was just us two – me pleading with him to relax and promising with my gaze that everything would be fine.

"I won't talk to him." Archer didn't have to explain who 'him' was because both Priya and I knew.

"Of course," Priya agreed. "I will tell him beforehand that he is not to address you."

"I don't want Hera to even look our way."

"I'll take care of it."

Finally, Archer cut our eye contact and looked at his mom. The frown was still present, but his body had relaxed. A little.

"I still don't like it."

His mom's only answer was a smile and an eyebrow raise. She knew her son better than anyone, after all, and she knew that he was going to cave.

At the sight of his mom's satisfied expression, Archer rolled his eyes. Oh, the man was annoyed but he couldn't deny Priya anything. I liked that a little too much.

"It'll be fun," I added with a soft tap on his hand. "Plus, I can't wait to have ambrosia again."

"We don't need to spend an evening in a pit full of snakes for that. I can buy you some,"

"I don't want to get drunk on my own, that's depressing. I want the full glam with it."

"And I want some peace and quiet."

"You're being grumpy again, Sunshine."

He gave me a dark look and I smiled before holding my hands up in surrender.

"What? Just thought I'd let you know in case you didn't realize."

Archer shook his head and couldn't quite hide the smile on his lips. I'd take that as a win.

Chapter Five

Sadie

Movies and books had the nasty habit of showcasing Paris as this beautiful, magical city of love and high fashion. The real thing was underwhelming.

I was currently sitting on a park bench speckled with dried bird shit, breathing in as much pollution as oxygen, and getting judgmental looks from the two women seated on the bench across from me. I had to admit that the architecture was impressive. However, the magical and romantic vibes must have come from another time because I sure didn't feel them.

Whatever. I wasn't here to sightsee or look for the love of my life in a high-end restaurant.

I was here to hunt.

Stars, how surreal. I still couldn't quite believe that I was on Earth as a Huntress for the twelve Olympians.

Old me would be ashamed.

New me didn't have the luxury of having the same moral grounds as before. New me had lost everything and needed escape more than anything.

So, here I was, pretending to read one of these awful celebrity magazines on the outskirts of one of Paris' fanciest parks, waiting for my target to leave his job.

Matteo Bailet must have been very efficient at hiding his powers because he was twenty-four years old. Most Coppers, especially the powerful ones, were brought to Olympus to participate in the Tournament around their twentieth birthday. More often than not, the magic that accumulated silently in Coppers' bodies overflowed after around two decades of life – except if a particularly traumatic event happened beforehand and caused the Coppers to use their magic earlier.

I had little information about him otherwise – just what Kellan had given me about his powers and a zoomed-in picture of the guy.

Matteo had definitely inherited the looks of his godly ancestors. Dark coppery hair, tawny skin that betrayed his mortal mother's Mediterranean heritage, dark eyes, and a tall built frame. Like most Coppers and Goldens, the guy could have come out of a Vogue magazine.

The first time a Hunter had gone to apprehend Matteo, it had been in a small coastal city in the south west of France. Since then, the Copper had moved to Toulouse, then a middle-of-nowhere village in the center of France, before finally settling in Paris. He might have hoped that, by hiding among millions of people, none of us would be able to find him.

Tough luck.

Unfortunately for Matteo, it was very hard for Coppers to escape Olympus, not when their magic called to ours.

Magic was intangible, something that flowed through our bodies but couldn't be seen. It was our atoms vibrating at a slightly different frequency. Maybe an invisible force that flowed in the emptiness of our atoms. Something that I didn't fully understand – some of the smart ones on Olympus had studied it in depth, but I had never been interested in science. But, even without knowing exactly what magic was, I knew that it attracted itself like the opposing poles of a magnet.

Magic recognized magic.

It manifested in small, hardly noticeable ways. A small electrical shock upon skin contact. Picking out someone within a dense crowd for no apparent reason. Feeling a weirdly strong connection to someone you had just met.

It was subtle, really. So subtle sometimes, that one wouldn't know what to look out for if they weren't actively searching for it. But it was there.

Once upon a time, this magical recognition had been a blessing – being able to recognize fellow descendants of the Gods was a great way to build community in a world dominated by humans.

Sadly, this ability had been perverted for too long now by the gods who had trained Hunters and Huntresses to hunt down every last one of the Coppers still living on Earth.

That meant that Matteo had had no chance to escape the clutches of Olympus.

Part of the limited intelligence we had on the guy was a mention that he had just started working at one of those restaurants where tourists payed an arm and a leg for an "authentic" French lunch comprised of frozen fries and beef that had seen half of Europe. I wasn't sure what Matteo did in this restaurant, but I had been sitting on this uncomfortable bench with a direct view to the entrance and patio of the restaurant for hours, and still hadn't spotted him.

I was hungry, tired, and cold. Matteo better show up quickly or I'd have to get in the restaurant to eat and grab him. In that order.

Ignoring my rumbling stomach, I tried to get back into my routine of pretending to read the magazine in my lap while discreetly eyeing the restaurant.

Walking on Earth meant I was not under Hecate's universal language spell anymore. Thankfully, someone – Hecate or maybe Apollo, I wasn't sure – had figured out a way to magically teach languages to Hunters and Huntresses before they left for their missions. It worked – I now spoke French and had never taken a single French course. However, using the language was painful – trying to read this stupid magazine was giving me a throbbing headache. Kellan had assured me it would pass, and I couldn't wait for that.

Another half hour passed by, and I was *this close* to abandoning the stealth plan, when the side door to the restaurant opened. Two people stepped out. A woman and a man. Matteo.

I immediately recognized him. The photo I'd received wasn't the best quality, but it didn't matter. I could *feel* the power flowing in his veins. This was no human.

How in the stars did that incompetent Hunter confuse Kalani for a Copper? There was no mistaking my target in the sea of humans.

Still sitting on the bench, I crossed my legs and turned a page of my magazine. I didn't remember a single word written on the previous page, but it hopefully ensured my cover remained safely up.

My eyes followed Matteo's movements, trying to be as discreet as possible behind my sunglasses. He was leaning against the outside wall, phone in hand, smiling at something the girl said. He looked relaxed, probably thinking he was safe after stopping three Hunters and moving to France's biggest city.

He wasn't.

Escaping the reach of the Olympians was tough. Any descendant of the Greek deities had a signature – a trace of their power that could be felt and followed by some of Hermes's children.

Changing his phone number, cutting contact with his mortal family, moving across the country… none of that would help Matteo escape Olympus. Escape *me*.

Although, I wouldn't do anything right now. I'd observe and tail the guy from afar, but I wasn't about to attack him right then, in the middle of his break. Not that I particularly enjoyed the surveillance work, but there were too many witnesses present. The street was bustling with tourists, kids walking back from school, and local people on their way to the metro station. Hecate's memory erasing spell was good, but I didn't feel like messing with the heads of thousands of people if a fight broke out between Matteo and me.

Plus, finding skeletons in the middle of the street in Paris wasn't easy. Based on what the guy had done to three of my unfortunate colleagues, I didn't want to face off against him with my only weapons being a smile and hand-to-hand combat techniques.

So, here I was, turning into a real stalker, hoping that my surveillance would reveal details about Matteo's life that I could use to bring him back to Olympus.

I watched as he joked around with his female coworker.

I watched as he finished work three hours later.

I watched as he said goodnight to two of his male coworkers before they parted ways.

I watched as he took the metro, sitting down one subway car away from him so I would remain inconspicuous.

And I followed him all the way home.

My chest was tight the whole time – this whole mission bringing forth a new wave of shame and guilt. I hated this new version of me who stalked a Copper who just wanted to live his life on Earth. I hated the way his simple life – with no use of magic whatsoever, so far – reminded me of my own before I was ripped away from my mom.

Unfortunately, I had no choice but to continue. Because I despised the version of me on Mount Olympus even more than who I was becoming.

Chapter Six

Kalani

Enough was enough. I'd given Sadie time. She had needed to deal with the consequences of the fourth trial, and to do so, she had needed to be by herself. It hurt, but I understood that.

However, it had been almost three weeks now. Three weeks without a word from her.

Today was the end of it. I would track Sadie down across the whole mountain if I had to, but I would get answers. I wouldn't let her isolate herself like this anymore. There had been no right way to end this Tournament. Søren could keep blaming his sister for his girlfriend's death, but I wouldn't let her continue to isolate herself.

Sadie hadn't killed Mei.

The deities had.

I wished I could make them pay for everything they had made us go through. However, I couldn't tempt fate after barely obtaining the right to live on Olympus. I didn't have anything on

Earth now that my family didn't remember me at all. Losing Archer, Sadie, and Søren… it would break me – or break whatever was left of me after the past three months.

So, here I was. Walking around the beautiful streets of Mount Olympus without Archer for the first time in over two weeks. He wasn't aware of this – neither of my goal for today nor of me walking alone. I felt slightly guilty for not mentioning anything when he left for work this morning and I promised him to be safe. I knew damn well that walking alone in the streets of a place where I was an outcast was not the smartest decision I'd ever taken. But I needed to get answers and there was too much history between Archer and the twins.

A lady out on her porch stared at me for a few seconds too long as I walked by. Praying she wasn't a member of the let's-hate-all-humans gang, I gave her a tight smile and continued on with my head held high. She didn't do anything – thank goodness, I didn't feel like fighting for my life this early in the morning – and I continued walking down the sunny street.

I had a vague description of where Nafula and Amara lived. I hadn't gone to Sadie's old apartment – Archer hadn't talked much to Søren in the past couple of weeks, but he knew she hadn't gone back to their shared place. Thus, I figured I would ask the other two Tournament survivors if they had any insight into where Sadie might be.

After walking thirty minutes from the nice neighborhood where Archer lived, I was finally there. Both Nafula and Amara had been given access to single apartments in a small complex on the outsides of the main city. From what Archer had told me, these apartments were given to the Coppers in the few years following the Tournament. It was the Olympian equivalent of low-income housing. From the outside, though, it looked much nicer than the ones we had on Earth.

The streets were narrower here, with taller, skinnier buildings. But the buildings were still made of those nice white rocks, with colorful flower bushes scattered everywhere along the streets. It was cute. But it wasn't as grand as the neighborhoods closer to the top of Olympus. Probably because the closer to the top of the mountain, the higher the percentage of ichor in one's blood – and vice versa.

The people living here, in the buildings around me, were all Coppers.

Funny how, no matter where you went, people always managed to put others in different social boxes based on purely biological things. Whether it was race, gender, or the amount of ichor in one's blood… there was always a way to discriminate other people, wasn't there?

Shaking my head at my thoughts, I took a deep breath and walked up to the entrance of the building where Nafula and Amara supposedly lived. There was a door blocking the entrance but, like most places on Olympus, there wasn't a lock. People didn't use keys all that often here – they usually preferred to use a protection-spell from Hecate which they could set up to allow certain people inside a house. It was pretty neat.

And, honestly, how essential was Hecate in the daily dealings of Mount Olympus? That lady seemed to have used her magic to create over half of the things that the deities and their descendants relied on. That was impressive as hell.

Anyway, the issue here was that, since I didn't live in the building, the spell wouldn't let me go through. There were really fancy magical phones available on Olympus – Priya Vasilias, Archer's mother, had one she used to talk with her fellow Golden friends – but they were rare and quite expensive, thus only reserved for the elite of Olympus. This meant that neither I nor my fellow victors had one – I had no way to contact them.

I probably should have thought of this before, since Archer had the same magical mechanism on his front door.

Oh, well. That just meant I was going to spend a few hours sitting on the front porch, waiting for anyone to pass that door.

Cheers to what was sure to be a *very* long day.

Thankfully, I only had to sit on the steps before the front door for fifteen minutes before someone walked out of the building. Looking around, I was surprised to end up face to face with Nafula.

Whoever was in charge of luck on Olympus must have been generous this morning.

"Kalani?"

Standing up, I smiled awkwardly at the Copper before me. "Hi, Nafula. How are you?"

Right away, it was terribly uncomfortable. We hadn't seen each other since that day. The day when we all killed someone and had to act like we were happy about it.

The day we had won.

She stood there in a white and red uniform that looked like a modern rendition of the one from *Baywatch*. In place of her afro, she now sported long braids with blue beads at the ends. The Copper looked sad, though, with tired eyes like she hadn't slept all night.

"Fine. How's life on the nice side of the mountain?"

I could feel the resentment pouring from her every pore. I had to fight to remain calm and not get defensive – after all, yes, I was living in Archer's fancy place, but it wasn't like people were very welcoming of me anywhere else. I was the outcast. And some of the gods and goddesses living here had tried to kill me – albeit indirectly – multiple times already. I wouldn't apologize for accepting the safety that came with my boyfriend's living conditions.

But I could understand if she was angry about it – she had been ripped away from her home, thrown into a deadly Tournament, and after she had won, she had been given a tiny apartment in the worst neighborhood of Olympus.

"I am not here to fight, Nafula."

"Why are you here, then? I thought you were happy enough to ignore all of us now that you earned a free one-way trip to a life of luxury."

"Come on, Nafula," I sighed at her tone. "Don't pretend like I didn't have to go through the exact same Trials as you did. I have lost my family, just like you. And I might be living in

Archer's apartment, but I assure you that I wasn't handed a fat trust fund with it. Plus, we weren't best friends, so don't come at me for not checking on you every day."

"Last I checked, you haven't been worried about your best friend either. From where I stand, it looks like you were happy enough to forget about everyone you used to survive once everything was over."

Nafula's words were a punch to the gut. I didn't need her to spell it out to know she meant Sadie. And yes, I hadn't come to see her. Because, from my point of view, it was pretty obvious that Sadie needed time away from all of us to deal with Mei's death and Søren's rejection. After all, she had avoided any contact with me or Archer. After Mei's funeral, I had tried to talk to her and she had almost run away from all of us.

But maybe I was wrong. Maybe she needed us to forcefully drag her out of her hiding place. Maybe I had failed at this friendship more than I thought.

And perhaps Nafula was right. Perhaps not contacting anyone during these two and a half weeks had been shitty of me. Perhaps my time on Olympus had changed me into a heartless monster who didn't care about others anymore.

I felt nauseous now, unsettled. And I couldn't quite meet Nafula's judgmental gaze anymore.

"Look, I just want to find Sadie. Do you know where she is staying?"

For long seconds, the Copper and I were stuck in a staring battle. I could see her debating whether or not she should help me out. Maybe what she saw in my eyes told her to answer. Or maybe she hoped her words would hurt me more than not knowing.

"She's gone."

"What do you mean?" Right away I had the horrible thought that she was gone forever, the same way that Mei was gone. But she couldn't be. There was no way she would have made that decision, was there?

"She left for Earth yesterday. Sadie is Olympus' newest Huntress." Nafula couldn't contain a wince at the words.

"As in, the Hunters and Huntresses that retrieve Coppers from Earth for the Tournament?"

The Copper nodded stiffly. I would bet that she had bad memories linked to Hunters – one of them had probably separated her from her family months ago.

"Why?" I was so confused because Sadie had seen how terrible the Tournament was first-hand. I knew damn well that there would always be Hunters and Huntresses there to retrieve Coppers still wandering Earth, but participating in the process? That was something I didn't think Sadie – or anyone of us – would ever do voluntarily.

"She couldn't stand to be on the same plane of existence as her brother or the rest of you."

What struck me first was the hurt in Nafula's voice. But I didn't have time to dwell on it because her words sucked the air out of my chest. My mind was spinning. My heart raced against my thoughts.

"I hope you all are happy with yourselves," Nafula sneered before leaving me standing alone in front of the door.

I didn't remember leaving the front porch. I didn't remember the walk back home either.

All I could think about was Sadie walking on Earth, chasing Coppers to bring them to Mount Olympus. And all of that to escape Olympus. To escape *us*.

Chapter Seven

Kalani

When Archer came back from work, three things happened.

First, he asked me how my day went.

Then, he freaked out when I told him I left the apartment. His blood pressure got so high that his jugular was pulsating. He was both arguing with me about my safety and checking me over for injuries. It was cute and frustrating at the same time.

Finally, he stopped ranting for long enough for me to actually explain what I had learned on my solo expedition. Then, Archer lost all of his anger and worry about the risks I had taken and fell completely silent. He was so shocked by the news that Sadie had left Olympus and signed up as a Huntress that he remained speechless for long minutes.

"I don't understand," he finally murmured, the incomprehension written on his face. His hands were in his hair, pulling at the roots as if the pain would help answer the unsaid question – why would Sadie feel the need to become something she despised so much?

I didn't think either of us had realized how much the fourth Trial had fractured our group. We knew things were very tense between the twins, and we had somehow removed ourselves from the conflict to avoid choosing a side. But Sadie's decision was so drastic that I was suddenly rethinking everything and wondering if Archer and my removal had made things so much worse.

"Nafula said she left yesterday, so I barely missed her. I hope she's okay."

My voice broke at the end, and Archer took my hand, pulling me to his lap. All of his previous frustration was gone. We were now desperately holding onto each other. Two people trying to prevent the storm around them from pulling them apart. His arms around me didn't make things all better, but they sure helped my heart remember I wasn't alone.

That was what I loved about Archer – among other things. We didn't always see eye to eye, and we fought sometimes. But we always leaned on each other when times were tough. We had each other's backs – always.

"Sadie is the strongest Golden I know, she'll be fine. I promise."

I nodded at Archer's words, but we both knew that he couldn't be certain she'd remain safe. Sadie was strong and powerful; she had trained for years in martial arts. But retrieving Coppers wasn't always an easy job – most of them did not want to come to Olympus to fight to the death, all because of powers they hadn't asked for in the first place. I did not want to know what would happen if she actually met with a Copper that wouldn't go down without a fight and had the power to back themselves up.

No, I couldn't go there. I had to remind myself that Sadie had completely whipped Nathan's butt without even breaking a sweat only a few weeks before. And Nathan, with his Hulk-like magic, had not been powerless.

She would be fine. She had to be.

"Do you think Søren knows?"

"Probably not, seeing as he has shoved his head so far up his ass that he can't think straight."

Normally I would laugh at Archer swearing, especially about his best friend – he still had some of those old-school manners that reminded me he was technically born long ago, since time went by much faster on Earth than on Olympus. But I couldn't laugh then. Not when I was so torn up about the desperation Sadie must have felt to make her decision to enroll as a Huntress.

I was about to ask if Archer could use his friendship with Hermes to get information on what was happening on Earth and where Sadie was, when he pressed me against his body and stood up. He slowly let me down, our bodies gliding against each other.

"We're going." Archer's voice was hard, his gaze determined.

"Go where? To Earth?"

"Not yet. We're stopping by Søren's first because this has to stop."

I didn't contradict him because he was right. We had allowed the feud between the twins to go on for way too long. Søren had to realize that there hadn't been a right choice that day in the Pit. The gods and goddesses had paired Sadie with Mei and only one of them could leave the Tournament alive.

Mei hadn't stood a chance.

The force with which Archer knocked on the wood made the door rattle. I was surprised that Søren's door held up.

Søren's voice came muffled from inside, screaming that he was coming. He better hurry because Archer was almost shaking with anger next to me. I had to put a hand on his forearm to stop him from forcefully breaking the door open.

"Breathe, Sunshine. He's coming."

Archer didn't answer but he did unclench his fists, which I took as a win. I was pissed at the whole situation too, and I sure wanted to slap Sadie's twin behind the head. But getting himself so worked up that his blood pressure would go through the roof was not the way Archer would knock some sense into his best friend.

The moment Søren opened the door, the tension between the two men became a physical thing. I knew neither of them had really talked in the past two and a half weeks since the Tournament had ended, but seeing them this way? It broke my heart. I missed the time when all of us were a team – a tight-knit family.

"You fucked up, Aska."

"Well, hello to you too, Archer Vasilias. To what do I owe this pleasure?" Sarcasm was dripping from every one of Søren's words.

"Do you know where your sister is right now?"

"I'm not her keeper."

"Sounds about right. You're barely her brother right now."

Søren's jaw clenched at Archer's words. He didn't answer and I could tell that Archer's words had hit him. Since the first moment I had met him, I had known that Søren prided himself in being a great brother for Sadie. She didn't need protection, but he sure gave some to her on top of his love.

As I watched the Golden in front of me, I felt a pang of longing in my heart. I missed Søren's smile and silly jokes. I missed his constant flirty remarks and the fun we used to have together.

But this Søren, with his hard eyes and unkept hair out of his usual manbun, was not our Søren. He was not the man I'd come to think of as family anymore.

I didn't know if there was any path that we could take to bring us back together.

Deciding that the death stare match between the two men would lead us nowhere, I cleared my throat and spoke. "She left Olympus. She enrolled as a Huntress and left for Earth yesterday."

Søren tried to hide it behind a heavy dose of indifference, but I saw the shock in his eyes. There might have even been a touch of concern there. But both emotions were gone in a flash.

"And? She is a grown woman. She can make stupid choices if she wants."

The shock at Søren's words was so intense that I had to blink and shake my head a few times to process it. It was inconceivable for me that Søren wouldn't care that his twin sister had made such a drastic decision.

I was about to… I wasn't sure actually, shake Søren so he'd stop being such an ass maybe? But Archer stopped me dead in my tracks by laughing beside me. Both Søren and I gave him incredulous looks, but the man continued to chuckle darkly.

"Is your pride choking you yet? Because it sure looks like it has sunken its claws so deep into you that you can't think straight anymore."

Søren snarled at Archer's words, his fists clenching hard. "I have every right to be mad at her for what she's done."

"And what did she do exactly, huh?"

"She killed Mei. She didn't even leave her a chance."

"A chance to do what?" Archer almost yelled by that point. "A chance to kill your sister? A chance to make their fight bloody and painful? What in the stars did you want, Søren? For your sister to die instead?"

"They could have refused to fight. We would have handled it."

Archer scoffed at his friend's words. "Your grief is blinding you, brother. The gods had punished us and there was absolutely no way either of us would have been able to break the rules this way. If they had refused to fight, both of them would be gone. Would that make you feel better right now? Is that what you would prefer?"

Søren opened his mouth to speak but closed it without a sound. And that left enough time for Archer to continue punching Søren in the face with a ton of tough love the blond Golden hadn't asked for.

"I love you, man, I really do. But you are being selfish, obtuse, and cruel. We all understand that you loved Mei, and we do want to support you in your grief, trust me. But punishing Sadie for surviving is extremely shitty. You should be ashamed of yourself."

The silence following Archer's words was deafening. I wasn't happy with how Søren had dealt with his grief, but my boyfriend's wake-up call was definitely violent. There was no gentleness in the way he had dished out every truth Søren had refused to face for over two weeks. But I trusted that Archer knew his friend better than I did – after years of friendship, he probably knew that Søren was too stubborn to listen to anything less than this.

"Søren," I murmured once I couldn't take the heavy silence anymore. "I am so sorry for what happened to Mei. And I am sorry you couldn't save her. I can't imagine how hard that must have been." I took a step forward and placed a hand on his forearm. "But Mei chose this. As soon as they announced both of their names, she knew that she wouldn't make it out. It wasn't Sadie's decision in any way. Mei didn't want to fight."

My words must have hit him in the cracks left by Archer's speech, because his eyes closed, and his face crumpled in pain. Maybe I should have told him earlier, but how did you tell someone their girlfriend didn't even argue for her life?

All at once, the big, strong Copper folded into my arms and started crying. It was so out of character that it took me a second to realize what was happening. But then my arms closed around him and I tried my best to hold him up as he broke down.

We stood there, immobile, for a long time before Søren stopped crying. Based on the desperation in his eyes, I was pretty sure this was the first time he'd actually cried since his girlfriend had died.

"I'm sorry, I—"

"Don't be," I interrupted Søren with a gentle smile. "Losing someone is hard. And as Archer said, we are here for you. Mei was also our friend, and we will both be here to support you through your grief. But you can't continue to hold Sadie responsible for Mei's death. Sadie needs to know you still love her and support her."

Søren nodded slowly and pressed his hands against his red, puffy eyes.

"I don't know how to deal with this, K." His voice was broken and so rough that it sounded like gravel. And seeing his pain was like a knife to my heart.

"I don't know either, Søren. I don't think there is a handbook for dealing with loss. But I think you need to let your emotions out and let people in. You can't do everything on your own. And you need Sadie, just like she needs you."

I gave him a long look with my last words. The twins were more than siblings – this rift in their relationship was destroying both of them.

Søren sighed and nodded, implicitly agreeing to at least trying to let go of his inane rage against his sister.

"Good, because we are going to bring her back home," Archer grumbled from behind us, surprising me. He hadn't made a sound for minutes, and I had almost forgotten Søren and I weren't alone in the apartment entrance.

"How?" From what I understood, becoming a Hunter or Huntress for the Olympians was somewhat like enrolling in the military – people sold away part of their lives for the cause and there was no getting out early. But, to be fair, Archer wasn't the kind of person that took things lying down. I wasn't surprised he already had a plan.

"We are going to go to Earth and contact her from there. I had already planned a trip to go and see your little brother tomorrow, so we will just leave early." Archer crossed his arms over his chest and, even in the middle of this emotional time, I couldn't not take an appreciative look at the way the shirt stretched over his shoulders.

"How the hell are we going to contact her? She could be anywhere on Earth right now!"

"Missions are confidential, too," Søren added with a frown.

"Hermes loves me," Archer shrugged with a cocky air that was both cute and deeply annoying. "I'll get her new phone number easily enough. Are you coming with us?"

That last question was aimed at Søren. The two men stared at each other for a few seconds before Søren finally nodded. Archer immediately relaxed and Søren gave him a tight smile.

Just like that, the underlying tension that had been present between the two of them fizzled out of the air.

Oh, *men*.

Somehow, the boys and I ended up in the streets of my hometown only an hour later. The Sun was up but it was only barely past breakfast time. The city was already bustling with people and cars.

Even after coming here a little over two weeks ago – in Olympian time, at least, – being back on Earth was a shock. What used to be home didn't feel like it anymore. I had gotten so used to the peace, quiet, and warmth of Olympus that the big city – with its pollution and constant noise – was overwhelming.

"Man, this is not what I expected California to look like," Søren complained with a slightly disgusted face at the busy street we were on.

"California is big and we're far from LA. Plus, March isn't the prettiest time of the year here. But, trust me, since we're in the Northern part of the state, the Fall is beautiful."

I wasn't sure why I felt the need to defend my hometown, especially since I wouldn't ever live here anymore. But it was hard to stop feeling like part of me was still stuck in these streets.

Søren shrugged at my words and quickly got interested in a big mural painted on the façade of a nearby building.

"Anyway, let's get started," Archer announced while getting a piece of paper out of his jeans pocket. "Ready to call?"

I got my phone – still mostly charged from the last time I'd been on Earth, when I'd decided that risking my family's mental health was too dangerous – and got ready to type in the number. It was an international number starting with the country code 33. A quick Google search before calling told me it was a French number. How odd, I wouldn't have expected that – which was dumb of me, since Coppers came from all around the world.

Both Søren and Archer were silent as I took a deep breath and tapped the call button. I put the phone on my ear and listened to the line beeping. Again, and again, and again.

I held my breath as I waited for Sadie to pick up and tell me that she was fine, probably enjoying some fun time in the French capital.

But she didn't pick up. Not on the first time I called, and not on the two tries afterwards.

Gods, I hoped she was fine.

Chapter Eight

Sadie

Having a coffee at four pm was probably not my best idea, but it was damn good. Actually, it was the only thing in this restaurant – Le Bistrot de Pierre – which was decently good. The rest was severely disappointing, even the ice cream. How could someone mess up ice cream?

This place definitely was a tourist trap.

A waitress came over and asked if I needed anything else. I knew a hint when I saw one – to be fair, I'd been sipping my coffee here for close to two hours. So, I smiled and ordered a crème brûlée. I was going to be here for a while, so might as well eat a barely sub-par dessert while I waited.

When the waitress came back with the dessert and a spoon, she gave me the tight smile the French loved to give strangers they made eye-contact with on the street. I thanked her and was grateful when she left me alone at my table in the corner of the room. I might have looked like a creep, sitting on my own at the table with the worst lighting in the room. But I wasn't there for fun – this table gave me the best view on the bar at the back of the place.

The bar where Matteo Bailet worked as a bartender.

Now, you might wonder, why wasn't the guy on Olympus already? Well, see, I made the executive decision that it would be better for the mission for me to observe my target a little longer. To understand him better and prepare myself to the best of my abilities for a possible fight.

So, this was my fourth consecutive day spending part of the afternoon or evening in this restaurant. And, in between pretending to read magazines or mystery books, I observed Matteo.

It was addicting to witness a normal life like his. He came here every afternoon and stayed until closing time, around eleven pm. He worked a normal job, joked with his normal friends, and enjoyed a quiet lifestyle. I didn't see him use even a hint of his magic. To anyone else, Matteo was a perfectly ordinary human man.

And that realization made it damn hard to do my job.

I remembered all too well what it felt like to have someone take me away from my life because of my magic. And I hadn't had to fight for my life afterwards – which he would have to do. Now that I was faced with actually having to remove someone from Earth against their will – someone who seemed nice, fun, and non-threatening to humans – well, it was harder than I had expected.

A ringtone started playing and it took me a few seconds to realize it came from my phone. It was the first time anyone had called me, so I was hesitant to answer.

"Hello?"

"Sadie Aska, this is Commander Kellan. How is your mission progressing?"

Per usual, Kellan was straight to the point. However, I would have liked an explanation for how he had managed to contact me. I thought contact between Earth and Olympus wasn't possible using cell phones. Maybe he was also on Earth to complete a mission or supervise another new Hunter?

"It's advancing," I answered after a second, not wanting to get into the details that I had been sitting at a French café for the past four days.

"Then how come the target isn't on Olympus yet? I thought the Aska twins had the reputation of being extremely efficient at their jobs."

I could hear the frustration in Kellan's voice, but I wasn't particularly sorry for taking my time. So, I took a bite of my dessert and gave a nod to one of the waiters who was staring a little too closely at me.

"I don't particularly want to end up like your previous employees, Kellan, so excuse me if I am taking my time. The job will be done in time, don't worry about it."

My boss hummed a noncommittal sound and I could tell he was still annoyed. The man wasn't used to being said no to. But I meant what I said – I didn't want to end up lying in a hospital bed, on the brink of death or complete madness, because I decided to rush through the whole mission.

"How much longer do you expect you'll need to complete the mission?"

"No idea. I am waiting for the right moment. But it'll get done, don't w—"

I stopped because my ringtone was going off again, this time much quieter. Moving the phone away from my ear, I was able to see that someone else was calling me. This was another unknown number. How strange, after not getting a single call for four days. I didn't know who other than Kellan would want to call me, though, so I clicked on the 'do not accept' icon and brought the phone back to my ear.

"Sorry about that, an unknown number was trying to call."

"Huh, it's probably a telemarketer trying to sell you insurance. Anyway. Aska, I won't be waiting for weeks. I'll allow you to continue to do whatever it is you're doing, but I am expecting you back on Olympus very soon. Am I understood?"

"Yes, sir."

"Good. Now, I need to go and take care of yet another mess up in Brazil. What a bunch of incompetents," he muttered, annoyed. "I will check in again soon, and I hope to hear better news."

Then he hung up on me.

Well, what a lovely time.

It wasn't that I didn't like Kellan – after all, he was only doing his job. But the reminder that I would have to be back on Olympus soon was not enjoyable. I was grateful to be on Earth and have the opportunity to forget the disaster my life had become during the past three weeks.

My phone started ringing again but I turned it off. I didn't want to talk to any telemarketer or give the opportunity to anyone from the upper chain of command to contact me again today. I wanted to focus on the here and now, not on everything I was trying to escape at home.

"Is this chair taken?"

Surprised, I snapped my eyes up to find someone standing to my right, a hand on the back of the chair. And not just anyone either – Matteo.

What a surprise.

"Not yet, no. Are you a worker here?" I asked innocently, as if I hadn't been stalking the guy for the past four days.

Matteo sat down and put his forearms on the table – he had very nice-looking forearms, now that I properly looked at them – and gave me a crooked smile.

"I am. I bartend over there. I could make you a drink if you decide to stay for a little longer."

"That sounds tempting. You look like you'd make a *very* nice cocktail." I added a flirty smile and twirled a strand of my hair around my finger. I was laying it on thick, but homeboy gave me a chuckle that signified he enjoyed it.

"What brings you to this side of Paris? Vacation maybe?"

"Not quite. I am here to find myself, I guess."

"Intriguing. What prompted the desire to find yourself, then?"

I remained silent for a second, debating what to say. Matteo seemed genuinely curious and I didn't think he suspected anything about my stalker ways. Instead, he was giving me the forearms and an intense look that might be qualified as a smolder.

"I decided to quit my job last week. It was kind of a spur of the moment decision. And now I'm trying to decide what I want to do next. Moving to Paris felt like what I should do, so here I am."

Matteo nodded and continued to give me all of his attention with his dark brown eyes. "I went through something similar a few weeks back and it is definitely tough. What were you doing before?"

"I was a martial arts teacher."

"No way! That's so cool!" Matteo exclaimed with an enthusiasm I'd lost long ago. He had a big smile on, and I had this weird warmth in my chest. "What kind or martial arts?"

"Oh, a little bit of anything but I focused mostly on teaching self-defense and mixed martial arts. I love boxing, though."

Once again, Matteo was speechless for a second, his face split by a grin. "I am so impressed! Does this mean you could put me on my ass super easily?"

I couldn't contain a laugh because this was so ironic. We were both pretending to be human, and I had to admit, he was good at letting me think he was a regular guy. He didn't know that I was a Golden. But I knew his powers were strong and, to be honest, I wasn't sure what a one-on-one fight would look like between us.

"We can try it and see," I offered with a seductive look.

Matteo shook his head with a grin. "Hell no, I don't play when I know I'm going to lose."

"Sore loser?" I taunted.

"Who isn't?"

"Fair enough."

We ended up looking at each other without speaking for a few seconds, and I didn't know what was happening because I couldn't drop his gaze. We were smiling at each other. I should be transporting this guy to Olympus – with or without his consent – but here I was, smiling at him like I was actually flirting with him and not just playing a role.

"Matteo! Break is over!"

The man who had called Matteo must have been his boss because he winced and started to stand up right away.

"Sorry, duty calls," he said with a wave toward the bar. "But maybe you could come and have a drink sometime…"

"Sadie."

Matteo smiled – he needed to stop that, his smiles were distracting – and he threw his hand out to me. "Nice to meet you, Sadie. I'm Matteo."

Oh, I knew. But I still said, "Nice to meet you, too, Matteo. I'll come and see you for that drink later on."

And I did. An hour later, after pretending to be interested in my book, I sat at the bar. I ordered an espresso martini – if I wasn't going to sleep, might as well enjoy the ride – and made small talk with Matteo.

By the end of the night, Matteo offered for me to join him the next evening at a club where he and a few colleagues were going to party. After all, he said, it was hard to move to a new city and he wanted me to make friends.

I promised I'd be there.

I would. I looked forward to it.

But, to be fully honest with myself, I didn't know if I wanted to be there because it would help my mission to get Matteo to trust me, or if it was due to the way his eyes looked at me like he *saw* me.

Chapter Nine

Kalani

At first, it was hard to focus on something other than Sadie and her disappearance. But once I laid eyes on Makaio, he was the only thing I could think about.

We arrived early enough in front of our – *their* – apartment complex that we saw Makaio leave with a full backpack and three of his friends.

My heart almost stopped when I saw him – all of the pain I'd been hiding away from for the past three months came back with a vengeance. For a second, I couldn't breathe as I took in Makaio's smile and excited gestures.

Gods, I missed him. So much.

Then, the doors to the lobby opened again and out walked my mom. I didn't know what surprised me the most – her smile, the massive cooler in her arms, or how she looked ten years younger than the last time we'd talked together.

It took all of my strength to stop the tears that welled up at the sight of my mom playfully teasing Makaio and his friends. I couldn't remember the last time I'd had a mom that teased me. And it hurt so much to watch, but it also healed some part of my broken heart to see the way Makaio felt supported and loved.

"Mayfield," Archer whispered before he wrapped me in his arms, his chest warm and comforting against my back. "We don't have to continue today. We can go home and come back another day if you need more time."

I appreciated Archer's understanding, but I couldn't leave now. Even if it hurt every single second to watch the family that didn't remember me anymore, I couldn't stop looking. Because not knowing how they were was harder than watching them be fine without me.

"I'm good, I want to continue," I said and gave Archer a thankful look.

We stared into each other's eyes for a few seconds before Archer nodded and kissed me softly. As he dropped his arms, I caught Søren staring at us with pain written on his face. Guilt slammed into me – hard. He had lost his girlfriend only weeks before, so I couldn't imagine how hard it was for him to see two of his friends show that type of affection. And, while I wouldn't apologize for loving Archer – we'd had to fight for it – I also didn't want to twist the knife of grief inside Søren's chest.

Swearing to myself that I would keep any public demonstrations of affection with Archer to a minimum in front of Søren, I turned back towards my old apartment complex.

We were too far to hear anything that was said by the boys or my mom, but I could imagine Makaio's excited tone as he joked with his three friends. One of them had a football in his hands and he threw it playfully at my brother.

Since when did Makaio like football?

He had always told me that football was too rough and muddy for him. But ten months was a lot of time for kids – plenty of time for him to get new hobbies and new friends.

Then the five of them were moving, walking down the street to the bus stop. The bus system wasn't the nicest or most reliable around here, so I was surprised to see my mom willingly get on one.

Either way, I started walking after them.

"Wait, where are we going?" Søren asked gruffly. "I thought we were just checking that the kid was still doing good."

"We are," Archer answered.

"But he's good! Look at him, he's smiling like he won the Olympics!"

"Søren, shut it. We're here already, so we are going to follow them for a little while longer."

Søren didn't reply to Archer's words, and I decided to pretend like I hadn't heard their conversation behind me. I didn't want to explain to Søren that, even though I was acting like a creepy stalker, I needed to feel like I still knew my brother. Even if it was only for a day, I needed to feel like I still belonged in Makaio's life.

And his smiles were addicting. His laughs were my favorite thing in the world.

I couldn't leave after just a look. I needed more. I needed as much of him as I could get in the few hours we could spend here, suspended in time.

An hour later, the guys and I were eating ice cream on a bench at the end of a pier, almost completely surrounded by the ocean. The waves crashed against the end of the pier and the rocks around it – the sounds were a sweet melody I had missed. The ocean air was like a balm on my soul. It brought back so many memories of hours and hours on the waves. It was a time when everything was simpler – just the routine of my life, back when I was a sister, a student, a teacher, and a bartender.

From where I stood now, Old Kalani had a much less stressful life than New Kalani did.

"Stars, I love ice cream," Søren moaned into his triple chocolate ice cream.

Archer half-sighed half-gagged. "Stop it, Søren, I can't enjoy this if you keep making obscene sounds next to me."

Just because he liked to annoy Archer, Søren moaned again, this time much closer to his friend's ear. As they started bickering, I couldn't suppress a smile. I had missed seeing them this way. Their brotherly banter was both annoying and heartwarming.

"Can you guys stop this? I'm trying to enjoy the view in peace, here."

"The view of what exactly? An expanse of cold water under a gray sky?"

I gave Søren a dark look and shook my head. "If you can't see the beauty of this," I said with a wave of my hand toward the ocean, "then you're truly a lost soul."

The blond Golden put a hand on his chest, pretending to be hurt. "Oh, my heart! Your words wound me, dear Kalani, and—"

Reaching around Archer, I swatted him lightly behind the head to interrupt him. "You're so annoying. Maybe we should have left you on Olympus."

"Agreed," Archer nodded solemnly. "Actually, I'll bring you back right now. Let's go!"

Søren playfully shouldered my boyfriend and I chuckled. I'd missed this – the easy fun we had together. If only we had Sadie and Mei with us, we'd be truly complete again.

The pain I felt at the thought of my two friends – both gone in such different ways – was sharp and deep. For a second, I wanted to let myself feel it, feel the bone-deep pain of losing two of my friends.

But I didn't.

Instead, I took a deep breath and focused on my brother, playing football with his three friends on the beach, not even fifty yards away from us. Mom was sitting on a beach towel, reading a book, looking like a cool mom from the movies.

Around her, the boys were playing football – or attempting to – and laughing when one of them ended up lying in the sand from trying to catch a pass. None of them would ever end up playing varsity or college football, that was for sure, but they had fun. It was all that mattered.

Soon enough, all four of them were covered in sand, their cheeks red from the wind and the exhaustion.

"Football is such a strange sport, don't you think? For me, it lacks some sophistication and elegance. All these guys just tackling each other like they're wild animals is just… bleh."

I raised an eyebrow at Søren, surprised by his words. For some reason, I didn't think he was big on human sports, but now that I thought about it, it made sense. Søren and Sadie had lived on Earth for fifteen years before they had been taken to Olympus by their dad.

"I much prefer soccer. That sport is truly a masterpiece," the blond Golden sighed with contentment. "I used to play when I was younger. I was a left winger and I used to score pretty often. And, trust me, the ladies loved watching me play."

He gave us a stupid grin and an eyebrow wave as he said so, and I wouldn't suppress a laugh. There he was, the Søren whose ego was often slightly too big, but who remained terribly endearing.

"I'll believe it when I see it," I said with a chuckle.

"What? The soccer or the ladies? 'Cause I could demonstrate both."

I rolled my eyes at Søren's cockiness while Archer sighed.

"Man, I've seen you when you work out, and you aren't one of Aphrodite's, trust me."

"Ouch, Arch, can you please be any more honest?"

Smiling, I took another lick of my ice cream – coconut and pineapple, because those were the best flavors. "And the current facial hair situation is not great either, so I don't think you'd attract very many *ladies*," I teased with a pointed look to his unkept beard.

"Please, K, I know you don't want to hurt Archer's feelings, but you can admit that my beard is sexy. It gives me a rugged look, and I know the ladies love it. You included." He added a wink and Archer threw him a dark look.

"Stop trying to flirt with my girlfriend."

My heart fluttered at the word. It still felt surreal to hear Archer say that I was his girlfriend – and not a fake one.

Søren was about to respond when I heard a whistling sound and a football landed right into Archer's chocolate-strawberry ice cream cone. The dessert splashed against his shirt before falling to the floor.

Instinctively, I bent to take the football from the wooden pier floor.

"I'm so sorry! We didn't mean to hit you," a small high-pitched voice said.

As I turned, my heart stopped. Makaio was there, right in front of us, breathing rapidly from running over to us. Suddenly, my throat was tight, and my voice gone.

From this close, I could see that he had grown a couple of inches and his hair was shorter than the last time I'd seen him. But his eyes… his eyes were exactly the same as before.

"I can pay for another ice cream, I have a few dollars in my pocket," Makaio added while frantically searching his cargo pants.

"It's fine, kid. No worries. It was a little cold for ice cream anyway," Archer smiled warmly at my little brother and I almost sobbed at the relief on his face.

Seeing him this close without being able to take him into my arms hurt like hell. But what hurt the most was the way Makaio then looked at me and gave me a shy smile.

I had the irrational hope that, maybe, being so close to me would spark something in my brother's memory, but there was no recognition in his eyes.

"Can I have the ball back, miss? I promise we'll be more careful."

Miss. Gods, I could swear my heart was bleeding in my chest from the wound of Makaio's words.

"Lani. You can call me Lani," I stammered awkwardly.

Then, because I didn't want to embarrass myself or Makaio, I threw my hand out. Little fingers grazed mine as my brother took the ball.

"Thank you, Miss Lani."

Tears welled in my eyes, but I blinked, willing them away. Then I nodded and smiled at him as he said sorry again to Archer and ran back to his friends.

Immediately, Archer's arm was around me and he was pulling me against him.

Maybe staying longer and following Makaio and Mom here was a mistake. Perhaps I should have stopped this after the first few minutes.

My heart couldn't take this – being this close to Makaio without being able to be his sister.

He was doing good. Everyone could see this. So, why was I subjecting myself to emotional lashings like this?

"We can go home if you want," he whispered in my ear.

I didn't answer right away because my eyes were glued to Makaio's back as he ran along the wooden pier toward the beach. I couldn't look away.

So, I saw the moment his foot got caught in a crack in the wood and he lost his balance, falling into the water.

Immediately, I was up and running. My eyes scanned the water, looking for a head of brown hair. Nothing.

The waves were strong, especially close to the pier. Sharp-looking rocks were clustered a few yards away and I didn't need to be in the water to know that the current would push Makaio toward them.

He still wasn't back up.

"Kalani!"

Someone shouted, but I didn't look back. I couldn't stop or slow down.

Another second and I reached the place where Makaio had gone down.

I didn't think.

I jumped.

The water was cold and, as predicted, the current was strong. I tried to look around for Makaio's body, but the water wasn't clear, and I could barely see farther than my hand.

Panic was settling in as I came back to the surface, hoping I'd see Makaio's head.

I didn't.

Gasping for air, I went back under and swam with the current, frantically looking around for a small body.

Come on, Makaio. Please, please, please, don't do this to me.

I wasn't sure who I was praying for, but something happened. The water stopped moving. The ocean became an unnaturally calm, tranquil body of water.

I didn't question it. Instead, I started swimming again and continued to search the ocean floor for a dark form that could be my brother. My lungs burned, my eyes strained, but nothing.

Until the water started moving again. This time, a current was coming toward me, but strangely enough, I wasn't moving. It was like I was attracting the water to me.

It didn't make any sense.

But I didn't care about that, because something was moving toward me. For a second, I worried it would be a shark. But I rapidly saw that whatever was coming to me was too small and too unmoving.

Makaio.

In seconds, he was in my arms and I was kicking the water to get to the surface. Here again, it felt like the water was helping me move faster, a current pushing us around the rocks and toward the beach.

My relief was short lived because when our heads broke the surface of the water, Makaio didn't make a sound. I had no in-depth knowledge of first aid, but even I knew that it wasn't good.

Voices were screaming around us, but I ignored everyone. My whole focus was on holding onto Makaio and swimming to the beach. By the time I reached the sand, my whole body was shaking from the cold and the exhaustion.

"Baby! Oh, my baby boy!"

Suddenly, my mom was here, taking Makaio from my loose hold. She was crying and frantically touching the boy all over his face and chest. Nonsensical words flew from her mouth in between sobs, and I didn't know what to do to make things better.

Still holding onto Makaio's legs, I forced myself to release them. Then I took his wrist and pressed my fingers to what I hoped was his pulse point. *Nothing.* I moved a little, searching for the tiniest flicker beneath my fingers, and—

"Kalani, I can help. Let me do this."

Archer's voice and presence was comforting, even in such a stressful situation. Because I had a vague memory of Archer telling me he'd gone through first aid training a few years back, I moved a few inches away.

So gently that it hurt to watch, Archer took my mom's arms and moved her away from her son, all the while reassuring her that he'd help.

In seconds, he had assessed the situation and was blowing air into Makaio's mouth and massaging his chest.

The next few seconds were the longest of my life – and that was saying a lot since I'd had multiple near-death experiences during the Tournament. I couldn't breathe or think as I waited for Makaio to do *anything* other than remain lifeless.

A cough. Water regurgitated. Wet breaths.

I had never felt so relieved before as when Makaio cried out in Archer's hold.

"Oh, Makaio," Mom cried out through her tears. "You scared me so much."

Their embrace was like a knife to my heart. I wanted to hold my baby brother in my arms so badly that it physically hurt. But I couldn't just impose on a family moment like this. Not when a mom had believed she would lose her only son.

"Thank you so much," Mom said after a minute of holding her son, her eyes bouncing between mine and Archer's. "You both saved my baby boy's life."

I had. And I wasn't sure how, exactly, I'd managed that feat. The water had been too rough and cloudy for me to do or see anything. So how the hell had I managed to get to Makaio?

"I— I'm glad he's okay."

Even though the beach had been pretty empty, a crowd was starting to form around us. I didn't need Archer to tell me that we should go. We weren't supposed to be on Earth and the gods had eyes everywhere. If the wrong deity learned of our little illegal trip, we might never be able to come back.

I had to leave. I had to leave before people started taking videos of the scene.

I put a hand on Makaio's ankle and squeezed softy, incapable of leaving without at least touching his skin now that he was back. His eyes snapped open to mine and we stared at each other for a few seconds.

Then the moment broke when someone shouted that an ambulance was on its way. Hurriedly, I stood up and turned around, speed walking to join Søren and Archer on the outside of the crowd.

We left as fast as we'd arrived. And as we were walking through the universes to reach Olympus, I couldn't shake the thought that, maybe, Thanatos hadn't been wrong.

No human could have saved Makaio today.

Chapter Ten

Sadie

When we moved to Olympus, our dad told Søren and I that the most important thing wasn't to be the strongest person in the room, it was to be the best prepared one. The advice stuck with me because Olympus, for all of its beauty and amazing food, was a pit of snakes where everyone was strong and wanted to beat everyone else. Power levels were important, sure, but not the most important thing you could do to ensure your safety.

Preparation was.

That was how I felt as I got ready for tonight's party with Matteo and his friends.

I had gone shopping today because the clothes I'd been given as a Huntress weren't exactly fitting for a party. At least, I was pretty sure that full-on leather outfits or the plain jeans and t-shirts weren't what girls wore to dance at a club.

If Kellan saw me right there, wearing this dress, he would probably freak out and drag me by my hair back to Olympus.

Maybe he would be right. After all, I wasn't sure if this – going to a party with my target and his friends – was a great idea or the stupidest, most insane thing I'd ever done.

Perhaps it was both.

Sighing, I tugged on the hem of the dress, wondering for the thousandth time why it was so short. It was barely long enough to conceal my shortest blade, tied around the top of my thigh with a belt. But, based on what the lady at the store said, this was perfect for the occasion.

Hopefully Matteo would also think so, even though I wasn't pairing the short midnight blue dress with heels. Tonight's outfit would include sneakers, because I wasn't about to try to fight anyone in heels. That would be a mess and undermine the whole 'be prepared' speech my dad still loved to dish out every so often.

After long deliberations around the timing of my arrival, I had decided to show up slightly late – or at least appear to. Matteo had told me that he and his friends were getting to the bar by eleven pm. I didn't want to appear too eager, so I was planning on arriving in the bar at least ten minutes late. But I wouldn't let myself be unprepared either.

That was why I spent part of the afternoon scouting the bar, checking for exits and other important safety information. On the off chance that this was a trap, I wouldn't be going in completely blind.

And now, here I was. Walking in the bar twelve minutes past eleven, looking more put together than I had in months. As I passed through the door and got assaulted by the loud music and sounds of conversation, I had a brief flashback of the last time I'd truly taken care of my appearance – the night of the Opening Ceremony before the Tournament started, when Kalani, Mei, and I had gotten ready in our beautiful dresses and laughed together.

I shook the thoughts away before they could bring out the sadness and forced myself to smile instead. I was good. I was fine. That night was all about the mission – gaining Matteo's trust so that he wouldn't be so quick to try to poison me to death with his plants when the time came for me to take him to Olympus.

"Hey, Sadie! You made it!"

I turned to the left, following the voice, and found Matteo waving from a high table. Two girls and a guy were sitting next to him, all sipping from their drinks and looking half-tipsy already.

With a wave and a smile, I started walking toward them. Tension was gathered in my shoulders and I had to force myself to relax as I approached the table. Things would be okay. I just had to pretend to be someone else for a few hours – nothing hard with that, not after everything I'd gone through in the past few months.

"I was starting to worry you had gotten lost," the Copper teased, a toothpaste-commercial grin splitting his face.

I chuckled but didn't have time to answer because the man bent down and brought his lips close to my face.

For a second, I had the wild thought that he was going to kiss me. Which was both completely dumb and improbable. But, right as his cheek touched mine, I remembered *la bise*.

Thankfully, I had done a quick research on the internet earlier that week for French customs, and I remembered that it was polite to imitate the sound of a kiss when touching someone else's cheek during *la bise* – so I did.

By the time the two cheek-touches-slash-air-kisses were done, I was weirdly flustered. Thankfully, there was no time to dwell on the strange things my body was doing, because Matteo introduced his friends to me.

"Sadie, this is Léa, Paul, and Clémentine. Guys, this is Sadie."

Matteo's three friends turned to me, and I gave them an awkward wave, hoping I wouldn't have to do *la bise* with them. Tyche, goddess of Luck, must have been looking down on me because they gave me waves too and that was it.

Thank the stars.

"Want something to drink?" Matteo was leaning against the high table, looking relaxed and staring straight into my eyes. I held his stare for a second before dropping my eyes to his crossed arms – where his dark tee stretched over muscles for days.

Stars help me.

"Yeah, a drink sounds great."

Matteo nodded and then we were both walking toward the bar. The place was decently packed, and I was glad to be taller than the average woman because it allowed me to breathe easier in the crowd of sweaty people surrounding me.

Once we finally managed to get to the front of the bar, Matteo flagged down the bartender.

"What will it be?"

"I'll do a rum and coke."

"Make that two," I added, almost screaming over the loud music.

Matteo gave me a surprised look and I raised an eyebrow. "What?"

"Nothing," he grinned. "I just pictured you as more of a sweet cocktail kind of girl."

I scoffed and grabbed the glass the bartender had just put down before me. "I am a lot of things, Matteo. But sweet sure isn't one of them."

Then I turned and walked back to the table, incapable of containing a small smile. And, while I felt Matteo following me, I didn't turn around.

Once we got back to the table, things became a little smoother. I sat next to Léa, and Matteo took a seat in front of me. We inserted ourselves into the conversation and I learned that Clémentine worked in the kitchen at Le Bistrot de Pierre, which is where she and Matteo had become friends. Paul was Clémentine's boyfriend, and Léa was their college friend.

Somehow, in the two months he had been working at the restaurant, Matteo had gotten really close to this group of people, and they had plenty of fun stories to tell. After an hour, I knew a lot of things about Matteo and his friends. From how Matteo had met Léa – he had stumbled into her as she was coming in the kitchen and spilled a whole cocktail on her uniform – to the poker nights they had every Tuesday. It looked like Clémentine was the card shark and beat them every time.

"You'll have to come for the next poker night, Sadie! It'll be fun," the girl in question said.

"You just say that because you want someone else to destroy and get money from."

Clémentine made a face at Léa but didn't deny her friend's accusations. The two guys then teased Léa for being the one who always lost the most money, and I couldn't suppress a grin. Witnessing this reminded me of all of the good times I'd had with my friends – back when Søren, Archer, Kalani, and Mei were still my friends.

I missed it.

I missed them.

"I've never played poker. I don't know if I want to start now, especially if my whole bank account is at risk," I added with a pointed look at Clémentine.

The young woman tucked a strand of strawberry blond hair behind her ear and shrugged as if to say, *Fair enough.* Homegirl was confident, and I liked that.

Then a new song came on, and barely five notes in, Léa stood up with a shriek of pleasure. "That's our song! Let's go dance!"

Clémentine chugged the rest of her drink, and then both girls were on the dancefloor. I watched for a second as they danced, but turned away quickly when the sight made me think of Kalani, Mei, and I.

Stop that, Sadie.

The sudden discomfort must have been visible on my face because Matteo shifted so his head was in my line of vision. "Wanna go get some air outside?"

I immediately nodded because, yes, the atmosphere around here was starting to become too much. Being surrounded by these friends was bittersweet – my heart was suddenly twisting in pain. I wished I could be in a time when I could still dance with my friends and have fun like this. Without the heavy weight of shame and guilt hanging over me.

I needed a distraction, and quickly.

As I stood up, Paul told Matteo he'd stay here and check on the girls – just in case they 'started dancing on tables.'

So, it was just us then. Matteo guided me with a hand to my back toward the entrance of the bar. When fresh air hit my face, my shoulders relaxed instantly. I hadn't realized I'd gotten so tense – my whole body was now relaxing, and I breathed easier.

"Feeling better?" Matteo asked once we were on the side of the bar.

I nodded and gave the Copper a thankful smile. The music was soft and far away now, and we were basically alone on the sidewalk. Maybe I should have felt uncomfortable being alone with an almost stranger. Especially seeing as I was lying to said man and also knew that he was way more dangerous than a regular human guy. But the silence between us was nice and comfortable.

And Matteo didn't trigger any of my defense reactions. I didn't feel unsafe standing next to him.

"They can be a little overwhelming sometimes," Matteo said with a small laugh, his breath clouding the night air between us.

"They're great. You are lucky to have such great friends."

"So, if they didn't scare you off, what happened?" I raised an eyebrow in surprise at his straight-forward question, and he brought a hand up in defense. "You don't have to answer if it is too soon for personal questions."

It was too soon. I wasn't anywhere near ready to talk about my friends and how I had lost them. Especially not with a guy who was supposed to be my target and didn't know the real me.

But I was supposed to get close to Matteo, wasn't I? This was the reason why I was playing this whole undercover game tonight.

"I miss my friends and family, that's all. All of you are close and it made me miss them."

Matteo nodded and looked at the sky for a few seconds.

"It's hard to be away from home. Sometimes, I look up at the sky and knowing I am under the same stars as my family makes it a little better. It's cliché, I know, but it helps."

"It *is* cliché," I teased him softly, "but I like it."

"Yeah?" Matteo asked with a sheepish smile.

"Uh-huh." I looked up at the sky next to him and, even though the light pollution was making it hard to see anything, I tried to imagine the stars and constellations above our heads.

I liked the idea of watching the same sky at the same time as my friends or Søren. If only Olympus and Earth were synchronized when it came to the position of the stars through time.

"Have you talked to them since you left? Your friends and family, I mean."

"No, I haven't," I answered softly, my chest twisting in sadness. "They don't really want to talk to me, lately."

Matteo turned toward me and stared into my eyes for a second, his gaze intense. "I don't see how anyone could stay mad at you for long, Sadie. Maybe you should try and call them. I'm sure they miss you too."

I wished that was true. But causing someone's death was not something one could forget easily, unfortunately for my relationship with Søren. But I appreciated the sentiment.

I was about to change the subject with something lighter, when I heard male voices getting close to us. Turning, I spotted six men walking from the bar entrance toward us. I couldn't see their faces in the dark, but their body language wasn't the most reassuring. They seemed drunk and were heading straight for us.

"Hey, there, pretty lady! You can leave your boyfriend, we'll take care of you," one of them slurred at me, while his friends made obscene gestures.

Well. This was my first time going out on Earth since the 80s when I was a young teenager, but I could tell this wasn't a great situation to be in. Based on the way Matteo was not-so-subtly looking around us, he agreed with me.

The issue was, we were pretty far from the entrance of the bar. We had moved away from the doors because the music inside was too loud. And it was late – way past closing hours for all of the other stores around here. The only thing open on this whole street was the bar.

Now, I wouldn't usually be too worried about six drunk human men who seemed dead set on *having fun* with me. I was Thanatos' daughter. I could control the dead bodies of animals and people. I had trained for half my life to become a predator, whether with my powers or my body.

I wasn't anybody's prey. Especially not a pathetic drunk man's victim.

But here I was, standing next to the guy who I had spent multiple days convincing I was human. If I started using superhuman strength and my magic, I would blow up my cover. And then Matteo would unleash his venomous plants on me, sending me straight to a hospital bed, back on Olympus.

I didn't want that to happen. At all.

So, maybe I should take Matteo's hand and run. It would be the smart thing to do – even though I would forever be ashamed of such cowardice.

Thus, after sparing another look to the group of men – now that they were closer, I could see they were in their thirties and looked like they were angry-slash-horny drunk – I sighed and took Matteo's hand. I tried to plaster on a scared look and gave him my best damsel-in-distress look.

"Matteo, we should run, I don't think—"

A roar sounded behind me and I shifted just enough to see that one of the drunkards had decided to run toward us, a… was that a knife in his hand?

We had seconds – not even that – to start moving before we were face-to-face with the lovely knife-wielding guy over there. We needed to hurry. I moved back a step, one hand reaching for the dagger strapped around my thigh, tugging on Matteo's hand with the other, but he didn't budge. There was a wild look on his face, and I saw the moment he made a decision. His face settled, resembling the statues of Ares before he went to war.

"You have to trust me, Sadie. I promise, I'll explain."

Then he moved in front of me and all hell broke loose.

The guy with the knife – it looked like a kitchen knife, who even went out with a kitchen knife as a weapon? – was only a few feet away from us, shouting something I didn't understand. Then, suddenly, the ground exploded.

To be specific, pieces of the sidewalk broke out and flew around as huge plant grew from the ground. One second there was nothing, and the next, three seven-foot-tall Venus flytraps were standing between us and the crazy drunk man.

One of the plants bent at the stem and closed around the knife-wielding man, before half-swallowing it. A second later, there were two legs frantically kicking at the sky as the guy was being swallowed alive by the plant.

Stars. I was stunned by the view, and I had been living on Olympus for almost ten years. I'd seen plenty of crazy powers over the years. But this?

There was nothing comparable to Matteo's powers.

Screams surrounded us, coming from both the guy in the plant and his five friends. If I hadn't been so surprised by the turn of events, I would have laughed – from both shock and irony, because how hilarious was it that Matteo was revealing his powers to me like this? Or maybe I would have tried to help the guy being eaten alive – it would have been the right thing to do, even though the idiot had been asking for trouble.

Instead, I watched in complete stunned fascination as the scene unfolded. The plant finished its dinner and the friends ran away, screaming bloody murder. And Matteo…

Well, he was acting all protective over me, with a defensive posture and a heaving chest from using his powers. I never had people defending me – except for my annoying brother. Was it strange that I liked it?

A few seconds passed. The plants shrunk back into the ground, we were alone outside again, and, if not for the destroyed sidewalk, no one would have guessed something had happened.

As Matteo turned around to face me, I realized that my heart was thundering in my chest.

I was slightly panicking, because I was now sitting in a tight spot. On one hand, I could pretend like I was still a human and thus panic, scream, and run away. It would keep my cover story intact, but it would make it very tough for me to continue to hang out with Matteo.

On the other hand, I could stop this masquerade and use this as an excuse to take Matteo away. After all, he had just used his powers to kill a human man. Sure, the guy had tried to attack us for no reason, but the gods would never see it that way. Kellan might have told me that it was time to cut to the chase anyway, so maybe this was the solution.

But there was this thing in my heart telling me that I didn't want this to end. I just didn't know what *this* was. *This* could be spending time with Matteo or being on Earth. Hopefully, it was just the latter.

Or… perhaps I could decide to go down another path. This man was sweet and kind, and the only reason he'd used his powers was in self-defense. He didn't deserve to go to Olympus and be forced to fight in the Tournament. Perhaps I could do my best to ensure no one ever found him and brought him to Olympus.

It would mean defecting from my job as a Huntress for the Olympians and being on the run. But I didn't want to go back to Olympus where everything reminded me of every one of my failures. And I hated the gods for everything they did to Coppers – and to my friends and I – during the Tournament.

Helping Matteo escape from Olympus would be the biggest middle finger to the gods that I could manage in my current position.

In a split second, I decided to go for it and put on the most horrified face I could. Two steps backward, a terrified gasp, and a hand to my chest.

"No! You're— you're one of them!" Then, using the fake-tear skills I'd learned early on in life, I continued, "Please, don't take me to Olympus! I promise, I won't use my powers here!"

Praying this was going to be enough to convince him, I continued to slowly walk away from Matteo, putting on the best panicked act I had in store.

My eyes were set on Matteo's face, so I saw the moment when the confusion let place to a partial understanding. His eyebrows raised in shock and he shook his head a couple of times, as if to shake his thoughts in order.

"Wait, you think I'm—"

"One of those leather-wearing guys who want to kidnap me to a magical world? Yeah, psycho, and I'm not going!" I interrupted Matteo, half screaming my last words.

Then, to really anchor my words, I raised both hands in front of me, as if I was readying myself to fight. Because that was what a scared Copper would do – fight with everything they had to escape the fate that awaited them.

A few seconds passed. Then, Matteo released a stunned laugh. "I'm not one of them, Sadie. I'm one of us!"

"How do I know you're not lying through your teeth? I've been hiding for weeks. I am not about to drop everything for a guy's pretty face."

Matteo's face split into a grin at my words before he became serious again. "I don't know how to prove it to you, but I am like you. I have been hiding for months. Three of them have found me already, and I managed to escape, but I…" he stopped and raked a hand through his curls. "I thought I was alone. I felt so, so alone."

My heart clenched at Matteo's words, at the way his voice cracked on that last sentence. I could only imagine what it felt like, to be hunted like game without understanding why. To feel so utterly powerless.

I hated myself for being a part of the problem now.

I hated myself for lying to Matteo for days. For lying to him right then, too.

But I had to. I couldn't bring myself to shatter the trust and hope in his eyes as he looked at me.

It was for the greater good. I was going to help him escape, even if it meant having to play a part and lie every waking second.

"I feel so alone too," I said softly.

At my words, Matteo's eyes shone like someone had dropped stars in them, and his facial expression changed – as if he'd seen a miracle. As if I were the miracle.

Then, his arms were around me and he was giving me the best hug I'd ever received. I melted in his arms, holding onto him like he was a rock inside a storm. Maybe I was his rock too, because it almost felt like he was shaking.

He was crying, and maybe I was too. Or maybe it was the pollen – I heard it was particularly bad this time of year.

"We need to go," Matteo murmured as he pulled away gently. "We can't stay here."

"Why?"

"They will find us. The magic always attracts them. We have to go." There was a slight panic in his words.

"Where will we go then?"

There, in the middle of the night, I saw the moment Matteo decided to fully trust me. I could barely see his face in the dark, the light from the few lampposts shading his front. But I still knew – I saw his face open and felt the way his body shifted to continue to hold me even as he looked backward at the bar entrance.

"I know someone. They are creating a refuge for people like us. We'll be safe there."

Chapter Eleven

Kalani

By the time we got home, I was still shocked. Dissociated from reality.

I couldn't quite believe that this whole day had happened.

Somehow, I made it back home, sitting on one of the chairs on the patio overlooking the sea of clouds. I didn't remember Archer transporting us back to Olympus. I didn't remember the walk back to the apartment or saying goodbye to Søren. Everything had happened as if I were on autopilot, incapable of connecting with the world around me.

Perhaps I was finally broken. Sadie leaving us, my brother almost dying in my arms, the possibility of Thanatos being right about my otherness… maybe this was finally too much for my sanity.

"Mayfield," a voice brought me out of my thoughts. "You have to stop this. Makaio is alive. He's okay."

Looking up, I found Archer staring at me with a worried frown. I nodded and tried to give him a reassuring smile, but it didn't ease his concerns.

"I am sorry we couldn't stay longer. People were starting to film the scene, and I couldn't risk us being discovered."

"I know, Archer. I understand."

And I did. I knew that us going to Earth was very much illegal and could put Hermes – the god who gave us free translocators to cross to Earth and back – in a lot of trouble. I wanted us to be able to continue to cross between the parallel universes that were Olympus and the Earth, and that required stealth.

I understood that, and I agreed with Archer. The situation on the beach had been too dangerous for us to remain any longer.

But it hurt like hell to have to leave my baby brother half drowned and frozen to death on a beach, without knowing for sure that he would be okay.

Archer nodded at my words, but I could see he was still concerned. So, I reached out and took his hand, squeezing lightly.

"Stop making that face, Sunshine. I am okay. I just need a little time to digest what happened."

Archer usually smirked at the nickname, but this time his face barely relaxed. Still, he sat down next to me and tugged me closer to him. I burrowed into his neck and breathed his relaxing stormy scent. I'd missed this since we came back – the easy comfort his presence gave me.

Closing my eyes, I tried to empty my mind of the worries, and instead focused on the calm surrounding me, only broken by Archer's soft breathing.

"You know I'm here if you want to talk about it, right? I can only imagine how hard today was for you."

It was hard. Seeing my brother and mother happy together – without me – was just as hard as the first time. And then the drowning incident…

"I keep wondering if our presence caused this, you know. If us breaking the rules to come to Earth led to Makaio being in danger. Like the whole butterfly effect, or karma, or something."

Archer sighed softly before hugging me tighter. "Bad things happen to good people for no reason. I don't think us not being there would have prevented him from falling in the water. And, it's actually good that you were there to saved him, isn't it?"

I heard the unasked question in his tone – how exactly had I saved him? Even without jumping in, the water looked rough and troubled. I was a good swimmer, but I wasn't *that* good. We both knew it.

And now, Thanatos' words kept repeating on a loop in my mind. The god of Death had talked about a ripple of energy in my soul, something that humans did not have. Ever. Was this whole water-bending thing a manifestation of the weird non-human energy?

But it couldn't be. I must have imagined everything, and the currents had just changed on their own. There was no way my dad – surf-loving, chill-living dad – was anything other than human.

Right?

Yes. There was nothing to worry about. And Archer didn't need to worry about me any more than he already was. He didn't need to know the crazy hypotheses the god of Death had come up with.

"You're right," I said, shaking my head to rid myself of every unhappy thought. "Of course. Everything has just been… a lot."

Archer hummed and, thankfully, did not press me for more answers. For a few seconds, we sat there in comfortable silence, enjoying each other's presence and the sun going down on the sea of clouds.

"We don't have to go to the show or the after-party tomorrow, if you don't want to."

It took me a second to connect the dots. Somehow, even after weeks of helping out for the preparations, I had completely forgotten about the fashion show happening tomorrow.

Did I want to spend the whole day working with Priya to troubleshoot everything that would surely be wrong before and during the show? No.

Did I want to spend the evening at a party where most of participants considered me either insignificant or particularly offending to their status as deity? Nope.

But I owed it to Priya to be present, even if I felt emotionally raw and exhausted.

"Don't you try to get out of this, Archer Vasilias. You will wear the outfit your mother prepared for you, and you will attend the after-party with me."

I added a pointed look and a smile saying, *nice try*. He chuckled and raised a hand in surrender.

"Okay, down tiger. We'll go, and I'll wear the outfit, I promise."

I felt his gaze on the side of my face for a little while longer, and I could sense the concern seeping from his body. Still, he didn't add anything, and didn't ask any more questions. He could probably tell that I needed some time to figure out how I felt about what had gone down today.

So, for the rest of the evening, I snuggled in my boyfriend's arms and watched the sunset on the clouds. It was peaceful, relaxing, and almost managed to stop the dark train of thoughts in my mind.

As I fell asleep, I was still repeating the same mantra in my head, hoping it would make it true.

I was human. It would be crazy to think otherwise.
Right?

As it turned out, running a fashion show was hard work. None of the movies I'd seen on Earth – not even the classic with the queen Meryl Streep – would have prepared me for the whirlwind of chaos that was models, designers, photographs, event planners, and interns running around backstage on show day.

By the time the show was half-way over, I was winded from running around to help all of the people who had suddenly needed something since that morning. My hair was probably a mess – the glossy brown curls a long-forgotten memory – and I didn't even want to see the state of my makeup.

Today had been rough.

So, when Priya stopped me from running yet another errand with a hand on my shoulder, I was grateful.

"What are you still doing back here, Kalani? I thought you were supposed to be in the stands with Archie."

She seemed genuinely confused, so I refrained from giving her an exhaustive list of every single person who had sent me on a wild goose chase since she had told me she didn't need me anymore.

"There's just been a lot to do, so—"

"No," the Golden interrupted me with a stern yet soft look. "You have done your part. You are done. Go make sure Archie is behaving."

She gave me a meaningful look at the last words, and I chuckled. Yeah, Archer and polite society weren't the best of friends.

With a thankful word and a wave, I was almost sprinting out of the huge tent we were working in. Luck must have been on my side because no one asked to me to hunt for yet another lonely high heel that had gotten lost in the wilds. *Small blessings.*

By the time I rounded the tent and the crowd, and finally found Archer's head of dark hair above the crowd, the show was almost done.

"Oh, Mayfield! Thank the stars you are finally here," Archer exclaimed when I finally managed to squeeze my way to his side.

"Yeah, sorry to be late, there was a lot to do back there, and—" I stopped abruptly at the way his face had changed. "What?"

Archer's eyes moved over my body, tracing a path of fire across my skin. When his eyes came back to mine, their intensity took me by surprise.

"We should make it to these fancy events more often if it means I get to see you in this dress again."

I wasn't sure if it was the husky voice, his eyes burning with desire, or the sexy grin on his lips, but I blushed. A lot. And, while I liked the attention from my boyfriend, I didn't enjoy the weird looks from the Golden lady standing next to me.

"Stop it, people are staring," I whispered to him, a hand covering the redness of my cheek.

"Of course, they are, my girlfriend is stunning," he replied with a cheeky grin.

Although I rolled my eyes in exasperation, I couldn't suppress a chuckle at the words. It sure was nice to feel pretty, even with the messy hair and overall winded composure. It made me want to stand a little taller and hold my head a little higher.

"How was the show so far?"

Archer gave me an amused look but didn't comment on my poor attempt at redirecting the conversation onto a safer topic.

"Excellent, everyone did a great job this season. I particularly loved the silver dress. It looked like someone plucked moonlight out of the sky and sewed it on a dress, before adding pieces of the stars. It was a showstopper, and the model did a great job showcasing it."

I had to agree. Priya had done an amazing job coming up with the concept for that dress, and while I hadn't seen it on the runway, I could only imagine it looked even better there than it had backstage.

As I watched the last four models walk on the runway one after the other, their clothes shimmering in the sunlight and reminiscing of the stars – the theme for this year's collection – Archer continued to give me his thoughts on the best parts of the show. I could feel the pride for his mother's work seeping from his every word. It was beautiful to hear.

Once the show ended with fairy glitters raining from the sky, as if the stars had descended on Olympus themselves, the crowd broke into applause. I couldn't lie, it felt incredible to have been a part of such as beautiful show.

Beside me, Archer was grinning, looking like a proud dad after his child's first show at daycare. It was cute that he cared so much about his mom's work. Especially for a guy who couldn't be bothered to wear nice clothes to most fancy events.

Soon enough, the people attending dispersed, either mingling, going home, or being directed to the after party.

The dreaded after party.

A lady dressed in a teal pantsuit was the one showing the VIP guests to the entrance of the after party. From what I'd heard, it was being held in a nice section of the garden, secluded away from the main part of the garden we were in.

I hadn't seen the list of people who were invited to the exclusive event, but I could imagine most of the gods would be in attendance. And that was what Archer was worried about too – I knew he hadn't seen his father since the day I'd almost died, and he'd begged for my life to be spared. He didn't want to see him or his stepmother today. Which is why I wasn't surprised when the man in question put his hands on my hips and turned me until I was facing him.

"We could go home and have some fun," he said seductively, his thumbs grazing the exposed skin from the open back of my dress.

I shivered from the words, and his touch, and the way his eyes promised me a great time. It would be nice, especially after everything that had happened the day before, to let loose and have fun with my boyfriend. I missed his touch, and his attention, and how he could help me forget all of the pain in my life. It sure wouldn't be hard to say yes and run away with him.

But I also knew he was using his charm to evade his responsibilities.

"Nice try, Sunshine. You promised your mom you'd be there, and I promised her I would make sure you behaved. So, we are going."

Archer slid his hand farther down my back, his fingertips leaving invisible tingling marks on my skin. He stepped closer to be, so close that our chests were brushing together. "Are you sure, Mayfield? 'Cause I know plenty of ways I could *behave* for you tonight, and—"

Ripping myself from his hold and the daydreams I was *this close* to falling in, I shook my head. "No, no, no. Stop using your sweet words on me, it won't work!"

Archer raised an eyebrow in challenge and opened his mouth, but I stopped him short. "Stop it, Archer Vasilias. Do *not* say another word!" Then, with determination to not let myself fall under his charm, I took his wrist and dragged him to the lady in teal.

Okay, he might have let himself get dragged, chuckling along the way. But still, I only turned back to face him once we were out of the small labyrinth and well within the after party.

Immediately, I was dazzled by the finery around us. Constellations had been magicked to appear all around us, making it seem like we were not quite on Olympus anymore. A fountain of gold liquid – probably representing ichor – was in the center of the clearing, creating a soft golden glow. And the gods and goddesses attending wore such brilliant, shimmery, beautiful garments that they illuminated the space too.

I couldn't quite believe I was there, attending a party with all of the gods and goddesses of Olympus.

From where I stood, I could recognize Hecate and Athena, deep in conversation with a guy who, based on his winged shoes, was Hermes. While Hecate wore one of her tiny leather dresses with dangerously high heels, Hermes and Athena looked like they could have been on the runway themselves.

Farther to our left, Dionysus was entertaining a group of ladies with a glass of what looked like Olympian wine in hand. He still had a flowery shirt on, his long hair flowing in the breeze, looking like he could be heading to the beach any second.

Thankfully, I couldn't spot Artemis. I didn't doubt that she would be here, but I was glad to not have to face her right away.

Similarly, while he remained tense at my side, I heard Archer release a small sigh of relief when he didn't immediately see Zeus or Hera. To be fair, I was also hoping we wouldn't be subjected to seeing them tonight. While the king of the Olympians had allowed for Thanatos to save my life, I couldn't think past everything that he and his wife had done to Archer throughout his life. Putting a thirteen-year-old boy into the Tournament out of spite because of Zeus' infidelity was horrendous.

"Archie! Kalani! You came!" Priya's voice rose across the murmurs of the crowd as she extracted herself from the conversation she was having with a blond man who looked very much like Artemis – Apollo maybe?

Then two things happened.

First, the crowd of gods, goddesses, and lucky Goldens quieted suddenly, to the point where all we could hear was the noises coming from the fountain and quiet whispers. It was terribly uncomfortable to be the center of all of the attention, but I had somewhat prepared myself for it. After all, Archer was Zeus' son who wouldn't obey the orders of the king of the gods, and I was the only human to have ever participated in and won the Tournament.

I knew we would garner unwanted attention whether we wanted it or not.

But what surprised me wasn't the quiet or the heavy looks. No, what shocked me was what happened a few seconds later.

Glass shattered on the ground, the sound jarring even with the soft grass absorbing most of it.

At first, I thought someone had inadvertently spilled a tray of drinks when Priya had called our names. But then more glass went down, followed by four more trays of drinks shattering on the floor.

An incredulous look around the clearing showed me that six waiters and waitresses had dropped their trays and now stood over piles of broken crystal glasses. And, while everyone around them were moving away from the mess, all of the waiters and waitresses were staring directly at me.

"What in the heavens is happening?" A voice boomed from the opposite end of the party. Zeus.

The silence stretched as the king of the gods made his way to the front, where most of the damage had happened. No one dared to speak while a such thunderous aura emanated from the god of the Sky.

"Well, I demand an explanation for such incompetence! Don't believe all of you cannot be replaced," the king of the Olympians threatened with a look at each of the staff that had dropped trays in the middle of the exclusive after party. "Humans are always replaceable."

And, as Zeus said the last sentence with a scalding glare at the waiter closest to him, I knew immediately what this was about. If these waiters and waitresses were humans, then—

"We refuse to serve you anymore. We might be humans, but we are not your slaves," the waiter in front of Zeus said with a voice of steel.

"You do not have a choice but to serve your gods. There is nothing humans can be other than servants on Olympus."

The human man puffed his chest, refusing to back down in front of the king of the gods. The next second stretched and my heart started beating like crazy, thundering in my ears. I knew what was coming. And it wasn't anything good. For me, at least.

"That is false, we have a living proof right there. If a human can be allowed to live freely on Olympus, then consider all of us done."

Well, shit had definitely hit the fan.

And based on the heated looks coming from all of the deities and Goldens around me, yours truly was back on Olympus' unwanted list.

Chapter Twelve

Sadie

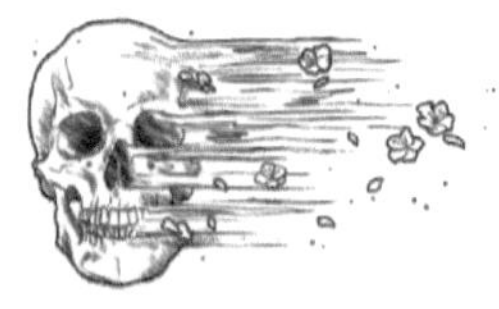

After Matteo revealed his powers to me, everything happened at the speed of light.

We didn't go in the bar to say goodbye to Matteo's friends. He sent them a quick text and then we were on the run.

We stopped by Matteo's apartment first. He was currently renting a room in an apartment with two other guys. In ten minutes, he had all of his things packed into two duffel bags. Seeing Matteo pack his meager belongings in such a clinical, efficient way made me wince.

This was a man who was already on the run. Because of people like me.

I didn't have time to dwell on the guilt I felt at the thought because we were gone again. Matteo drove his old, slightly beat-up black car to my hotel. He was surprised by how close I lived to his place – barely three minutes away.

What a coincidence.

I cooked up a half-assed story about how this was the first hotel I'd seen online, and I was still searching for a more stable place to stay before… well, before we decided to run away together. It must have been convincing enough because Matteo did not ask any other question, even when he saw how few things I owned.

In five minutes, I had my brand-new backpack and duffel bag filled with my three changes of clothes, a couple extra sweatshirts, toiletries, and a few weapons stashed in the bottom. Before leaving the room, I turned off the phone Kellan had given me and removed the SIM card, storing both in the bottom of my backpack. I hoped that this would prevent the Hunters from being able to trace our movements, at least for a little while.

Two minutes later, I had checked-out and was back in the car.

The first few kilometers were uncomfortable. The only sounds filling the car were the heater and the rumbling motor. Neither of us really knew what to say, now that we were heading off somewhere together.

Did I feel guilty that Matteo felt the need to run away again, because of other Hunters and Huntresses? Yes. And did I feel guilty that I was playing on his desire to not be alone to gain his trust in a moment of high emotional instability? Also, yes.

But here we were, and it was officially too late to turn back. I just had to remember that I was doing this for the right reasons — to make sure that he never had to compete in the Tournament, even if that branded me a traitor and prevented me from ever going back to Mount Olympus. Somehow, I knew that protecting Matteo from the horrors of Mount Olympus would be worth it.

"Where are we driving to, exactly?"

Matteo almost jumped at my voice before regaining his composure. I didn't need Archer's powers over the mind and its electrical waves to know that the Copper was confused, worried, and stressed. A bad combination when driving in the middle of the night.

"I am not sure yet."

I scoffed in incredulity. "What do you mean? I thought you said you knew of a place where Coppers are safe."

Matteo swallowed roughly before putting on his blinkers and getting onto the highway heading south of Paris.

"Well, I know this place exists, but I don't know exactly where it is. I do know where to find someone who will know, so that's where we are going."

Stars, I wasn't expecting that. This road trip was becoming more and more of a poor idea.

Maybe I should just take control of the situation and take us to the middle of the deepest forest or desert until we were as hidden as possible. It would probably be better than traveling through France in Matteo's own car, basically asking for my colleagues to find us. Especially when our current plan was so… nonexistent.

But I couldn't quite get myself to shatter the hope glinting in Matteo's dark eyes.

"How do you know this person will help us? How did you two even meet?" I might have sounded very skeptical, but how could I trust this plan?

"We met on social media. I was searching for information about people like us, back when I used my powers for the first time. Somehow, I ended up talking with this guy who made some tweets that everyone thought were crazy. But they were exactly what I had been experiencing. Especially once the first one of *them* showed up."

While I wasn't sure what 'tweets' were, I didn't need clarification to know who 'them' was referring to. I was one of *them*, Matteo just didn't know it yet. To say I felt like shit at the thought was a euphemism.

"We started talking, and after a few weeks, he decided I was deserving of his trust. He gave me the location for a woman who should be able to verify our identities and direct us to the safe haven for people like us."

There were a ton of unknowns in that plan. First of all, that man could be playing Matteo, or he could be completely psychotic. And then there was the whole several layers of knowledge about the 'safe haven for Coppers' which did not make me feel confident we would ever find such a place.

Matteo must have felt my skepticism because he winced before speaking again. "Look, I know it sounds crazy. I'm not dumb, I know people can say whatever they want online. But," he trailed off, searching for the right words, "I don't know. I just feel like this is the real deal you know. And if we were lucky enough to find each other like this, then maybe I was also lucky enough to find those other people."

To say that I was uncomfortable at the words Matteo said was an understatement. He was there, full of gratitude at not being alone anymore, and I… well, I wasn't the friend he thought I was. And the more time passed, the shittiest I felt about it.

And, still, I couldn't force myself to put a stop to my foolish mission.

So, instead of doing my job and stopping this masquerade – which would be the sensible option, really, instead of deciding to upend my life forever – I turned to face Matteo's profile in the dark. He looked uncomfortable and self-conscious.

"I don't think this is crazy per say, just a little…" I waved my hand around, hoping to find the right word, "hopeful?"

Matteo laughed but it was a hollow, weak sound. I missed the cheerful Matteo I'd gotten to know over the past few days.

"You don't have to pretend otherwise, Sadie. I know how this sounds. I just don't think I have another choice right now." He looked away from the road for one second to give me a tight smile. "You don't have to do it, though. I can drop you off at a train station close by, and you can continue on your own if you prefer."

I wasn't surprised by the offer. In the little time since I had officially met Matteo, I had started to see that he was a generous man. He wanted friendship but would never ask his friends for something that would be too much of an inconvenience. He didn't want to impose on others. Even when he cared a lot. And, based on the look on his face, I could tell he dreaded being alone again.

"I am feeling adventurous right now, so count me in on this treasure hunt."

Matteo didn't turn to face me, but I saw the corners of his lips turn up.

A minute passed when we both stared at the dark road, empty except for us. It was deep into the night, and I knew neither of us would be able to remain awake for hours on end.

"We should still stop somewhere to sleep a few hours," I said after a while when Matteo yawned.

"You're probably right. We'll stop at the next exit."

I nodded but couldn't bear to let silence settle again in the car. So, instead, I decided to attempt breaking the wall of awkwardness that had been raised between us. Conversation had flowed so easily between us before, there was no reason we couldn't get past the events of tonight.

"We should probably talk about it. What happened earlier, I mean."

Matteo tensed and nodded tersely. His powers were clearly a sore subject for him.

"How long have you known you were not quite human?" I asked after Matteo opened his mouth and closed it multiple times.

"Almost two years. I was coming back from an evening shift at my job and a group of guys tried to rob me. I kind of… exploded magic? I don't know. One second I was held at gunpoint, and the next, I was surrounded by gigantic plants and three lifeless bodies."

Well. That sounded like a traumatic experience. To be fair, Coppers usually had pretty terrible ways of revealing their powers for the first time. Their magic remained dormant until particularly strong emotions forced them to involuntarily use their powers. It was a hidden defense mechanism that often saved their lives, but also alerted us on Olympus that there was another Copper to retrieve for the next edition of the Tournament.

"So, you didn't know before that? Your parents didn't tell you anything?"

"I was mostly raised by my grandparents. My mom used to have custody of me, but she has been a little unstable mentally for years now. She was diagnosed with paranoid schizophrenia when I was three. And when she started telling everyone that my unknown dad was a god… well, let's say people thought she had gone completely crazy and wasn't fit to take care of me anymore." He let out a humorless laugh at the irony of the situation. "Turns out she was right the whole time."

My heart clenched at his words. Discovering his mother had been telling the truth after not believing her for years must have been heartbreaking.

"Did you know before your powers came out?"

For a second, I debated lying and telling him that I'd discovered everything when my powers had appeared. It would help me separate myself from the person I was creating with him – I desperately needed some separation from the charismatic and vulnerable man next to me. But, here again, I couldn't get myself to lie any more than I already was. After what Matteo had told me about his mom – the raw emotions in his voice – I couldn't give him anything other than the truth. Or as much of it as I could safely tell.

"I always knew something was different with me, or at least, I knew for so long that I can't remember a time when I thought I was fully human. I didn't need anybody to tell me, though, because my powers showed up very early. I started seeing ghosts as a child, and I learned pretty quickly that it wasn't normal."

Matteo scoffed and it warmed me to see some light back in his eyes.

"Is that your powers? Seeing ghosts?"

"Kind of. It started that way, back when I was a child. I learned to block their energies out, so I don't see them anymore.

Sometimes, a particularly strong spirit will manage to make itself seen and heard, but it is very rare. My real powers came out a few months ago, when I started being able to control dead matter."

"Dead matter?"

"Corpses. Skeletons. Of humans or animals, it doesn't matter."

I winced a little at my words, expecting the usual horror that accompanied the realization that I could do necromancy. People usually didn't understand my powers – they were scared or disgusted by my magic, not awed like they were with my brother's gifts.

"Holy shit! That is so cool!" Matteo exclaimed with a huge grin. "I love Zombie movies, so you'll have to show me what you can do at some point!"

The excitation in his voice was so unexpected that I remained speechless for a second. No one, except for my dad, had been excited to hear that I could control the dead. Ever.

"People are usually freaked out about it."

"People are dumb, Zombie girl. That's just how it is."

"Oh, is that my new nickname, then? 'Zombie girl'?" I asked, completely astonished by his reaction. "Is death a fetish for you? Should I be worried that I am in a car with you?"

Matteo laughed, his face transforming with a joyful expression that I liked a lot. How had we even gone from depressing thoughts of his mom being gaslit her whole adult life to laughing about my necromancy powers?

"Yeah, I like it, it has a nice ring to it. Don't you think, Zombie girl? And, no, I don't have a death fetish, but I do seem to enjoy all of the weird things you do."

There were flutters in my chest, and I blamed them on how nice his laugh was – it was contagious and joyful, the kind of laugh I hadn't heard in a long time.

"Plus, based on your powers and skills at martial arts, it seems like maybe I should be the one scared to share a car with you. If you decide to beat me up, can you avoid hitting my face? And also, I tend to scream in a very high-pitched tone when I'm scared, but I'd appreciate it if you don't mention it to other people. I have a reputation to uphold, you know?" He added in stage whisper.

"It'll be tough, but I'll keep that to myself, I promise," I winked at him, stifling a laugh at his antics.

Matteo sighed dramatically in relief, running a hand through his dark coppery curls. "I'm so glad we found each other," he said after a beat, his tone sincere. "Really, I am. It's good to not be alone in this anymore, you know?"

He gave me quick look, the light of the dashboard reflecting in his dark eyes. My heart pounded against my ribs, as if I'd sprinted seconds ago. This guy could take my breath away with just a few genuine and vulnerable words.

"I do. I am glad I met you too, Matteo."

By the time we stopped for the night at a hotel and fell asleep, we had spent another thirty minutes talking about our powers and our next steps in this wild goose chase. And, yeah, it felt good to be able to talk to someone as my own person, and not as one half of the Aska twin two-for-one deal.

I was just me. Sadie. The girl who just wanted to be appreciated for who she was, dark powers and all.

And, for the first time in weeks, I didn't feel completely alone anymore.

Chapter Thirteen

Kalani

I had never realized how quickly unrest could spread through a group of people. Sure, I had witnessed what could happen when students – and especially girls on their periods – were denied the right to go to the restroom during classes: a high-school-wide protest. Soon enough, hundreds of teenage girls wore red outfits and refused to enter the classrooms of professors who didn't allow them to leave their class when they needed to go. A week later, restroom passes were reinstated.

Anyway, my point was that I had seen how quickly anger and frustration could spread, but I didn't think it could go quite *this* quickly.

Barely two hours after the shit-show of an afterparty during which six humans quit their not-so-voluntary positions as waiters, two-thirds of the human servants on Olympus had stopped working.

By nightfall, not a single human servant was still working their assigned job.

This protest would be quite impressive, and I would usually support the movement – after all, I was a human myself, and didn't approve of the treatment my fellow red-blooded human beings were being given.

However, since I was somewhat responsible for this situation and was now hated by almost everyone on Olympus… well, I felt slightly apprehensive about publicly supporting the social movement.

Because, you see, humans had been tasked with all of the worst jobs on Olympus – all of the jobs that deities, Goldens, and Coppers did not want to do. Human workers were waiters, housekeepers, maids, garbage collectors, construction workers, and so on.

To make things worse, these human workers had often been tricked into coming to Olympus. They had been offered a dream position, and once they had signed on the dotted line, they had found themselves stuck on Mount Olympus, with their whole life erased from Earth.

Interesting way to keep the workforce happy, am I right?

So, was it surprising that these human servants were extremely angry at seeing little old me, fellow human, living on Olympus as a free woman? Not at all. I understood their pain and rage. They had every right to protest their living conditions.

My main issue here, was that most, if not all, of the deities, Goldens, and Coppers, were now blaming me for the social unrest and the work that wasn't being done.

Unsurprisingly, many of the Olympians and their children had trouble cooking on their own or cleaning their houses without the help of overworked and underpaid human hands.

So, now, less than twenty-four hours after the fact, tensions ran high on the mountain.

Nobody knew what was going to happen next. The deities and their descendants would not let all of these humans live in their world freely. And, as the involuntary and unofficial mascot for the free-the-humans movement, I was worried I'd bear the brunt of the blame and be punished along my fellow humans.

"Can you stop pacing like a lion in cage? It's stressing me out."

Archer stopped abruptly and turned to gape at me. "This is what's stressing you out? Not the stars-damned shitshow happening at the moment? Olympus is going to literally fall apart without the humans working, and they are not going to start their jobs again unless they feel they are being listened to. Do you think the gods will even pretend to listen for a second? No! This whole situation is going to end in a massive execution of all of the human servants who refuse to take back their jobs. And after that happens, do you know what the gods will do? They will try to get rid of the reason their social order fell apart in the first place. You!"

I had never seen Archer like this – he was seconds away from ripping at the seams from worrying too much. And, while I always liked to see evidence of his care and love for me, I couldn't bear to see him in pain like this.

"I know that, Sunshine. But your pacing around is not going to fix anything, is it?"

Archer crossed his arms on his broad chest and stared defiantly at me for a few seconds. When he sighed and finally sat down on one of his comfy chairs across from me, I couldn't suppress a satisfied smirk. He knew damn well that I was right.

"When did you become so rational, Mayfield?"

"Why, are you impressed? I can give you some tips if you want."

"No, I'm annoyed," he said with a dark glare I knew wasn't truthful. He loved me too much for that. "And stop changing the subject. We need to figure out a plan."

"I don't think there's much we can do. It's not like I have any pull with the other humans on the mountain. I had never met any of them until yesterday."

"Well, we'll have to find something to show you're not with them. That you aren't part of their rebellion. Maybe the gods will forget about you if you publicly claim to be on their side."

Just the idea of claiming to agree with the gods and their unjust social order made me nauseous. It was easy to pretend like Olympus was the perfect place to live once I was away from the Tournament and everything it represented. But now that I was faced with yet another ugly side of the land of the gods... I wouldn't be able to live with myself if I pretended to not see how awful and cruel the Olympian social hierarchy was.

"I'm not, though."

"What do you mean, you're not?" Archer asked with a confused look, as if all of this was a no-brainer.

"I can't say I am on the gods' side when I'm not. What they're doing to those people is awful. I can't stand for that."

Based on his open mouth and wide eyes, it appeared I had rendered Archer speechless. That was a first.

"But—" He stopped to blink a few times, seemingly confused by my words. "But if you publicly support the unrest then the gods will destroy you. They will strip you of your right to live here and..." He took a deep breath before starting again. "You have to say you stand with the gods, Mayfield. Even if you don't mean it."

I could see the fear in Archer's eyes. The panic he felt was clear in his words, too. He was scared that I wouldn't be allowed to live with him anymore. And it scared me too. Archer and I had become so close over the past few months, that I had a hard time believing that we had started out as reluctant allies.

But I had been forced to do so many things I didn't agree with or believe in to survive. I had hurt others, sometimes even condemning them to death through my actions. I had lied and I had fought.

And I had excused all of it, because I'd done it to survive.

I couldn't do one more despicable thing today. For once, I needed to do something that my moral compass agreed with. I *had* to do the right thing. Even if it terrified me.

"I am sorry, Archer, but I can't. These people could have been *me*. I could have—"

"Oh, come on!" Archer exclaimed, raising his hands in both frustration and anger. "They agreed to come here! And you did what none of them dared to do – you fought for your right to live here. None of them did that."

"None of them had the chance to do that! And, if not for Hecate, I would be dead right now, and all because there were no more 'human servant' positions available. None of these people were given the option to participate in the Tournament," I scoffed, bewildered by Archer's words. "And that's not even my original point. These workers were tricked by the gods and Goldens, convinced they were signing up for a cool job on a mysterious island where everything would be fun and exotic! Do you think any of them would have said yes if they were actually told that everyone on Earth would forget them? Do you think they were told they would be sequestered on Olympus and forced to work the most unwanted jobs until they died? Because I sure don't."

Archer stared at me then, jaw clenched so hard that I was worried for his teeth. His eyes, usually the color of the ocean right before a storm, were much darker now. And it felt like there was an ocean between us now, growing larger and larger by the second.

"You can't do it, Kalani." Archer stepped forward, close enough that we could touch if only we reached for each other. "You can't do against Zeus and win."

"You did."

The laugh that came out of Archer's chest was full of pain. "I wouldn't call two participations in the Tournament a win. My hands will forever be stained by all of the blood I shed. And, still, I know that Zeus could send me back a third time, and there's nothing I could do about it. That's not winning."

Archer never talked about that first time he'd been in the Tournament, when he had been thirteen. I hadn't pried either, since I could only imagine how traumatizing the whole experience would have been for him. But now, as he stood there, right in front of me, I could see the pain and shame in his eyes.

"Then what am I supposed to do, Archer? Spend the rest of my life agreeing to everything Zeus asks of me, even if it leads to the death of dozens of other people?"

"Yes, that's what you do. That's what all of us are going to do, because we'll never win against the gods. Not against Zeus, and not against Artemis either. So, if you have even an ounce of self-preservation, you'll do as I suggested and play nice with the gods."

This was a determining moment. Not just for our relationship, but for the rest of my life, too. I could choose to take the easy road and play nice with the gods. If I tried hard enough, I might even be able to convince myself that I wasn't responsible for the potential deaths of the humans of Olympus.

And, to be fair, Archer wasn't wrong when he said that going against Zeus and Artemis was madness. I knew it was. But I was standing there, at that crossroad, and I couldn't, for the life of me, start walking down the easy path.

"I can't do it," I murmured finally. "I need to be able to look at myself in the mirror once all of this is over, Archer."

My boyfriend – was he still my boyfriend now that we were clearly heading towards different life paths? – closed his eyes for a second, clearly reeling in his emotions.

"There won't be an 'after' this. Not if you refuse to listen to me. Zeus and the rest of the Olympians will destroy you and us by association. I won't..." he took a deep breath before meeting my gaze again, "I won't be able to protect you again, not like I did in the Tournament. They won't let me. Søren is still half drowning in grief, and Sadie is gone. You'll be alone, and we both know you won't survive on your own. Not here, among us."

Those last words hit me like a knife to the chest. *Among us*. It was the first time since we'd first met that Archer had made it perfectly clear that I wasn't really a part of this world, that I wasn't his equal and never would be. There was a barrier between us, one that I forgot all too often. But he was almost a god, and

I was… well, I wasn't quite sure what I was, but it wasn't anything close to a descendant of the Greek gods.

"So, this is it, then? I'm supposed to spend the rest of my life agreeing with Zeus and the gods, no matter what? Are you going to do that? If Zeus demands that you become an enforcer for him, that you torture prisoners for him, will you say yes?"

A muscle popped in Archer's jaw and he crossed his arms. Well, who was becoming defensive now?

We both knew that Archer and the twins had ended up competing in the last edition of the Tournament because Archer had refused to become an enforcer for his father. I understood why he had refused – using his powers to inflict pain onto others and torture his father's enemies would have destroyed him. But that was just my point, wasn't it? That when it came down to it, Archer had risked everything for his values.

"You know that was different."

"How was it different, exactly? Was it going against your morals? Would you have been responsible for the death of people?" I raised an eyebrow, making sure Archer got the irony of it all. "Because it doesn't seem that different to me."

Archer's chin dropped and he frowned. I knew right away that he wouldn't back down. I loved that man, but he was stubborn. More than was reasonable, sometimes.

But maybe that was hypocritical of me, because I was ready to stand my ground, too.

"The difference is that I have the means to survive any punishment Zeus can put me through. We both know you can't say the same thing."

Here again, the words hurt me more than I cared to accept. I wasn't delusional. I knew very well that without Archer and the twin, I never would have made it out of the Tournament alive. Without their help – or the help of other people – I would never be able to survive another Tournament.

Still, hearing Archer say it loud and clear was painful.

"Then, I guess we are at a dead end." I leaned back in my seat, crossing my arms to hide my shaking hands.

Panic crept in Archer's gaze and he took a step toward me, his hands dropping to his sides, fingers clenching slightly. "Please, Mayfield. We will find another way to help the humans, I promise. But this… you can't go against Zeus like this. He'll punish you and I'll have to watch you die, *again*." One of his hands shifted as if to reach for me. "I swear I'll help you, but you publicly standing against the gods is not the right decision."

He gave me a pleading look, and my heart clenched. I loved him. So much. And I could tell he was terrified. But I couldn't let him think he could make decisions for me. I was my own person, and I would make the decisions that I needed to make. For the both of us, yes, but for myself first.

"I can make my own decisions, Archer. And I don't know what I will do yet, but I will *not* pretend to agree with the messed-up social order the gods have implemented here. No matter what, this will not happen."

Archer's jaw clenched at my words. He nodded slowly, his eyes hardening as he realized that I would not change my mind.

"I see." His tone was ice-cold, his posture stiff.

We sat in a tense silence for a few seconds – and I was itching to get closer to him, because I still loved him, even during heated arguments – when the someone knocked on the door of the apartment.

Immediately, I stood up and almost ran to the door. I opened it without looking through the peephole – which was probably very stupid, seeing as I wasn't the most popular girl on Olympus right then. Luckily, dear old Søren was on the doorstep.

"Oh, thank goodness!" I exclaimed, relieved beyond measure.

"Wow, I love these kinds of welcomes! I'll come more often if you miss me so much, K. You know, I could even move in here to be closer to you and—"

"Shut it, Søren," Archer barked from inside.

Søren whistled, his smile still firmly in place. That man must have seen Archer in worst moods over the years, because he didn't even flinch at his friend's harsh tone.

"To what do we owe this pleasure, Søren?" I asked, hoping Archer would tone down the terrible mood.

The blond Golden leaned against the door frame, looking all chill and confident. "I am here because Priya wants to organize a crisis reunion. You guys holed up in this place for too long, it's time to face the music."

What an exciting prospect. I couldn't wait to spend some time with my pissed-off boyfriend – who I was also angry at, – his mother, and his best friend. Somehow, I knew all three of them would be on the same page. Because, no matter how much I cared for them, I was aware that they had been raised with different priorities and visions of social justice than me.

None of them knew what it was like to be the prey in a room full of predators.

None of them knew what it was like to be terrified of everyone around you.

But I did. And I could relate to all of the other people who had been taken away from their home on Earth and landed here, unaware that their human lives had changed forever.

It was fine, though. If there was something I'd learned today, it was that I could stand my ground. So, I would.

I had become the mascot of this human rebellion without my consent, sure. But I wouldn't turn my back on all of my people who had started fighting for more rights.

I would stand with them, because that was the right thing to do. And I was tired of making the easy choices – most of them had the bitter aftertaste of wrongness.

Chapter Fourteen

Sadie

After a whole day of travel, we had finally arrived in a tiny village on the border between France and Switzerland. Driving had been terrible because of a sudden snowstorm the day before. Plus, Matteo had insisted on taking the back roads, as if us driving on the highway would somehow make us more vulnerable.

Unsurprisingly, seeing as I – the Huntress Matteo wanted to evade – was sitting in the car, we arrived at destination without an issue.

The address Matteo had was that of an antique shop with a faded sign half hanging loose from the storefront. Had I not heard all about the store and owner from Matteo, I might have thought the place was uninhabited. After all, the display window was so clustered and dark that the place looked abandoned.

"Are you sure this is it?"

"Of course," Matteo said with feigned confidence. "It looks like the picture Thomas sent me."

From our lengthy conversation on the topic, I knew Thomas was the guy who had talked to Matteo on Twitter. He was the man who swore he had created a safe haven for Coppers.

"If I'd seen a picture of this place, I never would've come here," I mumbled as Matteo opened the car door with as much zest as he could muster.

With a deep sigh – because how was I always putting myself in these sketchy situations lately? – I gathered my bearings and got out of the car.

The air was cold and biting against my cheeks. The snow crunched against my boots, reminding me of home – the one I had before moving to Olympus. For a second, I felt a pinch of nostalgia. But, as quick as it happened, I snuffed the thought to focus on the present.

"Let's get going, Zombie girl," Matteo called when I lingered next to the car.

I rolled my eyes at his overly cheerful demeanor but started moving. I knew we had to go in, I just didn't particularly want to discover what was inside the place, seeing as the outside looked creepy as hell.

Ironic for a necromancy girl, I knew.

When Matteo opened the door, the first thing that I registered was the smell. It smelled like cookies baking. *Good* cookies. Was this an antique shop or a bakery?

Next, my gaze fell on shelves upon shelves full of old-looking books, fancy kitchen ware, and creepy dolls. What an odd assortment of things to sell.

"Customers! Hi, hi, hi! Come on in!" A cheery voice exclaimed from the back of the store.

I couldn't see the speaker, but it sounded like a teenage girl. Was a teenager in charge of the shop? Were we here to see a young girl? Was a *teenager* in charge of giving out directions to the place where Coppers could live in peace? Who in the stars had made this decision?

Let's just say that, if I'd been in charge of security, I wouldn't have given the keys of the kingdom to a kid.

Anyway. Matteo did not seem to think anything was strange. He trudged his way in between the overflowing shelves and I followed, because while I didn't trust this whole situation, I would not be a coward.

Sure enough, after making it through the unending clutter of random stuff through the store, we finally reached the back of the room where, sure enough, a teenager was standing among a pile of boxes.

Upon seeing us, the girl smiled brightly, revealing pink braces, and moved a pile of cardboard boxes to allow for her to move closer to us. She wore black leggings and a pink sweatshirt with a doll pictured on it. Her whole persona was like a splash of color in an ocean of darkness – she stuck out like a sore thumb in this place.

"Hi! Welcome to Anna's Curiosities!" she exclaimed, adding an energetic clap at the end. Was she a cheerleader or something?

"Are you Anna?" I asked with a raised eyebrow.

"Oh no! That's my grandma! She has dementia, so she doesn't work here much. I mean, she loves it, this shop is her favorite child. Don't tell my mom this, of course," she laughed, as if this was an inside joke or something. "But, you know, she tends to forget people have to pay, when she works here. She also forgets to close the shop. And she gives our stuff to people on the street. She's really nice, that's why! She loves people and wants to make them happy. Gifts are her love language, which I am grateful for, believe me! Christmas is my favorite time of the year!" she laughed. "But it doesn't help for the turnover of the business. So, anyway, here I am! Sofia, at your service!"

She ended the monologue with another bright smile, and I was rethinking all of my life decisions. I did not have the patience to deal with an overly talkative teenage girl in need of a bestie.

Thankfully, Matteo was quicker to recover from the whirlwind that was Sofia.

"Great," he exclaimed after a long second, forcing a tense smile on his face. "Nice to meet you, Sofia."

"The pleasure is all mine, dear customers! How can I help you, today? We have a special promotion on 1950s silverware, and this is the last day for our very special sale on horror books."

"Oh, that sounds great, but—"

"You should also check out the new arrival section," Sofia interrupted Matteo, rummaging through one of the many boxes around her.

"We will, but first we—"

"Look at this!" the teenager almost yelled, brandishing a creepy doll like a trophy. "Isn't this amazing? It's giving haunted house, don't you think?"

I could tell the girl was about to go on a tangent, explaining everything that made this doll special, and I just couldn't to it. Five months ago, I would have gently smiled and nodded, patiently waiting for the teenager to finish. But, since then, my whole life had gone up in flames, and I didn't feel like being patient anymore.

"Stop!" The word exploded out of me like a bomb, cutting off Sofia's monologue.

The girl snapped her mouth shut and stared at me with doe-caught-in-headlights eyes. She looked seconds away from crying. *Holy stars.*

Sighing, I tried to put on a reassuring smile. "I am sorry for being harsh, Sofia. It's just that we are in a bit of a time constraint, here."

Sofia's face lit up, and she nodded enthusiastically. "Of course. Sorry for that, I can get a little excited sometimes." What an understatement. "What can I do to help you, then?"

I gave Matteo a *Well let's go then, dude* look, and he swallowed nervously.

"Sofia, we are here for Thomas' safe haven."

Matteo added a weighed look to his last words, which was met with the teenager's blank expression. For a long second, I worried that we weren't in the right place, or that this whole adventure had been a bad prank from a weird guy on the internet.

"Oh, my goodness!" Sofia finally exclaimed; her eyes wide as saucers. "You're two of Tommy's friends! You should have told me that from the start!"

We had tried to. And, here again, I wondered who had chosen to trust a teenager with no filter to handle the kind of important information that surrounded a safe haven for Coppers.

"Alright, let me go get my notebook, I have all of the instructions in there," the teenager called as she ran to the backroom.

For the next few seconds, all I could hear were drawers opening and closing frantically. Was she going to have to upturn the entire place to find the notebook?

After thirty seconds had passed, I shifted to look at Matteo. He was leaning against a shelf full of mini troll figurines, arms crossed over his chest. Our eyes met and he winced. "Don't give me that look, Zombie girl. I know what you're thinking. She is a little…" he waved vaguely around the place, seemingly unable to find a word to accurately describe the whirlwind that was Sofia. "But I know that we are at the right place. It will be worth it. I promise," he added with a pointed look.

Right then, Sofia released a high pitch squealed, and I couldn't suppress an eye roll. Still, I didn't say anything else and even put on a small smile when the girl came back, brandishing a sparkly, hot pink notebook in the air.

"I found it!"

"You did," Matteo chuckled awkwardly.

"Alright, now I can do my job properly!" Sofia sat on a nearby stool and opened the notebook to a middle page. "Who wants to go?"

"Oh," Matteo exclaimed with a nervous look in my direction. "She's with me. But I'm the one who contacted Thomas so is it okay if I'm the one you test?"

"For sure!" Sofia smiled. "If you pass, there will be more in-depth procedures for both of you to go through once you reach your destination." Then, with a look in my direction, she murmured, as if she was sharing a secret with me, "I understand the fear of blood, I faint every time I get my blood drawn. Something about seeing my own blood out of my body, it just doesn't sit well with my stomach. Or my heart, for that matter. I should probably talk to a medical professional about it, because I think I might be getting panic attacks in those situations, and I feel like—"

"Sofia!" I interrupted her once again.

The girl blushed bright red, her eyes widening in realization. "Oh my, I am sorry! I'll stay on track, I promise!"

Matteo stepped forward, suddenly looking slightly nervous. He was probably right to be, because the girl looked a little too excited about the prospect of whatever was coming next.

However, I felt utterly relieved. During our drive in, I had told Matteo that I was terrified of needles and very uncomfortable talking about my upbringing and magical powers to strangers. I had added a few tears to showcase the anxiousness I was portraying. I had felt slightly bad about my lie – yet another one – but it was a necessary evil. There was no hiding the golden sheen of my blood, characteristic of the high percentage of ichor in my veins.

Thankfully, either the security measures surrounding the coordinates of the safe haven for Copper were lax, or the teenager was particularly bad at her job, because she didn't seem to want to check both of our identities.

I wouldn't complain about it, though.

"Good. First, can I have your full name? To check Thomas did put you on our monthly list."

"Matteo Bailet."

"No middle name?" Sofia inquired, focused on writing the information in her notebook.

"No, my parents ran out of ideas after my first name."

"Well, that's nice. My mom uses my middle name like a weapon of mass destruction."

And I could imagine there were often occasions when Sofia's middle name was needed – at least based on her current scattered energy.

After a few seconds of writing – Matteo's name wasn't that long, so what was she doodling in there? – Sofia looked back up expectantly.

"Can you please show me the color of your blood now?"

Matteo choked on air at the words. "Uh, sorry?"

"Are you deaf? I thought you people were superhuman. You are breaking a myth here."

This time I couldn't suppress a snicker at Matteo's reddening cheeks. Sofia could be fierce when she wanted – it made me like her a little more.

"No, I heard. It's just that…" Matteo cleared his throat nervously. "How am I supposed to show you my blood?"

Sofia produced a small knife from her back pocket and handed it to the Copper. Why in the stars was she carrying a knife in her back pocket? That seemed really unsafe for a teenage girl who tripped over herself and enjoyed creepy dolls a little too much. There were much safer ways to handle and store weapons.

I didn't have time to dwell on Sofia and her knife for too long, because Matteo pricked his finger. A drop of blood bubbled to the surface, glinting copper in the dim light.

For a second, I stared, fascinated, at Matteo's blood. Seeing the ichor in his blood was a stark reminder of our differences – his coppery, mine golden.

Then, I remembered that I was supposed to be terrified of blood, and I made a show of turning around and putting a hand on my mouth, as if nauseous.

Matteo gave me a reassuring pat on the shoulder, and I made sure to ask if the bleeding had stopped before turning around. When I faced the Copper and teenager again, I did my best to look uncomfortable.

Truthfully, it wasn't that hard to pretend, because this whole situation was making me uneasy. I was telling myself that I was helping Matteo out, making sure that he arrived in one piece wherever he was going and that he remained safely away from Olympus, but it was hard to forget about the lies and trickery I was using along the way.

So, I stood there, watching as Matteo answered the last of Sofia's questions. I watched the girl beam with pride as she gave us the address for where Thomas and the other Coppers were hiding.

The gleam in Matteo's eyes – his relief and joy – was a knife in my heart.

The guy was terribly endearing, and I was worried about the moment when he finally discovered that I was a fraud. The enemy. He would be appalled at learning that he had shared the location of a pocket of Copper resistance with a Golden.

But I couldn't get myself to leave him alone.

So, I didn't do anything. I sat in the car as we started driving again, the translocator burning a hole in my pocket. And I tried telling myself that I could find a way to make things better. I wasn't sure what I was going to do, but I would find something.

Chapter Fifteen

Kalani

Unsurprisingly, the walk to Priya's house was silent and tense. Archer wouldn't look me in the eyes. I didn't want to acknowledge him and his ridiculously controlling ways either. And Søren, while clearly confused about what had happened between Archer and I, had wisely decided not to enter the battlefield.

I was almost relieved when we entered Priya Vasilias's sprawling mansion. Maybe the Golden of Innovation would have some insight on more than just the social unrest that had started on Olympus.

I had never been inside Priya's house, but I didn't have the heart to look around and marvel at the decoration. The walk through the house was a blur, my brain stuck on my argument with Archer.

The more time passed, the angrier I felt about him thinking it was okay to decide things for me. I knew he was older and wiser – what with time moving much slower on Olympus than Earth – and I understood that Zeus was not someone you could dismiss easily, but I wasn't some silly little girl who needed her boyfriend's guidance.

I could make my own damn decisions.

So, I followed Søren through the house, trying to ignore Archer's angry footsteps behind me.

To say I entered Priya's living room seething was an understatement.

However, I quickly went from anger to surprise, because Nafula was standing right next to the window, arms crossed and leaning against the wall. The shock of seeing her there – especially after how our last interaction had ended – was enough to stun me into place.

"Nafula?" I asked, surprised by the turn of events.

"What are you doing here?" This time it was Archer asking.

Nafula didn't cower under what I knew to be Archer's stone-cold gaze. She raised an eyebrow – clearly meaning *Really? Are you going to be a bitch about this?* – and pushed herself off of the wall.

"I want answers. About Sadie and about what all of you are doing lately that is bringing chaos everywhere. Obviously," the Copper added with a smirk directed at Archer.

"I think that is what we are all here for." I jumped in surprise at Priya striding in the room from behind us. She was all business – her jaw set, eyes calculating. In that moment, she looked a lot like her mother, Athena. Priya usually radiated a warm aura and provided others with heartfelt support and smiles. But today?

Oh, today, Priya Vasilias seemed ready for war.

Someone might have said that I was a little intimidated by my boyfriend's mother, and they might have been right. But who wouldn't?

"We have a lot to get through," the Golden declared as she settled in the biggest sitting chair in the room. "Please, sit."

Søren almost immediately dropped down on one side of the couch, manspreading until only a third of the space was available anymore. Nafula took the other sitting chair.

I could have decided to sit on the opposite couch, next to where Archer was heading. Usually, I would have leapt at the chance to sit close to him and feel his comforting warmth.

But today…

Well. Today, I was pissed at him and his lack of trust in me. So, while it was probably the pettiest thing I'd ever done in my entire life, I decided to squeeze my way next to Søren, ignoring his incredulous look and muttered curse when he was forced to sit properly on his half of the couch. The whole time, I made a point not to look in Archer's direction.

I knew him too well anyway. I didn't need to look into his eyes to know that my actions would have caused him to clench his jaw and become closed-off. I could almost feel his gaze burn the side of my head, his powers barely tickling the mental barriers I always kept in place.

Priya was either oblivious to our quarrel or she didn't care – which was more likely – because she crossed her hands on her lap and cleared her throat. "Alright, let's tackle the easiest part first. Earlier, Nafula mentioned that Sadie was on Earth, acting as a Huntress for the Olympians. Have any of you heard from her since she left?"

All of us shook our heads sheepishly. Søren tensed next to me, his fingers curling tightly around his knee, joints white from the pressure. I wasn't sure how he felt. Sure, he had been able to talk to me about the situation a little bit, about the trauma of losing Mei in such a public, unexpected way. But the guy needed more than just a quick chat. He needed therapy and to talk with a professional – he needed help to deal with his grief and stop blaming Sadie or himself. I just wasn't sure this kind of mental health support was available on Olympus.

"Well, that is problematic. I was hoping to have Sadie help us in the next few days," the Golden murmured, a frown on her face. "I will contact the manager for new recruits at the

Hunting center, to see if I can get some information on Sadie's whereabouts."

"It would be great, thank you, Priya," I said with a grateful nod. Knowing that Sadie was alright – because she couldn't be anything other than good, right? – would ease my worries a thousandfold.

Athena's daughter inclined her head gracefully before turning her attention to her son. For the first time in minutes, I looked at Archer. He was sitting, arms crossed over his chest, looking like a sullen, pissed off god. I had to bury the want to go and run my hand through his dark hair or try to make him smile.

I was mad at him, dammit. I needed to get a hand on my feelings.

If only Archer wasn't as hot, maybe it would be easier to stay mad at him.

If only I didn't love him so much.

"I need a full report on the situation from your point of view, Archie."

Archer nodded and started reciting everything that had happened since the night before. Every word was clinical and straight to the point. Thankfully, he didn't talk about our earlier argument. But even without the mention of the fight, I was uncomfortable hearing the facts from the party laid-out in the cold light of day.

I had never wanted to cause any trouble. If not for someone messing up their job, I would not even be here in the first place. Obviously, I had never aimed to be some grand revolutionary movement's figurehead. My only objective after I had set foot on Olympus had been to survive. Everything I had done in the Tournament, everything I'd bled and fought for... it had all been for a faraway dream of being with my family again.

So, while I definitely cared about the living situation of the other humans on Mount Olympus, I couldn't pretend like my intentions had been to prove that humans could be equals to the Coppers.

No, I'd been much more selfish than that.

How horrible was it that, up until a day ago, I was barely aware that humans were forced to work on Olympus?

Maybe if I focused on my anger against Archer, I'd be able to avoid the guilt. Forever. Or, at least until things calmed down, both on Olympus and in my mind.

Priya hummed in agreement and jotted down some notes on her antique-looking notebook. Where in the hell had she gotten the notebook from? Or the quill, for that matter?

"Now that we are all on the same page regarding last night's events," Archer's mom started as she finished writing whatever she deemed important, "let me add a few points. First of all, I received reports an hour ago that over ninety-eight percent of all human workers have joined the protest and stopped working their assigned jobs."

Even hearing it from Priya Vasilias's mouth, I couldn't quite believe it. I'd only spent a few months on Olympus, but I already knew full well that the gods could be cruel. And unnecessarily strict. Especially toward those they considered lesser.

Like us. Humans.

Which was why I knew all of these people protesting and refusing to work were risking much more than just their jobs. They were risking their lives.

"This is bound to anger the gods and Goldens. Sooner rather than later." Priya emphasized her last words, and even though she didn't look my way, I felt like her words were directed right at my chest.

"And if the Coppers are forced to pick up the slack, that could cause even more trouble," Søren added gruffly next to me.

I almost scoffed at that. Were the gods and Goldens so incapable that they couldn't feed themselves or have clean clothes without help from the humans? Or from Coppers who they had also forcibly removed from Earth?

I was about to chime in to remark that, maybe the inhabitants of Olympus learning how to take care of themselves like grown adults was a blessing in disguise, when a loud knock resonated in the house.

All of us stopped dead in our tracks and a tense silence settled on the room for a long second, before the knock sounded again.

Someone was outside the house. And that someone was impatient.

With one hand raised to signal us to wait quietly, Priya left the room, her heels clicking away on the marble floor. And while I strained to listen for the door opening or someone talking in the entryway, I couldn't catch anything over the sound of my heart frantically beating.

I had no idea who was at the door, talking to Priya. For all I knew, it might be the Olympus equivalent of the Girl Scouts trying to sell their cookies. There was no reason for my heart to beat this fast or loud.

"Shit," Archer cursed, nervously raking his hands through his hair. "This is such a mess."

I had to clench my fists to stop myself from reaching out to soothe him. Comforting him, letting him know I was there for him through words, looks, and soft touches… it had become a reflex and a need. And, usually, I loved the deep connection I felt with Archer – the way it was almost like our souls touched right along with our bodies.

But right then, as our argument still hung in the air between us… well, I really wished I could turn off my feelings for him.

"Will you stop it with the whining, little lightning prince?" Nafula sneered in Archer's direction, standing up to walk away from us. "It's grating on the nerves."

Archer sent her a dark glare and crossed his arms on his chest. "What does that even mean?"

"Nothing. Although, worst comes to worst, you'll just ask daddy to clean up said mess, right?"

Right as Nafula dropped the last words, I felt the air crackle with tension. The hair on my arms stood up, and for a second, I almost felt as if Archer had really inherited his dad's lightning powers. I wouldn't have liked to be on the receiving end of his glare, but Nafula took it like a champ.

"Don't speak about things you don't know, Nafula."

"Funny," the Copper scoffed, "because you sure seem to have a lot of opinions about the way Kalani should deal with this situation, but based on your skin and blood color you've never been a part of any minority, have you?"

Well holy cow, I sure enjoyed the way Archer was speechless right then. And, while I knew Nafula was still very mad at me – and rightfully so – for the way things had gone down with Sadie, I was happy to see that part of her was on my side on this particular issue.

Next to me, Søren was almost giddy with pure excitement at the prospect of a fight. He was such a sucker for drama, and while I usually laughed along with him, I was way too stressed about the whole situation to let myself relax.

Archer clenched his jaw, his cheek muscle ticking under a shadow of a beard. He looked half a second away from strangling the Copper. "You should really—"

He stopped abruptly when the door to the living room opened to reveal Priya, and behind her, Hermes. The messenger of the Gods.

The god was tall, with a head of dark curls that fell over his forehead in a boyish manner that clashed with what I was sure to be advanced age. After all, weren't the Olympian deities thousands of years old?

He wore a red sweatshirt, dark jeans, and white high-top sneakers with little wings beating lazily from the sides of the shoes. If not for the winged shoes, he could have passed for an American college student. It was odd, seeing as most deities and Goldens chose to mix Earth fashion with more traditional Olympian clothing. But, after all, Hermes was probably the God that traveled the most to Earth – blending in with the human crowd must have been a practical choice.

"Well, what a lovely reunion we have here!" Hermes clapped his hands and seemed utterly oblivious to the tension that still permeated the air between all of us. "Archer, my man! Long time no see!"

Ensued the weirdest fifteen seconds of my life during which Hermes and Archer proceeded to give each other a very long bro hug filled with back claps and a whole lot of 'what's up'. Had I landed in an alternate universe? Hermes was thousands of years old and Archer had grown up on Earth when Michael Jackson was still a minor – how the hell did they know this bro hug routine?

And I wasn't the only one really confused because my eyes met Nafula's and we exchanged a clear *what the hell* look before shaking our heads at the display.

After a few seconds of watching the two men embrace like they hadn't seen each other for a decade, Priya cleared her throat and they finally separated.

"My bad, mama Vasilias, I got distracted," the god said with a prayer sign in Priya's direction. "I was asked to transmit an invitation for Kalani Mayfield to join my brothers and sisters at the throne room."

"Your brothers and sisters?" I asked, confused whether this was a courtesy call or something more.

"The other Olympian gods and goddesses, of course! We are all children of the Titans, living as family on this beautiful mountain," he added with smile, acting weirdly like a cult guru.

This god was the most disarming one I'd met yet, but I didn't have the time to worry about him any longer because my heart rate had picked back up. I was being summoned to meet the deities ruling Olympus, and I was pretty sure it wasn't for a cup of tea and biscuits.

Shit, I was in trouble.

"Is there a way to get out of it?" Archer asked, all business again.

This time, it was Priya who answered, her voice somber. "Unfortunately, when the king of Olympus calls, one answers."

Archer's face went hard at the mention of his father, and my heart squeezed painfully as I remembered what Archer had told me about his dad – how much pain being Zeus's son had brought him.

"All right dear Kalani, shall I give you a ride?" Hermes exclaimed like he was offering to take me to Disneyland.

I closed my eyes to gather the strength to deal with the overexcited puppy that was Hermes but didn't say anything. After all, what could I do? Like Priya said, when the king of Olympus requested my presence, there was nothing I could do but obey.

Palms sweaty from the anticipation of having to face the twelve Olympian gods in what was sure to be a trial with twelve judges and no jury, I took a step toward Hermes.

"She's not going on her own."

The words were like thunder, splicing the air in two.

"I was told to only bring Kalani," the messenger god said cautiously.

"I don't care," Archer continued, moving so he'd be between me and his friend. "It's either the both of us, or neither of us. Your choice."

The two entered a staring contest, and while I could only see Archer's back, I knew his face clearly conveyed that he wouldn't back down. A few seconds passed, my heartbeat pounding in my ears in time with the mounting worry in my chest. Were they going to fight? Was Hermes going to make Archer pay for daring to go against the words of a god? Was he—

"Alright, homeboy, let's roll!"

Then, with a smile and a mock salute in the direction of Priya, Hermes grabbed both of our arms. A second later, Archer and I were not in his mom's house anymore, but on a patio facing twelve thrones, all but one – Hermes's – filled with deities ready to find a culprit for the uprising.

With my luck, I wouldn't even have the chance to say two words before Artemis convinced everyone that getting rid of me would be better than dealing with this.

Based on the way Artemis was staring at me with a devilish smile like I was a deer she dreamed of hunting down… well, let's say I wasn't particularly enthusiastic about the next half hour.

Chapter Sixteen

Kalani

Life was so ironic sometimes. Months ago, this place – with its lush green grass, imposing marble and gold thrones, and small army of leather-dressed soldiers – was the first glimpse I had had of Mount Olympus. The last time I had stood on this patio, my whole life had fallen apart and desperation had made me sign up for a deadly tournament against the grandchildren of the gods.

How fitting was it that, after winning that awful Tournament and trying to rebuild myself after everything that had happened, I was back in this exact same spot?

Full circle moment, right?

"You sure took your time, Hermes," Zeus grumbled from his spot on the tallest, most imposing of the twelve thrones.

Hermes rolled his eyes and grumbled something I couldn't quite hear as he walked to his own throne. However, godly hearing was probably much better than mine, because Zeus's eyes darkened, and the thunder resonated from behind me. It was slightly dramatic, but I guessed immense powers called for immense displays of said power.

"Why is your newest bastard here, honey?"

I was so busy looking at the Hermes and Zeus show that I hadn't even taken the time to properly look at the other deities also present. To be fair, I might have also been avoiding looking in their direction to make sure I didn't have to see Artemis's smug smile. But now that she had spoken, I couldn't ignore Hera anymore.

Sitting to the right of her husband, Hera looked every bit like the queen of Olympus she was. With a long red dress that hugged her frame and long, shiny dark hair, she looked like a model. If only her hateful sneer in Archer's direction didn't clash with her beauty.

Archer tensed beside me at his stepmother's disdainful words and I had to stop myself from reaching out to take his hand – not because of our argument, but because I knew he wouldn't want to appear vulnerable in front of Hera and Zeus. Still, the hatred that filled my heart was so potent that I was surprised it didn't become a physical thing. How could someone decide to force a thirteen-year-old boy to compete in a deadly tournament against adults just because of his father's infidelity? How could someone be this cruel?

"Let's not get into this, my dear," Zeus answered with a compromising tone and a hand squeeze. "We are here for more important matters, are we not?" Then, with a look in Archer's direction, "I trust that you will not cause issues."

Archer nodded stiffly, looking tense as a statue. On her throne, Hera huffed haughtily but didn't add anything else, allowing for the change of topic.

"Yes, let's get this done," said a red-haired god who was probably Ares – at least, based on the bulging muscles and war helmet resting on his thigh.

There was a grumble of agreement coming from a few of the deities assembled, making me realize that not everyone was feeling particularly concerned by the issue at hand. This might actually play in my favor.

"Kalani Mayfield, you have been summoned in front of the Olympian council, to explain your involvement in the human protests that were started yesterday on Mount Olympus," Zeus declared with a very formal tone. "Athena, if you will."

The goddess of military strategy and wisdom leaned forward in her seat and seared me with her intense gaze. The goddess was destabilizing in a unique way compared to the rest of her family – she wasn't the most imposing or the most beautiful, and she didn't have the most impressive powers, but she had this aura that made me incredibly uncomfortable. It felt as if she saw every minuscule detail about me, as if she registered my every move and thoughts, and made calculations about the best outcomes at all times. And, somehow, that made my body react as if she were more dangerous than Ares, for instance, and he was the god of war!

Although, to be fair, smart women could be a thousand times more dangerous than strong men.

"Kalani Mayfield, thank you for presenting yourself to us today," Athena started with a benevolent smile. As if I'd had any choice. Still, I nodded and pretended like I was oh so glad to be there.

"We are gathered today because we want to investigate the genesis of this protest movement that is spreading amongst the humans living on Mount Olympus. Would you be able to share with us how you became acquainted with the social movement?"

Athena's words, while outwardly unsuspecting, turned my mouth dry like paper. My whole existence might depend on my answers in the next few minutes. And, while I had nothing to hide – really, I had become the mascot of this revolt without my consent – I also couldn't in good conscience *not* support the movement. Now, I just hoped that my stance on the issue would not cost me my life.

"I had no idea a social movement was going to happen until it started. This was a surprise for me, just as it was for many people on Olympus."

There, that was pretty non-threatening, right?

Athena hummed, her eyes never leaving my face and her features remaining impassive. "And how close are you to the leaders of this social movement?"

"I… I mean, not at all? I have not met them, nor do I have any contact with them."

Again, Athena waited for a few seconds before speaking, as if to make sure I didn't have anything else to add. "Alright. Then, how come your name comes back whenever humans reach out to negotiate their demands? It seems as though your position on Mount Olympus is driving the protest forward. How do you explain that?"

I felt Archer shift next to me, but he thankfully didn't intervene. Our argument from earlier replayed in my mind, and I knew that under his harsh words, he was terrified for me. His presence here, in front of both his father and stepmother, was proof of that. And, while I was still mad at him for not respecting my position on the strike, I could also understand his stance. Now that I was faced with having to officially choose a side, I understood that the words I used to answer Athena's questions could very well define the rest of my life.

Cautiously, I pursed my lips, trying to find the best way to answer.

"I cannot really explain it, since, as I just mentioned, I haven't personally met any of the people involved in the protest. I am not aware of the specific demands or claims made by the protesters, and any use of my name was done without my consent or knowledge."

I vaguely registered a few sighs coming from the deities assembled before me – I might even have recognized a slight snicker coming from dear old Artemis – but I remained entirely focused on Athena. Still, I could not see anything on her face that betrayed her thoughts. She was utterly impassive, and it did not help the mounting tension in my body.

"Convenient, isn't it?" Artemis chimed in with a smirk that didn't foresee anything good for me.

Athena gave her sister a look that very clearly said to let her handle this, before turning back toward me. "I see. Well, since you are not involved in this social movement, you will be more than willing to speak in support of the rule of the gods, won't you, Kalani Mayfield?"

Ah. There it was. The question that would probably seal my fate as a troublemaker and send me straight to death. How exciting.

I couldn't see Archer from where he stood slightly behind me, but I knew that he was half a second away from putting a hand on my mouth and answering in my place. And, to be totally honest, now that I stood in front of the twelve Olympian gods in all of their magical glory, I didn't feel as confident as I had been that morning. Standing up to the gods had gone from a vague thought to a reality, and I wasn't ashamed to admit that my hands were shaking as I cleared my throat.

I opened my mouth to answer but Archer stopped me with a hand around my forearm. "Please," he murmured, so low that I barely heard him. "Don't do this. We will find another way to support them, I promise."

His voice broke on the last words, and my heart clenched at the sound. Even after our argument, and even while being mad at him, I couldn't stop loving him. Doing something that made him this distraught was breaking my heart.

However, I couldn't continue to act against my conscience anymore. I'd bartered with myself, bent my own morals, and done things I would forever be ashamed of. I *needed* to do something good. Something I agreed with wholeheartedly.

So, I gave Archer a soft look, one I hoped conveyed that I wasn't doing this to go against his wishes. I just had to be true to myself. Even if it had painful repercussions.

I saw on Archer's face the moment he knew that there was no changing my mind. His pleading eyes closed, his jaw clenched, and he dropped my arm. My skin felt freezing cold in his absence, and I almost reached out to hold his hand. But I needed to do this on my own. I had to find the strength to stand on my own two feet and defend my values in front of everyone.

This was the moment to prove that the Tournament hadn't turned me into someone younger Kalani would despise.

"With all due respect, you do not want me to take a public stance on this issue, because I will not lie and pretend like I can't understand the claims that are made here."

Lightning broke the sky in two at my words, thunder cracking loudly in the air, translating very clearly Zeus's thoughts at my words. And, while none of the other gods had dramatic reactions to my words, I knew that I hadn't made friends right then.

Still, Athena barely reacted to my words, keeping a perfectly calm face. Her eyes almost sparkled though, which made me wonder if she was excited to see someone stand up to the king of the gods. However, I couldn't tell if she was more entertained because she was surprised by my audacity or because she enjoyed the unexpected challenge.

Artemis opened her mouth to speak, probably thinking this was a great time to chime in and vote for them to get rid of me, but Athena stopped her with a raised hand. If I weren't so stressed about the outcome of this little hearing session, I would have laughed at Artemis's shocked face at being shushed that way.

"I see," Athena nodded slowly, her eyes never leaving mine. "Well, that might prove to be a complication. What could make you change your mind and speak in favor of our council's ruling?"

Were the gods so desperate for me to support them that they were really trying to negotiate with me? How strange. I hadn't been expecting this at all. Rage and unnecessary cruelty, yes. But trying to change my mind without any veiled threats *yet?* No, I certainly hadn't been expecting that.

Play along, Mayfield. For the love of the stars, do not antagonize them any further.

I tensed as Archer's voice resonated in my mind. He had only used his powers to mind speak to me a couple of times, and only during dangerous situations. But still, having Alexei break into my mind during the Tournament had left marks and I hated feeling like the privacy of my thoughts was invaded by anyone, including Archer. So, I didn't particularly enjoy feeling Archer in my head, even if I knew he was only doing it because of what was currently at stakes.

Trying to calm my thundering heart, I took a deep breath. I now had two choices. The first one was to do what Archer was pleading for me to do and smooth things over with the gods. Or, I could continue to follow my beliefs and refuse to back down.

My throat was dry as Athena continued to spear me with her intense gray eyes. My thoughts were all over the place, and I wasn't sure whether to follow my morals or my screaming survival instincts.

Someone clicked their tongues in annoyance and my gaze snapped to Artemis. She looked at me with a mixture of glee and haughty contempt, as if I were an ant she couldn't wait to squash under her feet.

And it made me oh so mad.

"I would be more than happy to speak in your favor if you decide to change the laws of Mount Olympus and allow the humans that work here to have better living conditions and be allowed to go back to Earth if they so desire. As long as the humans you took from Earth are stuck here, working without many rights or benefits, I can't in good conscience speak out against their strike."

Athena raised her brows right as the sky shattered from Zeus's lightning again. This time, the thunder was so loud that I worried I was going to get electrocuted any second.

"Do you dare to insinuate that my rule over Mount Olympus and its inhabitants is not fair?" Zeus bellowed.

I wasn't ashamed to admit that I took a small step back at the sight of Zeus's glowing, rage-filled eyes. The man was scary as hell, and I was this close to apologizing and asking for forgiveness. And, while I wanted to be brave and hold my ground, it was impossible to not be slightly terrified when the god of the sky stared at you like he wanted to burn you to the ground. Well, let's say it didn't make it easy to act like a courageous woman.

My eyes widened in a mix of shock and terror as Zeus stood up, his lightning scepter glowing in his right hand. Was he really going to fry me alive with one of this lightning bolts? Just because I had answered Athena's question truthfully?

I couldn't believe that this was going to be the end of me. After everything that I had overcome in the past three months, it seemed terribly anticlimactic that I would die from the wrath of the king of the gods mere weeks after beating dozens of Coppers during the Tournament and earning my place on Mount Olympus.

"Do not even think about it," Archer growled as he stepped in front of me, posture menacing. Was it terrible that I was relieved that he was willing to fight his father to protect me? I was supposed to be a brave independent woman who didn't need her overprotective boyfriend to make decisions for her, dammit!

"Are you going to defy me too, son?" Zeus's voice was ear-splitting now, so loud that I could feel it in my bones. "This human girl has the hubris to think that she can contradict my rule. She has the audacity to support the ridiculous strike of a group of ungrateful pests. Your plaything deserves punishment. I will not stand to be ridiculed any longer!"

Thunder rattled the ground and my whole body on his last words. Facing off a rageful Zeus was more terrifying than anything I'd experienced before, and it made me realize just how far out of my depth I was. The Tournament had been an awakening on how different humans and Coppers were. But seeing one of the twelve Olympians use his full powers was on a whole different level.

"Athena asked a question, and Kalani answered her truth. If none of you had summoned her here today, Kalani would not have expressed those opinions in public," Archer argued, his body shaking with what could have been either anger or frustration. "And you cannot be foolish enough to believe that hurting Kalani for something you asked of her would be okay with me. I don't think you want to make an enemy out of me, *father.*"

Archer almost spat that last word and I shivered at the view of my man defending me in front of the most powerful beings in the universe. I might have been mad at him, but I could still appreciate how attractive he was in that moment.

Thunder continued to resonate in the distance, and I could almost see the anger coming off of Zeus in waves. As Archer and his father continued to face off, my gaze snagged on a delighted Artemis. She was spinning a golden arrow on her pointer finger, watching the confrontation like this was an episode of her favorite TV show.

"To be fair, Zeus, I did prod the girl for an answer," Athena chimed in with a sigh, as if this whole situation was a bother to her.

The king of the gods seemed to calm down at the goddess of wisdom's words, and I felt my chest relax a little with hope that things would diffuse down.

However, I could always count on Artemis to make sure things remained interesting – and dangerous – for me. And here she was, about to come through. Again.

"Although, as the situation remains, we only have two choices on our hands," the goddess of the hunt exclaimed with poorly hidden glee. "Either we yield to the humans' demands, or we squash them like the pests they are, starting with making an example out of their figurehead." She sat back with a smirk, staring me down. "After all, once it becomes a choice between their current living situation or not being alive at all, I am sure the humans will reconsider their stance on the strike, will they not?"

The other deities seemed to agree with Artemis's argument. I spotted Poseidon, Aphrodite, and Ares nodding along. Hera seemed almost ready to take it upon herself to deal with the problem – aka, me.

While Athena sighed in what seemed like frustration at her sister's words, Zeus also seemed like he was seriously considering making an example out of me. At that point, I was seriously starting to feel defeated. There was no way I would be able to make it out of this situation alive if the majority of the gods assembled before me decided to execute me – and Archer would not be able to stop a dozen of the most powerful gods on Olympus.

Was it too late to try to go back on my words and promise I'd speak in favor of the gods? After all, Artemis wasn't wrong – being held at metaphorical gunpoint sure made me reconsider my choices.

Then, three things happened so quickly I could barely keep up. First, Zeus made the executive decision that, yes, his sweet daughter Artemis – cue sarcasm – was right and making an example of me would for sure solve all of their problems. Right as he started announcing his verdict, I caught Hermes making a few hand signs that I was pretty sure were directed at Archer who was still standing protectively before me. And then, before Zeus could even finish declaring his decision, Archer grabbed my hand and reached in the pocket of his jeans at the same time.

I blinked and we weren't in front of the gods anymore. Instead, we were on the beach, facing the ocean, and it smelled like home.

Chapter Seventeen

Sadie

I wasn't sure what I had been expecting a hidden lair for Coppers on the run to look like, but it was not a half-destroyed cottage on the side of a mountain.

"Don't make this face, Zombie girl," Matteo chirped with entirely too much excitement. "This is what we've been waiting for! Oh, I can't wait!"

The man quite literally skipped away from the car. I rolled my eyes at his antics, but still followed. I wasn't about to leave him to fend for himself. Seeing as he was a golden retriever in human form, he might get killed without even realizing it.

After closing the car door, I sighed and resolved myself to trek through the snow to follow in Matteo's footsteps. Stars be damned, I missed the balmy weather of Mount Olympus.

Before I was even halfway there, the Copper was knocking on the wooden door that looked half rotten. To be honest, if this really was the safe haven we'd been promised, I was confused why no one had stopped us from getting so close to it. Did these people have no security system whatsoever?

After a few seconds of silence, Matteo raised his hand to knock again. The door rattled on its hinges, and it almost looked like the cabin itself was seconds away from falling over.

I reached Matteo's side, and still, no one had come over. Either this place was really abandoned or the people living in it hoped that, by pretending it was, they would be left alone by everyone but other Coppers desperate for refuge. It seemed like a decent plan to remain hidden, but I sure didn't feel like waiting around for hours in the cold and the snow to find out.

As Matteo started knocking a little louder and calling out for someone through the door, I tried to extend my awareness of magic to scan the inside of the cabin. In theory, if Coppers were hiding inside the rackety house, I should be able to sense their magic. Not knowing what type of magic I was looking for made things harder, but as a Golden, I had enough ichor in my veins and strong enough powers that sensing others' magic was often easy enough.

Except, even after a solid minute of magically scanning the space next to me, I couldn't find anything.

There wasn't anyone in there. Or, at least, there wasn't anyone with any kind of ichor-based powers.

My heart clenched at the thought. This would hurt Matteo. So much. He was dreaming of this safe haven, of a place where he would be free to be himself without being forced to compete in a deadly Tournament. Finding out that this place of freedom and acceptance didn't exist would break something inside of him.

Another minute passed and still no one had come to answer the door. I was slowly losing feeling in my nose and ears from the cold, and Matteo's face looked equally flushed.

"Maybe they're sleeping? Or maybe they can't hear us from the back of the cabin?" Matteo asked with a slight panicked edge to his voice that made my chest hurt. "You know what, I'll go around the back and try to find a window or something. I'm sure not all of them are covered up and—"

"Matteo," I stopped him with a hand on his forearm.

He stopped dead in his tracks but refused to look at me. His whole body was tense, and he stared at the side of the cabin. I didn't need Archer's mind speaking powers to know that the Copper was trying to pretend like things were fine in order to avoid destroying the little hope at escape he still had.

"Look, this place is abandoned. We can regroup and we will find somewhere else to hide. We can—"

"No, we can't give up," Matteo said, shaking his head vehemently. "We need to find them. I can't continue on like this, I can't…"

He didn't continue, his voice breaking, but I knew exactly what he meant. He couldn't continue to flee, to be afraid. And my heart broke all over again because this was the gods' doing. They had gone to Earth to have fun, and now, hundreds of children and young adults were forced to either flee or fight for their lives. After being forced to compete in the Tournament alongside Søren and Archer, I knew first-hand how deadly and traumatizing it was.

As I looked at Matteo's stricken face, barely hanging on to the last shred of hope that he had finally found a place to live in peace, I had the certitude that I would fight for him.

I would not let Matteo end up in the Tournament.

Ever.

The man had been forced to fight to survive this long away from Olympus. He had done ugly things to survive, and I knew they weighed heavily on his conscience. But I would not let Olympus destroy what was left of his hopes and dreams.

The gods had sullied and broken too many things already. They would not get their hands on Matteo Bailet.

I had failed at protecting my friends these past few months. Mei had died because of me. Kalani had been so traumatized by the Tournament that she had suffered nightmares every night for weeks and almost died under my eyes. Søren had lost his girlfriend because of me. And I hadn't been able to help Archer avoid having to compete in the Tournament for the second time in his life.

But this time, I wouldn't fail.

"It will be alright," I promised him, trying to convey reassurance through my eyes. "We will find somewhere to stay, and—"

I stopped because the air rippled with power. For a second, I worried that another Hunter had found us. Maybe Kellan, my new boss, had gotten tired of waiting for me to do my job and had decided to take control of things.

It only lasted a half second, but the panic did set in. My mind raced to find escape routes and my body tensed, preparing for a fight.

"Step back!"

The words ripped from Matteo's throat, and suddenly it made sense. Matteo was losing control over his powers. The surge was coming from him. And now that I paid attention to his body language, I could tell that he was on the brink of a panic attack.

Stars be damned.

The last time I had stood next to someone about the give in to panic, Mei and I were about to enter a duel to the death for the last Trial of the Tournament. For a second, I lost myself in the awful memories associated with that instant – I could hear the crowd cheering, Kalani and Mei crying, and Søren shouting from the other side of the Pit.

No, Sadie, get a grip!

With a mental slap to get myself back to the present, I tuned back to Matteo and the ticking time bomb he had turned into.

See, even though I hated the fact that the Gods made Coppers leave everything they knew to go on Olympus and fight to the death to earn the right to become a permanent resident, I also understood why having unchecked and untrained Coppers on Earth was dangerous.

Our powers were linked to our emotions. With training, most of us Goldens and Coppers could learn how to control our powers even under strong emotions. Unfortunately, Coppers like Matteo didn't have any training, and fits of anger, fear, or panic could lead to catastrophic events.

Especially when you could create human-sized plants who could either poison their preys to madness or eat people alive.

I didn't feel like getting eaten today.

"Alright, Matteo," I said with as calm of a tone as I could. I took a slow step back but remained close enough to him that I would be able to physically restrain him if needed. "It's going to be fine. You just need to take a few deep breaths with me, okay?"

Except Matteo didn't seem to be able to concentrate on me long enough to take those deep breaths. He was hyperventilating, his eyes were wide open and frantically moving, and his whole body was shaking.

"I can't— I can't—" he ran his hands through his curls, desperate. "They're going to find me, I can't—"

His eyes started to glow faintly. I could feel stronger ripples of magic coming from him – like waves crashing against my skin.

I was going to need to find a solution and quickly, because I could tell that Matteo was too terrified of the consequences of not finding this safe haven to be able to calm down by himself.

"I'll protect you, Matteo, I promise! No one will be taking you to Mount Olympus. But you need to calm down or your powers are going to blow both of us up."

For a second, Matteo stared at me, and I hoped that he would believe my words. All too soon, though, he was pacing again, fingers frantically gripping at his hair.

"I can't continue on like this. I can't continue on like this. I can't—"

The ground shook under our feet and I knew it was too late. Being on the run for months, feeling like he was constantly being hunted by the gods, having had to defend himself, and now losing the only hope he had of finally being safe… well, it had broken something in him.

We were seconds away from a point of no return, and I was going to have to defend myself. I didn't want to hurt him, but I also didn't want to spend the foreseeable months in a venom-induced madness because of his deadly flowers.

"Matteo!" This time, the danger of the situation was making it hard to keep a cool and collected tone. "You need to try to control your magic. I know it's hard, but you have to try to hold it in."

The Copper's eyes were now full-on glowing. I could tell that Matteo had heard me, though, because he was now focused on my face. "I don't know how to," he panted, panic swimming in his eyes. "I can't control it. I can't control anything! I'm scared, Sadie!"

My heart broke a little more at the sight of Matteo completely overwhelmed by his emotions, terror so potent I could feel it from where I was standing.

The ground was still shaking, and my body was screaming at me to move backwards, to distance myself from the Copper. But I couldn't do that – I couldn't show Matteo that he was making me scared. Right then, his eyes told me that the only thing stopping him from completely exploding was my gaze holding his focus prisoner.

So, I did exactly the opposite of what every instinct was telling me to do and took a step closer to him. Hands held in front of me, I had my power ready to access at any instant. I was trying to defuse the situation, but I also wasn't about to die.

"Don't come too close, I'm dangerous," Matteo's voice broke at the last word.

"I've seen much worse, Matteo. You just need to bring your power back into its usual resting place, okay? You do that, and both of us will be fine, I promise."

Matteo nodded shakily, swallowing the nervousness. "Okay, okay, I can try that."

I nodded slowly and gave him my best reassuring smile. He just needed to calm his heartbeat down and ground himself. Really, once he did it once, he would be able to control his powers much more efficiently. He just needed to—

"Well, what a great show!" someone exclaimed from behind us.

At the sudden words, Matteo's focus snapped from me, and he lost the little control he had managed to gather. The ground started to split right before my feet, a deadly flower growing. And I didn't want to hurt Matteo – somehow, I'd gotten attached to the guy – but my powers answered instinctively. In a split second, I had an exhaustive map of every single animal – and human – who had died and been buried near us. There was plenty to work with.

A plant burst through the snow mere inches in front of me. My heart was beating frantically. Palms spread, I called for the bones of the foxes that had died close to us months ago, but I wasn't sure who to direct my powers to first – Matteo's plant or the unknown individuals behind me who could very well be extremely dangerous too?

"Matteo!" I shouted as the plant grew and I jumped back, turning so that I could try to assess the potential threat behind me. "You have to reign it in, focus on—"

And then everything stopped. Matteo's flower stopped growing and disappeared. The ground stopped shaking. My two fox skeletons dropped as I lost control of them. And I couldn't feel magic anymore.

What in the ever-loving stars was happening?

Now that Matteo wasn't about to kill me, I turned around to face the three individuals who had arrived. Two men and a woman. They looked to be in their early twenties, and they didn't appear to be scared of what had almost happened in this clearing.

These people weren't scared of our powers. There was only one explanation for this – they were descendants of the Gods themselves.

I just had to figure out if they were allied with the gods or not.

Ignoring how vulnerable I felt without access to my magic – how was this even possible? – I took a defensive position in front of a still shaken Matteo.

"Who are you?"

The man on the left took a step closer to us, hands nonchalantly put in the pockets of his black winter jacket – as if we weren't a threat at all and he didn't need to stay on his guard. It was slightly insulting.

"Now, now, is that the way to thank the people who saved you from a nasty fight?" the man asked mockingly.

Alright, so they really were responsible for our sudden loss of magic. That was more than concerning. Who were these people, and what did they want with us?

I tried to remember if I had ever met someone on Olympus with the power to remove another person's magic, but nothing came to mind. Had Hecate made a new toy that could do that? She did enjoy creating all kinds of magical objects and playing around with the limits of what was possible. Although, the Titan didn't seem like the kind of person who would risk creating something that could remove her own powers.

Now that I wasn't focused on Matteo and his loss of control, I took the time to observe the three newcomers more closely. The man who had walked closer to us was average height, with red hair fashionably cropped short of the sides and longer on the top. He wasn't particularly attention-stopping, and if not for the aura of arrogance coming from him, I wouldn't have looked at him twice.

Behind him, the other guy was much taller – taller than even Archer or Søren – and imposing, with a strong bone structure and skin as dark as the night sky. He wore a long winter jacket but even with most of his frame obstructed, I could tell that the guy was dangerously strong.

And, finally, the last member of their trio was a young woman with short blond hair in a pixie cut and the biggest, roundest blue eyes I'd ever seen. She seemed almost as tall as me, and she wore weirdly colorful clothes compared to her *friends.*

"It is when I don't know them," I answered coldly. I didn't particularly care if these people could hear the distrust in my voice.

Behind me, Matteo was finally starting to get a hold on his emotions, and he moved closer to me. For a second, the crunch of the snow made it seem like he was going to step in front of me. I stopped him with a simple raised hand, still staring at the three strangers.

As if I needed Matteo's help handling whatever was coming for us.

"You don't trust easily, do you?" the red-headed man laughed, his voice echoing slightly in the still clearing.

"You still haven't introduced yourself," I quipped back with a pointed look.

"Sadie, I can't feel it anymore, my…" Matteo stopped himself before saying the word 'magic' but we all knew what he meant.

It was time to play and find out exactly who these strangers were.

"Well, you might want to ask these lovely people over there, since they were nice enough to prevent us from accessing our powers."

The woman chuckled, the mountain of a man remained perfectly stoic, and the red-headed spokesperson raised his eyebrows in amusement.

"No need to worry, Matteo and Sadie," the red-haired guy said with a pointed look in my direction at the mention of my name. "We aren't here to hurt you."

Sure, and I was the queen of England. The disbelief must have been visible on my face because the girl decided to stop letting her friend handle the social interactions.

"We are Coppers, like you. We are from the Refuge."

Matteo immediately perked up at the word. "The Refuge? So, it's real?" I could hear the relief and excitement in his voice.

"Of course, it is. And you guys found it," the ginger said with a self-sufficient smile that gave me irrational thoughts of strangling him.

"This place? Really? It's falling apart. It's not quite the impressive place I was expecting."

"Sadie!" Matteo whispered in a panicked tone. "We can't antagonize them, we need them!"

I rolled my eyes but refrained from commenting further on the state of complete disrepair the cottage was in. The ginger guy gave me a mocking look as Matteo stepped around me, bouncing like an excited puppy.

"It's all right," the girl reassured Matteo with a clear British accent and a soft smile that grated on my nerves. "Your friend is right to be cautious. But I promise you, we are only here to help. My name is Bella."

"It's so nice to meet you Bella, I'm Matteo."

To say I rolled my eyes at his reddened cheeks and the *looks* him and Bella were exchanging was an understatement. Stars, the man trusted way too easily. Plus, these people clearly knew him, seeing as the cocky ginger guy had said both of our names.

"Well, Matteo, the talkative guy over there is Thomas, and the quiet one is Liam."

Matteo barely looked away from Bella, and I suddenly wanted to drag him far away from this clearing – or from this country, actually. To be fair, I could probably protect Matteo better on my own than anyone else could. Even if these people really were organizing this *haven* for Coppers, they were probably one mistake away from bringing a whole squad of Hunters right to their door.

Plus, I didn't make a habit of easily trusting people who could somehow separate me from my magic.

Matteo was about to open his mouth – surely to compliment Bella or to thank her for simply being there – but I stopped him with a hand on his forearm.

"Let's just stop with the small talk, alright? Let's pretend like I believe that you are here as members of the Refuge. Why are we still standing in the snow instead of entering said Refuge? And why are our powers still not accessible to us? It seems like, as the welcoming committee, you aren't doing a great job of making us feel *welcomed*."

Thomas laughed at my words; hands still nonchalantly slung in his pockets. "Well, honey, we aren't going to let either of you inside until we make sure you aren't a danger for our community. After all, you don't seem very welcoming either, do you?"

I grinded my teeth at his smug face. I already knew that Thomas and I weren't going to get along any time soon.

"And how are you going to determine if we're dangerous, exactly? Are you going to do a background check on us?"

Matteo gave me a look that clearly meant I should shut up. But I had seen too much and been used by too many people to trust as easily as Matteo did.

"We have better than that, darling. Thanks to Bella's power, neither of you can access your magic right now. And you'll be delighted to learn that my godly ancestor was kind enough to gift me with the ability to detect lies."

Oh stars. A human lie detector. How great.

"And what about Liam's powers?" Matteo asked with the curiosity of someone who had spent years wondering about himself and had finally found people that shared his uniqueness.

For the first time, the tall black man opened his mouth to intervene. With a low voice and a slight accent that I couldn't quite place, he spoke over the clearing, "Trust me, boy, you don't want to know."

Matteo gasped quietly, and I sighed in desperation. Stars help me, this man needed to learn how to stop showing his emotions on his sleeve and grow a spine. It was a wonder that he had survived this long on his own. Thankfully, I was there to ensure he would remain safe for the foreseeable future.

"Well, then, let's do it." The challenge in my voice made Thomas raise his eyebrows in surprise. Somehow, I managed to keep a calm and composed façade. Inside, I was slightly worried. After all, one wrong step could lead to Thomas, and thus Matteo, discovering my real upbringing. But I'd be damned if I allowed the human lie detector to see me sweat.

Chapter Eighteen

Kalani

“**W**here are we?”

It was so anticlimactic to be standing there, in the middle of an empty beach, the moonlight barely bright enough for me to see Archer’s tense body next to me. My whole body was still thrumming with tension, adrenaline racing through my veins, heartbeat erratic and blood pumping in my ears, as if it couldn’t quite understand that we were now… safe? Were we?

“I think we are on the beach we visited a few days ago. With your brother and his friends.”

Archer sounded unsure, but now that I actually paid attention to my surroundings, I did recognize the pier where we ate ice cream cones while watching my brother play football on the beach.

“And how in the ever-loving hell are we here?” I asked, still slightly disoriented by the rapid succession of events. I could see the moonlit ocean, feel the breeze on my skin, smell the water… but, somehow, my body still reacted as if I stood in front of Zeus.

"Hermes gave me a new translocator right before he took us to the council, when we greeted each other. Just in case we needed a quick escape."

"Well, that was good foresight, wasn't it?" I couldn't keep the bite out of my words, even though I knew very well that Archer wasn't to blame for anything that had happened with the gods.

Archer simply grunted in a noncommittal way while observing our surroundings, and I felt strangely annoyed that he hadn't decided to start an argument with me. I felt unsettled, and maybe some part of me wished to expel some of my anger and frustration on the only person that was close to me right then.

"We should find somewhere to spend the next few hours until the translocator is recharged," Archer finally said after a long minute of silence.

I was still confused about translocators and how they allowed us to move between realms, bending time and space. I knew Hermes used his magic to power these little machines that one could activate to move through space. And I was guessing that it worked through some sort of mental imaging of wherever the person wielding the translocator wanted to go. But how exactly this happened, how the machine was constructed, or even how it recharged itself were all questions I had no answers to.

"And then what? What's the plan here? We go back to Mount Olympus and hide in your mom's basement until things calm down?"

Archer scoffed and shook his head at my words. "No, Mayfield. Trust me, they will hunt us down. There is nowhere we can hide on Olympus."

I shivered at his words – thinking of the gods hunting me down like an animal was terrifying.

Everything had fallen to pieces in such a short amount of time. Three weeks ago, I had stood on the sand of the Pit, blood staining my hands, and won the right to live freely on Mount Olympus. How could I have destroyed all of that so quickly?

And how had I brought Archer down with me, especially after everything he had already gone through for his freedom of choice?

Now that I stood there, facing the reflection of the moon on the surface of the ocean… everything seemed less black and white, right and wrong than before.

Sure, refusing to speak against the humans that just wanted to be respected by the gods was the right thing to do. But my actions had ruined Archer's precarious safety on Olympus and would probably drag the Aska twins in the mud too – at least Søren, since Sadie was still missing in action. Was my decision still the right one?

If I was in the process of destroying not only my life but also the futures of my friends, was it still the right thing to do?

I shivered as the cold wind blew my hair into my face. I hadn't dressed for the Californian early spring weather, and the goosebumps that formed on my arms were a stark reminder that we were not on Mount Olympus with its perfectly warm and sunny weather anymore.

Somewhere behind us, the siren of an ambulance started, and I jumped in surprise. I almost laughed at my reaction. Once upon a time, I had been so used to the sounds of the city that I hadn't been able to sleep without them. And now…

A hand folded around mine, and all of my thoughts stopped.

"It's going to be alright, Mayfield," Archer whispered, his fingers clinging to mine in the night. "We will figure it out. Together."

And, while there were still the unsaid remnants of our argument between us, neither of us wanted to break the physical contact. Holding Archer's hand was like holding on to a raft in the middle of a terrifying storm.

I shifted and lost myself in his endless blue eyes. Gods, I'd missed him. Knowing he was there, right next to me, was all

I needed to know to feel safe. After all, I knew from past experiences that this man would go to the ends of the world, even bartering with Death himself, in order to save me.

"Together," I repeated with a gentle squeeze of his hand. "I am holding you to that, Sunshine."

He smirked at the nickname and brought me closer to him. As soon as my side was flushed to his, my body melted into his – unconsciously reaching for the comfort and support that he provided.

I hadn't quite forgiven his hurtful words from our earlier argument. And I knew he was still mad at me for my choices. But this hug? This whole moment – both of us, alone on this moonlit beach – was a truce.

After all, love wasn't just for the happy moments, was it?

"Here you go," the waiter exclaimed as he dropped our order on the table. "Do you need anything else?"

"We're good, thank you," I smiled at him.

If the guy wondered why Archer and I were both dressed for summer and completely disheveled, he didn't comment on it. Thankfully, none of the employees of the fast food restaurant seemed to want to make conversation.

"What is that again?" Archer asked with a frown as he picked up his food.

"A bacon double cheeseburger. You'll like it," I assured him as I opened my own burger.

"If it's poisoned—"

"If I wanted to get rid of you, Sunshine, I wouldn't do it on Earth, in public, or with a burger."

Archer raised an eyebrow, clearly surprised by my words. "Do you think about ways to kill me often, Mayfield?"

"Only when you piss me off, which happens quite a lot, actually."

He laughed and the sound warmed me from the inside. How could this man make me feel at home and safe whenever I was near him?

"I'll keep that in mind, Mayfield. Although, we both know who would win in a fight, don't we?" he asked with an arrogant smirk that made me want to put his theory to the test.

"Oh, trust me, Sunshine, I'd find a way to make it hurt. The twins taught me *plenty* of fun things over the months," I added with an overly sweet smile.

"I'd love to see you try."

Archer's eyes twinkled with humor, and he hummed with a distinct challenge. Was I imagining the heat that came through his eyes and smug face?

Archer finally opened the wrapping around his burger, but he still had a look that clearly said that he wasn't sure whether this would we edible at all. I couldn't contain an amused smile at the sight, because I often forgot that Archer had grown up on Earth a long time ago. He had left the Earth when he was barely older than ten years old, which was decades ago in Earth timeline. A lot about the world had changed since then, and while he'd been able to visit the Earth every so often with the clandestine help of Hermes, he still hadn't been able to experience most of the things I took for granted.

Like bacon double cheeseburgers from fast food restaurants that somehow managed to be both terrible and weirdly satisfying.

Archer took a bite and his eyebrows raised in surprise. I chuckled as he chewed, staring curiously at his burger. By the time he had taken two more bites of his burger, I was close to full-on gloating. Dammit, it felt good to be right.

"Gods, I should have put more poison in there, it was supposed to be fast acting," I gasped in mock shock.

Archer rolled his eyes at my antics, but he did smile back at me. And as we both continued eating our food, I felt much better about our predicament. Sure, maybe we were stuck on

Earth and hunted by the Greek gods, but at least we were together.

As time went by, though, everything that had happened in the past few hours came back crashing to me. The after-party, the argument with Archer, the meeting with the gods… so much had happened and the realization that my life had changed forever – *again* – was hard to come to terms with.

Archer must have seen the change on my face because he also became closed-off. And then the table seemed like it lengthened until we were far, far from each other. Separated by so many unsaid and hurtful things.

He'd said things to hurt me, I'd said and done things that hurt him. We'd both been ugly and unfair. But I wasn't sure how to make things better between us. Not when he was both the man who'd deliberately hurt me with his words and the man who had been willing to sacrifice his freedom to help me escape the gods. The dichotomy was causing me whiplash.

Archer must have felt equally unsure of what to say or do, because the heavy silence sat between us for what felt like forever.

As the city started to wake up, both of us knew we needed to figure out our next steps. So, pushing my empty fry basket away from me, I decided to bite the bullet and break the silence.

"So. What are we doing next?"

"Well, the translocator should be recharged by now, so we just need to figure out where we want to go next."

And that was the billion-dollar question, wasn't it? It wasn't like I had been to many places on Earth – Mom hadn't had the time or extra money to take us on fancy vacations. And between school, my jobs, and taking care of Makaio, I hadn't really had the time to daydream about vacation spots either. Plus, I wasn't sure what would keep us hidden the best. Would it be better to go to hide in the desert or in the middle of the biggest city on Earth?

"Won't the gods be able to track you with your powers anyways?" I took a sip of my mostly melted milkshake, but it tasted like ash. Thinking of the gods was making it hard to appreciate anything. "Don't they have little trackers for magic or something? And that's how they find all of the Coppers still on Earth?"

"You're right, the gods and powerful Goldens can feel others' powers. Magic attracts magic, which means that when Coppers first reveal their powers, the sudden burst of magic can be felt and followed by the Hunters and Huntresses that work for my father. But there are ways to dampen our powers so that we are less visible to others. Not using my powers and focusing my energy on power blocks should work well enough."

"Power blocks?"

"It's like the mental blocks I taught you to prevent invasions of your mind. But instead of making walls so that people can't penetrate your mind, the goal is to make walls around the source of your magic so that it cannot escape. It can be very exhausting at times because we are made to use our magic often or we quite literally lose our minds. But a few weeks should be fine."

"Well I don't want you to lose your mind or hurt yourself, Archer." Suddenly, prospects felt a lot darker. I hated the idea of Archer physically suffering for my choices. Even when I was mad at him, I couldn't stand the idea of him being in pain. "And what if it lasts more than a few weeks? What are you going to do then?"

Before I could continue to anxiously ask about the timeline of everything, Archer put his hand over mine and it quite literally stopped me in my tracks. Our eyes met and we both lost ourselves in each other, letting the world become quiet around us.

"Breathe, Mayfield," Archer urged me with an insistent look, waiting until I reluctantly took a deep breath. "There you go. Nothing is going to happen to me, alright? I have done it before and it's just a habit to take, I'll be just fine. But we have to decide where to—"

"Oh, my stars! I had forgotten how cold it could get on Earth! We should probably go on a quick shopping spree. What do you think, darling?"

I jumped in surprise at the loud voice. Archer and I had been the only customers in the restaurant for quite some time now, and the sudden interruption was jarring. But what was even more surprising was the person who had spoken.

"Søren? Nafula? What are you doing here?"

"Way to make us feel wanted, K," Søren pouted playfully before crossing the restaurant and taking a seat next to Archer. "But it's nice to see you guys."

Nafula didn't say anything before sitting next to me, her body tense as if she were ready to be attacked any second. Being back on Earth was probably hard on her, after everything that had happened since she'd been forcefully taken to Mount Olympus.

"How are you here? And how did you find us?" Archer was suddenly all business and his soft eyes were steel again as they scanned the periphery, searching for threats and any god that could have also found us.

"Your buddy Hermes dropped us off after he managed to escape Zeus and Artemis's wild goose chase around Olympus for Kalani," Nafula explained with a frown. "I don't know how exactly he knew where the two of you were, but he did ask us to tell you that staying so close to Kalani's family was a poor idea."

"He dropped you off? Why?" I was so confused. What was the god of travel playing at?

"Well, obviously, we all know you guys need someone to make sure you remain safe. I mean, honestly, how would you even survive without m—"

"Søren," Nafula interrupted him with an exasperated hand raised, "please, shut up." She took a deep breath as if gathering the courage to deal with all of us. "For some reason, Priya Vasilias believed that it would help keep Kalani safe for us to be there. And she had some type of leverage on Hermes, but I'm not sure what that was, exactly. So, either way, we're both stuck here with you."

Archer nodded before asking Nafula if his mom had given her any other message.

"Not really, but Hermes did say that it had been way too easy for him to track you guys down, and we should all find a better hiding place, and quickly," the Copper declared while still holding a finger up to shush Søren.

As Archer and Nafula continued to exchange about Hermes' warning and the next steps we were supposed to take as a group, I couldn't contain a smirk at Søren's shock at being shushed by Nafula. The man was so overly confident that it was particularly satisfying to see him speechless for once.

"Okay, so we are searching for a remote location, then?" Nafula asked with a thoughtful look on her face. "Would that help keep us hidden?"

Archer frowned pensively and shook his head at her words. "Not exactly. Søren and you aren't trained in containing your powers and keeping them invisible to the gods, so we should maybe plan on moving around more often than I had initially planned. However, the good thing is that the gods need to focus on a relatively small part of the Earth to be able to pinpoint the location of a Golden or Copper. So, if we find a location that is relatively remote and away from any place where the gods know one of us has emotional attachment to, we should be able to remain safe enough for a few days."

Days. Our best hope was that we would be hidden and safe for a few *days* at a time. What a joyous prospect. And again, those words were another stab of guilt in my chest.

"We could go to the Saharan desert," Søren interjected with an excitement that was entirely out of place when talking about trying to hide from vengeful gods. "I've always wanted to see camels!"

"And spend days surrounded by sand and cooking under the sun? No thank you," Nafula added with a look of disapproval to Søren.

"But—"

"Hawaii."

Everyone stopped and three inquisitive faces turned to focus on me. "Hawaii?" Archer asked, confusion written on his face.

I hadn't even realized the word had come out. And now that it was out in the world, I felt a little foolish for requesting a hiding place when I was part of the reason why we were all in this mess to start with. But also… well, Thanatos had said that my potential powers might come from my dad's side of the family. I knew he came from Hawaii, but I'd never been before. Maybe this situation was a blessing in disguise, and I would finally be able to answer some questions about the strange things I'd been able to do to save Makaio.

"Yes, Hawaii. It's isolated, far enough from any continent that the gods shouldn't find us easily. And I've always wanted to see the place where my dad came from."

Søren announced that he was down to go to the beach, and Nafula complained about dangerous marine wildlife – which I found slightly ironic seeing as she was Poseidon's granddaughter – but Archer remained focused on me.

I could tell that he knew I wasn't telling the whole truth. The man was smart. He knew I had other motives for this trip to the Pacific Ocean. And, maybe, he even had suspicions about those hidden reasons.

Whether he had his own theories about my hidden truths, or he wanted to vacation to Hawaii for a few days, one corner of Archer's lips inched up.

"Hawaii it is, then."

Chapter Nineteen

Sadie

"Let's get it done, then, *Tommy*. I'd like to not freeze to death."

Matteo gave me a look but didn't voice his disapproval. After all, he was shivering in the cold too.

Bella snorted at the nickname I used for her friend, and I tried to not be annoyed at the way Matteo's attention snapped to her. I was only noticing all of this because I was still looking for any signs of danger. This wasn't anything else. It couldn't be anything else.

At the end of the day, Matteo wanted to stay on Earth more than he wanted to breathe, and I wouldn't be able to escape my life on Olympus forever.

Not that it mattered.

"I see someone is enthusiastic, aren't you Sadie? Alright, first off, can you state the reason why you are here today?"

My heart started beating faster from the anticipation. Sure, I was slightly worried that *Tommy* would find out I was bending the truth and had nothing to do here with them. But I was also excited by the challenge this interrogation presented.

I liked challenges. And I liked winning even more.

"We are looking for somewhere to hide. Both of us have been attacked by people who claim to want to take us to Mount Olympus. I don't plan on being taken anywhere against my will, especially when I have this gut feeling that what's on the other side isn't great for me."

Matteo's words must have rung true because the human lie detector nodded before shifting his inquisitive eyes on me.

It was my time to shine.

"I am here because I am tired of running. I've been running away from my problems for too long, and I want to be able to stay somewhere and feel safe for a while. Hopefully that place is here."

Nothing about that was a lie. After all, I was running from my problems – namely, my brother's dead girlfriend, and Gods that had a habit of forcing kids to fight to the death. I was just hoping that the red-haired man would not be able to tell the difference between a truth and the truth he wanted.

Tommy frowned and remained silent, his eyes unwavering from mine. A few seconds later, he inhaled sharply and gave a sharp nod in Bella and Liam's direction.

Oh, this was so good. Feeling this victorious was already addicting.

"And how did you two meet, exactly?" Thomas asked in a clipped tone.

"At the restaurant I worked in, in Paris. It was a coincidence, really. Sadie spent a few afternoons there, and I decided to go and talk to her."

"So, you only met recently?" Bella asked with a gracefully arched eyebrow. "It seemed like you were close earlier."

Matteo opened his mouth, but no sound came out, and I couldn't tell if it was because of the question itself or the woman asking it.

Ignoring the pinch of annoyance in my chest, I gave Bella a sweet smile. "We clicked rather quickly. Sometimes you just can't explain it."

Bella's big blue eyes crinkled as she smiled back. "You're right! I'm so glad you guys found each other. Having friends is important during times like these."

Oh stars, she was so sweet that it was really hard to keep up with the annoyance.

"Let's get back on track, girls. So, can each of you give us some information about your upbringing and your relationship to the world of the Greek gods?"

Oh boy, that was going to be a tricky one. Thankfully, Matteo took one for the team and started answering first.

"I was mostly raised by my grandparents. My mom lost custody of me because she was diagnosed with paranoid schizophrenia and wasn't fit to care for me anymore. She used to tell me that my dad was a god with magic from another world. Everyone thought it was the words of a crazy lady. Me included," Matteo scoffed darkly, face shrouded in pain and regret. "Anyways. Some guys tried to rob me a year ago and my powers just appeared from nowhere. Since then, I've been on the run, and I never got to ask my mom any more explanation about my dad."

Well, I had plenty of answers for him, but there was no opportunity for me to share them without destroying my cover.

"That is unfortunately the case for most of us," Thomas said in a serious tone. "While some of us have been visited by our demigod genitor, most haven't had that chance. We can't ask questions about our parentage without allowing for the henchmen to take us away."

Everyone nodded solemnly, silence settling down for a few beats on the clearing.

"What about you, Sadie?" Liam asked in a deep, slightly unsettling voice.

Here we go, time to spin some truths into a believable and safe story.

"I grew up with my mom and brother. She never hid my parentage from me, but I never really thought about the way my life would change until I started manifesting strong powers."

"And when was that?" Tommy stared at me intensely and I knew that he was waiting for me to mess up.

"Things changed a few months ago. My life went from pretty calm to completely hectic. I guess the gods decided I was too much trouble to leave alone. At first, I thought I could stay with my friends and protect everyone from the gods. But…" I trailed for a few seconds, closing my eyes and showing pain that wasn't fake. "But then a friend died, and I had to leave. Since then, I've been running and trying to figure out what to do with my life."

Again, Thomas' frown conveyed how suspicious he was. But there weren't any lies there. Everything was true. It wasn't my fault if his questions weren't precise enough to stop me from choosing which truths to tell and which ones to withhold.

If living with the gods since I was sixteen had taught me anything, it was how to play games.

And how to win them.

"Come on, Tom. I'm freezing over here," Bella complained when he took too long to ask the next question. Liam grunted in agreement next to her. And, for once, I agreed with her, too.

"Okay. Do you have any intentions or desires to harm any of the individuals living in or associating with the Refuge?"

"None at all," Matteo answered with fervor.

For once, I wasn't going to have to walk around the truth. Somewhere along the way, I had gone from just wanting to escape Mount Olympus for a few weeks to deciding to help Matteo – and whoever was willing to help him – escape the gods at all costs. That meant that there was absolutely no scenario in which I'd allow any of the Hunters to hurt anyone that lived in this Refuge. Not even *Tommy*.

"No."

The truth must have rung clear and loud, because the human lie detector raised an eyebrow in surprise.

"Are we done here?"

"Not yet, Sadie. I have one more question. Do either of you have the intention, desire, or even obligation to share the location of the Refuge, or any detail that would reveal its location, to anyone that would be associated with the gods of Mount Olympus?"

Well. This one was going to be more complicated to talk my way around. *Stars give me inspiration.*

Thankfully, Matteo was still playing for my team because, here again, he answered first, sounding all shocked that his newfound friend would even insinuate that he might be working with the *evil Greek deities.*

By the time everyone's eyes turned to me, I knew I had thought over it for too long. If I remained silent any longer, it would become very clear that I was stalling, and everyone would become suspicious.

See, my issue was that, while I had absolutely no intention or desire to give anyone the location of this Refuge, I still had technically signed a contract that bound me as a Huntress for the Olympians. And, while I didn't mind squandering my obligations towards the Olympians, I still had those obligations.

So, maybe my only choice was to rephrase the question myself and hope for the best.

"And who would I even contact? It's not like I've made friends with the people that hunt Coppers down."

"You don't have to be friends with them to give them the information they need to capture all of us," the red-haired man retorted.

"You seem slightly paranoid that people are out to get you, Tommy. Trust me, you don't have to worry about that from me."

The Copper scoffed and crossed his arms over his chest in a closed-off posture.

"Weirdly enough, Sadie, you don't inspire trust from me right now. And if you had to care for dozens of people instead of just yourself, maybe you would understand what it is to actually have responsibilities. As it stands—"

"Tom," Bella interrupted him. "She answered your questions truthfully. Both of them did. Let's not antagonize our new guests before they even make it into the Refuge."

Ensued a tense second during which the British young woman gave him a long, hard look. Thomas rolled his eyes but didn't argue any further. Stars, she was good. Maybe the two of us would get along after all.

"Let's get a move on it," Liam ordered in a deep voice that still unsettled me.

"What about the car?" I asked, wondering if we were supposed to just leave it parked near the small path.

"We'll take care of it," Liam answered without even turning around.

And that was it, we were supposed to follow them.

Matteo gave me an excited look, his smile brighter than the Sun. Seeing him so happy made me smile. The man had the same energy as a puppy. It was impossible not to smile at his happy face and bright eyes.

Snow crunched as Liam and Thomas started walking toward the cottage that was still falling apart. Matteo almost sauntered his way behind them. However, Bella remained behind, clearly waiting for me to join her.

Oh joy.

Still, because I knew that I had to play nice with the British girl – especially after she had taken my side against her friend only minutes ago – I walked toward her, and we fell into step behind the guys.

"Sorry about all of that. I know it must be stressful to arrive here and be interrogated like this. Especially after all of the stress Matteo and you must have been under."

Oh stars, she was nice too.

"I understand that you have to make sure people are trustworthy before letting them into your safe space," I reassured her with what I hoped was a genuine-looking smile.

"I'm glad you are understanding. In the past, we have had some people feel very betrayed."

I could imagine why. Stars, I would have felt very uncomfortable if I hadn't lived among predators for years.

"It's all good, Bella. I do hope we will be able to get access to our powers back sometime soon, though. I haven't had them for long, but it feels unnatural to be without them."

That wasn't my most subtle hint, but not being able to feel my powers made me feel way too vulnerable for my liking.

"Oh yes, no worries Sadie! I keep everyone's powers in check until we get to the Refuge. It's standard protocol. It keeps us hidden from the view of the gods. But don't you worry, you will be able to sense your powers again as soon as we are all safe inside."

I had so many questions – like how were they keeping the whole Refuge hidden from any magical searches, especially if they had dozens of Coppers living in it, like Thomas had suggested earlier? And how was this girl suppressing our powers? Was she creating a shield between us and our powers? Was she snuffing them out like a flame? Or was she siphoning them into herself, thus potentially making it possible for her to use them?

How dangerous was she behind her sweet smiles and cute doe eyes?

But I didn't ask, because I was playing the part of a new Copper who barely knew anything about how magic and this new world worked. So, I ground my teeth in frustration and held on tightly to the straps of my backpack, trying to pretend like I was excited to be trudging through snow toward an unknown destination.

If Søren were here, he'd be loving this. My twin had always loved surprises and adventures a lot more than I did. I enjoyed challenges and danger, but only when I had a modicum of information about what I was about to face. In contrast, Søren was as unpredictable and impulsive as was his power over hellfire – he would jump into the unknown in a heartbeat if he thought something fun might be on the other side.

Stars, I missed him.

Ahead of us, Matteo was chatting with Thomas and Liam as if the three had been friends for years. Gone were the shadows in his eyes or the fear on his face. He seemed so happy. And, while he was clearly trusting these people way too quickly, I couldn't repress the part of me that hoped that everything would go well in the Refuge. Just so that Matteo's hopes wouldn't be crushed to pieces.

I was observing the men talking when I realized that they had started walking away from the cottage. We had first started walking around it, as if to go to a side door, but now we were walking away from the creepy cabin and starting to walk toward the denser parts of the snow-covered forest.

"The Refuge isn't in the cottage?" I asked, trying to play it cool but secretly alert again. Where were we going? And had we just walked into a very well-thought-out trap?

"Oh no," Bella laughed softly, "this place is falling apart and full of nasty things. The last time I went in there, there were some of the biggest spiderwebs I'd ever seen."

I shivered at the thought – spiders creeped me out. How ironic coming from someone who could control actual skeletons and dead bodies. Kalani always made fun of me for my irrational fear of the eight-legged arachnids.

"Don't worry though, we've found a very nice place to settle in, and I promise you'll be comfortable."

"No spiders?" I joked to try to show Bella that I was friendly.

"Not usually, but we'll ask Liam to check your room before you move in!"

"Does he scare them away?"

"He scares everyone away," Bella laughed back. "Once you get to know him, he's a real softie, though." Then she stopped, eyes widening, and stage whispered the last part, "Don't tell him I said that."

I chuckled along as the big man turned his head around to look at us. He was too far ahead to have heard our conversation. But he must have felt that we were talking about him because he raised an eyebrow in Bella's direction, and she waved at him with a smile and a blush.

Oh. That was a welcomed new development.

"You guys are together?"

Bella blushed even deeper, and Liam gave her a heated look before turning back to face the trees in we were walking toward.

The girl cleared her throat, flustered, before answering in a shaky voice. "We… we became an item a few weeks ago, yes."

That explained why the man had stood protectively over her during the whole interrogation period. I wasn't sure exactly what he'd been scared of, since Matteo and I had been separated from our powers, but men tended to become overly protective of their girlfriends.

The thought reminded me of Archer and Kalani – specifically of how my friend had tried to hide his feelings for the human but had miserably failed. Every time she was in danger, he'd acted like a fool in love. I'd known about his feelings long before he *finally* gathered the courage to admit them to himself and to her.

"Nice, girl. I can see the appeal." Liam was a little too mountain man for my tastes, but he did have rugged features that made him attractive and I had a feeling that he was the kind of guy who gave women a really good time.

Bella nodded before dragging her eyes over her boyfriend's body. The dreamy look that came over her face was enough to make me laugh. Maybe I'd get along with her after all. She was funny, and more importantly, she was very much already involved in a romantic relationship.

Not that it mattered.

"As if you're one to talk. Your mate over there must have been a golden retriever in another life. I can see the appeal too," she added with a knowing smirk in my direction.

I wasn't sure how to explain the way my heart skipped a beat. "Oh, we're not… he's not…" I coughed. "We're not together."

The girl hummed but her smile said that she didn't believe a word I'd said. But I was right. Matteo and I couldn't be anything other than friends. After all, I had lied to him since the moment we'd met, and I couldn't imagine myself starting a relationship on so many lies. Even if I decided to come clear, he'd never trust me. Not when he'd realize that I was a part of the people that were destroying Coppers' lives.

There was no future in which Matteo and I were an item.

I just had to repeat it a few more times until my heart stopped beating erratically anytime I looked at Matteo.

Thankfully, I was stopped in my thoughts of impossible relationships by the sight of what looked like a huge fallen tree against the rocky cliff. And we were heading straight to it.

"Is this it?" I asked Bella with disbelief. Maybe the creepy cottage was better than whatever was over there.

The British Copper shrugged with a secretive smile on her lips. "You'll have to wait and see."

How fun.

Still, I followed along dutifully and didn't even comment when the three men ducked beneath the fallen tree and disappeared in the shadows that hid the space between the snow-covered branches and the cliff.

Really, sometimes I wondered why I had decided to leave Olympus with its sunny, warm weather, and environment that I knew mostly by heart. The snow, cold weather, and potentially spider-filled hidden caves were making me reconsider my decision to move away to Earth.

I couldn't suppress a shiver as I bent to move beneath the fallen tree. The tree was so massive that the space between it and the cliff was almost pitch black.

"Keep going, it's straight ahead!"

I rolled my eyes at Bella's words from behind me. As if there was anywhere to go but ahead. This was really one of the weirdest situations I'd ever put myself in – half-crawling under a snowy tree to enter what I assumed was a cave that could be filled with anything, for all I knew.

Stars, I really hoped that there weren't spiders crawling everywhere in these caves. I wasn't strong enough for that.

My backpack got caught in a branch and a pile of snow fell on my head as I struggled to get free.

Needless to say, by the time I made it into the dark cave, I wasn't having a great time.

As I straightened and shook snow off of my hair, I took a couple of seconds to observe my surroundings. The cave was pretty small, only big enough to have a dozen of people stand around comfortably. The only light came from the electric lamp in Thomas's hand, casting a cold white glow over the three men's faces.

"Welcome to the Refuge," Bella exclaimed as she stood up from the entrance behind me.

"How impressive," I drawled as I looked around at our very drab surroundings.

"I have to agree here," Matteo added in a hesitant tone.

Had we really come all of this way for a small empty cave? I still wasn't sure what Twitter was, but it sure didn't seem like a place to meet trustworthy people.

"You guys haven't seen the cool part yet," the young blond woman said with a couple of excited hand claps.

What next? Another empty cave? See, I didn't like these kinds of surprises. Not at all.

Next to me, Thomas mumbled something I didn't catch before walking closer to the wall of the cave. He touched multiple places along the rocky wall until a door appeared.

Well. Fun trick. I was curious who had this power over illusions among the Coppers that were present in the Refuge. Probably one of Apollo's many grandkids. The god was responsible for half of the overpopulation problem on Mount Olympus.

Thomas pushed the door open and light came through. Seconds later, I was faced with a huge room with dozens of people sitting at tables and eating together. It all seemed like another world, with a few children running around laughing, mouthwatering food scents, and light that seemed way too natural for a place that had to be within the mountain.

"Now, we can officially welcome you both to the Refuge," Thomas announced, narrowing his eyes at me as he said the words.

He might be welcoming me inside this place, but he clearly didn't trust me. That was fine. I just had to pay attention to my words and make sure he had nothing to pin on me.

So, I smiled and stared right back at him.

"Thanks Tommy, I can't wait to be a part of this big family."

Chapter Twenty

Kalani

Mom hadn't had many things that used to be dad's. By the time I was old enough to actually make memories and wonder who my dad was, most of his things were packed away in boxes and hidden in the dark corners of our apartment.

When I asked my mom who my dad was, she usually got either angry or sad. She hadn't been the type of person to tell me bedtime stories about how she'd met my dad, or how awesome he was before the car accident that took him away. If not for the handful of friends my mom still had from before I was born, I would have almost no information about who my dad was.

The thing was, my mom's one true love had died after they'd been together for a few months of a life-changing love story, leaving her heartbroken, heavily pregnant, and alone.

Seeing as my mom hadn't been raised by loving parents who preached taking care of one's mental health, she had decided that the best way to move forward was to bury her pain and every mention of the love of her life. At least, she had tried to do so. Unfortunately, she had mostly failed, especially on the first count.

When I was twelve, I had decided to snoop around the dusty boxes in the back of her closet. I knew she'd be pissed – she never took it well when I tried to force her to tell me something about dad. But damn it, I wanted to know about the man I'd gotten my green eyes and tan skin from.

The first box had been filled with a couple of sweatshirts that still smelled like the ocean, three autobiographical books – two about surfers and one about a guy who had climbed Mount Everest – and a few knickknacks that made me want to know why my dad loved sea turtle figurines and harmonicas so much. But then, at the very bottom of the box, there was a pile of photos. Some of my dad with his surf, long hair wet from the ocean, salt covering his cheeks, and a big smile on his face. He had kind eyes and a smile that was contagious.

Other pictures showed my parents together, before and after mom had become pregnant with me. They always looked so happy together, exchanging looks that screamed how much they loved each other.

And, finally, at the bottom of the pile, was a picture of my dad as a teenager with a middle-aged couple and a kid. His family. They all had the same sun-kissed skin, smile lines around their eyes and mouths, and sparkling green eyes.

Just like mine.

I had stared at the photo for a very long time, trying to memorize every single detail. There was a whole part of my family out there, somewhere. I had no idea who they were, what their names were, or whether they knew about me. But I could stare at them, sitting on the sand in front of a beach bar named 'The Crazy Coconut', and imagine myself with them.

Unfortunately, my mom had completely freaked out when she'd seen me with the picture and dad's things spread out all around me. I'd been grounded for weeks and she'd fallen back into a depressive episode that had scared me away from digging some more.

My point was that this picture had almost been tattooed in my mind. I remembered it perfectly, like it was still in my hand.

And 'The Crazy Coconut' hadn't changed one bit.

"Oh, I could go for a pina colada! I haven't had one since that last time we snuck out, you know, when we met those yoga girls in Australia! We had such a great time, right Arch?" Søren exclaimed with a suggestive smile in Archer's direction.

Nafula sighed, pinching her nose with her fingers. "You are exasperating, Aska."

"And you are a killjoy, Nafula dear."

I ignored Nafula's sarcastic response and turned to Archer. "Australian yoga girls, huh?"

Archer's cheeks reddened slightly, and he nervously ran his hand on the back of his neck. "You know Søren, he's exaggerating. There were girls doing yoga on the beach, and we were just eating at a restaurant in front of said beach. There weren't any interactions, I swear, and—"

"Relax, Sunshine." I gave him a soft tap on the chest. "I can't say anything about you looking at hot girls doing yoga on the beach before we met, since I also looked at hot guys surfing bare-chested. I just like to mess with you."

Relief crossed his face, swiftly followed by surprise and… was that jealousy? "What do you mean hot guys surfing bare-chested?"

"There's no way they're hotter than you, Archie, don't you worry," Søren interjected solemnly.

They really weren't, but I didn't say anything because Archer's concern was way too fun. And the petty part of me thought it was as good a way as any to make him pay for *the argument*.

Instead, I took a deep breath and climbed the wooden stairs that led to the beach patio of 'The Crazy Coconut'.

My chest clenched as I stood there, on the patio filled with lounge chairs and people drinking fruity cocktails with little colorful parasols.

Once upon a time, my dad had been right there, where I stood.

I felt so close to him, as if we were standing next to each other. For a heartbeat, I almost felt his hand in mine – our fingers intertwined, there for a second before it disappeared.

"Aloha! A table for four?" A lady with a green apron and a warm smile asked.

Throat still slightly choked from the emotions of being there, where my dad had grown up, I nodded and croaked out a yes. Two minutes later, all four of us were sitting at a high table, sipping on fruit smoothies or, in Søren's case, a pina colada.

"What now?" the Golden asked before taking a loud slurp of his drink. What a distinguished gentleman.

"Now, we need to find somewhere to lie low for a week or so." Archer narrowed his eyes at Søren. "That means no shenanigans, Aska."

"Shenanigans? How old are you, grandpa?"

"Søren, I swear, sometimes I want to—"

"Kiss me until neither of us can remember our names and you fall deeply in love with me? You're not the first one to tell me that, actually. But I'm glad to see that my charm is still working strong."

Archer sighed; eyes closed like he was asking for mercy. The two men fell into one of their usual friendly arguments, and I couldn't stop the warmth that spread through my chest. Seeing Søren joke around and laugh at his best friend was a sight I'd worried I would never see again after Mei's death. Sure, his smile didn't quite reach all the way to his eyes, and every so often, his eyes would become unfocused and he'd look so sad. And that was understandable – he'd lost his girlfriend a few weeks ago. But he was there, he was trying, and we would support him through his grief. At least, he wasn't alone anymore, and our group was almost complete again.

We just needed to bring Sadie back.

And we might need to find a way to survive the next few weeks without being killed by deities that believed I was the figurehead of a very inconvenient rebellion.

"Are they always like this?" Nafula asked me in a whisper as the men continued to argue about… who ran the fastest? How had they gotten to that point anyway?

"Pretty much, yes. You'll get used to it."

She seemed skeptical at my words but didn't comment further. Instead, she focused back on the guys, watching them like she was at the theater.

Soon enough, I stopped paying attention to the conversation at hand, my eyes focusing on all of the little details around us. The palm trees, the ones lining the path that went from the patio down to the beach, were slightly bigger than they had been on the picture. But the painting on the wall near the door that led to the inside of the restaurant was the same – a woman wearing traditional Hawaiian clothing and holding a pile of coconuts.

Gods, how I wished I could be here with my dad, if only for a few hours. I had so many questions for him, like what his dreams and hopes had been before he'd died, or what his favorite meal was. Sure, I had more than one question regarding why exactly Thanatos, god of Death and father of two of my best friends, had found weird magical waves in my soul. But more than that, I wanted to know what had made him the man who smiled on that picture with his family, and the man who had fallen in love with mom.

And, while my father wasn't in any condition to answer those questions from beyond the realm of the living, I couldn't suppress the stupid hope that I'd find someone else on these islands with answers for me.

I just had to find the people who had stood next to my dad in that picture taken over two decades ago.

Yeah, that promised to be *so easy*. Especially with my three tag-alongs that had no idea I'd chosen Hawaii with ulterior motives.

"No, Søren," Archer sighed once more. "We are here to lie low. Do you know what 'lying low' means?"

"Of course, I do, but it's not like the gods are going to know if we hang out at pool parties all day. I don't think your dear old dad will be checking social media looking for us."

"Fair enough," Nafula interjected, agreeing with Søren for the first time since we'd all arrived on Hawaii.

Søren did a double take on Nafula before grinning like a kid who'd been offered a whole bag of candy. "Really?"

"Don't get used to it, Aska. I just wouldn't mind having some fun since I've been 'voluntold' into this hide-and-seek game."

The waitress who had welcomed us walked past our table again, heading toward the inside of the restaurant. Based on the interactions I had seen her have with the other clients and waiters, I was pretty sure that she was either a manager or even one of the owners of the place. And if she was that high up in the hierarchy of 'The Crazy Coconut,' then there was a chance that she had been working here for a long time. Maybe long enough that she had met my dad.

"I'm going to go to the restroom really quickly. I'll be right back."

I didn't wait for either of my friends to answer before standing up and speed walking inside the restaurant. Inside, Hawaiian music was playing, and two men were throwing darts in the back of the room.

"Can I help you, honey?" the lady who had welcomed us asked when I stepped up to the bar.

Suddenly, my mouth was so dry that I wasn't sure I'd be able to speak. But the lady – Leilani, as written on her name tag – had such a warm smile that it made me feel comfortable. And I would never forgive myself if I didn't ask her any questions and had to leave Hawaii before finding out more about my family.

So, I took a deep breath and wet my lips nervously. I had survived a deadly Tournament and fought against bloodthirsty Coppers. I had refused to cower in front of the most powerful gods on Mount Olympus. I had survived against all odds for months on end. After all of that, I could have a civil conversation with this lady about whether she knew my dad or not.

"Yes, actually. I was wondering if you had already been working here around twenty-five years ago."

"I've been here since we opened this place with my husband, almost thirty years ago now. Time flies, right?" she added with a warm laugh. "Why do you ask?"

"I ask because my dad died when I was a baby and one of the only photos that I have of him is in front of 'The Crazy Coconut' with his parents and younger sibling. His name was Keanu Hale. He grew up here, in O'ahu, and he moved to California a little around twenty-two years ago. Do you by any chance remember him or his family?"

"Oh, sweetheart, I am so sorry to hear that." Her eyes softened and I could almost feel the love coming from her. "Let me go and ask Greg, he has much better memory than I do when it comes to names. Wait right here, okay?"

I nodded and she disappeared in what I assumed was the kitchen. I tried to listen for the sound of any conversation, but my heart was pounding so loud that it drowned out anything else.

An eternity flew by before the door to the kitchen reopened to reveal Leilani and who I assumed was Greg. The man looked in his early sixties, with a green shirt covered in little coconuts and a white chef hat on his head. What a combo.

"Here she is, Greg!" Then, turning to me, "Don't worry, honey, we will figure it out!"

The man introduced himself as Greg, Leilani's husband and co-owner of this establishment, before asking me to give him the details I knew about my dad again. So, I repeated the information I'd given Leilani and added everything I remembered about his physique: tall, shoulder-length black hair, and sparkling green eyes. The same as mine.

Greg frowned for a few seconds, deep in thoughts, before asking, "And he had a sibling you said?"

"Yes, or at least on the picture there was a younger boy who looked very much like him. Probably five or six years younger."

The man hummed, nodding along. His wife seemed to deflate the longer it took, and soon enough, my own hopes were dwindling down. It was fine, though, I told myself. I'd find someone else who might know Keanu Hale. Maybe some older surfers in O'ahu? I bet they had a tight-knit community here too, and someone had to rememb—

"I remember! The Hale family, that lives on the north side of the island, near Hau'ula! You know, Kawehi and David Hale, they come here at least once a month."

Leilani's hand went to her chest and she gasped. "Oh, dear god, yes. They did lose their oldest son a while back. What a tragedy." And she did seem genuinely moved at the thought.

My whole body perked up at the couple's words. "Are they still living close, then?"

Greg nodded enthusiastically. "Yes, they live maybe twenty minutes away. I don't have their exact address, but that can be found."

My chest tightened and my eyes watered a little bit. Not much, just a sheen. I wasn't about to cry. But I did feel a little emotional because, if Greg was right, then my grandparents might be only twenty minutes away.

Kawehi and David Hale.

"Oh, honey, it's all right. Come here." Leilani wrapped me in a hug, the kind that I'd dreamed my mom could have given me over the years. "I'll make some calls, all right?"

I nodded against her shoulder, feeling something loosen in my chest. This hug and the generosity this woman I had just met was giving me were something I hadn't known I needed. But after months of feeling one step away from death, and after being worried about the rebellion, Sadie disappearing, and my potential magical powers… well, this physical show of comfort was such a relief.

"Thank you, Leilani and Greg. It means a lot," I said as I stepped away from the woman. "I lost my phone, but I can stop back here in the next couple of days to see if you have found the address?"

Greg put a hand around his wife's shoulders and gave her a side hug. "Of course. We will have it by tomorrow evening at the latest," he trailed off.

"Kalani."

"Well, Kalani, I hope we will be able to bring you and your grandparents together soon. Come back here tomorrow in the late afternoon."

I thanked both of them greatly, hope swirling in my chest. There were so many things I wanted to know about my dad and grandparents, and I felt almost giddy about the possibility of meeting people from my family in a matter of days. Hours, even.

Just as Greg was saying his goodbyes to me and turning back toward the kitchen, Archer walked through the patio door, calling out my name.

"We have to head out. Are you ready to go?" he asked with a hesitant look as his eyes shifted from me to Leilani.

I straightened up and gave Leilani a final smile before turning on my heels and joining Archer. "Yeah, let's go."

I caught Archer giving Leilani a weird look – the man was too mistrustful for his own good – but I put a hand on his chest and pushed him back out of the door before he could continue to stare at her.

"What were you two talking about?"

"I was just asking about this painting in the women's restrooms. Nothing important."

I really hated lying to him, but I also didn't want to explain everything surrounding the unknown side of my family until I had more information. Plus, we still hadn't talked about *the argument* and there was this tense awkwardness between us. I wasn't about to reveal all of my secrets to him, not in the current state of our relationship. And he was still completely freaked out about having to hide from the gods, so I didn't want to add to the stress by telling him that I was trying to find my grandparents who may or may not have answers about my potential magical powers – which I still hadn't talked to him about, either.

The pile of lies was growing too fast for me to keep up.

Thankfully, we were already back at the table. "So, have you guys figured out where we are staying?"

"Yes," Nafula answered with a sigh, twirling the mini parasol that had been in her drink between her thumb and forefinger. "We are going camping. In the wild. Kill me now."

Chapter Twenty-One

Sadie

Twenty-four hours later, I had gleaned a lot of information about the Refuge. First of all, there were thirty-two people living in this place – thirty-four now, with Matteo and me. And all of these Coppers lived right under the nose of the gods of Mount Olympus.

I loved knowing that the Olympians were getting played by so many Coppers. The petty part of me found it extremely satisfying.

The Coppers were from almost all over Europe, North Africa, and the Middle East. It was impressive to see how well the leaders of this Refuge had been able to organize such a big rebellion movement with so many people. And all of it was so well hidden.

To be fair, it all relied on Bella. This whole concept had started with Thomas, Bella, and her twin brother named Ken. From what I'd understood, Ken and Thomas had been online friends for years when Ken and Bella's powers had emerged on the same day. I wasn't sure exactly what had happened for the two of them, but it had ended with Ken talking to his online friend about it. And Thomas had been lucky, because he had been able to hide his powers for years – he was fortunate enough that his gift was not the type to cause big waves of magic. The three of them had decided to meet and hide from the Hunters that were coming after them.

And Bella had been their salvation.

After all, what was the best way to evade people tracking one's magic but to be able to snuff out said magic?

Bella was an invisibility shield, and she'd worked to strengthen her powers from protecting her brother and friend, to hiding over thirty people. And she did it with a smile and an upbeat demeanor.

I wasn't sure how long this Refuge had been open, but it was long enough that two babies had been born here, and they'd built a mini city. Long hallways and dozens of rooms had been created under the mountain, courtesy of Ken who could manipulate the earth. And because of the Coppers they' recruited along the way, they had figured out how to have light in the rooms, running water within the three huge bathrooms and the kitchens, and even air flow through the rooms to make it feel like human-made buildings. I was more than impressed by the infrastructure they had built and the community they had created.

And Matteo loved everything about the Refuge.

For hours after we'd arrived, he'd gushed over everything that was here, asking thousands of questions, and gazing over everything with big, wide eyes. I would have been annoyed if he hadn't been so freakishly cute. So, I'd followed along and smiled as he got excited about the two baby Coppers and the magical bathing pools that twinkled like they were filled with stars.

I wished Kalani could see this too. She would have stars in her eyes at the views and people there.

At the thought, my heart clenched in a way it hadn't in a few hours. I missed her so much. Competing in the Tournament together had brought us close and I missed our friendship. Seeing the people here, living happily away from Olympus and the back-stabbing gods that lived on it made me wish for another life with my brother and friends.

Stars, I couldn't stop wishing for impossible things, now. Like wishing someone had created this Refuge years ago, back when I'd been a teenager hiding my powers, scared I'd be moving to Olympus without my twin brother. If I'd been able to join the Refuge then, my life would have been so different. I probably wouldn't be hiding away from everyone I loved and dreaming about the fourth trial every night.

That was why I was going to make sure Matteo never had to participate in the Tournament. Or any of the Coppers living in the Refuge, for that matter. These people deserved happiness, and Olympus would not bring it to them.

"Why are you looking so nostalgic and sad, Sadie?"

I jumped at the voice driving me away from my thoughts. Bella was standing next to where I sat, looking at a group of Coppers playing football. The non-American kind.

"It's just been a long few weeks." I gave her a smile as she sat down next to me.

"It can take some time for your mind and body to realize that you're safe now. And I do agree that watching your man is a good way to make yourself feel better." She giggled before adding in a whisper, "It's a shame we had two available rooms instead of one, because the 'Only One Bed' trope always works to bring people together. Plus, it's my favorite trope."

Bella had a shit-eating grin on her face at the words and I rolled my eyes, fighting an irrational urge to look at Matteo. I wasn't sure what a 'trope' was, but I imagined that the book-loving girl was referring to Matteo and I sharing a room.

"We've already gone over this Bella, he's not my man."

"Huh-uh, sure mate. I'll pretend like I believe you."

I shook my head at her words but couldn't contain a tiny smile. From what I have seen in the past twenty-four hours, Bella was a bookworm and hopeless romantic. She'd shown me the way to her room after we'd settled in the day before and one wall was covered in romance books that had been read and loved many times over.

"So, what are you thinking of the Refuge? Pretty neat, huh?"

"Yeah, it's pretty impressive. I hadn't realized there would be so many people living here."

"We've been recruiting an exponential number of people in the past two years. The few of us who have had contacts with our godly parent before going into hiding have been able to get some information about what is waiting for us on Mount Olympus, and it has spread through the community of Coppers who are on the run. The place has held up for almost four years now, and we doubled in size over the past year. And we will continue to welcome more Coppers here, because none of us want to leave our world."

I understood that. I'd been scared to move to Mount Olympus, and there hadn't been a deadly Tournament waiting for me there. Some of the Coppers living here were barely older than kids. Unfortunately, some Coppers revealed their powers much earlier than others. And, unsurprisingly, young teenagers rarely made it out alive of the Tournament.

All of it was unfair and cruel. I was grateful that at least some Coppers could find a solace in this Refuge.

"I'm glad this place exists." And it was the most truthful thing I could say.

A young girl scored, and cheers erupted from the players farther down in the gymnasium. The smile on Matteo's face was brighter than the Sun as he high-fived his teammate and congratulated her on her goal.

After having seen him fall into a panic attack at the thought of having to continue to run away from an endless stream of Hunters only a day before, my relief at this view was huge.

Matteo turned toward us as he joined the other players toward the center of their make-up field and our eyes met, colliding like magnets. His head tilted to the side and made a thumbs-up, asking if I was fine. I smiled and nodded, but he waited a few seconds before turning back toward the game.

"And you are saying he's not your man," Bella snickered next to me.

"You need to stop reading romance books, it's making you see love stories everywhere."

"It's only making me aware of men who are book boyfriend material. Since I don't love dark romances, my standards are aimed more toward green flag men. And when it comes to your Matteo over there, the flag is so green that it's blinding."

Even though I had never heard of green flags before and wasn't sure what were the criteria to be categorized one, I had to admit that Matteo was everything that I wanted in a partner – kind, gentle, supportive, smart, and I had to admit, very good looking.

None of that mattered though. Even if Matteo was interested in starting something with me – which wasn't even a known thing – there was no way anything could work. I was lying to him, to everyone here. And I was too broken to hope to start a committed relationship anytime soon. I could still barely close my eyes without hearing Søren's screams as Mei and I entered the magical cage during the fourth trial.

A shiver ran through me at the thought of Mei, and I quickly forced myself to think of something else.

"You don't have a meeting to go to, right now?" I inquired with a smile, so she knew I wasn't actually trying to get rid of her.

"Thankfully, no! I hate those bloody meetings. I mostly let the rest of the council deal with everyday issues and only show up for assemblies or when it comes to things that only I can do."

"Yeah, I can imagine they are a bore."

I couldn't, though. None of us had ever had a thing to say about the way we were ruled on Olympus – it was the Olympians' show and all of us were pawns in their games, powerless to do anything but follow their rules. Instead, here, a council of nine

Coppers made decisions, and there was an assembly every month so that the rest of the inhabitants of the Refuge could ask for changes in the way the Refuge was run.

"I heard down the pipeline of information that you are trained in martial arts," Bella suddenly commented in a tightly controlled tone.

I had to fight to remain relaxed next to the Copper. Matteo was too trusting and sociable for his own good. I knew damn well that he hadn't been acting in a malicious way when he'd told someone about my competency in martial arts. It probably had been a throwaway comment, something he hadn't thought about for more than two seconds. But if I wanted to remain here, I had to maintain my cover, which meant keeping Thomas as far away from me as possible. If he started to see me as a potential threat, he would come sniffing around with his powers, and there was only so much I could do to not lie when asked the right questions. I wouldn't last a week in the Refuge with that kind of scrutiny.

"Yeah, I started pretty young and I was a self-defense teacher until a few months ago."

Bella hummed, waiting until the same girl as before tried to score – and failed – before continuing. "Would you be open to teaching a class? A lot of people defended themselves with their powers until they were able to come here, but most have little to no training in physical combat."

"Are you planning on them having to fight anytime soon?"

"Hopefully not. But I want to make sure people feel more confident in their ability to defend themselves even without their powers. For many of us, the day we discovered our powers was very traumatizing, and we don't have a psychologist on hand here. Not having to rely on their magic might help people feel better."

Learning how to punch and kick and defend themselves from physical attacks would not save them when they faced the gods, or even a group of very determined Hunters. But I wasn't about to tell that to Bella.

I really didn't want to say yes. The last time I'd trained someone in physical combat, it had been Kalani, before we both had to fight in a deadly Tournament against a group of unlucky Coppers that hadn't found the Refuge. And, while training Kalani had brought the two of us really close, what had followed wasn't full of happy memories. I had absolutely no desire to immerse myself back into everything that had happened during the Tournament.

But I couldn't say no. If I refused to help, I would lose the trust Bella currently had in me. She was an important member of the Refuge, with political and magical weight. I needed her on my side. So, really, I had no choice but to pretend to be excited about teaching this class.

"Sure, I'd love to help."

Bella smiled brightly, looking relieved that I'd accepted. "Awesome! I'll make an announcement tonight in the mess hall. We'll get it started tomorrow!"

How exciting.

Still, I smiled and acted excited too, because I needed this girl to like me. I needed to become important to the Refuge, so that when I inevitably got discovered, people would think twice before killing me.

Plus, I knew that I was playing with fire there. Kellan, my boss for the Hunters, had given me the mission to find and apprehend Matteo. When he didn't hear from me for a few days and couldn't find a way to contact me – what with me having turned off my phone and removed its SIM card – he would know something was up. And he'd come looking.

Maybe it was a good idea to prepare these Coppers to fight. I would not be able to make them into skilled fighters anytime soon, but I might be able to give them a few tricks that would help them survive a little longer against the gods of Mount Olympus.

Because this safe haven wouldn't last forever. As much as I was impressed by the work Bella and the others had done to protect their people, something would go wrong at one point. Someone would talk to the wrong person, or someone would ask the right questions to the right person, and the Hunters would find this place.

Maybe what I could do was help prepare them for that inevitable moment, no matter how painful it was to relive the bad memories training would bring back to me.

This could be my penance. And my revenge against the gods.

"Do you ever wonder what it looks like? Mount Olympus? Sometimes I wonder and try to imagine where my dad lives and what he looks like." She paused for a second, deep in thoughts, before asking in a small voice, "Do you think it's dumb? That I'm dreaming about that place when I'm here, doing everything I can to escape it?"

I remained silent for a long moment, debating what to say. I knew too much about Mount Olympus to answer this without thinking long and deep about what I could and couldn't say.

"In my dreams, Mount Olympus is beautiful. The most beautiful place to ever exist. But I don't think there can ever be a place with only beauty, there always has to be a balance. So, even if I can't see it, I know that there has to be ugliness on Mount Olympus too." I shifted to look at Bella, holding her gaze. "And I don't think it's dumb to wonder what Mount Olympus looks like, or what your dad is like. I think you can have a deep desire to know more about something without wanting to be a part of it. You're not selfish for wondering about what's out there, Bella. All of us want to know where we come from. It's only natural."

She nodded; her eyes misty. For a second, I thought she was going to say something more about my thoughts on Mount Olympus or my golden parent. But, instead, she blinked rapidly and turned back to the game.

"Well, it's a good thing we'll never have to see the darkness on Mount Olympus, right?" Her small laugh was more sadness than happiness.

I hummed along, focusing back on the game too.

"Will you need someone to help direct the classes?"

"I mean, it'll depend on how many people decide to show up," I frowned, wondering how I would manage to teach up to thirty people on my own. "Who would even be competent to help me out?"

"Liam used to be a boxer, so he'd be great at it, but he does make many people a little frightened. Otherwise, Thomas could—"

"No, it's all right," I interrupted her right as I heard his name. There was no way I was going to spend any extra time in the presence of the human lie detector. "I'll be fine, no worries."

Bella gave me a look that said very clearly that she knew what I was doing. "He is not so bad, I promise. Once you get to know him, you get over his attitude."

"Really?" I scoffed, incredulous. "I can't see any universe in which Thomas, and I would get along. He decided he didn't like me the very first moment he laid eyes on me."

Bella winced but didn't contradict me. "He's a little distrustful, sure, but he does have a lot of responsibilities. It doesn't forgive his bloody attitude, but it does explain it."

I rolled my eyes at her words but hummed in agreement. Sure, it explains Thomas's terrible attitude. But it didn't mean that I was in any hurry to make friends with him.

"Anyway, I'll do the first classes on my own and if there are too many people for me to run them on my own, I'll ask Liam. And if needed, I'll also ask Thomas."

"Sure, I'll pretend like I believe that," Bella laughed.

Right then, the other team scored, and I watched as Matteo's head bent down in defeat. In seconds, though, he was standing tall again, giving his teammates encouragements and hyping them up for the rest of the game.

The flag really was green, wasn't it?

Chapter Twenty-Two

Kalani

As it turned out, camping with Archer, Søren, and Nafula was an experience, and not in a good way. Before Nafula and Søren had left Olympus, Priya had given them cash in a few different currencies, including US dollars. It was enough to last us through a few weeks, but in the optic of being responsible with the money we had, we had decided to only buy two tents.

Right away, Nafula had refused to bunk with Søren, claiming that she was going to lose her mind if she had to 'listen to Søren whining nonsense all day and night,' then she wouldn't survive with her sanity intact. I probably could have argued, but I wasn't mad at having an excuse not to spend hours alone with Archer.

I knew this was ridiculous. Archer had sacrificed a lot for me, even after *the argument*. But there were so many hurtful things hanging between us, and I didn't feel strong enough to deal with them yet. Not when there were so many other things on my mind.

Plus, bunking with Nafula was a blessing in disguise because the girl didn't pry.

So, when I sneaked out from our makeshift camp the next evening while Archer was busy teaching Søren how to suppress his powers – which were quite strong since he was a Golden and not a Copper – she didn't even ask where I was going.

I knew it was stupid of me to sneak out like this, especially with Artemis hell-bent on making me pay for simply existing as a human in her world, and dozens of Hunters probably looking for me and my runaway friends. But I needed answers, and I wanted to have some time to process them before having to share them with everyone else.

The walk to 'The Crazy Coconut' was short, less than ten minutes on back roads. A few months ago, back when the most dangerous part of my day was serving alcoholic drinks to bridesmaids on weekends, I would have been anxious at the thought of walking alone on such isolated roads. But the advantage of having been trained to fight against Coppers with very dangerous magical powers was that, while I remained conscious of my surroundings, I felt relatively safe.

I had to find the positives in this whole ordeal I had been thrown into or I'd start crying.

My heart started beating faster as I climbed the stairs up to the back patio of the restaurant. I had so much hope about this; so much hope that I'd finally find information about my dad and where I came from.

But I'd be lying if I said I wasn't also terrified. I'd lost my family, and while I'd found amazing friends along the way, I still felt a little alone in this world. If the people Greg had thought of actually were my grandparents and they didn't want to meet me… something in my heart would break.

There was very little of my heart still whole, I didn't want to lose those pieces too.

Anxiousness riddled my nerves as I opened the door, ukulele music floating to my ears.

The place was less crowded than the day before. I also hadn't managed to leave our camp until later in the afternoon than I'd hoped, so most of the patrons had already left the beach restaurant.

The first person that I saw as I entered was Leilani. The older lady was stacking menus on the bar counter and dropped all of them as soon as she saw me.

"Kalani! Honey, you came! I was worried when I didn't see you earlier in the afternoon."

Slightly shaking from the nerves, I stepped toward her and gave her a small smile. "I'm sorry, the day was a bit hectic today." I swallowed roughly, heart pounding in my ears. "Were you able to get the address?"

Leilani reached for my hand and squeezed softly. "We did better than that, honey. We brought your grandparents here."

Time stopped for a second.

One heartbeat.

Two.

Three.

"They're here?"

Leilani nodded, her eyes soft and kind as she watched me break at the seams from the inflow of emotions. Fear. Excitement. Anxiousness. Hope. I didn't know what to feel and what to do and what to expect.

"Really?" I asked, still wondering if I was dreaming this conversation.

"Yes, honey, they are here, sitting on the beach patio."

The next few seconds were a blur. Leilani almost dragged me to the door that led to the patio facing the ocean. I heard the waves and saw the descending sun over the water before anything else. Soft music played from the restaurant's outdoor speakers. It was a great setting for a family reunion.

The patio was empty except for two older people, sitting close together on one of the beachy couches. They were facing away from me, so I couldn't see their faces, but I could see their hands held tight together. There were empty glasses in front of them, and their heads were down, as if they were feeling defeated. My heart raced at the thought – were they disappointed at the idea that I wasn't going to be there to meet them?

Leilani squeezed my arm softly, turning my attention to her, before nodding, her eyebrows raised, wordlessly asking me if I was still up for this. I nodded stiffly once, and she smiled.

"Kawehi, David," she called out.

The couple turned around, and I was faced with two older versions of the people from the photograph. For a second, I had this feeling that I had traveled back in time and my dad would appear from somewhere, ready to pose for the picture.

"Kalani?" the man asked, his voice breaking at the word.

I nodded but my throat was too tight to speak.

The woman walked around the couch, a hand over her chest and her eyes filled with unshed tears. "Oh, my baby's daughter." A sob came out of her and she visibly struggled to remain composed. "Can I hug you, Kalani?"

I was on the brink of tears too, overwhelmed by the possibility of getting a new family after losing Mom and Makaio. "Yes," I croaked out.

Half a second later, I was engulfed in the warmest, nicest hug I'd felt in a long, *long* time. My whole body relaxed, and I melted into her arms. Her body was shaking, betraying her tears. And somehow, I knew these tears were a mix of happiness and grief – joy to meet me, but sadness that I was reminding them of the son they'd lost.

The hug might have lasted for a few seconds or an hour, I wasn't sure. When Kawehi – my *grandmother* – and I separated, I felt both drained and relieved.

A quick look showed me that Leilani had left the patio, and it was now empty except for the three of us. My grandparents and me.

"Come and sit, granddaughter," David said, his voice low and soft, a watery smile on his face.

With a tentative smile, I stepped forward and went to sit on the padded chair next to the couch. My grandma went to sit next to her husband again, and both of them took me in slowly. I felt like squirming under their gazes, but Kawehi's next words relaxed me.

"You have our Keanu's eyes."

It was like a punch to the gut. I had known that my dad had greenish eyes from those faded pictures in the box full of memories hiding in my mom's room. But hearing from his mother that we shared this feature was heart-stopping. And it made me want to know even more. I knew we shared our love of surfing, but was there anything else that I'd taken from him, even without ever knowing him?

"How was he? I've only seen pictures, but I have never seen any video."

Once again, there was a split second when I couldn't do anything but hate the way my mom had handled everything. It was hard to hold on to my resentment when I had seen her so happy with Makaio after she'd forgotten me. She'd still been my mom, and I knew that nothing forgave her behavior as I'd grown up. But maybe having me right after she'd lost the love of her life had made healing from her grief impossible. Maybe that explained things, even if it didn't make the years of abandonment go away.

"We can show you pictures and videos honey, and we'll tell you everything you want to know about your dad. But can you tell us about yourself first? We never even knew that your mom was pregnant," my grandma said, her frown conveying how betrayed she felt at that realization.

I wasn't surprised at her words. While I had a feeling that my parents had shared the great news when they'd discovered they were expecting me, I knew that the memory-erasing spell that had been cast over me when the Hunter had taken me to Olympus had probably erased that from my grandparents' lives.

Now came the weird moment when I had to talk about my life. I wasn't sure what to say about the past six months of my life but decided to just pretend they hadn't existed. Instead, I went over the big strokes of the painting that had been my life for the first twenty years of my life.

I talked about my passions for surfing and gymnastics. I talked about my brother and how much I loved him. I shared my enthusiasm for learning about science and especially marine biology – which had been my college degree. I described how much I had loved teaching little kids how to flip, and how excited I'd been about the prospect of becoming a science high school teacher after college. And through it all, my grandparents listened with sparkling eyes and wide smiles.

When it came to questions about what I was doing now, I remained evasive and changed topics as quickly as possible. Similarly, I remained vague about why I was in Hawaii right then, letting them think that I was on vacation for a few days with some friends, but that I wouldn't be able to stay for very long.

Soon enough, it was their turns to tell me everything they could think of about my dad. They told me about my dad's love for the ocean since before he could speak – how he spent every free second of his time swimming, free diving, or surfing. They told me about his love of teaching others how to dive and how to appreciate the marine wildlife. They explained how he had dreamed of traveling the world and seeing every ocean. They shared how much my dad had enjoyed teaching his little brother, Lokela, how to surf. And they told me how bright his personality was, how easily he made friends, and how everyone loved him.

Moving to California to become a scuba diving and surfing instructor had been a first step in his dream of traveling the whole wide world.

He'd met my mom and fallen in love.

I knew they'd become pregnant after a few months of their love story, and they'd decided to remain in California until I was a little older before leaving to travel.

They hadn't had the chance to even start realizing their shared dream.

By the time we were mostly done with reminiscing, I had cried and laughed and smiled and felt more things that I had in a long time. It felt good and it hurt to learn all of those things about my dad. This information filled the empty void in my heart but also made me wish I'd met him even more.

A group of teenagers ran past, laughing all the way to the ocean. The interruption made me look at the clock above the door: two hours had passed already. Archer would freak out soon about my departure, if he hadn't started doing so already.

I needed to get to the touchy question about why the god of Death thought my budding magical powers came from my dad.

What a fun topic of conversation for the first time I was meeting my grandparents. I really hoped they wouldn't start to believe I was completely crazy.

It would suck to lose my grandparents because they thought I was a crazy girl they should order a restraining order against. However, I needed answers about the strange things I'd been able to do to save Makaio. No human was able to control the ocean like that. And I was almost completely sure that my mom had nothing to do with these strange powers.

Since my dad wasn't there anymore to answer my questions, my only option was my newly acquainted family.

"I have one last question before I have to leave tonight, but it might sound weird."

Kawehi scoffed, waving a hand in the air. "Don't worry, dear, you can ask us anything you'd like."

Well, I was sure she wasn't quite expecting this line of questioning, though. Although, if my mystery magical powers were inherited from my dad, then at least one of my grandparents had to be involved, too.

However, if my powers were not inherited from my dad… well, meeting my grandparents for an evening was a gift in itself, wasn't it?

"Again, this might sound crazy, but I've been experiencing some strange… things, lately."

"Strange things?" David frowned.

"Yes. I've been able to do things that no one is supposed to be able to do." I stopped, looking for a reaction on either of my grandparents' faces that would reveal that they understood what I was trying to hint at. There weren't any surprised looks on their faces, though. They were either truly unsure what I was talking about, or they had incredible poker faces.

"What exactly are those *things* that you can do?" Kawehi asked in what sounded like a genuinely confused tone.

I closed my eyes for a second, doing my best to remind myself that I had to continue on with this conversation. I needed to understand what was happening to me, and I needed to do it now. Pretending like I was joking around would be easier and less uncomfortable in the event that I was completely wrong about my dad or grandparents' involvement in magic, but it wouldn't solve my problems.

If I wanted to stand a chance at escaping the fate that Artemis and most of the other Olympians wanted for me – namely, death – I needed all of the weapons I could get my hands on. That included any obscure, non-Greek-gods-related magical powers I might have.

"Hmm, well, a week ago, I jumped in the ocean to save a kid who had fallen in and wasn't swimming back up. There was a very strong current and I couldn't find him. I started panicking and then…"

"And then what, dear?"

"And then the water stopped moving, except for a small current that brought the kid directly to me."

I'd been looking more closely at my grandma and saw the moment her eyebrow flinched. She didn't let anything else go through, though, and David didn't either. "That is a strange story indeed," he drawled softly.

Deep breath in, I decided to be brave and just come out with it. "Look, this might sound completely ridiculous, but did my dad ever have similar episodes? Did he ever experience anything that didn't make sense or seem normal?"

David opened his mouth but closed it after a second, no sound coming out. Instead, he turned to look at his wife. From the way they looked into each other's eyes, I knew they were having one of those wordless conversations that only decades of marriage could enable.

Both of them were silent for so long that I was almost sure they were not going to answer. And with each tick of the clock above the door of the restaurant, I knew that time was running out. I needed to go back to our camp site and deal with an Archer that was sure to be freaking out.

I was about to laugh it off and pretend like I had been messing with them, when Kawehi finally turned back to me. She had a serious look on her face, her smile gone and replaced by something more closed off.

"What exactly are you asking, Kalani?"

It was the first time she'd used my name instead of a term of endearment, conveying that she meant business. And based on how her eyes were set and her mouth wasn't stretched in a smile anymore, we had gone past the friendly getting-to-know-each-other phase and had slid right into the potentially-dangerous-and-very-serious zone.

Could I play this in any other way than just laying all of my cards on the table? Probably not. But I really didn't want to talk about my experience on Mount Olympus if I could avoid it. For some unknown reason, I felt like I wasn't supposed to be talking about this place and the gods that lived on it with anyone on Earth. Like something bad would happen if I did.

It was probably me being paranoid, but I'd still try to avoid the topic of conversation if I could.

However, I needed to be more explicit with my words if I wanted my grandparents to reveal their own hands.

"I want to know if my dad had magic. If he could do things that most human beings cannot do. Like me."

Another look shared between Kawehi and David. A beat of silence. Then Kawehi spoke again.

"If he, hypothetically, had such magical powers. What would you do with that information?"

I inhaled a sharp breath at her words. Interesting. "I would ask you two for advice on how to control the powers I have. Because if my dad had those magical powers, then one of you two must have them too."

David scoffed but didn't contradict me. And based on the way he was letting Kawehi talk, I'd bet everything I owned, which admittedly wasn't much, that my dad and I had inherited our powers from her.

Who the hell was she? If she wasn't descended from the Greek gods, then how had she been able to give the both of us our powers? This whole story was turning into a mystery that I was excited to solve, so I couldn't wait for Kawehi to finally react to my words.

"I see, child," she mused with the ghost of a smile appearing on her lips. "Well, I don't think this is the best place to talk this through, so why don't you come to our house tomorrow morning?"

Some part of me balked at the thought – were they trying to drown this conversation out before I could get any answers? Were they even going to give me the real address to their house? Was it a tactic to cut all ties to me and my pesky questions? Panic was creeping in at those thoughts, and I had to take a deep breath to calm myself down.

I knew moving this conversation somewhere else made sense. Talking about magic at the patio of 'The Crazy Coconut,' close enough from a group of teenagers on the beach that we could hear their laughs as they played Truth or Dare… well, it wasn't the most ideal place for sneaky business.

Plus, Archer was probably losing his mind over my disappearance. I was actually surprised that he hadn't tried to force my mental shields down to invade my mind and find out where I was, yet.

Stopping myself from freaking out, I agreed to meet the next morning and wrote my grandparents' address on a mini green napkin with a coconuts printed all over.

By the time I left the patio and my grandparents behind with a promise to meet them at their house the next day, my stomach was knotted with apprehension. While I was scared of not having been given the right address and never being able to get the answers I desperately needed, I was also terrified of what those answers might be. I wasn't sure I'd be able to survive another world of bloodthirsty gods who had no consideration for humans like the Olympians did.

Chapter Twenty-Three

Sadie

The girl screamed like a banshee and tapped out, slapping the mat in frustration. The boy she'd been paired with had a huge grin on his face as he stood back up. "Hell yes! I'm a beast!" he bellowed.

"You're a baby giraffe at best, Nolan. Let's not get ahead of ourselves, here, all right?"

The boy's cheeks reddened slightly, and he nodded at my words before scooting away toward his older brother. Both of them had arrived in the Refuge together and the older one was particularly protective of the younger teen. It was expected after everything they'd been through to escape the Hunters after them and get here. But I wasn't about to cower under the dark glare that the older guy was sending me right then. I was here to train all of these Coppers, not baby them.

"Do you have a problem, here, Tim?" I challenged him, hands on my hips, clearly conveying that I wasn't backing down.

"He was excited, you could have let him have that."

"Sure, I could have let him have that win against an untrained fourteen-year-old girl. But that's not going to make him ready to fight against the people that want to bring all of us to Mount Olympus. What would you prefer him be able to do then, Tim?"

The young man grumbled, a hand ruffling his shaggy brown hair, before he rolled his eyes and turned around. That had gone well. Cue sarcasm here.

Sighing because this hadn't been the first interaction of the sort that I'd had in the past two days since I had started teaching those self-defense classes, I turned back toward the rest of my students.

Surprisingly enough, two thirds of the inhabitants of the Refuge had decided to show up for the first class yesterday morning. Today, almost everyone was here. These people needed to feel like they were being productive, and I was offering a perfect opportunity to do so. Thankfully, Liam had been able to come and help me with today's class, because this was a lot of work.

Most of the Coppers living in the Refuge had very little training in hand-to-hand combat or self-defense. I had needed to teach how to properly form a fist to a dozen of them so far. We weren't anywhere close to having efficient fighters, but at least they were eager to learn. For the most part.

As I surveyed the dozen pair of fighters that were reproducing the simple jab-jab-hook combo I had shown them earlier, I had the eerie feeling of being back in the Pit, training Kalani for the Tournament. This gymnasium wasn't anything like the Pit – there was no sand on the ground, no warm Sun above our heads, and no pressure from trials that might kill us. Not that I'd ever really been worried about my fate in the Tournament. After all, as a Golden, my powers were significantly stronger than most of the Coppers alive.

Still, if I closed my eyes and focused on the sounds around me, I could almost imagine Kalani, Archer, and Søren around me. Sometimes, if I shifted my focus quickly enough from one student from another, I could almost see Kalani standing there, a few meters away. It made me long for my friends even more than I usually did.

But this was good. I needed to find myself again, away from everything that had defined Sadie Aska on Mount Olympus. And I was actively acting to undermine the gods, which was all benefits.

So, I plastered a smile on my face and gave gentle corrections to a teenage girl who looked ready to flee at any second. I needed to focus on the here and now, on what I could do for these Coppers at that moment.

As I made my way around the gymnasium, I tried to force myself to forget about all of the good times I'd had while training Kalani and playing around with Søren and Archer. These times, before we'd lost anyone and seen the horrors of the Tournament, were nostalgic. But they were also a distraction I didn't need and couldn't afford when I had to focus on keeping my cover up and airtight.

Especially when a certain human lie detector was creeping near the entrance of the gym, talking animatedly to Bella.

Making a point of ignoring Thomas and Bella's conversation, I walked to Matteo who was training with Liam. Somehow, Matteo had managed to make the big guy smile as they sparred. *Of course, he would be so friendly*, I thought as a grin crept up to my lips too. Seeing him so excited to learn and make friends with literally anyone was heart-warming.

"Good job, Matteo, but don't forget to keep your core engaged. And don't let your guard down when you throw your hook, okay?"

Matteo turned his head to look at me and his grin was almost blinding. "Yes, captain Zombie Girl!" He even added a mock salute, his dark brown eyes glinting with amusement.

"Let's get back to it." Liam crossed his arms over his chest. "We don't have all day."

"Aw, stop that, Liam. I know you love playing around with me."

"I really don't, Matteo. I am only here because there was an uneven number of students."

But even as he complained, the big man couldn't stop the corners of his lips from going up. I couldn't blame him – Matteo was really good at being genuine and likeable.

The two Coppers went back into position and went through the combo again. Matteo was a quick learner and had a decently good form. And his memory of being hunted by the Olympians' minions was very fresh. Fear was a strong motivator to learn how to defend oneself. He would be one of the easiest to teach.

For the next couple of minutes, I offered Matteo some corrections and asked Liam to show him a slightly more complicated version of the combo they'd been working on. Soon enough, I would need to start separating people into groups of different levels because teaching young beginners that were afraid of throwing a punch was very different from teaching grown adults who didn't have a lot of experience but were excited to learn and fight one another.

But that would be a problem for the next few days. So far, I needed to give these Coppers confidence in their own ability to defend themselves with their bodies instead of their magic. Once everyone got their confidence up, it would be easier to—

"Sadie!"

I jumped at the loud voice, turning on my heels to find Thomas striding toward me, smiling wide. My whole body tensed at the view, and I had to force myself to appear relaxed.

"Thomas. What can I do for you?"

From the corners of my eyes, I could see that many people had stopped their drills to look at our interaction. Somehow, I was sure they could feel that neither of us liked or trusted each other.

"I wanted to see what these new classes of yours looked like. Seems like they are a success so far."

"We only started, but yes, there is a great turnout so far, and I've been able to assess everyone's abilities. We will start working on building everyone's strength and developing their self-defense techniques over the next few weeks."

My body was tense as if it was worried Thomas would discern a lie that wasn't even there. Everything I'd said was the truth and both of us knew it.

"I can see that. I wasn't sure about this whole endeavor when Bella proposed it, but I can see the appeal now. I do wonder, though, how someone so young can be so knowledgeable about fighting techniques."

"Is there a question there?"

Thomas chuckled at my words and the sound echoed in the now silent gym. My body was screaming at me that this was a trap and I needed to escape this situation. But there was no escape and judging from the way Thomas's calculating eyes glinted with satisfaction, he knew it too.

"No need to become defensive, Sadie. I just want to make sure our people are being given the best possible training. You know me, always looking out for my people."

Yeah, and I could hear the threat just fine in that last sentence.

"Thomas—"

The man raised a hand to stop Bella in her tracks and stepped closer to me. "And because you know that I look out for the Refuge and its people, you can guess that I can't just let a newcomer teach everyone how to defend themselves without looking into it. Don't you agree that it would be unreasonable, Sadie?"

"Of course, that would be unreasonable, Thomas. And I can confidently say that nothing I'm teaching here, or will be teaching, will be meant to cause any lasting physical damage or put anyone here in severe danger."

Thomas snickered, his eyes narrowing at me. "Choosing your words carefully, aren't you Sadie?"

Behind Thomas, Bella gave me a look that said she was sorry for her friend's behavior, but she couldn't stop him from continuing this very public interrogation. Because this was what it was. The Copper was hoping that being surrounded by witnesses would cause me to lose control, allowing him to catch me in a lie.

But I had learned how to twist words and play much deadlier games a long time ago. I wouldn't go down without a fight.

"Well, learning any martial art is not without risks, I'm sure you know that, Thomas. I can't promise that my students won't leave these classes bruised or sore."

A laugh left Thomas's chest at my words. Stars, that man was like a cat playing with a mouse. He enjoyed the chase way too much for my liking.

"So, are we done here, or do you have any more questions? I have students to teach."

"Of course, I'll let you go back to your class." He crossed his arms over his chest, a self-sufficient smirk on his annoying face. "Although, Sadie, I think your students would benefit greatly from seeing you in action. So, let's give them an educational show, shall we?"

And he seemed all too excited to spar against me. What was his angle there? Did he want to judge how well I fought or was he still trying to catch me in some sort of lie? Would fighting against me help him figure things out about me that I was trying to hide? Would he be able to tell that I wasn't a Copper and had been on Mount Olympus for years just from my fighting style?

My insides had locked up at his words, but I couldn't escape this. If I refused to fight against Thomas, he'd know something was up. And there was no excuse I could come up with that would be efficient and true.

There was no choice, really. So, I met Thomas's challenging stare with my own and summoned my best self-assured smirk. "Game on, Thomas."

There was a wave of excited murmurs through the crowd as the both of us headed toward one of the makeshift rings Liam and I had created with tape.

Before I could get close to the ring, someone grabbed my forearm and stopped me from following Thomas. Matteo's gentle eyes met mine, and he looked worried. "You don't have to do this. All of us trust your capabilities as a teacher. And he seems a little… mean. Unhinged."

I had to agree, there. But I didn't want Matteo to worry like this. No matter what happened next, stars knew that there was no way Thomas would best me in hand-to-hand combat. I wasn't quite as good at it as Archer was, but I was still one of the best on Mount Olympus.

"I'll be fine, don't worry. And it'll be good for me to work out a little," I added with a wink before gently removing his hand from my forearm. "I appreciate the vote of confidence, though." I squeezed his hand, trying to tell him with my eyes that I would be fine.

By the time I turned back toward the ring to meet Thomas, my skin was warm from the emotions I'd seen swimming in Matteo's dark eyes. Knowing he cared made me feel stupidly happy, and I needed to squash that before I entered the tape-delimited ring.

"You can still back out, Sadie," Thomas taunted with a toothy smile. "No one will fault you for not wanting to face me."

"Oh boy, I'll have a lot of fun destroying you." And it was the ringing truth. "First tap out wins?"

"Are you scared of first blood?"

I laughed at the audacity of the man. He needed to be brought down a peg. And now that I was in the ring, the adrenaline of the challenge was running through my veins and my heart was pumping with excitement.

At my heart, I loved challenges. And this was a great challenge I couldn't wait to win.

"First blood it is."

Chapter Twenty-Four

Kalani

Before I even came close enough to the camp to see it through the bushes and palm trees, I could hear the argument. It was Archer and Nafula yelling back and forth, with Søren interjecting every so often to place a snarky comment that made both Archer and Nafula snap at him.

I sighed. This promised to be *so much fun*.

Trekking through the bushes and hoping that no animal would jump out of them, I prayed – not to the Olympian gods, thank you very much – that my friends would let me explain without freaking out even more than they already were. Highly unlikely, but one could hope.

To be fair, I probably should have talked about this whole issue surrounding the unknown side of my family and my newly discovered magical powers before leaving earlier. It might have helped the current situation. But meeting my grandparents had felt like something that I had to do on my own, something personal and private that I didn't want to share with anyone else until I was ready.

Unfortunately, I probably wouldn't have the privilege of keeping this private anymore.

"—stop acting like a freaking hard ass and let us live a little," Nafula almost yelled at Archer.

"Do you even realize how serious our situation is? The gods won't—"

"There are some animals trying to sleep out there, you guys," I tried to joke around as I left the shadows of the wooded area. All three of them stopped arguing and turned to stare at me, seemingly shocked to see me there.

"Kalani? Where were you—"

Archer interrupted Søren by striding toward me until he was right in front of me. "What in the stars were you thinking, Mayfield? Do you think this is a joke? You completely disappeared on us! We're here to hide you from the gods. The least you could do is stay where we can protect you!"

Even hidden against his anger, I could feel the hurt and worry in Archer's words, see them in his eyes. He had been scared for me. And after everything that had happened these past few days, I couldn't suppress the guilt that rose in my chest. It was impossible to be mad at his reaction then, even though his words stung a little.

"Look, I'm sorry, I should have told you guys I was leaving. But I needed to do something alone."

Archer's eyes narrowed and his cheeks reddened in anger, as if he couldn't quite comprehend my words. I winced as he raised his hands in the air, speechless.

"Well," Nafula snickered behind Archer. "It's funny how I was berated for not preventing her *kidnapping* by the gods, and she left on her own. Oh, this is fun!"

Ignoring Nafula and her shit-eating grin, I followed Archer as he strode away. He wasn't speaking, but I could tell that he had plenty to say. He just didn't want to speak right then, probably so he wouldn't say anything he would regret later on.

But I needed to explain myself. Guilt churned in my stomach. It wasn't fair that I had made them – and Archer especially – so worried. He deserved better than that.

"I'm sorry, Archer. I should have told you earlier. I'm sorry for not saying anything. But I promise that it was worth it for me to leave. It had to be done, and I couldn't go with all of you scaring them off."

"Scaring *who* off?" Archer's voice dropped low, sounding dangerous. If I didn't know that he'd never do anything to hurt me, I'd be scared.

The point of no return had arrived. I had to share this part of myself – this new part I had just discovered – with them. If I wanted to keep their trust, there was no other option.

"My grandparents."

While Nafula didn't know much about my family history, Archer and Søren looked taken aback by my words. "I thought you only knew your mom's side of the family, from California. And the memory-erasing spell should have removed you from their memories, right?" Søren asked, confused.

"Yes, I only knew my mom's parents, before everyone forgot about me. But my dad was from here. From Hawaii. And I found his parents."

"So that's why you left all of us here, scared you'd been taken back to Olympus? To meet your estranged family?" Archer asked, incredulous. "And you couldn't just tell us that?"

I tried not to let the frustration rise up at Archer's words. Meeting my grandparents wasn't just an afterthought – it mattered. A lot. But I also tried to remind myself that this was his fear talking.

Thanatos's words came back to my mind as I readied myself to reveal the secret I'd kept for the past month. *I strongly recommend that you keep this information private*, the god of Death had said after revealing that he believed I had magical powers that had been unearthed as I died. I had tried to do just that, but I couldn't see a path that would allow me to continue to explore my magical heritage with my grandparents without Archer, Søren, and Nafula knowing what was going on.

"First, you guys need to swear on Lethe that you won't share what I tell you with anyone."

Søren's eyebrows shot up and he swept a hand through his wind-blown shoulder-length blond hair. "What's with the secrets, K? Do you not trust us?"

Søren chuckled, as if waiting for me to tell them this was all a joke. But I wasn't playing. Sure, I trusted my friends. But Thanatos had advised me to be careful, so I was. An oath on Lethe was binding, which meant that my friends would physically not be able to break their promise. I needed that assurance. So, I crossed my arms and waited for them to take the magic-binding oath.

Long seconds passed by before Nafula huffed, mumbled something I didn't quite hear, and took the oath. Then, Søren followed suit. Once both of my friends had taken the oath, I turned my gaze to Archer. He was somber, his jaw tight and eyebrows pinched. He looked hurt, and it made my heart stutter. But I didn't – couldn't – cave on this.

Finally, Archer swore on Lethe to keep my secret and my shoulders dropped from relief.

I had heeded Thanatos' warnings, and while I was worried about my friends' reaction, a part of me was excited to share the news.

"I wasn't just meeting my grandparents. I was trying to get information about something Thanatos felt when he brought me back to life." My mouth was terribly dry as I tried to get the words out.

This felt like a turning point in the relationship I had with Archer. There was no avoiding the change that was coming to the way he looked at me.

"What do you mean? What did my dad say?" Søren asked, moving a couple of steps closer to us.

I turned to face him, and it was easier to look at him than at Archer's face. Easier than facing the betrayal he was surely going to feel when he realized I had lied to him for weeks. So, I continued to look at Søren as I told the whole story – how Thanatos had come to see me and revealed this huge secret, how I hadn't believed it until the moment I had jumped in the ocean to save Makaio and the currents had worked with me, and finally how I had decided to find my paternal grandparents to search for answers. By the time I finished explaining that I was to meet my grandparents the next day to talk about my magical powers, all three of my friends were dead silent.

No one spoke for a few moments, my heartbeat quickening with each second. After everything my friends had abandoned to follow me on this run as fugitives, I could understand if they felt betrayed and violated to learn that I had been lying to them and had used them to come to Hawaii.

I would have understood if they lost their minds at my words. But instead, Søren, usually the jokester of the group, frowned and thought aloud. "That would explain why the Hunter got confused and brought you back to Mount Olympus. They get cheat sheets with the identity of their targets, but they also use their powers to recognize other people's magical signatures. Since his actual target was dead, his magic might have latched on to your powers, even though they were hidden and not very strong. That might have made him believe you were his target, even though you didn't fit all of the criteria he was given."

Huh. Yeah, that would make sense actually. Those strange powers might have been the reason why I had been taken to Olympus months ago. Somehow, knowing that I hadn't just been at the wrong place at the wrong time didn't make me feel better about everything that had happened since that fateful day I had met a Hunter for the first time.

"And your powers aren't coming from the Greek gods?" Nafula frowned before shifting to ask Søren. "How is that possible?"

"No idea. I have never heard of anyone having magic outside of the realm of Olympus." The Golden ran his hands through his long blond hair. "I can't believe my dad didn't even trust me enough to tell me something was going on."

Guilt swarmed through me at his words. I knew the past few weeks had been very rough on Søren and I could only try to imagine how he felt now that he was realizing that his dad hadn't wanted to share this critical information with him. After losing both Mei and Sadie – in two different ways but just as painful – I didn't want him to think that he'd lost his father's trust.

"It wasn't like that, Søren. Thanatos just wanted to let me decide when to share my secret. It has nothing to do with how much he trusts or loves you. I promise."

Søren nodded but his eyes remained sad, even after he took a deep breath and forced a smile on his lips. "It's all good, I like surprises better anyway."

There was one person who remained silent, though, and it was Archer. Shifting, I looked at him and found him sullen, jaw tight.

Things had already been tense between us lately, especially after the argument we'd had regarding the way to deal with the rebellion. I loved him, and I knew he loved me, but I had a feeling this conversation was a new tear in the trust we had between each other. Would we be able to build that trust back? I wasn't so sure.

"Archer…" I started, but his hard eyes stopped me in my tracks.

"You knew this for weeks and chose to not tell any of us." Archer's voice was cold, with a hint of pain behind the harsh edges of his words.

"I—"

"We could have found information on Mount Olympus. I know my mom could have helped. But instead, you chose to keep this to yourself for a month, until you were backed into a corner and had no choice but to share."

And his eyes shown with anger as he spoke – anger that I had waited until there was no other way out before sharing this secret with him.

"Archer, I really didn't mean it like that. I honestly didn't even believe Thanatos until a few days ago, when we went to check on Makaio. I really thought Thanatos was just looking for something that wasn't there, and then after I realized he was probably right… well, we had a lot of other things to worry about, didn't we?"

"She has a point, there," Nafula interjected, and I wanted to hug her.

Archer huffed and crossed his arms over his chest, clearly not agreeing with the Copper. But he didn't push the topic further. Instead, he started making a plan, which was both very on point with him and extremely frustrating. But I wasn't about to start the argument back up either.

"Alright, so we will all go to Mayfield's grandparents' tomorrow morning to find out what they know. We'll get there early and scope out the place. I want answers and quickly, but I don't want any surprises either once Mayfield enters the house. We also need to try to find answers on our own about these powers. Anyone have any ideas how we could do that?"

Nafula shook her head but Søren was deep in thought, fingers tapping against his jaw. "Oh! We could ask Hermes? That guy knows everything about everyone, so if someone has been talking about magic that doesn't come from the Greek gods, he will know about it!"

"I am not sure if I want to tell an Olympian. Thanatos was very clear that he didn't think the gods would be happy to learn about my magical heritage, and I don't know that telling the gods of messages and gossips is the safest bet."

"I trust Hermes. He's the only brother I like and would trust with this kind of information."

I was taken aback for a second before remembering that, yes, Archer and Hermes were brothers. Both were Zeus's children. Sometimes I forgot how powerful Archer was, and how impressive his direct family was.

The Kalani from six months ago would have been completely mind blown at the idea of meeting Zeus's son or

Hermes's half-brother. Oh, how things had changed since then. And how I'd changed too.

Sometimes I remembered the me from before, and it scared me how much I couldn't recognized myself anymore.

"Still, I don't think we should get to that point until there is no choice left. We should focus on my grandparents first."

"So, you still don't trust my judgment then?" Archer's words were full of anger, full of resentment. They were like a knife to my heart.

"Don't make this about us, Archer. Please. I was advised by one of the strongest gods on Olympus to keep this under wraps. This has nothing to do with your relationship with Hermes."

But even as I said the words, I could tell that, in Archer's eyes, there was no way to make this *not* about us. This had been about us since the moment I'd made the decision to keep my conversation with Thanatos to myself. And a part of me understood Archer – after all, weren't we supposed to fight together against the world? My lies and omissions had widened a ridge in our relationship that had been started by our different views of the world and of social justice.

Our gazes met and held – anger and hurt running between us like a two-way street. My heart was crying out for him, for a hug and those gentle loving looks he used to give me before we both frayed our relationship. But I couldn't back down on this. Archer was mad and he wanted to be right. But I trusted Thanatos's advice that this had to remain as far away from Olympus as possible.

I wouldn't back down on this, no matter how hard it was to see the way Archer's face closed off from me.

"If we don't have answers from your grandparents in the next forty-eight hours, we'll contact Hermes. That's the best I can do. I won't ignore a possible source of information on a potentially dangerous and untrained power."

Archer's eyes challenged me to complain, but I knew this was as much of a compromise as I would get from him while he was in this state of mind. So, I ignored the hurt I felt at his implication that I was a ticking-time bomb, and I gave a tight-lipped smile.

"Sure."

"Good."

"Is this a good time to ask when we're going to try to find Sadie again? Because that's basically why I'm here, so…"

I broke the staring contest Archer and I had going on to look at a Nafula that looked extremely entertained by the situation. And she had a good point. I was still extremely worried about Sadie and where she had gone. Being stuck on Earth was the perfect opportunity to not only get information about my powers, but also find out where Sadie was hiding.

"You're right Nafula, we should try again. We can buy a phone tomorrow on our way to my grandparents' and try calling her again. And if we can't get to her, we will think of what we can do next, okay?"

The Copper didn't seem particularly happy that our only path of action so far was to call the phone number we'd been given for her, but she still nodded at my words.

And then we were back at this stalemate, with everyone looking at everyone else, unsure what to say and where to go from there. The rest of our time on Hawaii promised to be interesting.

Seeing the entrance of my grandparents' house was a relief, and not only because I was desperate for answers. No, I was relieved because I needed to get away from the dark cloud that surrounded Archer and was spreading to all of us.

Getting some answers would be nice, too. Especially with the threat of talking to Hermes looming over me.

"Let's do a perimeter search around the house. Stay far enough away that they won't see us from the windows. Søren and Nafula, you start on the right, we'll go on the left."

With that, Archer left, walking with determination toward the trees that surrounded the left side of the house. Nafula gave me a look that said 'Good luck with him' before half-dragging Søren in the other direction. Which left me there, forced to speed-walk to catch up to a brooding Archer.

Wish me luck.

By the time I finally reached Archer, I was slightly out of breath. I needed to get back into working out.

"So. How long can I expect this cold shoulder to last? A day? A week? More? Just asking for a friend."

"We're supposed to be walking a perimeter and checking for any traps. That requires silence, Mayfield."

"Oh, come on! As if you can't multitask or use your powers to check this whole perimeter in a few seconds. Let's stop playing games, here."

The man scoffed. "Let's stop playing *games?* Are you being serious right now?" He stopped and turned to face me. "That's all you've been doing, lately. I feel like I don't even know you anymore."

I rolled my eyes, annoyed by the hypocrisy of it all. "Are you serious, Archer? You lied to me for months about being a Copper. I never held that against you because I understood that it was a matter a safety for you to keep that quiet. This is exactly what this was about – my safety. I apologized a dozen times already and explained extensively why I didn't say anything earlier. So, quit sulking like a baby and grow the hell up."

Silence met my words, but for once, I didn't want to try and fill it up. If Archer didn't want to understand that my choice to keep my powers secret was a matter that had nothing to do with him, then it was his loss. I loved him, but I refused to be treated like I'd just killed his puppy under his eyes.

It was ridiculous.

Meeting my grandparents and learning about my powers were important to me and I had the right to decide when I wanted to share that news with my other loved ones. Not to mention that *the argument* still sat heavily between us and hadn't made it easy for me to share in the first place.

"Is that the end of the secrets?" Archer finally asked with a sigh.

For half of a second, I felt myself become defensive. What was that supposed to mean? That he thought I had a closet full of skeletons, still? But then, before I could let my anger burn up again, I met Archer's eyes and they looked so tired. We stared at each other for a second and I felt just how exhausted and hurt he was.

Archer's vulnerability blew out the flame of my anger and frustration, and we were both standing there, silent, our hearts half broken by each other.

I nodded; my throat too tight for words.

Archer inhaled sharply, his eyes never leaving mine, before murmuring, "Okay."

My heart stuttered as he started walking again. What was happening there? Was it a good okay or a bad one? What did 'okay' even mean?

"Wait!" I exclaimed as I ran to catch up to him. "So, that's it? We're good?"

Archer remained silent for a few of the longest seconds of my life before he finally answered. "I need some time. I think we both do."

The pain was physical at his words – my heart squeezed painfully, and I started feeling nauseous. Was that his way of breaking up with me? Minutes before I was going to go and see my grandparents again? With no way for me to process the information on my own? When we still had to live together for the foreseeable future while we fled the gods and their Hunters?

"Wait, stop those thoughts right there, Mayfield," Archer growled softly, his fingers grabbing my chin and forcing my eyes to meet his. "I can tell you're panicking, but I am not breaking up with you. I just need some time to learn to be just your boyfriend and not your protector. You don't need me to protect you anymore, at least not in the same way I did during the

Tournament. I need time to accept that, and to come to terms with you having a life apart from me."

His fingers slid from my chin to my throat, his thumb tracing slow circles against my pulse point. There was no way for me to hide how fast my heart was beating, now.

"I still love you. Stars, I love you so much that it hurts, sometimes. When you are in danger or when I don't know where you are, my whole body aches, calling for me to ensure that you are safe. And even when I am mad at you, I can't stop thinking about you. About your body, your gentle soul, your determination to help others, your loyalty to your friends…" He stopped and dropped his forehead to mine. "I couldn't stop loving you even if I wanted to, Mayfield. You are a part of my heart, of my soul, and I never want it to change. But we can't continue to hurt each other like this. You need time to discover who you are. And I need time to learn how to trust that you will be okay on your own. Not because I want to break up, but because we both need to be able to stand on our own, side by side, for this to work."

I wasn't sure how to feel because this was both the most romantic thing that he had ever said to me and the most frustrating decision he'd ever taken. After his declaration, all I wanted to do was jump in his arms and kiss him until we were both breathless. Spending the past few days close to him but not *with him* had made me crave for his touch.

Unfortunately, I understood what he meant. We had started our relationship during the Tournament, in the middle of some of the most traumatizing times of our lives. I had relied on him to survive, and it must have been a heavy weight on his shoulders too.

But if I really had magic, then I might not be as defenseless as I'd been before. Which would also mean that he wouldn't need to carry the responsibility of keeping me alive on his shoulders at all times. More than that, we needed to learn to rely on each other equally, the way a healthy couple would.

We both needed time to learn to trust each other in a world where we were equals – at least as much as we'd ever be.

So, as much as I wanted to bury my head in the sand and pretend like we were good again, I had to agree with Archer that we both needed to take some time to learn how to be good on our own so that we could be great together.

"So, is that a break, then?" I murmured, my hand grabbing Archer's shirt even though I knew I should move back.

"I don't like that word," Archer growled, his lips so close to mine that I felt his words on my skin. "But I guess… yes. You're still mine, and I'm still yours, but we should spend some time as friends."

He shuddered on the last word and I chuckled. "As friends? So, like me and Søren?"

Before I could continue to tease him, Archer kissed me, his lips taking control of mine until I could barely think straight. "No," he murmured an eternity later, "like friends who love each other and will be back together soon. Really soon."

"Okay."

Then he kissed me again and I could feel his desperation and love as his hands tightened in my hair. By the time we separated for air, my heart was pounding again.

"That's not very friends-like, Sunshine," I teased him softly, a smile blooming on my face.

Archer shook his head, pretending to be annoyed, but a corner of his mouth tipped up.

We both took a step back, still staring at each other, and my heart felt lighter than it had in weeks. We weren't in a great place yet, but we were getting there. And it gave me butterflies.

Archer reached his hand out, palm turned toward me. I intertwined my fingers with his and didn't comment on how this wasn't very "friend-like" either. After all, we could be friends who held hands.

"Let's go, Mayfield. Your grandparents are waiting."

Chapter Twenty-Five

Sadie

The thing with hand-to-hand combat was that it usually wasn't very bloody. Fighting with blades, whether swords or daggers or knifes, was the easiest way to draw blood. But, since Thomas didn't seem like the kind of guy to carry a knife in his preppy sweater or dark wash jeans, I was expecting that we weren't going to use weapons.

Which meant that the fastest way to draw first blood was going to be to aim for the face.

Stars, I really didn't want to sport a black eye tomorrow.

Although, black eyes would only be a problem if I got hit. And I wasn't planning on letting this fight last long enough to get seriously hurt.

Plus, I couldn't afford to show my golden blood. It would for sure ruin my cover as an innocent Copper.

As I stepped into the makeshift ring, Thomas turned his back on me and removed his sweater – the one that gave him the look of a private prep school, old money young man. He folded the sweater carefully before giving it to Bella. Then, he turned to me with the swagger of a man convinced he was going to win.

Oh, how cute. I *loved* it when men underestimated me.

It made me feel alive to show them how wrong they were.

"Are you ready, Thomas? Or do you need to remove those fancy loafers of yours?"

I heard a few snickers behind me and couldn't quite suppress a grin of my own.

"If I were you, I wouldn't be quite so impatient to start, Sadie, seeing as this will be a short fight," Thomas declared with the overconfidence of a mediocre white man.

"Let's just get to it, then, shall we? I can't wait for this *short* fight to start."

Thomas's eyes flashed with annoyance, but he didn't try to flaunt his capabilities anymore. Small mercies.

The crowd around us quieted down. Thomas settled into a fighting stance, and my whole body shifted into the focused mind space that I had developed specifically for fighting. In half a second, my emotions were settled, senses laser focused on every movement Thomas made.

Through the haze of this hyper focus I had practiced thousands of times, I barely registered the encouragement coming from Matteo.

Thomas and I circled each other for a few moments, observing the other's footwork and technique. Based on the way he moved, I was pretty sure that the guy was a boxer – he probably preferred to remain standing rather than having to do floorwork. I also wouldn't be surprised if he was a more traditional fighter with pretty technique. This man didn't fight dirty.

If there was something I'd learned since I was a child training with Søren, then later on with Archer, it was to win no matter what, even if it meant fighting slightly dirty.

Surviving the Tournament had required all of us to learn to survive no matter what – that included learning that fighting dirty was necessary sometimes.

Plus, while I also preferred to stand during fights, Søren loved wrestling and Brazilian ju-jitsu, which meant that I was more than proficient at floor work.

Thomas attacked first, throwing a jab directly at my nose – as if I'd be dumb enough to leave my guard wide open – followed by a hook I easily evaded. This combo did help me see that I was right, though. The Copper had perfect footwork and beautiful technique.

He wouldn't be *that* easy to destroy.

Still, he wouldn't be good enough to best me.

The next time Thomas attacked, I was ready to not only defend myself, but also counterattack. My opponent went for a few quick and powerful jabs, followed by a left hook. With as few movements as possible, I dodged his fists and used his close proximity to throw a sharp elbow into his liver. Thomas inhaled sharply and bent over in pain, which allowed me to knee him right in the forehead.

Sadly, no blood in sight. Yet.

In his defense, Thomas wasn't a coward. Even with the liver shot and a red welt onto his forehead, he stood back up and moved back a couple of steps. "You like dirty shots, don't you, Sadie?"

"I offered to teach self-defense, Thomas, not French boxing. And I have most of my training in mixed martial arts, which means I am not scared of getting down and dirty."

Thomas scoffed at that, but he wasn't so quick to attack anymore.

The next few minutes were filled with each of us attacking and trying our best to break the other's skin. Even though it pained me, I had to admit that Thomas was good. Really good. I would have quite a few bruises blooming on my legs and abdomen tomorrow to prove it.

But he hadn't been able to hit my face. So, no blood was showing.

For his part, Thomas had a black eye, a swollen forehead, and hopefully a couple of sprained ribs. However, I hadn't been able to hit his eyebrows, nose, or mouth yet – all of which were great places to aim for when one wanted to break the skin of their opponent.

Clearly, I needed to up my game.

The next time I got close to Thomas, I had one goal: get him on the ground. I used the opportunity of him throwing a kick to grab his leg. And pulled. Soon enough, I was behind him, his arm stuck in an arm lock. He tried to punch me with his second arm, but he had suddenly lost most of his bearings since he couldn't very well use his boxing skills anymore. The punch caught my jaw and I hissed in pain. *Stars, that would bruise too.*

I couldn't get distracted, though. I needed to end this fight, and quickly. As Thomas was trying to escape the arm lock – and failing to do so – I threw my elbow right in his nose. A hiss of pain accompanied a small river of blood down his face.

Immediately, I dropped the Copper and stood back up. Winning felt awesome. Especially when I saw the people around us murmuring and excitedly pointing at me.

I wasn't a winner of the Tournament and daughter of Thanatos for nothing.

Thomas was still on the ground, cradling his bleeding nose with a sullen expression. Based on his dark eyes as he stood up shakily, I knew this fight hadn't made us into friends. Oh, well. That man was never going to like me anyways.

"Hell yeah, Zombie girl!" Matteo exclaimed as he rushed to me and twirled me around in his arms. He laughed as he did so, and I couldn't do anything but join in. No one had ever made me feel so good after a win.

After a few moments and at least a half dozen turns on himself, Matteo dropped me back to the ground, his hands slowly moving from my hips to my shoulders, leaving a trail of goosebumps in their wake. And as my feet touched the ground, my eyes remained glued to Matteo's dark irises.

We were in our own bubble, the sound from the crowd around us muffled and far away. All I could feel were his hands on my body, all I could see were his eyes. And my heart was beating like crazy – much faster than it had during the fight.

"You scared me a little bit, out there," Matteo whispered, so low that I barely heard him.

"Really? You were worried for me?" Somehow, that thought made me feel better than it should have.

Matteo's cheeks colored slightly, and his fingers pressed against my shirt. My breath caught in my lungs as his eyes darkened and dropped to my lips. "You make me worry even though I know you can handle yourself better than I could ever hope to myself. There's something about you, Sadie, that makes me care. A lot."

Oh. My. Stars. I had butterflies in my stomach and now it was my face that felt hot. How could this guy make me feel so much with just a few words?

Before I could answer or go against all of my best intentions and just kiss him already, someone bumped into me, breaking the spell between us.

Then, everything came back into motion around me. People were talking and laughing, and Thomas was walking in my direction. Most of the blood had been wiped away from his face, but he still looked in pain. That might make me a bad person, but I was satisfied with the wince of pain he couldn't contain as he stopped before me.

"Nice job, Sadie," the man said through gritted teeth. He reached his hand out and I shook it.

"You too, Thomas. I hope that clears up any misconceptions about whether I'm qualified to teach this class or not."

The red-headed Copper gave me a tight-lipped, very fake smile, and hummed along. A second later, he was walking to the door, trying to hide a slight limp.

Oh, how sweet victory tasted.

"Oh, Sadie!" Bella walked up to me with a huge grin, her arms up in the air. "Mate, you ate and left no crumbs!"

With the way she clapped excitedly, and hip bumped me, I figured that it was a compliment. But, honestly? I had no idea what she had just told me. I had left Earth way to long ago to understand this new generation's slang. But I had to pretend to fit in, so I laughed along.

"I told you guys that she was badass," Matteo chimed in. He and Bella high-fived and I stood there, happy and bittersweet.

It felt like I was slowly building new friendships with Matteo and Bella, maybe even with Liam whose quiet company I enjoyed. I just wished that Kalani, Archer, and Søren could be there too.

But they weren't. And it was my choice that I was here, away from them.

Most days I didn't regret that choice to leave Olympus and find myself somewhere else, as someone other than the girl who had killed Mei.

But, sometimes, I had those moments when I was so happy that it made me sad again. Sad that I couldn't share those happy moments with my loved ones.

Liam joined us and went to stand behind Bella, an arm around her shoulders. "We'll have to actually spar one of these days, Sadie. Although I'm not that excited to get destroyed, so we'll wait for a few weeks, alright?"

"Sure, Liam, works for me. And, trust me, I'm not looking forward to your right hook either, big guy."

Bella snickered before going on her tiptoes to whisper something in his ear that made the Black man visibly embarrassed. Knowing the British girl, she had probably told him a wildly inappropriate thing that would be only acceptable in one of her dark romance books. I didn't even want to know what kinds of things she was reading in her room – some of the book covers I'd seen with shirtless men on them had scared me.

Matteo must have seen the same embarrassment on Liam's face because he threw me a cheeky grin, like we were both in on an inside joke.

After a few seconds, Liam recovered from whatever Bella had told him and kissed her cheek before stepping back. "I think practice is definitely over, but I'll go and prep some things for tomorrow. Are we still meeting at two-thirty to go over next steps for the class?" he asked me directly.

I nodded and he left without another word. Soon enough, Bella was leaving too – she had to go and talk to her brother about something related to the wards that protected the Refuge.

And then it was only Matteo and I left in this big, empty gymnasium.

"So, now that you've warmed up against Thomas, are you finally ready to go against me? I promise I'll go easy on you, Zombie girl." He even jumped around like a boxer, pretending to fight me. *That man*, I thought with a grin.

"Oh yeah? I wasn't expecting to have to face you today, I'm shaking in my socks," I played along.

"I'll make it quick. Promise."

Then he charged at me and put his arms around my waist, trying to take me to the ground. I could have easily blocked him off. After all, the man was decently strong, but he had absolutely no wrestling technique. But I wanted to see where he wanted to take this, so I continued to play along and made a show of falling to the ground.

Matteo fell over me with a grunt followed by a victorious – and surprised – cry. Then he moved up over me and grabbed both of my wrists, pining them against the ground. I moved my hips up to dislodge him, and he fell forward, bringing his face right up to mine.

We were close enough that I could feel his breath against my lips.

Our eyes met and remained glued to each other. Matteo's hips went down, almost resting against my own, but his face remained just as close to mine. We were locked in that moment, in this place where only the two of us existed. Time slowed to a halt. The world stopped spinning.

His eyes fell to my lips again, mine fell on his, and for a second, I thought of shifting up so that our lips would touch.

But then the realization that I *couldn't* kiss Matteo hit me like a lightning bolt.

I couldn't kiss him when he didn't even know the real me. I couldn't take any more of his trust than he had already foolishly given me.

Even though it hurt my heart to do so, I flipped Matteo onto his back and landed above him, before disentangling myself from him and standing up. It was almost too easy to do, and I wished he'd tightened his grip on me, wished he hadn't let me go that easily.

As soon as my body didn't touch his anymore, chills ran up and down my body, like I was missing the part of me that gave me warmth. Matteo's confused expression was like a band around my heart, tightening painfully as he opened his mouth and closed it, looking lost and hurt. Stars, it hurt to see the frown on his usually smiling face.

"Nice job, you almost had me there," I said in a playful tone, hoping to ease the awkward tension between us.

Matteo hummed in agreement but didn't add anything. I offered him a hand to get up, and he stared at it for a couple of seconds before cautiously taking it, as if it were a potentially dangerous move. I helped him up and then we were standing awkwardly next to each other, the playful flirting we'd had now long gone.

"Should we go to the mess hall? Get some food?" I was desperate to make it up to him, to bring that smile back to his face.

"Sure, I could eat."

And he started walking ahead of me, acting like everything was fine. But his shoulders were rigid, his fists closed, and he had a tense half-smile on.

Nothing was fine. And it was my fault.

The next few hours went by in a haze. I barely remembered eating and then meeting Liam to discuss how we wanted to set up the self-defense class for the next few weeks. I tried to be involved in the whole planning, but I felt off the whole time. I couldn't get Matteo's confusion or the his poorly hidden hurt at my rejection, out of my mind.

Who would have thought that I would be stuck on a guy?

Not me, that was for sure.

But here I was, walking back to my room from the almost-three-hour long meeting with Liam, and I still couldn't shake the guilt. The regrets. It was maddening, and it made me angry at the world and at myself.

There was no way to change things now, though. If I'd met Matteo in that restaurant as the Sadie Aska that hadn't been to Mount Olympus yet, then it might have worked between the two of us. But now that I had spent years among the very people that Matteo and the others in the Refuge wanted to avoid at all costs, now that I had lied to them for days and weeks, now that I wasn't the real me in Matteo's eyes... there was no path forward where we could be together.

I just had to accept that instead of dwelling on everything I couldn't have anymore.

Focusing on this doomed attraction to Matteo was ridiculous when I was supposed to worry about bigger problems such as the Olympians wanting to throw all of the Coppers within the Refuge into the Tournament. I knew first-hand how traumatizing the Tournament was, so I should focus all of my energy on that. Not on frivolous things and—

"We can't do anything about it?"

I stopped short right as the words floated beneath the door I was walking by to my ears. It sounded like Bella. I hadn't seen her since the end of the self-defense class this morning. Was she still in that meeting with her brother about the magical wards around the Refuge?

The hallway was empty, and I couldn't hear any other voices around except for the faint sound of the conversation within the room next to where I stood.

While the door seemed utterly common, I knew I'd somehow made it to the council room. And I'd bet anything that there was an important meeting going on in there. A meeting I could listen to for a few minutes, as long as no one entered this hallway.

"No, we don't have the manpower for a rescue mission. And even if we decided to try to help her, it would be way too dangerous for us to expose ourselves this way. We can't afford that."

I had never talked to Bella's brother, but I could hear the same British accent to his words. And who in the stars were they talking about? Who was that person Bella wanted to help? A 'rescue mission' made me think of a Copper that had tried to come to the Refuge and failed to escape the Hunters, but I could be wrong. I didn't have enough context to fully understand the conversation that was happening.

"She's only thirteen! We can't leave her to their hands! She won't survive a minute in their competition."

I had to agree with Bella there. Even if I'd never met the girl they were talking about, I knew that there were very little chance that such a young Copper would survive the Tournament. None of the young Coppers from the last edition had made it out.

"I know, Bells, but do you want to risk all of the people we have here to try and save her? We can't risk that many lives. We gave our word that the Refuge would be safe. We can't just throw everything out of the window for one person."

Well, Ken, way to make Bella feel like a selfish person for being compassionate about this young Copper's fate. Although, I couldn't disagree with him either. If that young girl had been taken by Hunters, then she was gone to Olympus already. There was no recovering her.

"What I'm most worried about is how close they were to the Refuge. Kendra was almost here. She was half an hour away from the meet-up point."

This time, it was my dear Thomas who had spoken. I could recognize his voice among thousands. But what made me pay even more attention was the implication that the Hunters had been very close to here. Had they been running around here to catch this Kendra girl, or were they searching for someone else too?

"You're right. This is concerning. And a whole group of them, too. Bella, are you sure the wards are still strong? We can't afford to have any magical emission escape the—"

"Of course, Ken. I always check the wards. Every day, without fault. They are just fine," Bella snapped defensively.

"I'm not trying to be mean, Bells. I just need to check every possible avenue, make sure we are covered. You know that I trust you, right?"

There was a short silence followed by soft murmurs I couldn't discern. Probably Bella telling her brother that, yes, she knew he trusted her. But the following silence was so long that I worried the conversation was over or the speakers had moved to another room that was too far away for me to hear their words.

Thankfully, right as I was about to leave my spying spot, Thomas decided to speak again. "Could it be that Matteo's explosion of magic a few days ago brought them here? Could there be remnants of magic that could indicate our location?"

"I don't think so. At least it's never happened before. We've had people freak out in the meadow before I could nullify their powers, and we've never had this many of *them* sniffing around afterwards."

So, there were a lot of Hunters around. And this was unusual. From what I could tell, the only thing that had changed in the Refuge was me – a Golden hiding within the Coppers living here. That meant one thing.

There was a good chance Kellan had found out that I had stopped doing my job, and they were hunting me down.

"…and close the Refuge down for a few days. Keep the doors closed and the wards safely in place. We just did our run for groceries, so we should be able to hide out for, what, a week?" Ken asked, seemingly getting closer to the door.

Was the meeting almost over? I needed to leave before any of them caught me spying on them.

"It should last us six days, maybe seven if we ration the food," Thomas intervened.

"I don't want to scare the people, though. If we start to ration the food, it will raise everyone's suspicions that something is wrong."

Bella was right. If food portions became smaller overnight, people would notice. Especially since everyone was now working out more regularly in my self-defense class. I was sure people wouldn't go hungry per say, but they would notice the sudden change and worry about it.

These people had been hunted down until they came to the Refuge. Fear would take hold very easily in their minds.

"I don't think we have a choice, but we can maybe—"

A laugh down the hallway interrupted Thomas's words, snapping my attention away from the conversation. I couldn't see anyone coming yet, but I knew people were coming. I had to leave. I couldn't afford to have people – especially Thomas and his nasty powers – doubting my trustworthiness.

Trying to remain as quiet as possible on the hard floor, I walked away from the door in the direction of my room. Right as two young men I'd met for the first time this morning appeared at the end of the hallway, I went back to walking normally and waved at them.

"Hi, guys!"

"Hey Sadie! Nice win earlier," one of them said with a wave.

We passed each other, smiling politely, and the second guy said he was excited for tomorrow's class. I nodded and pretended to be excited about it too, my heart pounding in my ears until I was out of the hallway.

I was barely in my room, door closed against the rest of the world, when I finally felt like I could breathe normally.

Stars, that had been close.

And now that I was there, leaning against the door and catching my breath, I couldn't stop thinking that things were getting complicated. Maybe I'd been very naïve to think that I could escape Mount Olympus and Kellan, my boss. I had believed that I could cut all ties with the world of the gods and leave here, in the Refuge, until... well, until I couldn't anymore because someone within realized I wasn't one of them.

But it looked like my decision to live in this place would be taken away from me much quicker than I had thought. If Hunters and Huntresses were sniffing around, searching for me, then I'd have to leave. I wouldn't let myself be the reason why the Refuge fell. All of these people deserved to leave happily here. If it came to the point where I was the reason they were in danger, I would need to leave and find a way to get the Hunters away from this place.

My heart bled at the thought of leaving this place. I'd only been here for a couple of days, but I loved living here. I loved being Sadie here, and not Thanatos's daughter, or Archer Vasilias's best friend, or Søren's twin sister. And I deeply enjoyed the new friends I was making here – even if things had gotten awkward with Matteo this morning.

Stars, I didn't want to leave and go back to Mount Olympus. I didn't want to be reminded of everything I'd done wrong and destroyed back home.

Taking a deep breath, I moved to sit on the bed, trying to get my bearings again. I would wait it out, at least for a few days. The lockdown might work just fine in leading the Hunters away from here. Everything might be fine.

But if Hunters remained around here, searching for me and the Refuge... well, I would figure it out once I got there.

For now, I'd lay low and continue to carve my place in this community.

Chapter Twenty-Six

Kalani

My palms were sweaty as I knocked on the door to my grandparents' house. I'd been extremely relieved when I had checked the mailbox and found their names on it. This really was their house, and they still wanted to see me. But now that I was at their door, waiting to be let in? Oh, I was very stressed.

Time slowed down as I waited anxiously for the door to open. Had I waited for an hour or a minute?

I could almost feel Archer's eyes burning holes on the back of my shirt from where he and the others were hiding in the bushes. Real classy, right? I had told them that my grandparents would probably open up more easily if I went in alone, so they were waiting outside – *keeping an eye on things*, as Archer had said. And even though talking to them about my situation had been rough, I was thankful that they were here, supporting me.

Should I knock again? Maybe I hadn't knocked hard enough. If they were in a room in the back of the house, they might not hear me unless I knocked harder. Yeah, that might be why they still hadn't come – they hadn't heard me yet. That made sense, right?

I raised my hand to knock again, fingers shaking slightly. My knuckles hit the wooden door. *Knock, knock, knock.* Hard enough that my skin stung. Now, they would hear, right? They had to. After all, they had given me the right address. It meant they wanted to see me again, right?

Right?

A few seconds – or minutes? – went by again and I could feel myself start to hyperventilate. Shit. I needed to get a grip on myself. It was fine. Maybe they were in the bathroom? Maybe they were in the shower? Or still sleeping? It was eight-thirty, so still early enough that—

The door opened.

A shuddering breath left my lungs as my grandfather's face appeared in the crack of the door. *Thank goodness.*

"Good morning, Kalani! Come on in, come on in!" His face was so welcoming and warm. "We are so excited to have you in our home!"

I gave him the sentiment back, expressing how I was also happy to be here. Walking in the house was a mind-blowing experience, mostly because there were pictures of my dad everywhere. Family pictures were exposed all over the living room, with my dad going from a young kid to a young man, smiling at the camera in various poses.

It was like a punch in the gut.

I had never had pictures of my dad displayed before. For fuck's sake, I had been forced to snoop in my mom's room to see his face! And now that I was surrounded by dozens of pictures of him, I wanted to go to each one and memorize them until they were tattooed in my brain.

Would it be rude if I took pictures of those pictures with the new phone that we had just bought an hour ago? We had bought an old phone without GPS tracker, which meant that the camera was probably trash too. But at least I'd have a reminder of the way my dad illuminated the room everywhere he went.

"Sweetheart!" Kawehi exclaimed as she walked out of a different room. She wore a flowy yellow dress and her mostly black hair – with quite a few grey strands – was braided down her back. "It's so good to see you!"

Then I was in her arms and she was hugging me tight. I had the sudden urge to cry, and I wasn't even sure why. I'd met them yesterday, so why was I feeling emotional?

I was going to put it on having all of those pictures around me, as if my dad was here, with us.

"Thank you for welcoming me into your home."

"Of course, Kalani! Our granddaughter is always welcome. Always," my grandmother added with a pointed look, as if to underline her last word.

David had moved into the kitchen – or I imagined it was the kitchen, from the sounds that were coming from the half-open door – and asked us if we wanted something to drink.

"A coffee would be great, thank you." I didn't usually drink a lot of caffeine, but I could tell that I would need it if I wanted to remain sharp and observant today.

A few minutes later, we were sitting on the couch, three mugs on the coffee table. We had done small talk – how was your night? Did you sleep well? Look at that nice weather! – but now that we were on the couch, it was getting obvious that we were dancing around the real topic of interest.

After we all took a few sips of our drinks, Kawehi finally decided to breach the topic.

"Thank you for agreeing to meet us here this morning, Kalani. We couldn't very well answer your questions around any Nons."

"Nons?"

"Non-magical beings."

Alright. So, we really were going to talk about this. No more playing around and pretending like they didn't know what I was talking about. This was precisely what I needed.

"I see. And are we? Magical beings, I mean."

David sat back in the couch, letting his wife take the lead again, which made me think again that she was in charge of sharing this knowledge. Indeed, Kawehi nodded at my words before clearing her throat.

"We are, yes. We both know that. You and I are able to perform things that shouldn't be possible based on the laws of physics as described by Nons."

Huh, so I was right, then. David wasn't capable of magic the same way that his wife could.

"Does that mean that my dad was also capable of magic?"

Kawehi hummed along. "Our magic is spread from parents to children. It has been flowing in our family for generations, taught to the newer generations as they become older. If we had known about you earlier, as a child, we would have made sure that you grew up with your power. You wouldn't have needed to discover it so suddenly. It would have been like a part of you, an extension of your limbs."

I could see in her face that she thought that it was a shame that I'd grown up without that knowledge and education. I couldn't say she was wrong – growing up with her teaching me everything she knew would have been more than incredible.

I wasn't sure what had happened after my dad's death. Had my mom cut all contacts with my dad's side of the family on purpose for all of these years? Or had they kept the pregnancy a secret, hoping to surprise my grandparents' when I would be born? Had dad never given my mom any way to contact his parents? Or had there been a feud between my mom and my grandparents? How come I'd never met this side of my family for twenty-one years?

There was no way to know, now. With Hecate's spell erasing my existence from the world, my grandparents would never remember if they ever knew about me. I would never understand exactly why I'd been so alone in California, without any family around except for Makaio and my mom's estranged parents we saw once every other year.

"What is that magic? And where does this power come from? Why does our family have it, exactly?"

"Our magic comes from Mother nature, from the Earth itself, and is strengthened by the spirits of our ancestors." Kawehi stopped to take a sip of her coffee. "There are other families like ours. Families that are able to ask of the world to change and move for us. And while my next words are not known facts, I and many others believe that those of us that have access to these powers are descendants of individuals that revered the spirits of nature. Since then, all of us have continued to believe that there are spirits that control the earth, and we are rewarded by being able to ask them to bend nature for us."

Huh. So, nothing to do with the Greek gods then? But how was that even possible? From the way people had talked on Mount Olympus, I had been convinced that the descendants of the Olympian gods were the only beings capable of performing magic.

"So, we can control nature, then?"

"No, we can't *control* Nature. We ask nicely, and Nature decides it if allows it," Kawehi explained with the same tone as my most impassioned college professors. "We do not force Nature in the way other people do."

"Other people? There are other people who do magic too?"

"Of course!" David scoffed as if this was basic knowledge. "Every myth, every legend has a part of truth."

What in the world?

"What does that mean?" I frowned, confused by what my grandfather was implying.

Kawehi sighed and gave her husband a look. "What David means is that all myths and legends have a part of truth. You might have read stories about Egyptian or Greek myths when you were younger?" She waited for me to nod before continuing. "Well, these myths are in part true. Gods and demigods existed, and still do in many cases. Some might call us witches, but many other legends are also real, such as lycanthropes or any of the other urban legends that humans have told for centuries. Magic is everywhere you look and everywhere you don't. We happen to be able to communicate with Nature on a level that most people can't, but we are not the only beings who can bend the rules of the world."

I was speechless. Everything was real? Not just the Greek gods, but everything else that humans had been believing in for centuries? Lycanthropes meant werewolves, right? I'd seen Elena change into a polar bear, but her power came from the ichor that flowed through her veins. My grandmother's words meant that there were people out there who could change into all sorts of animals without having ever interacted with the gods of Mount Olympus.

And other urban myths… did that mean that vampires also existed? I'd watched plenty of vampire movies in my early teenage years and romanticized the bloodsucking monsters for years. But knowing they really existed put everything in a new light.

How come I hadn't learned about this when I was on Mount Olympus? How come Archer and Søren, who had lived with the Greek gods for years, hadn't known this was possible? Was this something that was hidden by the Olympians to the rest of the population living on Mount Olympus?

"I… I don't know what to say. It's hard to believe that everything is real." I swallowed roughly, trying to shake the shock of this revelation. "Have you met any of these other magic users?"

This time, it was David who answered. "There is a clan of shark lycanthropes on this very island. Nice people, really. They just get a bad reputation."

Shark shifters. I couldn't believe it.

"And they just live here peacefully? Among humans?"

"Yes. Just like we do, they hide their otherness from the Nons, but they live in plain sight. You know, Kalani, most of the magical beings on Earth just want to live their lives peacefully, practicing their form of magic and communing with their powers discreetly. You could live your whole life next to a clan of witches or a family of shark lycanthropes and never know it."

What Kawehi was saying made sense, even if an irrational part of my brain was worried that I was going to get assaulted in a dark alley by a vampire. Most of the people living on Mount Olympus just wanted to be themselves and live in peace and quiet. Having powers didn't have to equal to having a desire to use it for nefarious acts.

"I know this is a lot to take in, Kalani," Kawehi reassured me with a hand over my forearm. "But you are a witch and you deserve to know your heritage. I know that if your dad had been able to, he would have shared his love for Nature and taught you himself how to communicate with its spirits. But if you would like to, I can teach you what I know."

"I do want that. I want to learn more than anything." Those words came straight from my heart. Learning about my heritage, about the things I shared with my grandmother and late father, was more than just a desire. It was a need that came from my soul.

Pride lit up my grandma's face. From what I could remember from our conversation last night, their second son, Lokela, was working in Honolulu and had never married or had children. I was the only grandchild Kawehi would ever be able to share her knowledge with.

Excitement coursing through my veins, I texted the number for the second phone we had bought this morning – the one Archer was for sure checking every thirty seconds for a message from me – and assured my friends that everything was going well and I had gotten many of the answers we were searching for. I also advised them to go and find something to do since I might stay for a few hours here. Archer's answer was that they'd remain 'close enough,' which was so *him* that it made me laugh.

"Are you ready, Kalani?" My grandmother called from a doorway at the end of the living room.

I followed her to a door that led to a small patio on the back of the house. The patio was small but cozy, with plenty of flowers and small trees planted around it.

Kawehi sat down cross-legged on the wooden patio and signaled with her hand for me to imitate her. I obeyed, feeling weirdly like I was back to those days of training with Archer to learn how to close off my mind from mental attacks.

"To start getting connected with your power, you need to feel the Nature around you and understand what each element feels like in your core."

Huh. Kind of abstract, but sure. I'd gotten used to trying to visualize very abstract things when training with Archer.

"Okay, and how do I do that?"

Kawehi smirked like she knew that I was somehow skeptical. "You need to feel. And not just with your five senses. No, you need to feel with that part of you that isn't quite human. The part that you inherited from you dad."

Here again, not the clearest explanations of what I was supposed to do. But I was determined to find that place Kawehi was talking about, the one I shared with my dad.

I closed my eyes and calmed my breathing. Once my sense of sight was gone, I was attacked by dozens of sounds and smells. Birds chirping, leaves rustling in the soft breeze, the small river gurgling peacefully hidden behind the trees, the smell of the flowers all around us, the faint fragrance of coffee coming from inside the house, the distant aroma of the ocean… it was almost overwhelming now that I was letting myself feel.

But I needed to feel with something else, something deeper than my senses of smell or hearing.

It took a lot of focus, minutes and minutes of hard work, but I managed to block these sounds and smells out from the front of my mind, until all that remained was a soft blanket of nothing.

And now I was waiting. Waiting for this place within me – the place that my dad had also had within himself – to make itself known.

It sure took its time. I kept trying to search for that other, magical sense, but it was like mediation – the more I tried to search for calm, the more intrusive thoughts appeared. After struggling for what felt like hours to force this special feeling to arrive while keeping my other senses away, I decided to change tactics and let it come to me. Maybe this magic was playing hard to get.

Instead of actively searching for the magic, I turned to the calm part of myself that had appeared as I tuned out all of my other senses. I leaned into it, into the tranquil warmth in my center that felt like the core of me. As I remained in that serene place, warmth spread to my chest, warming my body and soul.

I was safe.

Tingles followed the warmth, as if I'd stepped into a hot, bubbly bath. The silence and comfort were so relaxing and—

Was that music? It was almost as if someone was singing a soft melody, the kind that was so beautiful it brought people to tears. It didn't sound like anything I'd ever heard before. No, it sounded like something ethereal, like the voice of an angel or…

Could this be what Nature sounded like?

I was vaguely aware of the breeze picking up its strength, blowing my hair over my face, and the song picked up in strength to match, the music enchanting and haunting all at once.

"Do you feel it, granddaughter? The music of the wind?"

My grandmother's voice should have been jarring after all of those minutes and hours of silence, and it should have broken my trance-like state. But it didn't. Now that I had connected with this song from beyond the human realm, I understood what my grandmother had said earlier.

I heard myself answer that yes, I could hear it, but my voice was muffled and far away even to my own ears. Instead, the song of the wind was stronger than ever, and the melody brought me to tears.

It was the most beautiful, otherworldly thing I had ever experienced.

It was lifechanging.

"Good. Now, I want to you ask the spirits of the wind to levitate the flower petals I just put in front of us."

Here again, it was strange because I heard Kawehi's words, but they barely breached the bubble that the music had formed around my conscience. Logically, I knew she was there, sitting in front of me, just like I knew that I was on her patio, surrounded by her house on one side and nature on the other. But my mind wasn't anywhere anymore. I was completely taken by the music, living in and through the melody and the otherworldly voice that gave me chills and brought me to tears and made me want to laugh until I couldn't anymore.

It took me a long time to register what my grandmother wanted me to do, because I was utterly transcended by the melody that was somehow both around me and within my soul. It made it hard to remember that I was supposed to do something other than listen and *feel*.

But, after some time, I remembered that I had something to do.

I had no idea how to go about asking the spirits of the wind anything. Was this supposed to be a conversation? Should I ask aloud or could they read my mind? Was there a protocol when it came to communicating with the magical spirits of Nature?

I wasn't sure either way, and I wasn't about to ask my grandmother for indications. Somehow, I knew that if I started asking her questions, this magical moment would break apart and the music would disappear.

I needed to figure it out for myself. This was my own connection to Nature, not my grandmother's.

The only time I'd used my magic was when I had asked the water currents to help me find my brother's body after he had fallen in. It wasn't like I had had a conversation with any spirit at that time. And I hadn't been thinking that I wanted the currents to move and obey me. No, I hadn't had the time or brain space to do any of that. The only thing I'd done was be desperate and beg for help. Any help.

Emotions had worked last time. Maybe this was what I needed to do now, too.

For half a second, I worried I would fail this exercise because I had no idea what emotion would work. What emotions would convey to these wind spirits the message that I would like them to move those petals? But then the music swept me away again, as if the spirits of the wind knew I needed their help.

And then all I could feel was thankfulness. As I listened and felt the melody of the wind through my body and soul, my heart grew with joy and belongingness. I shared these emotions with the world and these spirits, with everything and everyone I could feel around me.

And they listened.

"Open your eyes, granddaughter," Kawehi's soft voice commanded me.

After a few seconds – here again, my mind took some time to process my grandmother's words – I opened my eyes, blinking away the tears that had come from this communion with the spirits.

And there, before my eyes, was a small whirlwind with dozens of colorful flower petals within it.

"Holy shit."

Kawehi giggled at my astonishment and joined her, eyes locked on the magic going on before me. I'd done that. I had asked the wind and it had answered.

I had powers. Real, magical powers.

Holy shit.

Chapter Twenty-Seven

Sadie

Growing up knowing that I was different, that my dad was a Greek god, I had been forced to learn how to lie, and how to do it well. See, it wasn't like I had been able to tell any of my friends growing up that my dad wasn't around because he was dealing with all of the people dying, back in the Underworld on Mount Olympus. Not that anyone would have believed me if I had, but I also hadn't wanted to be labelled as crazy.

My point was that lying had become second nature for my whole childhood and teenage years. I'd pretended like I could only see the odd ghost to my family and that I was a perfectly normal girl to everyone else. Lying hadn't always been easy, but I had done it well.

It wasn't hard to fall back into old habits.

For the past week, I had smiled and talked to Bella like I hadn't spied on a meeting she'd had with her brother and Thomas days ago. I had pretended like I had no idea why we couldn't get seconds during meals anymore. I had continued to put on this fake persona of the Copper searching for a safe place to hide from Mount Olympus. And I had lied when people asked me if I was fine.

I wasn't fine.

It had been a week since I had learned that there were Hunters sniffing around the Refuge, and I couldn't shake the thought that I had led them here, somehow. And the guilt was becoming unbearable.

I wasn't the only one lying, though. Bella, Ken, and Thomas were doing a fine job hiding and bending the truth on their own. They had closed down all entrances and exits to the Refuge, pretending like Bella needed to work on the wards and the magical construction work required all of us to remain inside. Poor excuse, but it had worked. People were gullible, these days.

The only thing people had been annoyed with this week was why they couldn't get seconds for French Fries Friday.

Thankfully for the leaders of the Refuge, people had plenty to talk about with the self-defense lessons. Liam and I had separated our students based on their level of ability, but this wasn't what had gotten people talking. No, what people were excited and worried about were the friendly matches we were setting up for them. Every week, two pairs from each group would spar in front of the whole class of students. The goal wasn't to punish them or stress them out, but to add some friendly competition. I knew from first-hand experience that healthy competition made people more eager to learn and get better.

The first exhibition matches were happening this afternoon, and the mess hall was buzzing with excited conversations.

"Sadie! I need to know if I'm fighting today! I know I can wow everyone," Nolan exclaimed with a toothy smile as he ran up to where I sat.

"You know very well that the competitors won't be announced until our exhibition class starts. Be patient," I added with a pointed look.

The young teenager – he was only twelve, brought here by his older brother since they were each other's only family – huffed and puffed but listened to me and went back to the table where a few of the younger inhabitants of the Refuge had gathered.

"You created a monster over there. The kid has been sneaking around and putting random people into arm locks, claiming he's a bloody master fighter, or whatever." Bella shook her head. "He's taking this way too seriously."

He really was, but it was cute to see him so excited to learn. I'd just have to spend more time curbing his overexcitement at the prospect of learning multiple ways to strangle other people. I was teaching him how to defend himself, not a step-by-step tutorial on how to kill someone else.

"He is, yeah. At least he's nicer to teach than his brother. The guy is always frowning and looks like someone's pulling his teeth every time he has to practice drills." I rolled my eyes at the thought, because Nolan's older brother really was a pain in my ass.

"Are you excited about those exhibition fights starting today, Matteo?"

At Bella's words, I couldn't stop myself from looking at the man in question. Things had been very awkward between us since the *incident* from a few days ago. Since then, we had both decided to pretend like things were fine, but it was hard to ignore the hurt look that still haunted his eyes every so often, or the guilt that was still trapped in my chest at the thought of lying to him and rejecting him.

My heart clenched painfully as Matteo avoided my eyes and focused on Bella instead. "I like to learn but I am no fighter, Bella. You know that."

"You do fight bloody well for a guy who doesn't like it," Bella remarked with a raised eyebrow.

He did learn very quickly for someone who had no formal training. I wasn't about to intervene in this conversation, though. First, because I was the coach and it wasn't my place to jump into a conversation between two friends. And, second, because the awkward tension was still there, thick and uncomfortable between us.

"Sure, I hold my own. I don't particularly love doing anything in front of a crowd, though."

The British woman waved a hand in the air, as if to say that it didn't matter. "Everyone dislikes public speaking and public demonstrations of skills you've barely learned."

"Nolan doesn't," I murmured just loud enough for Matteo, Bella, and Liam to hear.

Bella laughed, Liam shook his head with a scoff, and Matteo snickered softly. Our eyes met and he painted on a deceptively happy face. It was the same falsely joyful smile that he had shared with me for the past five days. And every time I saw it, it made me feel like shit. Because every line on his face betrayed how everything had changed between us.

But Matteo was a nice guy. An amazing guy. He wasn't about to make me feel like shit for rejecting him. No, instead he pretended like everything was fine all the while looking at me like a kicked puppy whenever he thought I couldn't tell.

It hurt even more than if he just yelled at me about it once and for all.

"Is he going to be on the ring, though?" Bella asked in a stage whisper with a look in the kid's direction. "And can you please put him against a really tall and strong guy?"

"He's twelve. You can't wish for him to get destroyed, Bella."

"I don't want him to get *destroyed*. But I wouldn't mind seeing him knocked down a peg or two. He's going around the Refuge acting like he's Captain America and it's annoying."

I wasn't sure who Captain America was, but I had witnessed Nolan's arrogance often enough to visualize what she meant. The kid had the hyper confidence of youth, paired with complete obliviousness of societal norms. A fun combo in such an enclosed environment.

"You'll just have to see, darling," Liam intervened, a hand closing over Bella's.

She turned to look at him, a bright grin stretching her lips, and bittersweetness invaded my mind. I longed for the closeness that Bella and Liam had – that gentle, easy companionship and love – and couldn't stop resenting myself for still not being able to find this kind of relationship. Even after leaving Mount Olympus, I still couldn't escape my past and all of its secrets I couldn't share.

I needed to stop with this. I couldn't afford to dwell on everything I couldn't have, right then.

I needed to remain focused on what I had to do.

"Alright, Liam. Let's go. We have a few things to prep before class starts."

I stood up and waved at the table before turning around to leave the mess hall. My whole body vibrated with frustration, fingers clenching and unclenching nonstop.

Why in the stars was I so emotional lately?

I heard Liam long before he caught up to me, his footsteps full of determination and leadership. Liam was a warrior, and even his stride was a picture of strength.

"Are you okay, Sadie?"

Not really, but I wasn't about to say that. Instead, I hummed along and continued to walk straight to the gymnasium. Today's class would be a great way to get my mind back on track.

"Sure," Liam mused with heavy sarcasm.

"And I thought you didn't do emotional talks?"

"I don't. I have no desire to discuss why you and Matteo are in this weird lover's spat. I'm just trying to be polite."

I rolled my eyes but didn't take the bait. Liam knew very well that Matteo and I weren't together, but I was sure that he was trying to fish for information to report to his girlfriend. Bella was nosy and a hopeless romantic, so she was probably *very* curious about the weird tension between Matteo and me. And while Liam wasn't into deep, emotional conversations, he also knew what to do to please his girl.

Thankfully, we arrived at the empty gymnasium quickly and started setting up everything. Soon enough, we were deep in our organization of the room and supplies, as well as finalizing the last touches on our pairings. We had separated the students in three groups of increasing level and confidence in hand-to-hand combat skills. To be fair, it was mostly different levels of beginners, since the only Coppers with heavy knowledge of martial arts were Liam and Thomas. Each group had between eight and twelve students, and it made teaching classes much easier.

After almost a week of classes, our students weren't anywhere near proficient in hand-to-hand fighting or most self-defense techniques, but they were at least not going to injure themselves while throwing a punch anymore. Small steps and all that.

When I was teaching the Coppers of the Refuge, I had no choice but to compare everything we did to what I had done with Kalani, back when we were training for the Tournament. She had trained with us for almost two months, and she had been a quick learner – much quicker than most people. It was eerie, how I saw her in every girl I taught, or how I saw Archer and Søren in Liam whenever he helped me demonstrate something.

We were finishing up the last few touches of preparation when the first students arrived. The three groups hadn't trained together for five days now, so they were excited to be in this space together again. Chatter surrounded us as the space filled out and people started warming up. Even though I hadn't been the most excited about teaching those classes when I had started, I couldn't lie and say that it wasn't nice to see everyone so excited to come and learn together.

Liam ran warm-up while I finished writing the six pairs of students that would spar in the next half hour. I could see a few Coppers trying to sneak looks at the white board I was using, but Liam kept them far away enough that they couldn't see the names written.

By the time everyone gathered in front of me, there was a noticeable energy over the group of Coppers – all of them were excited to see what was going to happen, even the ones who had been the least enthusiastic about the idea of weekly fights. This wasn't about fighting in itself, though. No, these weekly check-ins were important because these Coppers needed to see that they were getting better and competing was the best way to remain motivated to learn.

I didn't want anyone to get hurt, but I also kept in mind that these Coppers were still being hunted by the soldiers of Olympus. These friendly fights would help keep everyone engaged without me having to scare anyone about what was waiting for them outside of the walls of the Refuge.

"Are you ready to show the order of the fights?" Liam asked quietly as he joined me at the head of the room.

The white board faced us, with my neatest handwriting showing six pairs of names. I really hoped the fights would be mostly evenly matched. Here again, this was a way to motivate them, not scare them away from the classes. I didn't want anyone to end up beaten up to a pulp.

Not that I would let anything go too far, anyway. Liam and I had agreed on a strict set of rules that would hopefully keep everyone as safe as possible.

With a nod in Liam's direction, I took a deep breath and got ready to get started with this whole endeavor. Hopefully nothing would go wrong.

"Alright, let's settle down, everyone!" I exclaimed loudly, gathering everyone's attention and giving a disapproving look to the few Coppers who kept on chatting along even after everyone else had quieted down. "Good. Now that we are all here, let's go over the rules again. The sparing matches will be two rounds of two minutes each. I don't want anything that could significantly hurt you or your adversary. That means, no fingers to the eyes, avoid the teeth, and nothing that could break bones or lead to knock-out of your opponent. No jewelry in the ring. Fights will end at the end of the timer, if one of you taps out, or if we stop it because some of the rules are broken." I stopped to add some weight to my next words. "If you break those rules and put yourself or your opponent in significant danger, you will not participate in those weekly matches anymore, and I might even kick your ass to make you understand those rules better. These are *friendly* sparring matches. Am I understood?"

Nods and yeses rang out in the room. Once I was satisfied that everyone had understood the rules, I sighed at the excitation that would surely explode in the room again and turned the white board around.

As expected, screams, laughs, and excited chatter came back in full force as people reacted to the twelve names written on the board. Stars, I had forgotten how hard it was to keep a large group of people under control. I used to have plenty of practice when Søren, Archer, and I used to teach the kids on Olympus – mostly Goldens but also a few Coppers whose godly mothers hadn't wanted to leave them on Earth for years until their powers manifested – martials arts and fencing. It had been months since I had been in front of these kids, though.

All the students were buzzing with excitation and my gaze passed over them before stopping on Matteo. He didn't look excited at the sight of his name written next to Tim's, Nolan's older brother.

He must have felt my eyes on him because Matteo's head shifted until he stared right back at me. He raised an eyebrow in question, as if asking why in the stars he was written on this board. And the following look was half-surprised, half-accusing me of doing him dirty.

It wasn't like I had chosen Matteo all on my own because of some misguided emotional reaction. Liam and I had agreed that he was one of the most hardworking and competent students from his group and deserved to show it off. Even if I knew that Matteo wasn't excited about the public aspect of this fight – or even the fighting aspect of it – I needed him to show the other

Coppers that they needed to get better and stronger to survive. Tim needed it more than most.

"Settle down, everyone. Stop acting like little kids and quiet down," Liam declared, his voice cracking like a whip. Immediately, silence fell upon the room.

I suppressed a laugh at the reputation that Liam had crafted for himself in the Refuge as a dangerous, cold-hearted man. It was funny when I knew that he was a big softie inside, especially for Bella.

But the tough act worked wonders on the students.

"First pair. Let's go. You have one minute to get ready and go stand in the ring formed by the tape in the center of the gym."

The two young teenagers whose names were written first on the white board rushed to get ready for their fight. Their friends tapped them on the back as encouragements and a circle of spectators formed around the fighting ring drawn out of tape.

We had decided to start out with the sparing matches with students from the beginners' group. It would probably intimidate them less to go first rather than go after the more experience and older Coppers.

That meant that, when the first two students entered the ring, the sight of these two young people made me a little sick. I could still see the young Coppers who had fought and died in the Tournament. For a second, there, this friendly competition brought me back to the last trial of the Tournament, when only half of us had been able to walk out alive.

Stars, I needed to get a grip on myself. I couldn't go down the rabbit hole that were my memories of the Tournament again. This was fun and educational. Nothing to do with the cruel games of the gods.

I was nothing like them. I wasn't forcing these kids into a traumatizing fight to the death.

Deep breath. All right. I was fine. *I was fine.*

"Are you both ready?"

The boy and the girl, both less than fifteen years old, nodded shakily at my words. They were bright-eyed and visibly antsy, but they weren't scared. Good.

"Good. You can go ahead."

The matches started and continued in a blur. Most of the Coppers were still very unsure of how to fight each other, standing and waiting around every so often. But they tried, gave their best, and most of all, respected the rules. No one got a broken bone or sprained joint, no blood was shed, and no eyeballs were attacked. By the time Matteo's fight arrived, I was more than satisfied about the way the afternoon was going.

Since Matteo was in the third and last group of students, his sparing match against Tim was the very last. As the previous students got out of the ring and shook hands goodheartedly, I couldn't stop myself from searching for Matteo in the crowd. He was talking with another Copper named Mehdi who was about our age and had arrived from Northern Africa a year ago. The two of them had gotten closer over the past few days and I was glad to see Mehdi hype Matteo up before his fight.

Before I could do anything stupid like going to see Matteo and give him a hug before his time to go in the ring, he started walking through the crowd to enter the ring. Tim took his sweet time before moving from where he stood in the back, but one sharp word from Liam's booming voice had him scurrying to meet Matteo.

The two men observed each other for a few seconds, sizing up their opponent. Once Liam announced that the timer was starting, the two Coppers started circling each other, waiting for the person who would strike first. If they continued this way, the two-minute round would pass without them even attempting anything.

Thankfully, Matteo was the kind of guy who might not enjoy this public display of skills but still became competitive. Quicker than I had ever seen him do so before, Matteo attacked and aimed a couple of jabs straight into Tim's upper chest, followed by a hook to the left side of his head. Tim managed to avoid Matteo's fists on the jabs, but he was too slow to completely avoid the hook. Immediately after getting hit, he stumbled back and brought his fists up, guarding his face again. Right above his half-opened hands, I could see dark eyes full of anger directed at Matteo.

A shiver ran up my back. I had this strange feeling that something was going to go wrong. That didn't make sense, though. Tim hadn't been involved in the classes much, and I was pretty sure he didn't have any desire to learn anything. There was no way he was going to beat Matteo.

Right?

As I stepped down from the box that I'd been standing on to watch the sparing matches, Matteo went back in for an abdomen hit, followed by a kick to the thigh. Both hits were hard on Tim and he continued to stumble back. Wasn't he even going to try to hit Matteo in return?

Squeezing through the crowd, I observed as Matteo continued to pepper Tim with quick, straight-forward attacks. Tim tried to throw a few hits here and there, but he was slow enough that Matteo had plenty of time to see them coming. Still, I had this weird feeling that something wasn't right.

Liam announced that the first two minutes were over and both Coppers walked to the side of the tape ring. Mehdi gave Matteo his water bottle and they talked for a few seconds. My heart wanted me to go and talk to Matteo, but I remained where I stood along the circle of tape, observing Tim as he also drank water.

Something was wrong. Tim wasn't great at boxing, but he wasn't usually *that* bad.

It wasn't like I could just stop this sparing match on a hunch, though. First off, I knew that Matteo wouldn't want me to do that and undermine his ability to deal with this situation on his own. And second, I couldn't accuse Tim of doing anything wrong – he was just acting like a particularly annoying brat who didn't want to put any effort into this exercise. But that was his prerogative, after all. I could teach these Coppers, but I couldn't force them to care or make them want to learn.

I had been preaching to all of my students that they were in charge of their own learning journey. Stopping this fight for no reason would undermine everything I'd told them before for days.

Both men went back at it as soon as Liam announced the second round was on. We had told everyone that the winners of each fight would get to not only have bragging rights, but also decide on a few drills that their groups would perform in the coming weeks. Based on the competitive look in Matteo's eyes, he didn't want to let those perks get away from him.

The first minute went well, and I wondered if I'd just become completely paranoid. As if to prove my point, Matteo hit Tim's knee with a low kick that looked like it hurt. A lot.

Matteo was going to win, no questions asked.

The dark-haired Copper brought Tim to the ground and got him into an arm lock. That was a technique that we'd just barely started to cover the day before, and I was pretty impressed by how well Matteo executed it. He wasn't holding Tim's arm too tight, so there wasn't a risk of breaking the arm, but it would still hurt. A lot.

Even from outside the ring and among the other spectators who were encouraging their friends, I distinctly heard Matteo ask Tim to yield. He was breathless, but his voice remained strong and confident. He had won, and he knew it. Really, there was no—

Quick as a snake, Tim's free hand shot up and his fingers dug into Matteo's eyes. Before I could even react, Matteo screamed in pain and released Matteo's arm. And then, because breaking one rule wasn't enough, Tim decided to try to permanently destroy Matteo's windpipe with his elbow.

I wasn't sure how I got from the outside of the circle of tape to straddling Tim on the ground. Things happened in a blur. But suddenly I had on hand on Tim's throat and I was squeezing.

Tight enough that he wouldn't be able to get even a tiny bit of air into his lungs until I would decide to let him breathe.

"What did you think you were doing, scumbag?" I didn't even recognize my voice anymore. The pure rage that had flooded my veins had taken all of my rational thoughts away. "I said earlier that if anyone broke a rule, I'd destroy them, didn't I? And what did you do, Tim?" I squeezed a little more, Tim's eyes and veins bulging from the lack of blood flow. "You broke a fucking rule."

I felt hands on my shoulders, trying to get me away from Tim. But the rage was blinding. Matteo was hurt, and this dipshit was responsible for all of that pain.

Someone crashed against me at full speed, effectively making me tumble to the left. I couldn't hold on to Tim anymore, and I vaguely heard him gasp. But there was a person lying on me, preventing me from moving.

"Bloody hell, Sadie, what were you thinking? You can't kill someone, even if they hurt your man!"

Bella.

Bella was on top of me, trying to restrain me from going and attacking Tim again. To be fair, if I really wanted to, I would be able to move away from Bella pretty easily. But the fight had disappeared from my body, right along the blind rage and my loss of awareness of the world around me.

Suddenly, I didn't want to choke Tim to death anymore. I just wanted to go and check on Matteo, which I should have done from the start.

"I'm sorry." My voice broke and I had to take a deep breath to stop me from crying. "I won't do anything else to him. I promise."

Bella remained stretched on top of me for a few more seconds before slowly sliding down to the floor. "Don't make me regret letting you go."

"You won't."

As I sat back up, I felt the emptiness inside me, a void where my powers should have been. Bella had trusted me enough to let me go, but she'd still temporarily removed my access to my powers. Not that I needed them to do some damage, if I really needed to. But it wouldn't come to that, because I wasn't a cold-blooded killer. I'd lost my temper for a second, but I wasn't about to go to Tim and finish what I had started.

I wasn't like them. Like the gods. I wasn't so ruthless that I could kill others without a second thought.

Standing up, I ignored Tim who was lying on the ground, a crying Nolan next to him, and turned to where Matteo was trying to sit up, Liam helping him. His eyes were red-rimmed and full of tears, and he seemed to have a hard time breathing. Guilt flooded my chest at the sight of him in pain.

Most people had left the gymnasium in the commotion, but there were still a few stragglers who gave me strange looks as I took a few steps toward Matteo. I was antsy to know that he would be fine, that he just needed a few minutes to get better and this fight I'd put him in wasn't going to have lasting impacts on him. I just needed—

"You should leave, Sadie." My steps stopped as someone grabbed my forearm. Thomas. "You've done enough as it is, don't you think?"

He wasn't wrong, was he? I was the reason why these sparing matches had happened in the first place, and then I had completely lost all control and almost choked to death a guy who might be dumb and aggressive, but surely didn't deserve to die.

"I just want to check on Matteo. I promise I won't do anything to Tim or—"

"Matteo will be fine. And you need to come with me." Thomas forced me to look at him, his grip tightening on my forearm until it hurt. "Now."

Chapter Twenty-Eight

Kalani

I left my grandparents' house with stars in my eyes and my heart full to the brim with wonder. I had interacted with spirits of Nature and asked the wind to move flowers petals for me. How crazy was that?

If someone had told me six months ago that I would have fought in a deadly Tournament against the Greek gods' grandchildren, lived on Mount Olympus, and now had magical powers I was learning how to wield with my paternal grandmother… well, I wouldn't have believed them. At all.

Kawchi had told me to come back the next morning so we could continue our lessons together, and I could barely wait for the time to come. I wanted to learn more about how Nature worked and how I could interact with its spirits. I wanted to know everything about what our family could do, and what other kinds of magic there were in the world.

But before I could go back to my grandmother to learn how to communicate with more Nature spirits, I had to go and explain everything I'd learned to my friends. I was actually pretty surprised to not see Archer standing at the end of the wooded path, waiting for me and ready to complain that I'd been in there for way too long.

As I walked down the path that led to the main road, a pep to my steps, all I could hear were the birds chirping and the far away sound of waves. No cars, no conversations, and no indication that my friends were anywhere around here. How strange.

I checked the phone but didn't see any notification. To be fair, there wasn't great service at my grandparents' house. They lived far enough away from the main populated areas of the island that phone reception didn't seem particularly reliable. Maybe I hadn't received a text letting me know that they had gone on a walk or something?

Even as I tried to remain confident that they were getting tanned on a beach somewhere, I couldn't stop the thoughts that maybe something had gone wrong and the gods had found us. Maybe coming here, on Hawaii, where some people might realize I had estranged family, had been a terrible idea. Perhaps fleeing to the middle of the Saharan desert would have been a better and safer choice.

What the hell was I supposed to do if the gods were here?

They would have already found me, though, right? Although I wouldn't put it past Archer to try to lead them somewhere away from me at his own risk.

Now that I had reached the main road, I was feeling more and more worried. I needed to reach Archer, but I wasn't sure I could trust phones anymore, not if there was a risk of us having been found. I did know one way to potentially reach my boyfriend, though.

Sighing because I really hated the thought of leaving my mind unguarded after everything that had happened with Alexei, I dropped my mental blocks down. After weeks and weeks of training and feeling terrified that someone would invade my mind again, keeping my mental shields up was second nature. Not having them made me feel naked and vulnerable. I hated it with every atom in my body.

I wasn't usually the one reaching out to Archer through whatever mental link he had access to. The few times we had talked this way, he had been the one to instigate the conversation and establish the link from my mind to his. But I couldn't just wait around and hope for the best, so I tried to mentally scream his name. I felt like a fool, but still, I kept yelling *Archer!* in my mind, hoping he'd hear and answer.

For what felt like minutes, I heard nothing back. Was I completely crazy to hope that my boyfriend would hear me mentally scream his name when he was nowhere to be seen? Yes, I probably was. But I still had almost no phone reception and my friends weren't answering to the one text that did manage to go through.

Should I go back to my grandparents' house? It might be safer and—

Mayfield? Are you okay? Why are your mental shields down?

The relief I felt at hearing Archer's low, husky voice in my mind was indescribable. My shoulders dropped and I felt my whole body relax. Thank goodness.

Yes, I am good. Where are you guys? You scared me.

There was a silence before Archer started speaking again. *We are at a beach bar down the main road from your grandparents' house. Nafula started feeling sick and she's been stuck in the bathroom for a couple of hours now. Sorry for letting you think we weren't waiting for you.*

Well, I had really gone down the deep end of overthinking this. I hadn't quite realized how stressed I had been about hiding from the vengeful gods of Olympus. But the past few minutes had been a great reminder that this trip wasn't a fun vacation or an opportunity to find my family and learn about myself. This wasn't fun – it was survival.

I had needed to remember that; remind myself that our lives were at stake there.

As I started walking down the road toward the coast, I took a quick look around me, making sure I was alone. My steps weren't so joyful anymore – being terrified that something had happened to my friends had sobered me up really quickly.

It's nice to talk to you this way, Archer murmured in my mind.

I rolled my eyes, knowing full well that he was trying to convince me to allow him to mind speak to me this way again in the near future. He knew I usually hated when anyone – including him – came anywhere near my mind. *It's not too bad, I guess. But don't get used to it, Sunshine.*

His laugh resonated in my brain, tingling my scalp. *Alright, Mayfield. I get it. Do you want me to leave?*

Did I want to have my mind back to myself? Usually, I'd say yes. But right then, I still felt the aftershock of thinking that I might have lost him to the wrath of the Olympians. *No. Stay. Until I get to the restaurant.*

Archer hummed and I could almost see his smug smile. *Good. I'll stay. So, how did it go with your grandparents?*

Should I wait to tell Søren and Nafula too? It might be easier to only tell everything once.

Just tell me the fun things. I missed your voice, Mayfield, and I miss you confiding in me.

For the next few minutes, I recounted how my grandparents had welcomed me and how I'd drunk coffee with them. We never really had good coffee at home, it seemed like a waste of money. Mom bought the cheap stuff – it got the job done well enough. So, I told Archer how surprised I'd been to like the coffee my grandfather had made. And then I recounted how many pictures I'd seen of my dad and how much I looked like him.

Words fell from my mind to Archer's, and it was liberating to talk about all of those little things that seemed so inconspicuous but meant so much to me.

By the time I reached the beach bar, I was smiling and felt much lighter than I had in days. Having this companionship with Archer, hearing his soft laughs and feeling his warm half-smiles in my chest, was a soothing balm on my heart.

As soon as I crossed the threshold, Søren waved me down to the corner table that him and Archer were sitting at. I walked in between tables with a few patrons reading the newspaper or watching basketball on the television screens over the bar, and then sat next to Archer in the booth.

"How did it go, K?" Søren asked with an excited grin.

"Good. Really good." I turned around to look at the hallway where the restrooms were located. "Should we wait for Nafula before I tell you guys what I found out?"

Søren shook his head. "Nah, she is probably still puking or something in there. Poor girl, I think she got food poisoning from her smoked salmon breakfast sandwich, this morning. It smelled kind of strange."

"Stop being annoying, Søren," Nafula snapped from behind me. She went to sit next to the Golden in question, and he scooted dramatically toward the wall. "I'm fine."

She didn't look fine. Her skin, usually glowing with vitality, looked ashy, and there was a dew of perspiration on her forehead. But if she wanted to pretend like she was fine, I wasn't about to mention anything.

"Okay, let's go through everything, then. Did you get any answers about your powers and where they come from, Mayfield?"

We could always count on Archer to make sure we remained on track. But I wasn't about to complain. We were on a time crunch, and we all knew it.

I checked around us discreetly, making sure that no one was going to be able to hear us. Thankfully, the guys had chosen a table that was away from all of the other customers of the beach bar, and the music playing through the speakers was loud enough that our words shouldn't be heard by anyone.

For the next few minutes, I recounted everything that I had learned about my powers and where they came from. It felt liberating to speak the words aloud, to explain who I was at my core to my friends. This new layer of my identity was as much a part of myself as being a gymnast – claiming it was so satisfying.

"Wait, witches? But those don't exist. They're just stories, right?" Nafula frowned in confusion.

"That's what I thought too. The only people with magical powers have ichor in their veins, from the Olympian gods. Right?" This time it was Søren, a hand rustling his long blond hair before putting it back into his usual man bun.

"From what my grandmother has told me, that's not true. Every myth and legend about magic or magical creatures are true, to some extent."

Archer's eyebrows shot into his hairline. "What do you mean?"

I hadn't been wrong earlier. Archer and the others didn't know about all of the other individuals who could manipulate the world in ways that weren't normal. Was this something that was voluntarily kept secret by the gods? Or were my grandparents just particularly well informed?

Ensued a lengthy explanation about all of the other magic-users that existed – allegedly – all over the planet. Based on the incredulous looks in my friends' eyes, I knew it was hard for them to believe my words. For years, they had been taught that being a descendant of the Greek gods was a gift that made them special beings. Discovering that other people also had those special powers without the deadly strings that attached them to the cruelty of the Greek gods… well, it might be a tough pill to swallow.

By the time I was done explaining everything, all three of my friends were dead silent. I had brought my mental shields back up – I still didn't appreciate the loss of personal space, thank you very much – so I couldn't talk to Archer anymore using our minds. But I didn't need this special link to know that he was trying to figure out what to do with this new information.

After a minute, the silence became more than uncomfortable. "Did I break you guys?"

"Of course not, Mayfield. It makes sense that if we, as descendants of the Greek gods, exist, then other mythologies might also be real. And you're a living example of someone who has powers that are in no way related to Mount Olympus. There's no reason to doubt your information."

"But?" Because I could feel there was a 'but' hiding after Archer's words.

He closed his eyes, sighed, and rubbed the bridge of his nose with his right index and middle fingers. "I just can't figure out why none of us knew this beforehand. I mean, I can imagine plenty of reasons why the gods would want to keep this information secret. But how has none of this ever leaked before? There are thousands of Goldens and Coppers, most of whom have lived on Earth for years. How has no one been exposed to anyone who had magical powers that came from another source? It just… it doesn't make sense."

That was a fair point. What was the probability that not a single one of the Coppers that had ever set foot on Mount Olympus hadn't ever encountered a witch, or a werewolf, or even the granddaughter of one of the Egyptian gods? And how come none of this had ever reached the inhabitants of Mount Olympus, even as form of gossip?

"And how haven't we heard about incidents caused by these people's magic? We're always told that magic users are dangerous to Earth, but if there are so many *other* people who have magic and live here…" Søren didn't finish his sentence but all of us knew what he meant.

Why were all of these magic users able to live on Earth and not Goldens or Coppers?

"Maybe our magic is stronger than theirs?" Nafula tried to offer as explanation, but her tone was unsure. This seemed like a flimsy reasoning. I didn't have any better explanation, though. Actually, I might have other ideas, but none that gave the gods the benefit of the doubt of not knowing any better.

Archer seemed to agree with me because he hummed noncommittally, eyes narrowed as he stared at the table. Søren, on the other hand, was nervously playing with his hair, tying and retying it in different ponytails and man buns.

"So… what do we do with this information?"

I pondered on Søren's question for a few seconds before answering. "I don't think we should talk to anyone from Olympus for a few days, until we can get some more details about the other magic users. Not even Hermes," I added with a look in Archer's direction. "We don't know why the gods haven't revealed this information to their people, but I don't think there is any way they don't know. They're hiding this from all of us, and it can't be for anything good."

I saw right away that Archer tensed at my mention of his brother. "Look, Sunshine, I know you trust him. But can you bet all of our lives on him not throwing us to the metaphorical wolves if we tell him what we know? He's a god. He has to know that other people have magic out there."

Archer's jaw worked from side to side, betraying his frustration, but he couldn't disagree with me. All of us knew that, whatever their reason to keep this knowledge under wraps, all of the gods had to be involved in it somehow. That made our situation even more precarious than it was before – not only were we fleeing for political reasons, but we also had knowledge that the gods might kill to keep secret.

"I agree," Nafula added softly. "I don't trust any god to protect us once they realize we know that we aren't the only magical people in the world. Can you even imagine what would happen if the people on Olympus knew?"

Oh, I could imagine that just fine. There would be an even stronger revolt on the gods' hands. Especially from the Coppers that were waiting to compete in the next edition of the Tournament.

The wince on Søren's face and the sigh Archer released told me their thoughts were along the same lines as mine. We had stumbled onto something that was so much bigger than us.

"Okay, so we keep this quiet for now," Archer conceded after a few moments. "But I want more proof. So, tomorrow, you need to get more information out of your grandparents, Mayfield."

That seemed fair.

"And we should decide where we want to go next. It's not safe to stay in one place too long."

My heart sank at Archer's words. I logically knew that we couldn't remain here, in Hawaii, for longer than a few days. Even with them trying their best to dim their powers, my friends were still beacon for the gods to find us. Moving was the safest option for us to remain hidden as long as possible – hopefully until we figured out a way for me not to be killed by the gods.

But still, knowing I'd have to leave so soon after meeting my father's parents was painful.

"We could go in the Himalayas? I've always wanted to see Mount Everest," Nafula offered after no one spoke for a while.

"Sure, I'm down for some hiking in the mountains. And seeing mountain goats in the wild is on my bucket list."

"You have a bucket list, Søren?" Nafula teased the Golden with a smirk.

"Wanna see it? I've only done about ten percent of the items so far, but I have high hopes for the next few years. After the mountain goats, I want to swim with orcas, go skydiving, do an ironman triathlon, and go see penguins in Antarctica. Plus, some other, even more fun things," Søren added with a playful eyebrow wiggle.

"No, I don't want to see your list, weirdo. Also, I thought we weren't supposed to go to Earth – how come all of your bucket list items are things you can only do here and not on Mount Olympus? Just how often are you planning on breaking the big rule of *not* coming to Earth?"

"Says the girl who's currently illegally standing on Earth."

Nafula rolled her eyes but I could tell she enjoyed those little arguments she and Søren always got into. Without having talked to either of them about the topic, I still knew that their annoyed banter was a way for both of them to deal with the grief and trauma the past few months had dealt them.

I wasn't stupid. I knew that Nafula and Sadie must have had something going on during the couple of weeks after the end of the Tournament. I wasn't sure exactly what that relationship had been, but it must have been something strong enough that Nafula had decided to break all of the rules on Olympus to flee to Earth with us – all in the hopes of figuring out where Sadie had gone.

And Søren… well, Søren had lost Mei in tragic circumstances, which then had led to him losing Sadie too. Even though he was working through his grief and learning to not blame his twin sister for his girlfriend's death, I still saw him staring into space with pain written all over his face whenever he was alone.

So, even though the both of them could get absorbed into their silly little arguments to the point that it got kind of annoying sometimes, I couldn't fault them for finding ways to work out their new selves.

"Alright, let's do Mount Everest. We'll just go on a hiking trail or something, it'll be a good cover," Archer agreed with Nafula, his eyes telling me he was sorry about it.

My heart clenched painfully at the thought of leaving, but I wasn't about to be the annoying girl who complained about it. I was grateful for all three of my friends being here, supporting me, and I would not start a pity party for myself.

That was why I gave Archer a quick nod, telling him that I was fine. He probably didn't believe me because he grabbed my hand beneath the table and started running his thumb in circular, soothing motions over the top of it. And my heart might have started melting a little at the casual intimacy we had finally found again.

"Okay, I think for the rest of the afternoon we should do something fun! Can you teach me how to surf, K?"

"I'd love that, fire boy." And the smile that came over my face conveyed all of the giddy excitement I felt at that prospect. I hadn't surfed in way too long.

Minutes later, we were getting ready to leave the bar and go find somewhere to rent boards. Søren and Nafula were back to bickering about something random – again – and Archer was trying to moderate the situation. I took this time to try and call

Sadie's number again. It was my third time calling today, so I wasn't surprised when no one picked up. Still, as I listened to the robotic female voice telling me I could leave a message, I had this strange feeling pressing over my chest – like something was terribly wrong.

Where the hell are you, Sadie Aska?

Chapter Twenty-Nine

Sadie

I knew the moment Thomas took me to that small, cold conference room at the far end of the Refuge that I was fucked.

I probably could have figured it out the moment I jumped on top of Tim and almost choked him to death for daring to fight dirty against Matteo. As a teacher, it was a big no-no to assault one of my students. And as an inhabitant of the Refuge, showing this much volatility and pent-up aggression wasn't a great look either. But I guessed some part of me had still been hopeful that the repercussions wouldn't be too bad.

Except now, I was sitting in front of Thomas and he looked like the cat who had gotten the mouse.

"Are you feeling a little more settled, Sadie?" The question could seem genuine, but Thomas' smug face and teasing tone were anything but nice. The man was happy, dare I say excited, that I had slipped up earlier since it would give him an excuse to interrogate me again.

It didn't take a genius to figure out why we were in one of the most remote rooms in the whole Refuge. Thomas wanted to use my heightened emotions to catch me in a lie. And he didn't want anyone to interrupt the interrogation.

The man hadn't trusted me since the moment he'd laid eyes on me, so it wasn't a surprise at all to find myself in this situation. To be fair, I had been waiting for this moment for days.

And here I was, about to start another interrogation session with the human lie detector I despised.

"Please don't pretend like you care, Thomas. We both know you don't."

The Copper scoffed, manspreading his legs like a guy who knew he'd already won. "Oh, I care, Sadie. I care about everyone in this Refuge, and I care about their wellbeing. Which means I care about making sure you don't destroy everything I've worked so hard to build from scratch."

I sighed, pretending like I was perfectly unbothered by what he was implying. "We've gone over this before. I told you that I have no desire to bring significant harm to the Refuge or its inhabitants. And you know that's no lie."

Thomas' eyes narrowed on me. "What I know is that you just assaulted one of us. And I know that you choose your words very carefully. A little too carefully for me to trust you, Sadie."

My heart started beating a little more rapidly and I fought the urge to wet my lips. I couldn't appear stressed or worried because Sadie-the-Copper had nothing to hide.

"I laid out very clear rules before the sparing matches started and I also told everyone what would happen if they broke those rules. Tim decided to go ahead and break the rules. I simply followed through."

"So, you're telling me that almost killing Tim was purely logical and totally deserved? Coming from someone who wasn't bothered with fighting dirty against me, I find that pretty ironic."

Stars, his arrogant smirk was so frustrating. And it was even more frustrating that he was right – my reaction had been stronger than necessary. I just hoped my loss of control wouldn't cause me to lose everything I'd built here with Matteo and my other friends. I loved living here, away from all of my problems and the ugliness of my life back on Mount Olympus. I liked the Sadie I was allowed to be here.

"Most of the students barely have any knowledge or skill to fight properly. If I let them fight dirty, they would all end up injured. That's not what I want, trust me."

"Huh." Thomas's right eyebrow curved up. "And how can I be sure that you won't try to kill another one of your *students* anytime one of them so much as lift a finger against your precious Matteo?"

I tensed at the mention of Matteo and quickly chastised myself for it. I had nothing to hide – or at least I had to make myself believe that.

I wanted to tell him that I hadn't wanted to kill Tim, that it was ridiculous to even think that. But that would have been a lie. At some point, when I'd seen Tim hurt Matteo, my brain had switched into a mode I'd only been in once – when Elena had stabbed Kalani after the end of the fourth trial during the Tournament. I'd wanted to make Tim pay, maybe even to the point of taking his life. And it had only been for a second, nothing more, but I couldn't pretend like it hadn't happened, especially not to Thomas and his lie detecting powers.

Instead, I had to find the only truth I could safely give him. "I can stop teaching that class if that makes you feel safer. But if I continue to teach, I can promise that the sparing matches won't happen anymore and that I won't try to purposefully hurt Tim or anyone else again the way I did today." I stopped for a second, searching for the best way to try to convince Thomas that I wasn't a crazy, dangerous person. "I don't usually lose control the way I did today."

Thomas nodded but didn't add anything else. Instead, he looked at me intensely, like he wanted to see right through me. And I was under no impression that my words had convinced him that I wasn't a threat to the Refuge.

Seconds ticked by and I had to forcefully refrain myself from squirming under his gaze. Pretending like I had nothing to hide was becoming harder and harder. If Thomas hadn't been stuck here because of his powers, he would have been a great cop – he had the interrogation techniques on point.

The silence became so oppressing that I could hear my blood beating in my ears in rhythm with my quickening heartbeat. My palms were sweaty, but I refrained from wiping them on my thighs. *I was fine.*

"You know what's interesting?" Thomas finally said after making me wait for what felt like hours.

"No, but I'm sure you're going to tell me, aren't you Thomas?"

The Copper snickered softly, a corner of his lips inching up in amusement. "We've been hidden here for years. That's a long time, don't you agree?" He raised an eyebrow and waited until I nodded before continuing. "In all those years, we've never had a breach in security. That required a lot of work, as you can imagine. But I, with the help of Ken and Bella, have kept a tight leash on everything that happens in and around the Refuge to keep everyone safe. And we've done it remarkably well."

Oh, stars, I had an inkling where this was going, and I didn't like it one bit.

"Do you know who Hunters are?"

"You mean the people who are trying to bring all of the Greek gods' grandchildren to Mount Olympus?"

"Yes, Sadie. Well you'll be glad to know that none of these Hunters have ever been able to track us here. Sure, we've had a few close calls here and there, with Coppers who have had strong reactions upon finding the empty cabin we use as decoy, kind of like your friend Matteo. It seems like strong usage of magic help them find Coppers. Neat, right?"

I hummed along, pretending like I was half-bored already by his monologue. Inside, though, I was getting increasingly worried.

"Anyway, my point is that we've managed to remain hidden away for years, even when things got a bit dicey here and there. But for the past two weeks, we have had Hunters camp around here, *hunting* for Coppers. They're so close they could probably be on us in minutes if Bella's shields broke down."

My breath caught in my chest as I came to the realization that this was over. There was absolutely no way this man was going to let me walk free. Or, at least, he wouldn't let me go without a thorough, lengthy interrogation that I would not be able to finish unscathed.

Before the Copper had even put the final nail in my metaphorical coffin, I was already gasping for air – for any escape from this situation.

"I've been trying to figure out why that is. It doesn't make sense that these Hunters would suddenly know where we are when we've managed to fool them for so long. But then I thought about the things that have changed since they started sniffing around here. And you know what? They started scouting the area since Matteo and you arrived. That's intriguing, isn't it?

"So, I've been asking Matteo a lot of questions, trying to understand if he's involved in bringing these Hunters around here. You'll be pleased to know that your friend is a completely open book, and he has nothing to do with these Hunters. So that leaves me with only one option. You."

Stars. I never should have come here. Instead of trying to help Matteo and undermine the gods in their efforts to gather all of their Coppers, I should have just gone and hidden in the wild woods or something. This fantasy I'd been living for the past two weeks was just that – a fantasy. And it was about to end.

That thought made me more desperate than it should have.

"You, Sadie, choose your words too carefully for me to trust your truths. And, today, you've fought like someone who has learned to kill. Being a martial arts teacher on Earth, in France, doesn't teach you that. So, I am going to ask you this, plain and simple. Have you been on Mount Olympus, Sadie?"

My heartbeat was frantic, now. Every atom of my body was screaming at me to either fight the guy or flee the situation. Sitting here, knowing that I had no way of getting myself safely out of this trap, was killing me.

My brain was desperately searching for a way for me to twist my answer so that I didn't blow my cover to pieces. But I couldn't see a way out of this. There was no way I could pretend like I hadn't been on Mount Olympus, since Thomas would smell the lie from a mile away. And I knew the man wouldn't let me get away with redirecting the conversation away from the question.

There was no exit. No way for me to escape.

I had to face this head-on and hope that the Coppers in the Refuge weren't as cruel and unforgiving as the gods of Mount Olympus.

"I have. But that doesn't mean I am a threat to the Refuge. I have no desire or intention to cause harm to anyone within the walls of the Refuge, and I am not the one who told the Hunters to come around here."

The laugh that came out of Thomas was full of absolute glee. "Oh, how good it feels to be right! Bella will be crushed to hear that her new friend was lying to her all this time. And Matteo… Oh, what a betrayal for sweet Matteo."

I hadn't realized it at first, but I'd closed my fists so tightly that my nails had almost broken the skin of my palms. It took all of my willpower to remain seated and refrain from hitting Thomas in the face with all of my strength. I hated the look of victory and pure excitement on his face. But more than that, I despised myself for getting into this situation in the first place.

Thankfully, the anger in my chest was a good way to drown out all of the other feelings I had at the thoughts of Matteo learning that I wasn't who I had said I was.

"Is there anything I can do to prove to you that I had no intention of being a threat to you or anyone of the Coppers in the Refuge?" I was grasping at straws. I knew it. But I wasn't too proud to ask – to *beg*.

"Do you mean, is there a way for me to cover your lies and betrayal? I guess it'll depend on the next few minutes and on your answers to my questions. First, are you a Copper?"

I winced at Thomas' words. Couldn't the man be too dumb or gullible to ask the wrong questions? Was that really too much to ask?

"No, I'm not."

"What are you, then?"

"A Golden."

Thomas' smile widened. It wasn't a warm smile. No, it was creepy and arrogant. It made my teeth grind.

"How exciting. Why are you on Earth and not with your people on Olympus?"

"I lost someone a few weeks ago, and my friend group kind of exploded because of it. I needed to get away from everything."

"Who was it? That you lost?"

Did he really need all of those details? "My brother's girlfriend. She was also a friend of mine."

"And how did she die?"

I had to take a deep breath before answering to calm myself.

"She lost the last trial in the Tournament."

This time, Thomas couldn't suppress his surprise. "So, she was a Copper, then. How did you two become friends, if she was a Copper and you are a Golden?"

"I was competing in the Tournament for political reasons. These have nothing to do with our current situation, so I'd appreciate it if we moved on to something more relevant."

"Touchy subject, Sadie dear?"

I didn't answer, but my face must have given him the satisfaction of knowing he was right.

"Oh, I love this so much!" Thomas even clapped to show just how much fun he was having. I couldn't relate. "Now, I am slightly confused because I thought Goldens weren't allowed to go to Earth."

"Is that a question?" I snapped, my patience running thin.

Thomas' smile stretched wider. "Yes. How did you come from Mount Olympus to Earth a few weeks ago?"

Well, this was it. This was the question that would blow everything I'd built here apart. Once I answered, Thomas would probably put me in the darkest, deepest hole they had available in the Refuge, before going around, gloating to everyone about how he'd arrested the biggest threat to everyone's safety. After today's events, I wasn't sure anyone would even try to take my defense.

"I enlisted as a Huntress for the Olympians. I have never agreed with their mission, though. Enlisting was a means to an end for me to escape Mount Olympus, and since then, I haven't intended to help the gods by bringing in Coppers to Mount Olympus. If there's one thing you can trust me on, it's that I despise and hate the gods more than anyone else."

Thomas' eyes glinted with excitement at my words. He looked like a guy who'd just won the lottery.

"My, my, Sadie, you surprise me. And I'm guessing you meeting Matteo wasn't accidental, then? Does lover boy know he was a target for your job as the enemy?"

My whole body tensed at the mention of Matteo. Somehow, I'd gotten way too attached to the man, and I didn't want to imagine his reaction to learning that I hadn't just stumbled upon him by chance in the restaurant where he worked. I didn't want to picture the pain in his eyes. I didn't want to imagine him losing even more faith in the world and people because of me.

"Again, I will not, nor do I have the intention, to deliver Matteo or anyone else to Mount Olympus. I might have lied and hidden who I really was, but I am on your side," I pleaded, hating the desperation in my voice. "The Tournament is a cruel and unnecessary practice and I don't want any of you to have to experience it."

Both of us knew I hadn't answered the question, but Thomas didn't call me out on it. Instead, he narrowed his eyes on me and remained silent, probably thinking through everything he'd just learned. I was too antsy to wait for him to take his sweet time thinking things through, though.

"Where do we go from there, then?"

"Well, we both know now that your Hunter friends out there are sniffing around the Refuge because of you. Based on your affections for Matteo, I am going to guess that it wasn't voluntary on your part. But it doesn't change the fact that they're there and that you are not one of us."

I couldn't say he was wrong. If the Hunters really thought I was hiding somewhere around here and had betrayed the Order of Hunters, then they wouldn't stop searching for me anytime soon.

And Thomas was right – I wasn't one of them. One of the Coppers Thomas would do anything to protect. If it came down to it, I didn't doubt that he'd throw me under the bus to save everyone else.

I wouldn't blame him for that.

"Alright. And what does that mean for me, then? Are you going to throw me out of the Refuge? Are you going to kill me to deal with the problem? What are you going to do, Thomas?"

The man didn't answer for a while, instead closing his eyes and leaning back in the same way people did to enjoy a sun bath. He knew exactly what he was doing, making me wait like this. He clearly had sadistic tendencies, and he enjoyed this little game – the one where he had won and could gloat his superiority over me.

Thankfully, the Copper reopened his eyes before I lost the last shreds of control over my temper. With a self-sufficient smile that made my jaw tense up, he sat back up and clapped his hands once.

"Let's go," was all Thomas announced before he stood up.

The Copper didn't wait for me to stand up too and grabbed my arm to pull me up. Then we were out of the room and walking down the empty back hallways. Thomas' hand never left my bicep, and there was no way for me to fool myself into thinking I wasn't a prisoner here.

The moment I had been forced to share my truth with Thomas, I'd lost any chance to live here freely. Now, it was time to face the music.

There was no other choice but to own up to my mistakes and lies with the hope that I would be at least partially forgiven.

Still, I didn't have much hope for forgiveness when Thomas pushed me inside my room and closed the door behind me. As the lock turned from the outside, I had the sinking feeling that the next time the door opened, everything I'd built there, in the Refuge, would be completely gone.

Blown away like smoke in the wind.

And all that would remain would be the broken-up version of myself I'd tried to escape.

Chapter Thirty

Kalani

The next morning, I was back at my grandparents' house, sitting cross-legged on the patio in front of a bowl of water. This time, finding the place within myself that could connect with Nature and its spirits was much easier. Establishing a voluntary connection with the wind spirits had opened a door within my mind and soul that led straight to the magical part of who I was.

As the world faded away and my senses dulled, I could feel the Nature spirits around me. Their songs and presence slowly invaded my mind, warming my soul from the inside out. Compared to the first time I'd communicated with them, when Makaio had fallen in the ocean, the Nature spirits were gentle and kind protectors. As they surrounded me, I knew I was safe, respected, and loved.

It was hard to describe exactly what happened as I communicated with the spirits of Nature. I wasn't sure the English language had the words I needed to express the emotions and sensations that flowed through me as I communed with Nature.

It felt like something from another world.

And I craved it.

This time, sharing my emotions with the spirits of water was like second nature – easier than breathing. Joyfulness and gratitude flowed through me, and I wasn't sure where I started and where Nature did. We were one in that moment.

Before I even opened my eyes, I knew that I had successfully asked the water spirits of Nature to perform magic for me. I wasn't surprised when I blinked and the water from the bowl was floating through the air, moving in a graceful dance around me.

Was that what power felt like? I could understand why some people became addicted to it.

Water continued to spin languidly around me, both a protector and a friend, and I couldn't contain a peal of laughter.

"It feels amazing, doesn't it?" my grandma asked with a gentle smile. "The water spirits can be the gentlest of them all, but also the most vengeful. So, be careful what you ask of them, granddaughter."

I heard the warning in Kawehi's voice even through the haze of contentment. Surrounded by their playful, gentle magic, it was hard to remember that those water spirits could also cause natural disasters.

Could I cause a natural disaster?

Anxiousness rose up in my throat as I wondered what would happen if I ever lost control over my anger or frustration. Would the water spirits cause a tsunami in my defense? Would they drown or kill someone for me?

Suddenly, I wasn't sure I wanted the responsibilities that came with the ability to interact with the spirits of Nature anymore.

Cool liquid caressed my cheek, so much like a comforting hand. *The water spirits.* They didn't appear in a human form at all, and I wasn't sure that they could even comprehend or communicate in the same way as we did. But they felt my anxiety and answered with comfort.

"I'll remember that," I assured my grandmother.

She nodded and we both remained silent for a few moments, observing the water moving in the air like dancing liquid orbs. It was a beautiful spectacle and brought me close to tears.

I wished I could show this to Makaio. He would have loved this.

Soon enough, Kawehi and I were leaving the patio behind, going to meet David in the living room. My grandfather was drinking a coffee and closed his crossword puzzle magazine when we sat on the couch.

"How was today's session?"

My grandfather always seemed excited when his wife or I talked about our connection to Nature. He couldn't communicate with the spirits like we could, but he had embraced the love Kawehi had for Nature and its wonders.

I was more than happy to share how well today's session had gone. It was hard to describe how intense the experience of connecting with the spirits of water had been, but I must have done a good enough job because my grandpa's eyes glinted with fascination at my words.

By the time we were done talking about magic and Nature and all of the incredible parts of the world that had just been revealed to me, it was time for me to leave. The others were prepping for us to leave soon.

As I told my grandparents that I had to go, David asked at what time I'd be back tomorrow and if I'd enjoy having pancakes for breakfast with them. My heart constricted painfully as I remained silent for a second.

"I probably won't be able to make it tomorrow. My plane leaves tomorrow morning and I don't think I will be able to modify it. I'll try to come back as soon as I can, though."

As soon as the words came out, my grandparents frowned and sat back in the couch. I could see the shock, and damned if I didn't feel horrible about it. I hated having to leave, and I hated lying to them about why I wouldn't be able to see them for a while. I just couldn't bring myself to tell them the whole truth about me – about where I'd been for the past few months and who my friends were. I didn't want to risk them seeing me differently after learning that I'd killed people in that Tournament.

So, I lied. And it killed me to do so, but I couldn't get myself to do anything else, even when my grandma's face fell with disappointment.

"Oh, I didn't realize you were leaving so soon."

My heart broke at her words. I put my hands beneath my thighs to stop them from shaking. After everything that had happened in the past few months, I was terrified of losing them, the last people that linked me to my family.

"Yeah, even I had forgotten about the trip back. But I'll be back soon. Really soon." I chewed my lower lip for a second, trying to keep the tears at bay. "I don't want to lose contact. I just found you guys, and—"

Kawehi stopped me with a hand on mine, gently pressing on my skin. "Oh, honey, you will not get rid of us anytime soon! You have our phone numbers to keep in touch, and I hope you know that you are welcome to our house anytime."

David hummed along before standing up and walking to the bookshelf on the other side of the living room. He grabbed something before walking back and giving it to me.

It was a small photo album with a soft black cover. I hesitated a second before opening it – it felt like something important was inside the album.

And I was right.

As soon as I opened the album cover, I was faced with a polaroid picture of my dad as a young man.

My dad's bright smile stole the breath from my lungs. Gods, how I wished I could have met him. Just for a second. Just for a hug. But the best I had were these dozens of pages filled with polaroid pictures of him.

"This is for you, Kalani. So that you don't forget him. Or us," David murmured with a sad smile.

"As if I could ever forget you, grandpa." This time, it wasn't possible to fully contain the tears, and I had to catch the stray drop before it fell. How had I gotten so attached to both of them so quickly.

Before I could get too emotional, my grandma clapped her hands and exclaimed, "But we can't let you leave like this! We haven't even met your friends, yet. We would love if you all came for dinner tonight. That would be nice, wouldn't it, David?"

My grandpa nodded and they were both looking at me with hope in their shiny eyes. And while I didn't want to risk my grandparents learning about my time on Mount Olympus and all of the terrible things that I'd done there, I also couldn't say no to them.

"Of course. I'd love that."

By the time I made it back to my friends, Archer and Nafula had packed most of our things. Knowing Archer, he was probably antsy to leave. Unsurprisingly, as soon as I told the two of them that we were invited for dinner at my grandparents' house, Archer's frown deepened. However, he didn't complain. Instead, he just nodded and announced that we would leave right after dinner.

I could tell that he was anxious about keeping us moving so that our group's magical signature didn't attract Olympus' Hunters, so I took his hand and squeezed it softly. "Thank you," I murmured.

He didn't answer verbally, but his face softened, and he squeezed back. A second later, he was packing the tent again.

"The lovers' spat it over, then?" Nafula asked as I approached her.

I rolled my eyes at her teasing tone. "I guess you could say that."

She snickered but didn't add anything. I wasn't surprised, since we were still very far from being best friends.

"Where is Søren?" I asked, finally realizing that the blond Golden wasn't in the clearing.

"On the beach, I think," Nafula answered distractingly before going back to rolling her sleeping bag.

Confused, I headed toward the ocean, acknowledging Archer's warning to 'not go too far' with a hand wave. Once I reached the beach, I took a second to admire the waves. They were just big enough that surfing them would be fun. For a second, deep longing hit me square in the chest – what would it have been like to come here with my dad for the summer and learn to surf with him?

Before I could let myself dwell on what could have been, I spotted Søren sitting on the sand, facing the water. Right away, I could tell that something was wrong.

I padded toward him, wondering if I should leave him alone the way our friends had done. Although, both Archer and Nafula could be as emotionally available as rocks when they wanted to, so I couldn't dismiss the possibility that they hadn't even tried to talk to Søren.

"Do you want a friend?" I asked as I approached the Golden, feet sinking into the warm sand.

Søren didn't turn around. "I won't be great company," he warned.

"That's fine." I sat cross-legged next to him. "I'm not your friend for the jokes, you know."

He scoffed but didn't come up with a playful comeback. Instead, he remained motionless, staring at the waves crashing on the shore in a calming rhythm. If I hadn't been able to sense the grief coming from him, his lack of response would have been indication enough of his emotions.

I wasn't accustomed to a sad Søren, so I wasn't exactly sure what I was supposed to do to help. For lack of a better idea,

I decided to just sit next to him in silence, offering him quiet comfort.

We remained like this for a while, wind blowing in our faces and the sound of the ocean lulling me to a peaceful state of mind I used to reach when I spent hours on my board. It was relaxing to enjoy this moment of calm together.

"Do you still miss your brother?" Søren finally asked, his voice hoarse. "I mean… I know it's not the same because she was only my… my girlfriend. But I can't stop missing her. I can't stop seeing places and thinking that she would have enjoyed the view. I keep wanting to tell her things, or I expect to hear her voice. And now I also feel like I might have lost Sadie forever and it just…" He trailed off, inhaling sharply. "It hurts. All of it hurts. So much."

My heart broke for him because for all of his swagger and impressive powers, Søren was just a young man who'd been thrown into something no one should have experienced.

He was still staring straight ahead, and I could tell that he didn't want to show more vulnerability than necessary.

"I do. I miss Makaio every day. And it's strange because he's still alive, but he'll never be mine again. It's strange to grieve the death of a person who's still alive." I blinked away tears and leaned forward, tracing shapes into the sand. "I am not sure that I will ever stop thinking of him, wanting to share something with him, or wishing he was with me. But I hope it'll get easier with time. And grief is hard, no matter who you lost or how it happened. We're both allowed to struggle with it."

From the corner of my eye, I saw Søren nod slowly. For a few moments, both of us remained silent, deep in thought. Then, he cleared his throat and murmured, "I'm so scared, K. I shouldn't have pushed Sadie away. But I was hurting so much, and I had so much *anger* in me. Sadie didn't deserve the way I treated her. And now that she is gone… what if something has happened to her and she won't come to us because of what I did to her?"

There was so much panic in his voice, and it echoed the fear that had plagued me for days. Not knowing where Sadie was or how she was doing was horrible. But we couldn't afford to be pessimistic.

"Sadie is the strongest woman I know. I am sure she is fine, and she'll be back soon."

She had to be.

Chapter Thirty-One

Sadie

The issue with living in a bunker-like compound beneath a mountain was that there weren't any windows. Some of the Coppers living in the Refuge had managed to create a lighting system that recreated natural light somewhat well, but it didn't allow me to use the movement of the Sun to estimate time.

For all I knew, I could have been locked in my room for the past ten hours, or it could have only been half an hour. Either way, I was getting more than antsy as I wondered what the leaders of the Refuge were going to do with me.

If the Coppers living here had even a tenth of their godly grandparents' ruthlessness, then I wouldn't leave the Refuge alive. Traitors were dealt with swiftly on Olympus, sentences ranging from painful death to centuries in Tartarus, forced to do an impossible task over and over again. Hopefully, Thomas and the others would be merciful enough to give me a quick death.

My mind drifted to my friends, back on Mount Olympus. I wish I was able to talk to them and ask for their forgiveness, especially Søren's. Even a month after the end of the Tournament, I couldn't stop searching for a way I could have ensure that both Mei and I had gotten out alive. I knew that it was a futile mental exercise, seeing as Mei wasn't alive anymore. But, every time I was alone, my mind returned to that point in time, when I had realized that everything was going to change forever. It was my own form of mental torture.

And it wasn't taking me anywhere.

There hadn't been a way for this to end in anything but pain and suffering. If it hadn't been Mei, then I would have died in that arena. This was how cruel the gods were – making us choose between death or years of self-disgust, not even recognizing who we were anymore and losing touch with our loved ones.

Still, I wished I could see Søren right then. He probably still blamed me for losing his girlfriend, but I'd take his scowl and disdain for a hug. Stars, I missed him.

And I missed Archer and Kalani. I missed our friendship, and I missed feeling like I was truly part of a chosen family.

I scoffed at the direction my thoughts had taken. Being put right smack in front of all of the things I'd done wrong – both on Olympus and here, with Matteo and the others – made me rethink all of my decisions. Most of them had been terrible. I could admit that.

Would it have been better for me to just suck it up and remain on Mount Olympus like a good Golden? It sure would have avoided this whole mess with the inhabitants of the Refuge discovering that I wasn't one of them and might or might not be a traitor.

I didn't regret everything that had happened since I'd left Olympus, though. Meeting Matteo, Bella, even Liam… it had been amazing to get to know them without seeing all of my mistakes reflected in their eyes as they looked at me.

My throat constricted at the thought of my new friends discovering my secrets from the mouth of a snug, utterly annoying Thomas. Imagining them learning that I wasn't quite who I'd told them I was, picturing the betrayal in their eyes…

Stop it. I had to keep my wits about me. I couldn't just let myself fall into a pit of despair, not when I had to find a way to escape this unscathed. I couldn't just let—

The lock moved in the door, rattling around as someone opened it. My heartbeat quickened and I stood up from my bed, readying myself for whoever was about to open the door. If it was Thomas, coming to gloat and announce that they were getting rid of me, I wouldn't go down without a fight. I didn't want to hurt anyone in the Refuge, not after how welcoming they'd been, but I also wouldn't give up my freedom or my life without a fight.

The door opened slowly, and I bent my knees slightly, getting ready to defend myself if needed. My hands flexed, anxious energy running through me like electricity.

Deep breath in, I tried to calm my frantic heartbeat. I was fine. I'd be fine. I had survived the Tournament; I wouldn't die in the Refuge. And Thomas could—

"Matteo?"

There he was, standing in the open doorway, and all of my fight left my body in one big wave. The first thing I saw on his face weren't the blooming black eye or the red marks around his neck, but the way his eyes looked incredibly sad. He looked at me like he wasn't sure who I was anymore. Like we hadn't spent the past two weeks holding onto each other like we were each other's lifeboats in a storm.

"Is it true?" he asked, his voice rough around the edges.

I wished I could disappear into a hole right then, to escape the way Matteo's voice and eyes made me feel. My throat was dry, and I didn't know how to make things better. I *couldn't* make things better. That was the problem, wasn't it?

When I opened my mouth, no words came out, as if my vocal cords refused to acknowledge my mistakes. Instead, I nodded slowly, every part of me feeling the shame that had overturned my heart.

Matteo's face shuttered at my voiceless admission, the last shreds of hope disappearing from his eyes. I'd be lying if I said that didn't gut me.

The Copper I'd gotten to know so well over the past couple of weeks, the guy I'd started feeling a lot of things for, couldn't even look me in the eyes anymore. He was staring at the ceiling, jaw clenching and unclenching quickly, and his fingers were tapping in a frantic rhythm against his thigh. Everything in the man's posture screamed pain and anxiety.

And it was my fault.

I never should have gotten that close to him, not when I knew damn well that he didn't realize who he was getting close to. The betrayal he experienced might have been easier to swallow if I'd kept my distance from him.

"You know, when Thomas told us that you weren't one of us, that you'd lied, I said it was impossible." Matteo scoffed. "How could I be so fucking blind?"

He laughed but it was a sad sound, filled with so much pain that it broke my heart.

"I never meant to hurt you, Matteo. I… It was never meant to go that far, and I never had any desire to take you or any other Copper to Mount Olympus. My goal has always been to undermine the gods by helping you, and later on the Coppers here, escape the Tournament. I just… none of you would ever have trusted me if I'd been honest about what I am."

"Your people have hunted us. I became a *killer* because of people like you," Matteo snapped, anger dripping from his words.

Technically, it was Coppers that had been charged with retrieving Matteo before I had enlisted. But I wasn't about to correct Matteo on that technicality. Because he was right, all of the inhabitants of Mount Olympus had gone along with the Tournament and its cruelty for way too long.

"I know. And I'm sorry about it. So, so sorry. I know that doesn't help. But I am." I knew nothing I could say would ease the pain and betrayal Matteo was feeling, but I still had to try to explain my choices. "Since the moment I talked to you, I've been trying to make sure that you would remain safe. If it hadn't been in the Refuge, I would have figured out somewhere else for you to be safe from the Hunters. I'm just sorry I couldn't be truthful about my past."

Stars, how I wished I could repair the damage my secrets and lies had caused. It was sadly way too late for that.

"I don't even know if I can trust that, Sadie." Matteo shook his head before running a hand in his dark curls. "How can I trust that you really wanted to protect me? I was a target for you to bring back to Mount Olympus! I just— I can't trust you anymore."

It hurt, but it was fair. I could only try to imagine how I'd feel if our roles had been reversed, and I wouldn't be forgiving either.

"I understand." I did, even if it hurt. "Where do we go from there, then?"

Matteo took a deep breath before glancing at me, our eyes meeting for half a second before he looked away again.

"I don't know. The others were still discussing your case when I left to come here. I needed to have answers, to understand…" He stopped for a second, closing his eyes like he was holding in his emotions. "Why? Why did you do it?"

I wasn't sure that knowing the reasons I'd chosen to pretend to be a Copper would help attenuate his pain, but I wouldn't deny him answers if he wanted them.

"I was forced to compete in the Tournament a few months ago with my twin brother and best friend. None of us are Coppers, but we got forced to compete because of political reasons – we weren't willing to compromise on our values, we'll say. On the last of the four trials, I ended up being paired against my brother's girlfriend. It was a fight to the death."

I had to close my eyes to avoid seeing the look of pity forming on Matteo's face. It was the first time I was actually speaking about this aloud, and I needed to make it through the whole explanation without falling apart.

"I made it out, obviously. She didn't. That created a huge rift in my relationship with my brother. And my other friends came out of the Tournament half broken, too. Once it was all done, I kind of broke down and needed to leave Mount Olympus. Becoming a Huntress for the Olympians was the only way I could leave Olympus legally, but I never actually intended to do a good job at bringing Coppers back. I hate the Tournament, with all of my heart. I would never subject you to that."

My hands were shaking, now. It didn't make sense that I was still so affected by just talking about what had gone down during the Tournament. Over a month had passed. When would I get back to a point when the wounds of the Tournament wouldn't hurt anymore?

"Here again, from the second I talked to you in that restaurant, I knew that I had to protect you. You were my chance to redeem myself. And then I got to know you, and protecting you became more than just a job I'd assigned myself." I took a deep breath, gathering every ounce of courage I still had. "I really care about you, Matteo. And I care about the Refuge. I care about protecting everyone within its walls. But if I had to choose, I'd always make sure you made it out unscathed. No matter what."

I opened my eyes back up, slightly worried that Matteo would be ready to leave and drop me like a used piece of garbage. But his eyes were filled with something that—

"Well, if that isn't a touching reunion!"

Unsurprisingly, Thomas is standing in the doorway, looking extremely joyful at seeing Matteo and I in this situation. That made me hate the red-haired Copper that much more.

"Drop it, Tommy," Bella said from behind her friend. Her words were short, her tone carefully controlled.

A second later, my room was becoming pretty crowded with Thomas, Bella, Liam, and Ken entering. The latter I'd barely seen before, but now that he was this close, I could tell that he was basically a taller, more masculine version of Bella. Both of them look so similar with their thin frames, floppy blond hair, and ice-blue eyes, that I would have been able to tell they were related without even knowing them.

"Are you all here to deliver my sentencing?" I asked, trying to fake confidence.

Thomas was the only one who smiled, seemingly excited to hear the challenge in my voice. The others, though, were somber enough to make me think that it was looking very grim for me.

"Sadie…" Bella stopped short, her big blue eyes welling with unshed tears. "Why didn't you tell us earlier?"

"Because none of you would have ever trusted me if I'd shown up announcing proudly that I was a Golden, even though I only want to help. I think what's happening right now is proof enough, isn't it?"

Bella couldn't argue otherwise. There was a rift between Coppers and Goldens, and I couldn't fault the Coppers for it. They were the ones who stood to lose their lives when arriving on Mount Olympus while Goldens lived the high life. It wasn't fair.

None of this was fair.

But here we were anyway.

"Let's get down to business, shall we?" Thomas intervened, his fingers giddily tapping against one another.

Stars, I couldn't stand that man.

This time, it was Ken who took control of the situation. He first asked Matteo to leave the room, but the Copper shook his. "I'm staying right here. I want to know what's going to happen to her."

I ignored the way my heart skipped a beat at Matteo's words – after all, he might not be acting protectively at all and might just want to make sure I was being dealt with effectively.

Ken and Matteo stared at each other for a few seconds before the leader of the Refuge nodded. Then Ken's icy blue eyes were back on me, ice picks piercing my skin and soul.

"We have never had a traitor in our midst before." Ken took a step forward, placing himself in front of the rest of the group. "In all of our years running the Refuge, we've never had anyone try, or be anywhere close to succeeding in invading our walls. And we've checked since Thomas found out about you."

I could only imagine Thomas going around the whole Refuge, interrogating all of the people living within its walls to make sure they actually were innocent Coppers and not spies for the Greek gods. I wasn't surprised that nothing had come out of the witch hunt, seeing as I'd never even heard rumors of Coppers escaping Mount Olympus before. I wouldn't be surprised that the gods believed themselves too smart – and Coppers too dumb – to be played like this.

"And?" I didn't particularly want to beat around the bush.

"We didn't have any protocol in place for this type of situation. But Bella, Thomas, and I have spent some time thinking on it, and we've taken into consideration the advice of other people who know you well," Ken bent his head in direction of both Liam and Matteo.

Oh, so everyone here had been involved in deciding my fate. How fun.

My throat constricted as I looked around at all of my friends. Liam, Bella, and Matteo… I'd gotten very close to them over the past couple of weeks, and I knew that I hadn't been truthful to them, but it still hurt to know that they hadn't taken my defense.

It was like the fourth trial all over again. I was losing everyone the same way I'd lost everyone and everything right as Mei was sentenced to death.

Weird how life repeated itself, right? The Fates must have been having a field day with my threads, making sure I always ended up there, alone and lonely.

"The suspense is killing me," I deadpanned, trying to build new walls around my heart to protect myself from what was to come.

No matter what happened, I would not crumble. They wouldn't see me cry or break down. I was stronger than this. And, even though Bella was currently suppressing my powers, I would fight to the bitter end with whatever tool I had.

"We are not the gods, so we refuse to stoop so low as to kill you. However, we cannot afford to let you reveal our secrets to the gods. We've all worked too hard for our freedom to let you ruin everything and put all of us in danger. So, we currently have two people working to build a cell for you to remain in for the foreseeable future."

I couldn't contain the laugh that fell out of me. Stars, how generous of them to offer me a lifetime of prison for my crime of having slightly too-golden blood. How ironic.

My eyes left Ken's severe face and passed over everyone else that was standing before me. It was like facing the jury that had decided on my sentence without me ever having the chance of defend myself. Wasn't there a lawyer – or even a law student – within this Refuge? I felt like I could have at least gotten the opportunity to explain myself to everyone before being sentenced to a lifetime of imprisonment.

"Nice. I hope the cell I spend the rest of my days in will at least have a TV. Might get lonely in there otherwise."

Matteo winced and Bella closed her eyes at my words. At least both of them felt somewhat guilty or sad at the thought of me spending the rest of my life in a cell.

There was one person who looked like he was frowning for the wrong reasons, though, and it was Thomas. The man seemed to be slightly bummed that the death sentence had been removed from the list of possibilities.

And, standing slightly in front of Thomas, Ken didn't seem to think my joke was funny.

"You will be staying in this room for the next day or so, under surveillance, and we expect to be able to move you to your new accommodations soon."

"Oh, thank you, Ken. How reassuring to know that you guys have such a great plan. I feel very cared for."

The humor didn't seem to lighten up anyone, and that was fine. Now that I had a timeline, I was going to be able to figure out a way to get out of here.

If they managed to put me in a cell that would for sure be in the deepest, darkest pit within the Refuge, I'd never get out. But I knew the way from my room to the entrance of the compound. I just needed to find a way to escape.

Hopefully, whoever would be in charge of my 'security' wouldn't be inclined to do a great job.

"Alright, if we're done here," Thomas started after a few seconds of heavy silence.

"Yeah, I'll let you guys go. After all, I'd like to enjoy my last few moments with a real room. I hear prisons cells aren't as comfortable. Not that I've seen any in person, you know, since I haven't been a criminal for very long." I scowled at Thomas, hoping he could feel how much I despised him through my eyes. Then, with a poisonous, sweet smile, I added, "I do hope you manage to get rid of the Hunters sniffing around here, though. It's a shame I can't go out and lead them away from here."

The Copper in question scoffed as if this was the funniest thing he'd ever heard. "As if we would let you leave the Refuge so you could give out our location and reveal all of our secrets to your friends on Mount Olympus?"

Oh stars, that man was so dense sometimes! "Is your little lie detecting power defective? Because I told you multiple times, very explicitly, that I have and never had any intention of putting any of you in danger. And for the record, if I'd wanted to sell the Refuge out, I would have done so much earlier! Why would I have spent two whole weeks here, taught a class for everyone to learn how to defend themselves without their powers, and let myself get comfortable enough to be caught? How stupid do you think I am, exactly?"

Based on Thomas' sneer, I had an inkling he wasn't about to say anything nice about me. He did choose to remain silent, though, and I was thankful for it because my patience was running thin.

From the corner of my eyes, I saw Bella and Liam frown at my words. It didn't make sense for me to be the enemy after everything I'd done these past two weeks in the Refuge. But even though the seed of doubt had been planted into their minds, my friends – former friends, probably – wouldn't allow themselves to rethink their decision. I couldn't quite blame them for it, seeing as they were clearly in a fight-or-flight mode, worried about their lives and the lives of everybody else in the Refuge.

I couldn't blame them, but it still hurt that they didn't believe me when I told them, as truthfully as I could, that I wasn't the enemy.

"Look, we—" Bella stopped abruptly, her eyes widening.

Immediately, I knew something was wrong, and it had to be related to the magical wards that protected the Refuge from being located through the equivalent of a magical GPS. The wards were an extension of herself, and with the Hunters sniffing around so close to the Refuge…

"What is it, Bells?" Ken asked his sister, suddenly very alert too.

The young woman looked my way hesitantly, as if worried about revealing her secret in front of me. I ignored the pang of hurt that hit me straight in the chest again and observed as Ken ordered everyone out of the room. One after the other, all of my friends left my bedroom, giving me farewell looks. And before he closed the door behind him, I saw the poorly hidden panic in Ken's eyes.

In seconds, I was alone again.

While I didn't know exactly what was going on, I knew enough from context clues to be confident that most people within the Refuge would be occupied with the potentially very important problem at hand.

If that wasn't an opportunity for escape, I wasn't sure what it was.

Maybe the Fates were on my side, after all.

I listened to the lock turn, then a flurry of hurried footsteps moving away from my room. Oh, the situation was bad, I could taste it in the air.

And I couldn't have asked for a better opportunity.

As an announcement rang through the compound, declaring the Refuge under lockdown for the foreseeable future due to a ward leak – *sure* – I looked around my room and gathered some essentials that would help me survive the next few days before I figured out what I'd do next.

I put on a thick sweatshirt, my jacket, the beanie I'd borrowed from Matteo, and the thick boots I'd arrived with. I checked that my blades, SIM card, and turned off phone were still in my backpack. The fact that no one had checked my room for weapons was a testament to how unprepared everyone here had been for internal betrayal.

Then, with one last look around the room where I'd lived and rediscovered myself for the past two weeks, I walked quietly to the door.

I squatted silently and watched through the keyhole in the door, observing for movement outside the door. After a minute, I could only see one person pacing back and forth in front of my door. Had they really asked *Benji* to stand guard? The guy was barely old enough to have finished high school, and he was half my size. What was he supposed to do to restrain me?

The situation with the wards must have been really dire if the only person Ken and Thomas had been able to assign to guard me was Benji. I would have expected Liam to remain behind the door, seeing as he was the most likely to hold his own against me.

Not that I was complaining. Far from it.

In the far background, I could hear people running down the hallways, yelling at each other, and probably freaking out because 'lockdown' didn't sound very reassuring.

But that was perfect for me. My hallway sounded pretty calm, which would allow me to deal with Benji somewhat discreetly. But the commotion in the rest of the Refuge should work in my favor when escaping.

I just had to open the door.

Thankfully, Søren had been a bad influence my whole childhood and he had had a couple of years when he had imagined he'd become a spy. He had learned how to do a lot of crazy and stupid things that a spy might do, and he had felt the need to teach me in return. Just in case we were destined to become twin spies, I guess.

Ironic that I was the one who had become a spy instead of Søren.

Still, the lock picking skills were pretty useful right about now.

Before I had left Mount Olympus, I had had the presence of mind to grab a few bobby pins from my stash. Deities and their children didn't usually use bobby pins or hair clips since we had magic, but all of our illegal trips to Earth with the guys had allowed me to gather some essentials – including hair tools that could pair up as spying essentials.

Thank the stars I had, really, because Bella's suppression of my powers was still very present and I could only feel a far-away outline of my magic, too unsubstantial to grasp. Not that I would have been able to do much with my powers, since digging whatever skeletons were beneath me would have been tough through layers and layers of rocks.

Through the door, I heard hurried steps – someone running. What in the stars was happening out there?

I didn't have much time to wonder about the situation outside of my room, though, because I needed to open this stupid door. Thankfully, when the Refuge had been created, no one had decided to use complicated lock systems on the bedroom doors.

Unsurprisingly, I heard the lock turning after only a few moments of me working on it.

Then, things needed to happen quickly for me to retain the surprise effect. In seconds, I was back up, bobby pins tucked into my pockets, and mind focused on what I had to do.

I would not get another shot at this. It was either I escaped right then, or I would spend a long, *long* time stuck in a cell that would probably be built with the goal to keep me in there.

There would be no time for mistakes.

Eyes closed, I focused on the sounds of Benji pacing in front of my door. Once I was sure that he was located right in the path of the door opening, I yanked the door open and attacked before the man could even realize what was happening. In half a second, I had Benji in a headlock and was restraining his left arm so that he couldn't reach for his walkie-talkie.

Five seconds later, it was lights out for dear Benji.

I felt slightly bad as I carried the man into my room and down to the ground as gently as possible. He didn't deserve his treatment, but things had to be done.

As soon as Benji was settled and away from prying eyes, I closed the door and took off down the hallway. In the background, I could hear people yelling orders around, and doors slamming. Thankfully, I couldn't hear any of this commotion anywhere close to me.

Still, I remained hyper aware of everything going on around me as I speed walked down the hallways. I knew the path to take to go from my room to the entrance of the Refuge by heart – it had been the first thing I'd ensured I had memorized during the first few days of my stay. If the Tournament had taught me anything, it was that I wasn't about to be caught by surprise and unable to leave anymore.

I was slightly surprised that the hallways were empty as I sped through them. The only time someone almost ran into me, I hid in a small alcove, and watched as Liam and another guy ran full speed past me.

This was too easy.

I wasn't too stupid or proud to admit that I should have encountered more resistance when escaping. Where was everyone? And what exactly was happening outside the Refuge that warranted this lockdown?

What was I going to have to face when I finally made it out?

If I left the Refuge and ended up right in front of a stars-damned deity, this day would really take a turn for the worse.

One more turn and I'd have to go through the mess hall before reaching the doorway that led outside. Hopefully, all of the inhabitants of the Refuge hadn't gathered in the mess hall – that would defeat the purpose of trying to be discreet in my escape attempt. And without my powers, I would never be able to fight my way through three dozen Coppers.

Moreover, I hadn't lied to Thomas and I didn't want to have to hurt any of the people living in the Refuge. Knocking Benji out already weighed on my conscience, and I wouldn't be able to face myself if I hurt other inhabitants of the Refuge. *Although, knocking Thomas out might be cathartic…*

Focus, I reprimanded myself, getting ready to push the doors to the mess hall. I would do what I could to escape, within reason.

Gently, I pushed the door open, holding my breath. No sounds came from the inside of the mess hall, which meant that it was unlikely that there would be many people gathered in the big room. Still, I remained cautious as I sneaked into the darkened room.

There were many shadows in the room, which made it hard to see clearly among the tables and benches. However, I couldn't see anything moving or reacting to my entrance in the room, which was a good sign.

I didn't stop to wonder how I could be so lucky and rushed as stealthily as possible across the massive room toward the exit. There were probably other exits to the Refuge – the leaders of the Refuge weren't stupid enough to have only one exit plan for their people – but I didn't know where they were, so I'd have to make do with this one.

When I finally reached the spot in the rocky wall where the door to the outside was hidden, my heart was racing with anticipation. I was so close to freedom that I could almost taste it.

"Sadie?"

The word drew the breath from my lungs, stopping me dead in my tracks.

What was *he* doing here? And how in the stars was I going to be able to finish my escape when he was there? I would never be able to resolve myself to hurting him.

"What are you doing here, Matteo?"

"Shouldn't I be asking you that question, seeing as you're supposed to be in your room right now?"

The man stepped forward until he was only a few paces away. From there, I could see how hard he was trying to keep a straight, severe face on. But the corner of his lips kept creeping up, betraying how he really felt. And he was amused to find me here.

Which meant he didn't quite hate me after discovering I'd lied to him for weeks.

Was it completely crazy of me to be relieved at that thought when I should be thinking about how I was going to escape a life-sentence in prison?

"You're probably right. But you know me," I added with a tentative smile in his direction, "I don't do well with small, enclosed spaces. I needed some air."

Matteo scoffed softly at my words, but that only lasted for half a second. Then he was serious again, his eyes boring into mine like he was searching for my deepest, darkest secrets.

"Are you going to betray us, out there?"

The vulnerability in Matteo's words was a punch straight to the gut. The guilt in my chest expanded like a dark, ravenous monster.

"No. I know it's hard to believe me after everything, but I can promise you that I wouldn't do anything that would endanger you, Bella, Liam, or any other Copper in here." I tried to convey how much he meant to me through my words, but I wasn't sure I even knew how to express those feelings. "I just can't stay here and allow myself to be imprisoned for who knows how long."

Matteo's jaw ticked and his fists clenched. In that moment, I wished I could use Archer's powers to know what was happening in the Copper's head. Did he believe me? Did he care enough about me and my wellbeing to let me go? Or did he trust Thomas' judgement over me?

"I'm sure it wouldn't be for very long," Matteo murmured just loud enough for me to hear.

I raised my eyebrows, containing a surprised laugh. "Really? Because I think Thomas has enough beef against me that the rest of my life would be too short of a sentence in his eyes."

And Matteo couldn't say he disagreed. Thomas was an asset to the Refuge and probably a great leader, but he also had a knack for holding a grudge.

"So, what are you going to do out there?" Matteo asked, his voice sounding tight. Was he sad thinking about me leaving?

"I'm going to find a way to make sure the Hunters that are staying around here leave this place alone. And I'll find a way to escape my life on Mount Olympus for a few more weeks until I don't have a choice but to go back."

I ignored the burn that started behind my eyelids at the thought of leaving and never coming back, ever again. I couldn't think about that right then.

"So, is that it, then? We won't ever see each other again?"

This time, I didn't imagine the way Matteo choked on his last words. It made me want to give him a hug and tell him I'd find a way to come back. But that would be a lie – our worlds were too different for anything between us to work, or for me to make that promise.

"I don't have a choice, Matteo. You need to stay here, where you're safe. And I can't stay here, because I am endangering all of you."

The Copper nodded slowly, eyes closed, his chest moving in rapid, shallow breaths. My fingers were tingling with the need to get closer to him and comfort him. But I shouldn't, right?

Finally, Matteo opened his eyes and they were shiny enough to betray unshed tears.

"I'll miss you, Zombie girl, even after everything that happened."

"Really?" I wasn't even ashamed of the unabashed hope that bloomed in my chest at his words.

This time, Matteo let a shy smile stretch his lips. Per usual, his smile brightened the world around us.

"Yeah, I will miss you. I won't miss the secrets, though. I can't fully understand why you did it, but I know that you don't mean harm to me or any of us."

Matteo's words were a healing balm on my heart. And suddenly, I couldn't hold on to the truths I'd buried in my chest for so many days.

"I care about you a lot, Matteo. A lot more than I should. A lot more than is reasonable."

Matteo took an involuntary step forward, his eyes widening slightly. "Really? But you didn't…"

He stopped, but I knew what he meant. "I wanted to kiss you that day, but I couldn't do it with when you didn't know who I was."

Matteo sucked in a deep breath and my heart screamed at me to run into his arms. But I didn't. And he didn't move either.

Instead, we both remained stuck in place, both close enough to reach out and touch each other, but far enough that whole universes could have separated us. And we stared into each other's eyes like we would find the solutions to our impossible story there.

We didn't. Obviously.

And when I opened the door and left, I felt Matteo's gaze burning a hole in my back.

Chapter Thirty-Two

Kalani

This was as close to having my dad meet my boyfriend and friends as I'd ever come. As my grandparents opened the door and let us enter their house, I was hit by a wave of sadness at that thought.

Thankfully, I didn't have time to dwell on how much I wished my dad was here because my grandma was hugging me tight.

"We are so glad you could make it tonight, sweetheart," she murmured in my ears, warming my heart. "Now, introduce us to your friends!"

The next few minutes passed by in a dream. It was surreal to watch my friends standing in my grandparents' living room. Watching Søren joke around with my grandfather, witnessing my grandmother show Archer and Nafula around the living room… it was like being in a weird fantasy.

It made me dream about impossible things, like a world where I would live happily with my friends and family on Earth, unafraid of vengeful gods.

By the time we sat around the dinner table, drinks in hand, my heart was ready to jump out of my body at any moment. I loved this. I loved seeing my family members and friends get along so well.

For a few minutes, I watched David ask my friends about themselves and a smile formed on my face. Maybe this wouldn't be so bad, after all. Maybe I wouldn't have to tell my only family members that I had lied to them since the moment I had met them.

Unfortunately, it was without counting on my grandmother.

"How did you all meet?"

I shifted to look at Kawehi and my heart dropped when I met her pointed gaze. Instantly, I could tell that she knew something was up. I heard my friends shift awkwardly beside me, but I couldn't look away from my grandmother.

I stood at a metaphorical crossroad there, and I was terrified of both options I had in front of me. On one hand, I could try to get myself out of this situation by spending the rest of the evening spinning lies and hoping my grandmother believed me. On the other hand, I could be honest and hope my grandparents wouldn't be disgusted of the choices I'd made, the things I'd done to survive.

As I looked between my grandparents, though, I knew that there was only one choice I could make.

I had dragged my friends on the run from the Olympian gods because I couldn't part with my morals. It would be hypocritical for me to lie now, when my newly found family was asking to get to know me and my friends.

"I haven't been totally honest when we first met," I started with a wince, avoiding my grandparents' eyes. "I knew about magic before I met you. Or, at least, I knew about the Greek gods and Mount Olympus."

Once I had opened the gates, everything came out. I talked about how I'd arrived on Mount Olympus by mistake, how I had ended up thrown into the Tournament with no knowledge of my magic, and how I had become unlikely allies and friends with Archer, Søren, and ultimately, Nafula.

By the time I was done, my heart was beating so hard that I couldn't hear the birds chirping outside anymore. I was terrified of my grandparents' reaction.

How could I have become so attached to these people in such a short time?

We had known each other for less than forty-eight hours, but I could already tell that I would never recover if they decided that my experience in the Tournament made it impossible for them to accept me. To love me.

"You must understand," Archer spoke softly after the silence lingered, "Kalani has done what she needed to do to survive. And she couldn't reveal all of this information to anyone without making sure she could trust you. Really, I was the one who told her multiple times not to reveal anything to the both of you."

My heart swelled at seeing Archer take my defense like this. I wanted to reach for his hand, but I didn't want to lose myself in him – not when I needed to keep my thoughts clear for this conversation.

Throat tight from worry, I looked away from Archer and forced myself to face my grandmother. She was completely unreadable. That was almost worse than seeing her openly angry or disappointed.

David, on the other hand, was an open book. His mouth was half-open, and his eyes were wide from shock. The man was completely speechless.

Seconds ticked by and I could feel the panic rising in me. Nervously, I wiped my sweaty palms on my jean shorts and faced my grandmother again. She was the one who would need convincing that I wasn't an awful person, even after all of the terrible things I'd seen and done on Olympus.

"I knew none of you felt like humans," Kawehi finally said, her gaze sweeping over my friends. Still, she didn't look at me. "I couldn't tell exactly what your heritage was, but your magic is strong enough to tickle my nose."

All three of my friends looked uncomfortable under my grandma's watchful eyes, clearing their throats and squirming on the couch, pretending to find a more comfortable position.

Finally, Kawehi turned to me and her gaze pierced through me, all the way to my soul.

"Child, I wish you had told us earlier. We have shared sensitive information with you regarding our people. We have trusted you, and—"

"Kawehi," David interrupted her, reaching over to squeeze her knee.

My grandmother took a deep breath, eyes closed for a second. "I am sorry, Kalani. I understand why you chose not to reveal this information to us until now. After all, we have only known each other for a few days." A corner of her mouth inched up in a half smile. "I do hope you will feel safe to share your adventures with us, now."

I released a shaky breath and nodded slowly. "Yes. I really want this to work. I want us to be able to trust each other and get to know each other like family."

Kawehi's eyes softened and David smiled at me. "We'll appreciate the honesty, but everyone deserves to have their privacy. And you keeping secrets won't make you any less our granddaughter. Right?" David asked with a raised brow in his wife's direction.

"Of course." Kawehi rolled her eyes. "Although, when it comes to your powers and the Greek gods, I'll ask for you to be as forthcoming as possible. It's a matter of safety. For you, and for the rest of our coven."

That was more than fair. And now that I knew I hadn't lost the last two members of my family before I had even gotten the chance to properly know them, I felt much better. Lighter.

"Then I guess I should probably explain why we're currently on Earth, shouldn't I?"

Archer tensed next to me, but I ignored him. I had already trusted my grandparents with everything else, so it only made sense to tell them that we might have put them in danger by coming here. If the Greek deities tracked us all the way here, my grandparents might become more involved with Olympus than they had ever imagined was possible. They deserved to know.

So, I started explaining the situation: how I had unknowingly become the face of the human rebellion on Olympus and how—

I stopped abruptly because my phone was vibrating in my pocket. Someone was calling. The only people who had this phone number were in this room though, so who would—

Holy shit.

"Sadie is calling." The words fell out on their own, and I stared for a second at the screen, shocked.

Archer asked "What?" in surprise, before shifting to look at the screen too. He swore under his breath right as I shook myself out of my stupor and answered.

"Sadie?" I asked, voice shaking with a mix of hope and dread. Was it even going to be her? Or would someone else answer and crush my hopes that we'd finally found her?

On the other side of the line, I could hear hurried breathing, as if the caller was running. What was happening? My chest constricted in fear.

"Kalani? Is that you?"

Tears burst from my eyes at hearing Sadie's voice for the first time in weeks. This was her. This was really her.

"Yes, it's me. Oh, my gods, Sadie! Where are you? How are you?" My words were rushed with the fear that the call would be too short for me to ask all of my questions.

I was so focused on the call that I barely registered Archer reacting next to me, hands in his hair and shoulders slumped in relief. Søren and Nafula were pacing, murmuring things I couldn't focus on.

"Thank the stars," Sadie breathed in relief through the phone. She stopped speaking for a second, her breathing still heavy and labored. What was happening on the other side of the line? "I wasn't sure who had been calling me so often. I was hoping it was a friend, but I wasn't sure, and I couldn't risk—"

Sadie stopped abruptly. It sounded like there were things crunching in the background – like leaves maybe? Was Sadie in a forest of some kind?

"I'm sorry Kalani, I can't stay very long. But I…" She stopped and dropped her voice down, speaking so softly that I could barely hear her. "I need help."

Minutes later, we were landing in the middle of a snowy forest, across the globe from Hawaii. I was still slightly overwhelmed by the thought that magic had transported us halfway across the world in a matter of seconds.

"Where is she?" Søren asked, his voice shaking. From the moment his twin sister had contacted us, he had been antsy to see her.

Unfortunately, she was nowhere to be seen. All we could see were snow-laden trees and bushes all around us. No sign of Sadie or anyone else for that matter.

"Are we sure we came to the right place?" I asked Archer, hoping that we hadn't messed up in the coordinates. Since the translocator needed at least a dozen hours to recharge after transporting all four of us along such a long distance, there would be no way for us to correct the situation.

"Yes. I used the exact coordinates Sadie gave us." Archer still frowned and looked around, as confused as the rest of us.

Why were we here, without Sadie in sight? And why did Sadie need us? She hadn't given me any other information apart from coordinates and a pleading to come as quickly as possible. The whole call had lasted less than thirty seconds before Sadie had announced that she had to go and wouldn't be able to answer the phone anymore.

It was all very secretive and worrying. What had Sadie gotten herself into, and where had she been all this time? Had she been hiding in this place for the past month? And why did she seem so panicked on the call?

"Why would she even be doing here?" Nafula echoed my thoughts, rubbing her arms to warm up.

This whole situation was strange, and I really hoped we would get answers soon.

Right then, snow cracked on my right, prompting me to shift and look through the forest for the source of the sound. And there, in between the trees and half hidden in the shadows, was Sadie with a man slung over her shoulders.

What in the—

"Sadie!" Søren rushed forward to reach his twin sister, grabbing the unconscious man from her hold.

Sadie seemed a little surprised at her brother's reaction. She stared at him for a couple of moments, mouth half opened, before breaking down in a sob. In the next moment, Søren brought Sadie in a one-armed hug filled with tears and so much emotions that I could feel their love from where I stood. And while I couldn't hear their words, I knew that they were saying the words they both needed to hear.

It was so good to see them like this, especially after the way their relationship had exploded after Mei's death. That moment meant so much more than just a hug – it was both twins showing their love and forgiveness for each other.

Archer put his arm around my shoulders and squeezed softly. The physical contact was a reminder that we had made it – almost all of us, at least. We had made it out of the Tournament, and now we were back together. It was full circle, and I knew we would find a way to make it out of trouble, together.

When the twins finally separated, they both looked like they had been through the ringer. Their eyes were red from tears, but they had smiles on their faces. They were the perfect picture of sibling love – except for the man still unconscious over Søren's shoulder.

It looked like we were going to ignore the unconscious guy, though, because Sadie stepped toward us, next.

Nafula was the closest to her, and they exchanged a hug that was long enough to suggest that I had been right in thinking that the two women had become much closer after the end of the Tournament.

Then, Sadie stepped closer to Archer and me. It was so good to see her after worrying for her for so long.

"It's nice to see you guys, although I didn't miss the nauseating love demonstrations," Sadie joked hesitatingly.

Archer shook his head with a quick laugh before taking the two steps that separated him from his friend. They exchanged a quick but strong hug, filled with all of the friendly love and care they had for each other after years of being in each other's lives.

It made my heart ache to see all of my friends back together. And as Sadie stepped away from Archer and toward me, I felt a twinge of guilt in my chest. I never should have given Sadie that much space after the Tournament, not after everything that had happened after the fourth trial. She had needed me, and I hadn't been there for her.

I was the shittiest of friends.

"I am so sorry, Sadie," I murmured, tears threatening to fall.

My friend smiled softly – the same smile as before, but her eyes were full of pain and shadows that hadn't been there a month before. Whatever she had been through since the end of the Tournament, it had changed her.

"It's all good, Kalani. I needed time to find myself, and I needed to do it alone."

And then we were in each other's arms and we were crying, and a part of my heart was sliding back into place. Finding Sadie back was healing.

We were meant to be all together, not separated like we had been for too many weeks.

"I missed you, K," Sadie whispered in my ear.

A laugh that sounded a little like a sob left my chest. "I miss you too. So much."

Gods, I was a mess of emotions, right then. But in the best way.

"Hey, guys? The man is waking up. Is that good news, or not?" Søren called out from where he stood.

Sadie immediately jumped out of our embraced and ran toward her brother. In seconds, she was knocking the man unconscious again with an elbow hit right in his temple.

"So, I'm guessing he is not a friend?" Nafula asked, incredulous.

Sadie winced and rubbed her forehead with obvious discomfort. "Not really, no. But I guess I should explain what has been going on and why I asked you guys for help."

A few minutes later, I was still reeling from discovering that Sadie had gone rogue on the Order of Hunters, had infiltrated a safe haven for Coppers hiding away from the gods, had almost been imprisoned for life after being discovered, and might or might not be in love with a Copper. That last part was more inference than straight-up information from Sadie, but I could tell from the way she was talking about that Matteo guy that there was more than what she was telling us upfront.

And the guy who was now taking a nice nap on a patch of ground that wasn't too snowy was a Hunter that Sadie had found sneaking around the entrance of the Refuge right as she was escaping. He had been part of a group, and while all of the other Hunters and Huntresses had left the premises, this dude had decided to stay a little longer and explore around the mountain where the Refuge was located.

Sadie explained that, when she had stepped foot outside of the Refuge, she had ended up pretty much face to face with the guy, and she had had no other option but to knock him out and take him with her as she fled.

Then, once she'd been far enough from the Refuge, she had finally turned on her phone. My new number had been the only one that had called multiple times and hadn't been saved beforehand, so she'd called back to see who it was, hoping it was a friend rather than a foe.

And here we were. All of us fugitives from Mount Olympus, and now kidnappers of a Hunter who had been in the wrong place at the wrong time.

What a day.

"And how come you guys weren't on Olympus?" Sadie asked once she was done explaining the mess that she'd found herself in.

"We were on our way to see mountain goats, actually, and—"

"Shut it, Søren," Nafula hissed with a tap on his chest.

This time, it was our turn to explain how we had ended up in the middle of a rebellion led by all of the human servants on Olympus and had been forced to escape from vengeful gods who wanted to kill us as examples – me more so than the others, but still, we were in this together. Then, I told Sadie about my powers, meeting my paternal grandparents, and learning about all of the other magic users that existed on Earth.

By the time we were all done with our stories, all of us were silent for a few seconds, trying to wrap our heads around both the delicate situations we were in and the dangerous implications of the information that we had collectively gathered.

Between groups of Copper resistance scattered throughout Earth, the humans rebelling against the gods on Olympus, and potentially hundreds of thousands of magic users who didn't have a drop of ichor in their blood... well, that was information that could bring down the order that the Greek deities had created in their perfect world.

We – and the knowledge we now carried – had become even bigger threats to the rule of the Olympians.

And that was an issue when we had a Hunter that was probably very loyal to the gods unconscious next to us.

"What are we doing now, then? With him," I nodded in the guy's direction, "and with the gods?"

My friends remained silent for a few seconds, before Archer spoke, choosing his words carefully. "The way I see it, we have two options. The first one is to continue to hide and stay on the run from the gods. We can hope that, in a few months, the rebellion on Olympus will be squashed and the gods won't be as determined to find us anymore. They will probably relax their search for a deserter too after a while," Archer added in Sadie's direction.

Well, that didn't sound like great odds. We would be hoping that the gods would get bored of hunting us and would decide to do something else with their endless time. However, I knew in my bones that Artemis could hold a grudge for a long time, and I represented everything she had been fighting against for a while, now. I wasn't so sure that things would die down anytime soon.

"And the second option?" Nafula asked, still shivering from the cold.

"We fight back."

The Black Copper raised her eyebrows at Archer. "We fight back? Against the gods of Olympus?"

"I mean, we have options, now. We know that there are quite a few groups of Coppers hiding on Earth. There's the Refuge, but I know there are others, and I know that the leaders of the Refuge would be able to contact those other communities of Coppers around the world." Sadie frowned, her gaze unfocused, deep in thoughts. "If we tell them that we have a plan to stop the gods from continuing to force Coppers to fight in the Tournament, they might be willing to fight with us."

"Do we have a plan to end the Tournament, though? People on Olympus seemed way too excited to witness our edition of the Tournament. And it's a power play for the gods, a way to control the Goldens and the Coppers." Nafula shivered but I knew it wasn't from the cold anymore – it was disgust for the methods the gods were using to control Olympus. "It's not going to be easy to put an end to it."

No, it wouldn't be easy. But now we knew something that could change everything. And all thanks to my grandparents.

"We know that the gods' rhetoric that the Tournament is necessary to keep Olympus hidden from humans is false. There are people out there who have magic and they manage to remain hidden from non-magic users without having to move to a separate realm. It would be possible for Coppers to be trained to use their powers responsibly on Earth."

Søren nodded at my words, his eyebrows furrowed in concentration. "And if we can show that the Tournament is not needed anymore, that should spur the Coppers that are still on Earth to fight for their freedom to remain on Earth, with their families. That could even help us gain the support of many Goldens who don't want to see their children die every year in the Tournament."

What if we really could do that? What if we could stop the Tournament from ever happening again? What if we could save all future Mei's and Charlie's from having to die for the right to serve the gods on Olympus for the rest of their lives?

A new energy grew in my chest from the anticipation of what could be – what we might be able to achieve.

"We might be able to do it." Archer buried his hands in his pockets before turning his gaze on each on us. "It won't be easy, though. We will have to convince the Coppers to stand with us. And we will have to find other magic users who are willing to act as living proof that it is possible to have magic and live safely on Earth. And neither Coppers nor magic users will be easily convinced to even listen to us."

Archer was right. This half-baked plan of ours would be almost impossible to achieve. But if there was even a small chance to stop the Tournament from ever happening again, I was willing to take it.

"I'm sure we can do it. I don't want to hide and run anymore. I want to make sure no one else has to fight in that awful Tournament ever again." My last words had power behind them, the kind of determination I hadn't felt in a long time.

Sadie met my gaze and we held each other's eyes for a few long moments. Whatever she saw in my eyes must have convinced her because she nodded. "Never again."

I turned toward Søren next. His jaw was tight, and I knew instinctively that he was thinking of Mei. He didn't say anything, but he nodded with such determination that I knew he was all in.

Next to Søren, Nafula seemed more unsure. As I met her eyes, she sighed. "I mean, I wouldn't be against stopping the Tournament forever. And I don't think we have much to lose in trying."

That was as much of an agreement as I knew I'd get from her. I could understand why she was being cautiously optimistic. After all, she'd seen first-hand how cruel the gods could be during the Tournament, and she hadn't had a tight-knit group to support her through it like I had.

Finally, I turned to face Archer. The last time I'd decided to do something kind of stupid – namely, standing up to the gods – he had not taken the news well.

"What about you, Sunshine? Are you ready to become Olympus' most wanted troublemaker with me?"

Archer rolled his eyes at my words and my taunting grin, but he couldn't contain a smile of his own.

"Of course, Mayfield. I'll be a troublemaker with you. Always. We're a team."

And I'd be lying if I said his words didn't make butterflies fly in my stomach. Damn it, I loved him. And I loved that we could decide to do something stupid and courageous together.

Right then, a soft moan came from our prisoner.

"Stars, I had forgotten about him," Søren groaned.

A strained laugh left all of us. This was a reminder that we were going to have to start our potentially ill-advised, probably dangerous plan right away.

But I wasn't scared.

No, I was excited. I couldn't wait to shake Mount Olympus up until the Tournament was in shambles. And we might put ourselves into a lot of trouble – a lot more than we already were in – but I was ready to leave my name in the Olympian history books.

What was this saying again? Something about nice women not making history, or something? Well, either way, I was done being the nice, quiet girl.

Now, I was fighting for what was right.

Chapter Thirty-Three

Sadie

The issue with deciding to go and take down an oppressive system that the Greek gods of Mount Olympus had created and reinforced for centuries was that we couldn't quite do it by ourselves. Destroying the Tournament as an institution and working to save hundreds of Coppers from death during the trials required a lot of manpower.

We needed allies.

Unfortunately, our potential allies didn't particularly love us, right now.

Far from it, actually, seeing as the leaders of the Refuge had been ready to imprison me for life when they had discovered that I was a Golden. How were they going to react when I showed up with my four friends in tow and a Hunter we were keeping as prisoner for lack of a better idea?

Stars, I could already imagine how poorly things were going to go.

Our first plan of action was to make allies in the magic-user communities around Earth. That started with Kalani's grandparents, seeing as they were the ones most likely to help us. Kalani's grandmother was our best bet to reach other witches and maybe even other magic-users throughout Earth.

So, here we were, waiting for Kalani to finish her phone call with her grandparents to ask them for support. Unsurprisingly, Kalani seemed to be having a tough time convincing her grandmother of the importance of the situation, especially through a phone call.

From where she stood on the other side of the small cave that we'd set up shop in, Nafula waved me over. I joined her, slightly uncomfortable around the woman because we had been close after the Tournament, and while we hadn't been *together*, I still felt weird about what had happened with Matteo. Not much had happened since we hadn't even kissed, but the emotional connection I had with the French Copper was very different from the small romantic connection Nafula and I had shared.

I just hoped Nafula hadn't decided to embark on this adventure with the hope that something would be rekindled between us.

Still, as I stood beside the girl that I'd shared a lot of fun moments with, I couldn't help but be thankful that she had come here. As a friend and, selfishly, as a Copper. She would have a much easier time talking to the people of the Refuge than the rest of us would.

"Do you think she's going to get through to her grandma?" Nafula asked softly, looking at Kalani who was now frowning in the emptiness.

Oh, so we weren't going to talk about *us*. I was more than fine with that.

"I hope so. I don't think we can do this if we don't have a proof that it's possible to live on Earth and have magic."

Nafula nodded slowly. "Am I the only one who's still shocked about all of this? Like, shifters, witches, centaurs, and vampires? It feels like being inside of a movie, which is so crazy because we literally have powers, too. But somehow it feels different to know all of these people exist."

"No, I feel that way too. I feel so blindsided to learn that there's this whole world of magic out there, and we had no idea. Can you imagine how people are going to react if we show up to Olympus with a shark shifter that doesn't have a single drop of ichor in their blood?"

Nafula chuckled at the thought and I followed along. I would pay good money to see the reactions of some of the people who acted like they owned magic from their homes on Olympus when they realized there was a whole other magical world out there.

Kalani started to pace in the snow, her face down and focused on the phone conversation. Both Nafula and I looked at her for long seconds, trying to determine whether things were going our way or not.

"What happens if we fail?" Nafula suddenly asked.

I didn't need to look at my friend to know that this was a very serious question, and that she was scared. It was almost out-of-character for Nafula to be so vulnerable about her fears, because she always put on a brave face and a tough act. But she was still a young woman who had been put through too much and was still fighting for something so much bigger than herself – it was normal for her and all of us to be terrified.

I just wished I could reassure her.

"I don't know. But we'll continue to fight for our lives and for what's right." I reached for Nafula's hand and squeezed her fingers softly, letting her know I was there with her. "And we'll do it all together."

It was the best I could offer, and I hoped it would be enough.

Before Nafula could answer, Kalani said goodbye and ended the call. The moment she turned our way, I knew that the vulnerable moment was over. We had to be focused and determined.

"How did it go?" Archer asked, jumping up from where he and Søren had been sitting on a rock and guarding our esteemed guest.

Kalani ran a hand through her dark hair, looking completely exhausted. "Not great. But they will talk to the people they know and try to gather a group of people that could testify for us."

It was good news, but all of us could see that the conversation had taken a lot out of Kalani.

Archer went to his girlfriend and wrapped his arms around her, comforting her and whispering something into her ear. Witnessing the love between them was incredibly bittersweet, and it reminded me of the mess I'd made of the situation with Matteo.

Stars, I wished I could hug him right then, and I knew that was completely ridiculous – I was supposed to be focusing on destroying the social hierarchy of Mount Olympus, not on feelings I might or might not have about a guy. No matter how sweet he was.

I needed to get a grip on myself, especially since we all knew what our next step was.

After a few moments, Kalani stepped apart of Archer, and after he dropped a kiss on her forehead, they both turned toward us.

"So, I'm guessing we are going to step two in our grand plan to save the world?" Søren asked, trying to break the heavy silence with a touch of humor.

A small smirk crept upon Kalani's lips, and she rolled her eyes at my twin. "I don't know about saving the world, but yes. I guess it's time to go meet Sadie's new friends."

My heart was pounding as I stepped in the cave that led to the Refuge. There was a mix of fear, anticipation, and excitement at the prospect of opening the door to the Refuge and seeing everyone I had left in it.

Things could go extremely wrong once I opened the door. Very, very wrong. And I was worried about how my friends and the leaders of the Refuge would interact. One thing was for sure, the leaders of the Refuge – and especially dear Thomas – would not be happy to see me come back like nothing had happened and with an entourage.

Frankly, I was surprised that they hadn't intercepted us before we even made it to the cave.

"I was expecting something more... impressive? Or maybe something more cloak-and-dagger, like a villain lair or something," Søren commented as he entered the cave, a firm hand holding the Hunter's bicep and forcing him to walk with us.

We hadn't found a great solution for the Hunter I had intercepted and quite forcefully stopped from looking around the Refuge. It was pretty ironic that I was about to open the door to the Refuge with him in tow, but we had no other choice. We couldn't very well let him go, because he had seen and heard way too much about the Refuge and our plans to bring down the Tournament. Leaving him tied up in a remote place was asking for trouble – Hunters were trained professionals and we couldn't be sure that he wouldn't manage to escape or that one of his coworkers wouldn't find him. The only other option would be to kill him, but I couldn't bring myself to do it. After all, this guy hadn't been given a choice but to participate in the system that the gods had created. He didn't know any better than the Tournament – for stars' sake, he had won the Tournament and probably believed that there was no other way to live as a Copper than to survive the trials.

It was a particularly cruel irony to force many of the Tournament winners to enlist as Hunters and Huntresses and have them bring the next batches of Coppers to the Tournament.

If we killed this guy just because he had been in the wrong place at the wrong time, were we any better than the gods?

So, here we were, carrying a disoriented and very unhappy Hunter around, his wrists tied as securely as we could behind his back and a makeshift blindfold over his eyes, hoping that our decision to give him mercy wouldn't come back to bite us in the ass.

"It's not supposed to be eye catching, Søren. Being inconspicuous is the whole point." I gave my twin a look that told him very clearly that he should try to be inconspicuous too.

"It seems strange that we were able to approach the place so easily, though," Archer remarked with a frown.

I agreed with him. It was strange that there had been no outward reaction to our approach. But I also knew that the leaders of the Refuge often relied on a defensive strategy that focused on hiding, locking everything down, and hoping that no one would find the entry to their bunker.

The issue for them was that I knew where the entry was, and I'd seen Thomas open it right before my eyes.

It took me only a couple of minutes to find the right part of the rocky wall to press. Then, it was only a matter of reproducing the movements that I had seen Thomas do two weeks before. And I had watched very carefully what was happening that day, knowing very well that I would need to know this one day.

When the door finally revealed itself and opened, I released a sigh of relief.

But the relief was short-lived, because as soon as the door opened, I felt the magic leaving my body. A second later, the door opened wide to reveal a mess hall where a half-dozen people were waiting for us with weapons and clear determination to defend the Refuge against us.

So much for a warm welcome home.

"Well, guys, I was hoping for a nicer welcome," I announced as I took a step closer to the six Coppers who stood in front of me.

I wasn't surprised to see Thomas, Ken, Bella, and Liam ready to defend their home. Standing next to Liam was Sarah, a girl who had been pretty proficient during the few classes I'd taught. But the one who surprised me the most was Matteo, standing on the outskirts of the group.

Our eyes met and locked for a few long seconds. I wanted to talk to him and tell him that I had missed him, that I wasn't here for trouble, that I was here to help.

Instead, I ripped my eyes away from Matteo's dark irises, and focused back on the biggest threat right then: Thomas.

The Copper in question decided to be the spokesperson – unsurprisingly – and took a step forward, his dagger glinting in the light.

"How dare you come back here and betray us?" he spat with so much hate that I felt it coating my skin.

I sensed my friends entering the mess hall and moving around me, showcasing their support. But I didn't dare drop my eyes away from Thomas and the others for even a second.

"Turn your powers on, Tommy. I am not here to betray you. I didn't bring my friends over there with the goal to bring you to Olympus to compete in the Tournament." I gave him a pointed look, making sure he could feel the truth in my words. "I am *not* the enemy."

Thomas' jaw clenched with what I knew was frustration because he knew that I was telling the truth. And that made him oh so mad.

"Why are you here, then?" Ken asked, his voice cold and sharp. I could see the distrust in his eyes. "And why did you bring so many of your *friends* with you?"

Well, this was going to be the moment of truth. I needed to convince these people that their best bet was to join us on our wild quest to destroy the Tournament. And based on their defensive body language, I wasn't sure they would even be open to the conversation.

But I had to try. Kalani had spent an hour convincing her grandparents to help us. Now, it was my time.

"We are here because we need your help."

As soon as the words left my mouth, Thomas exploded in a sardonic laugh. "Oh my god, the irony!" he exclaimed with way too much glee for my liking.

Around him, the others looked both confused and surprised. Bella was staring at me with a deep frown, and Liam's eyebrows were ready to hit his hairline.

"Let's listen to her, guys," Matteo interjected, looking at me with what I could only define as hope. Hope that I was going to redeem myself in the eyes of the Refuge leaders.

Thomas opened his mouth, surely to say something nasty again, but Ken gave him a strong look that shut him up instantly. Thank the stars for that.

"You have two minutes to convince us that we should let you walk in the Refuge," Ken announced, his voice slapping in the silence like a whip.

I could have laughed then, because there was nothing the six Coppers could do to prevent us from fully entering the Refuge if we wanted to. My friends and I had been trained by the best and tested through fire and pain. Even with Bella restraining our magic, we were a hundred times stronger than the leaders of the Refuge.

But I didn't say any of that out loud. Ken was offering me an opening, and I would be stupid not to take it.

"My friends and I are currently on the run from the gods of Olympus. We all competed in the last edition of the Tournament. While most of us are Goldens and were forced to compete for political reasons, Nafula here is a Copper, and Kalani is a human who was mistakenly enrolled in the Tournament. We survived, but we didn't do it quietly. Since then, a lot has happened, too much for two minutes of explanations. But the main point is that we are currently fugitives from Olympus." I nodded toward Kalani to my left. "Kalani has become the figurehead of the human rebellion on Olympus, specifically from the human servants who are fighting for more rights and freedom. The gods want to make an example out of her, and we can't let that happen."

Archer took a small step closer to his girlfriend, as if to protect her from the mere mention of danger.

"On my part, I have obviously deserted the Order of Hunters by deciding to help Matteo come to the Refuge and then refusing to take all of you to Olympus. Gods don't take kindly to deserters."

"And where do we come in? Do you want a place to hide?" Bella asked, still confused but genuinely trying to understand where I was coming from.

"No, we want to ask you to fight with us." I stood taller and tried to convey confidence through my posture and words. "While I was here, in the Refuge, my friends were hiding on the other side of the planet, and they discovered that there are a lot of magic users on Earth who are not descended from the Olympian gods."

Nafula was the one who continued the explanation. As a Copper herself, she was in the best position to relate to the Coppers in front of us. "We want to destroy the Tournament once and for all. The gods have kept hidden the fact that there are people out there who live among humans their whole lives and contain their magic just fine. Our plan is to prove to every single person on Mount Olympus that the Tournament is useless and that there are other ways to ensure that the human world doesn't learn of our existence."

In front of us, the six Coppers remained silent for a long moment. They exchanged a few looks between themselves and seemed to replay our words in their heads. And I could understand that the explanation was hard to believe and wrap their head around, but I needed them to fully grasp the implications of what we were proposing.

"If we manage to destroy the Tournament, none of you will have to hide in here any longer. This would mean freedom for you and all future Coppers."

Matteo's gaze latched onto mine and his eyes were shining with unshed tears of hope. That man dreamed of having a life of his own, of having choices and opportunities. None of this was truly possible within the Refuge, and I was offering him everything he dreamed of.

For that reason alone, I was determined to make sure our plan worked and the Tournament never happened again.

I would make sure Matteo was able to walk outside of the Refuge without fear of being hunted down again. No matter what, he would be free. All of them would be free.

"And what about the guy who's restrained? Is he one of your friends too?" Thomas sneered at us.

"No. If you want to know, he is one of the Hunters that was sniffing around the Refuge. Sadie took care of him for you all," Søren drawled with nonchalant dangerousness.

Warmth spread through my chest as Søren defended me. Stars, I had missed feeling like I mattered to him, like we were closer than blood.

Søren's glare must have been icy because Thomas's shoulders slumped forward and he shifted away from my twin. The satisfaction I felt was entirely unnecessary and petty when we were trying to save hundreds of lives.

"And why do you need us, exactly?" Matteo asked, his voice shaking with poorly hidden excitement.

This time, Kalani took control of the situation. "We need the support of Coppers who will refuse to participate in the Tournament. A lot of Coppers. And we know that you guys have ways to contact other groups of Copper resistance through Earth."

Tense silence fell onto the room. I couldn't blame the Coppers for being wary of the situation. After all, we were asking them to contact the other pockets of resistance around the world and face the gods with us. It was scary, and it was everything they had been trying to avoid for years.

But the promise of freedom was valuable. These people had been on the run for so long, hiding and scared of the shadows around them. And now that we were putting their freedom on a silver platter…

Well, they were interested, even though they didn't want to be.

"So? Can we sit and discuss the situation?" I asked with a hesitant smile.

Ken frowned but still nodded. "Bella will maintain your powers under lock for the time being, but yes. Let's sit and talk."

Chapter Thirty-Four

Sadie

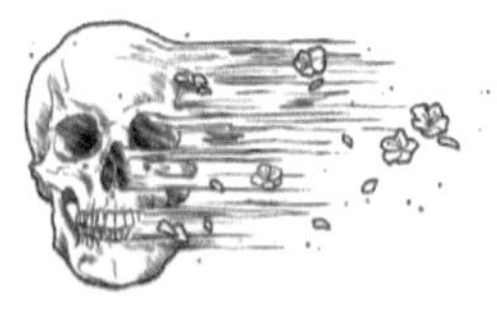

Three hours later, we were finally taking a break from discussing goals, strategies, and everything that could possibly go wrong under the sun.

I was exhausted. Mentally and physically, the day had completely drained me.

And it wasn't over.

We had agreed on many points, including that the six Coppers currently representing the Refuge would ask the rest of their community members if they wanted to join our endeavor. But we still had a lot of things to figure out. For instance, how were we going to transport potentially dozens of people to Olympus with only two translocators, mine and Archer's? Should we even go to Olympus or should we try to bring the gods to Earth? What happened if none of the other Coppers throughout Earth wanted to join us? And how would we retreat if things didn't go well with the gods?

"Where is everyone else? I thought you said there were like thirty people in this place," Kalani whispered to me as everyone started standing up and stretching around us.

That was a good point – we still didn't know where all of the other Coppers were hiding. Were they all locked in their rooms, worried about what was happening outside of their bubble of peace?

Bella who had gotten closer to us must have heard Kalani's question because she quipped a response. "We have a part of the Refuge that is hidden and closed off from the rest of the compound. It's kind of like a safe room. Everyone else is in there."

She didn't offer to show us where it was. We were still foreigners and I respected that she was going to protect her people no matter what. But the way she smiled softly at me was clearly a peace offering.

I couldn't wait a second to take that peace offering – I had missed Bella so much in the past couple of days. That girl had quickly become a great friend, and it had been heartbreaking to see her believing that I had betrayed her and her family.

"That's good. I'm glad you guys were prepared."

At my words, Bella's shoulders dropped, and the corners of her eyes relaxed in relief. This was my peace offering back. And she was taking it too.

She reached out for my hand and squeezed it softly for a second. "I'm glad you came back."

Then she was running off to talk to Liam and her brother, the latter of which looked like he was holding the weight of the world on his shoulders. Sarah and Thomas were deep in conversation on the other side of the room, and Matteo…

Matteo was making a beeline for me.

And he looked determined, his eyes fixed on me with an intensity that made my whole body burn.

With a laugh and raised eyebrows that said 'Damn, girl,' Kalani stood up and left me alone. A second later, Matteo was standing in front of me, his mere presence washing over my body like a wave of electricity.

"Can I speak to you for a second?" Matteo swallowed roughly and I couldn't stop staring at his Adam's apple with way too much fascination. "Alone?"

My 'yes' sounded too breathy, but I didn't care. I was too busy following Matteo out of the mess hall and trying to calm my heart from pounding like I was running a marathon.

As soon as we turned into the hallway and the chatter from the others died down, my whole body started vibrating with anticipation. I had never been this close to Matteo without my secrets holding my heart prisoner. This was the first time that Matteo and I were standing in front of each other without anything muddying the atmosphere between us.

It was just the two of us, staring at each other's souls in the silence.

"You're back," he whispered suddenly.

"I'm back," I repeated, a smile creeping onto my lips. He looked so overwhelmed and slightly unsure if this was real. It was heartwarming, somehow, to see him so affected by my return.

"You scared me when you left. We didn't hear from you or from whoever was tripping the wards beforehand, and I…" He stopped and shut his eyes, as if to keep his worried thoughts away.

"Hey, I was fine. I can take care of myself." I reached for his hand and intertwined my fingers with his. "But I couldn't wait to come back here."

Matteo opened his brown eyes, pupils so dilated that his eyes almost looked black. "For your plan to take down the Tournament?"

Oh, I knew where he was going with this. He wasn't that subtle. After everything I had put him through, I could be the one to take a leap of faith, there. "Yes, but not just for that. For you, too."

The smile that bloomed on Matteo's face was so bright that it rivaled the sun. I was almost blinded by it.

"Good," he drawled, his voice gravely and sexy as sin. He tugged on our joined hand until I took a step forward, so close to him that I could feel the heat coming from his skin. "And do you have any more secrets that would make me look at you differently if I learned them?"

I shook my head slowly, knowing exactly where this man was going with his questions. I could remember our last conversation word-for-word, so I knew that he was referring to the last sentence I'd told him before leaving the Refuge.

I wanted to kiss you that day, but I couldn't do it with when you didn't know who I was.

And now that he knew who I was…

"So, if I try to kiss you, will you be okay with it?"

"Yeah. I might be easily convinced."

Stars, who would have thought that consent was so sexy?

Matteo hummed at my agreement and dropped his gaze to my lips. My whole body was vibrating with anticipation and excitement. I had never been so excited for a kiss before and this—

"Good to know," Matteo deadpanned before turning on his heels.

What in the stars? What was happening? I shook my head to try to shake what was sure to be an illusion. But no, there was the French Copper, walking away from me with a pep to his steps.

"What—"

Matteo turned his face to look at me, a shit-eating grin on his face. "Did you think I was going to make this so easy? No, no, no, Zombie girl, you'll have to work for it."

And then he walked back into the mess hall, leaving me alone in the hallway, still shell-shocked.

What in the stars had happened?

Unsurprisingly, I kept receiving dark looks from the Coppers assembled in front of us. Farther in the back of the room, Søren, Archer, Kalani, and Nafula were getting suspicious glances, but I was the one being ostensibly glared at by most of the Refuge inhabitants.

I couldn't blame them, seeing as the last they'd seen of me was the little incident where I had almost choked Tim to death and then disappeared from their lives.

On top of that, most of them had spent the past day in a separate bunker that was hidden in the depth of the Refuge, not knowing what was happening around them. The stress had heightened everyone's emotions.

They had every right to be wary and distrustful of me being back here, standing in front of them next to their leaders.

Now, did I wish that everyone would be excited to see me, or at least positively curious about my whereabouts from the last couple of days? Of course. It would make the current situation a lot easier. Turned out, convincing people to go to metaphorical war against gods was tough when they didn't trust or like you much. And I didn't want to resort to fear or threats, so my only hope was that the inhabitants of the Refuge would decide that fighting for their freedom was a better plan than hiding here for the rest of their days.

"We still have some things to figure out, especially regarding how we will approach confronting the Olympians." Ken's voice was strong and confident as he addressed his people. He was really good at conveying the impression that everything was fine, and that this assembly was not a matter of life and death. "But we wanted to ask for your opinion on this. You all have a right to decide on what we are going to do. As a group."

"If the majority of people want to do this, will everyone else be forced to fight, too?" A young girl who wasn't older than fourteen asked, her voice shaking.

Bella shook her head emphatically. "No, honey, no one will be forced to do anything. If some people want to fight against the Olympians, that would be awesome. But no one will be blamed for not wanting to do something. The Refuge will remain open for everyone that desires to remain here."

The young girl nodded, but her body didn't quite relax. There was a heaviness that had settled over the crowd of Coppers in front of me. When Ken had talked about fighting for their freedom and being able to live on Earth without the fear of being hunted by the Olympians' minions, many people had had stars in their eyes. But the mere mention of going to Olympus and fighting the gods… well, the glint of hope in their eyes had dimmed. Very quickly.

"We are hoping to know your answers by tomorrow morning. Things won't be set in stone, but we do need to know if you would be willing to fight or not. Either way, we will do our best to keep all of you safe," Bella announced with a gentle smile to the crowd.

"And how do we know it's legit? We don't know these people," Tim hollered, pointing at my friends standing along the back wall, "and Sadie hasn't been the most reliable person ever. So, why should I decide to fight for them?"

Stars, the man's sneer was still just as annoying as it had been a couple of days ago. But I couldn't roll my eyes at his question – not when it was more than legitimate.

"I'm not asking you to fight for me," I retorted before Ken or Bella could answer. "I'm telling you that we have an opportunity to make sure no one ever has to compete and die in the Tournament again. Now, if you want to stay here and hope that Hunters never find you, that's your prerogative."

Tim was the first one to drop our staring contest, rolling his eyes and shrugging in that 'I don't care' way.

A few minutes later, everyone was splitting out and going to get dinner. Quiet chatter continued as small groups of Coppers discussed the situation and what they wanted to do. While I couldn't hear any of these conversations, I could tell based on the hunched shoulders and wide eyes that people were scared about the prospects of going to war against the gods.

"Well, you sure know how to work a room, Zombie girl."

I didn't have to turn around to know that Matteo had joined me on the makeshift stage we had made for the announcement. His every word dripped with amusement.

Even though the announcement hadn't quite gone as I had – naively – hoped for, I couldn't keep my frown on when Matteo was standing there, soft laughter leaving his chest.

I glanced at him from the corner of my eye, and he seemed way too happy about the situation. "I must have failed the class on how to motivate people to enlist in war. I'll complain to Zeus about the failings of the Olympian education system," I deadpanned.

Matteo chuckled and bumped his shoulder against mine. "Be sure to do that, because this was shameful. I mean, Tim could have become your war general, if only you hadn't antagonized him."

I almost choked on air at the thought of Tim having any sort of important position in whatever we were trying to do – could it be called a revolt? A rebellion? War seemed too strong, but rebellion sounded too soft.

"Oh, what a waste," I pouted playfully, irony dripping from my every word. "I might have to continue on with the antagonizing, just in case he didn't quite feel it the first time."

Matteo hummed along, looking at me with mirth in his dark brown eyes. He didn't say anything, though.

"What?" I asked, feeling slightly vulnerable under his watchful eyes.

"I just missed this." He didn't elaborate but he didn't need to – I knew exactly what he meant.

"I did too." My cheeks felt warm and time slowed down until it felt like everything had stopped around us. It was just the two of us, staring at each other's eyes, close enough to reach out and touch.

It was hard to forget about the world and completely lose myself in Matteo's eyes when there was so much riding on the next few days.

"Do you think they're going to want to fight with us?"

"I don't know. I hope so." One gentle finger under my chin, Matteo made sure I was looking in his eyes before continuing. "Either way, we will make it work. I believe in your plan. I believe in *you*, Zombie girl."

Was it possible for someone's heart to melt into goo just from a few murmured words and intense eye contact?

Someone called my name from somewhere behind me, but I couldn't escape the trap set by Matteo's gaze. I shouldn't be so easily distracted by a guy, not when there were so many important things to figure out and do still. Some part of my brain knew this was ridiculous. But here I was, incapable of thinking about something other than what it would feel like to kiss him.

The Copper must have been able to read my mind – or my face was an open book in that moment – because he smirked and dropped his forehead against mine. "I won't kiss you now, Sadie. We deserve a special moment." He sighed, as if this was also painful to him. "But I can't wait for it. And I'm proud of you for fighting for us."

I had a feeling that his words referred to fighting both for the two of us and for Coppers in general. It was moving to know that my actions were truly making a difference for him.

A second later, he was gone, striding toward Liam. But I was still stuck there, my heart swelling with the vulnerability that he had shared with me.

And as I joined Kalani and Søren at a table where they had brought some food for us to share, my heart was divided between hopeful joy and worry.

What if none of this worked out?

What if we failed miserably and all of the Coppers around me ended up forced to compete in the Tournament?

And based on the ambiance around the room, I wasn't the only one doubting our ability to succeed in destroying the Tournament once and for all.

Chapter Thirty-Five

Kalani

Our first night in the Refuge, I could barely sleep. Things had been moving so quickly lately that I was too overwhelmed for my brain to let me fall asleep peacefully. Even cuddling with Archer hadn't managed to make my thoughts slow down long enough for dreams to come.

By the time morning came and I opened my eyes from a fistful night, I was still exhausted.

And I was worried sick that none of the Coppers living here would be willing to fight against the gods.

What would we do then?

What were we supposed to do if we didn't have the support that we needed to convince Olympus that the Tournament would not need to happen ever again?

Will my friends and I be forced to remain on the run for weeks? Months? *Years?*

And even if we managed to stop the Tournament from happening ever again, would the gods let me stay alive? Or would

I still be made an example of in the hopes that it would stop the human servants on the mountain from continuing to rebel from their living conditions?

Was any of this worth it anyways? Or were we ants trying to go against Goliath?

"You're thinking way too loud for a morning, Mayfield."

Archer was still half asleep, his voice gravelly and rough. His eyes were still closed, but he reached with one arm and pulled me against his chest.

Even with the worried thoughts still spinning through my mind, I couldn't help but burrow closer to Archer.

"Sorry, I didn't mean to wake you up."

He shook his head slowly before nuzzling his face in my neck. "You know I love waking up next to you. Even when your cute brain is worrying too hard."

The man dropped a sleepy kiss against my skin and wrapped me tighter in his arms. The embrace was like being immersed in a bubble of safety and warmth. Knowing my Sunshine was there, with me, might not remove all of my worries, but it was the best way for me to relax and feel supported.

A part of my brain reminded me that cuddling in bed together wasn't very *'let's take a break to learn to be apart so we can be better together'* material, but I wasn't about to complain about it. So many things were happening around us lately that I needed to feel his presence grounded me in reality. We could continue to do our break thing once the day actually started.

"Maybe we should go and see if there's anything we can do to finish convincing people. Or maybe we should go and check on Sergio?"

Sergio was the Hunter that Sadie had knocked out when she'd escaped the Refuge a couple of days ago. We had been forced to put him in the only room in the Refuge that could be fully locked from the outside and kept secure. From what I understood, the room had initially been created to lock Sadie up when the leaders of the Refuge had discovered that she wasn't a Copper. That, and locking someone up in the first place, made me very uncomfortable. The issue was that Sergio had heard and seen too much, and he wasn't loyal to us but to the gods.

"Or maybe we should stay here, together, and enjoy our last free morning for what could be a while," Archer murmured against my skin.

"Where's my Sunshine that wants to control everything and make sure we always remain safe, especially if that means being prepared for everything at all times?" I asked playfully, pretending to look around for him.

The laugh that shook through his chest was loud against my ear and it brought a smile to my face. I loved this – feeling so close and comfortable with him. It made everything that had happened worth it, somehow, that I had found someone who I could be myself and feel loved with. Him, and the twins were blessings in disguise from the past few months.

At least, my friends and Archer made it as worth it as it could ever be, when competing in the Tournament had been so traumatizing for all of us.

And maybe he was right. Perhaps there wasn't much to do or say anymore, not when we wanted to let every Copper make their own informed decision without any coercion from our part.

So, I relaxed in my Sunshine's arms and decided to hold onto this moment of peace.

None of us knew what might come after today, and I wanted to absorb every last drop of happiness possible.

Just in case.

"So, what we are going to do is that whoever is willing to stand against the Olympian gods and help in the effort to bring down the Tournament, please go and stand to my right," Ken announced to the mess hall full of Coppers. "If you prefer to remain here, in the Refuge, then stay where you are. Again, there will be no blame laid on anyone based on their decision."

There was a tense energy floating through the room as people anxiously looked at their friends. There were only a few young children, but they were clinging to their family members, fear painted on their faces.

I couldn't imagine how hard it was for these people to make this decision. After all, they had been on the run for months, if not years, and facing the gods was probably among their worst fears. Weighing the hope for potential freedom against the certainty of danger… well, it wasn't easy. Especially not when they were living in this place, where they had evaded the Hunters and Huntresses of Olympus for years.

I had never had a choice when it came to my arrival on Mount Olympus. I also hadn't had a choice but to fight in the Tournament – not when the other option was *elimination*. And, to be honest, knowing what I did about Mount Olympus, I wasn't sure if I would have volunteered had I been in their situation.

Next to me, Sadie was as tense as a bow string. She had been exchanging murderous glares with the red-haired guy who held himself like he believed everyone should kiss his feet in admiration. I wasn't sure what was the beef between them, but the guy seemed like he was willing to go to extreme lengths to annoy my friend. I just hoped he hadn't gone around the Refuge making sure no one volunteered just to spite Sadie.

But we would be done wondering in the next few seconds, once everyone made their decision.

Except no one was moving. The nerves were mounting in me. What if no one wanted to try their luck against the Olympians and their Tournament? What if—

A guy finally moved from the crowd and walked to Ken's right side. At first, I couldn't see him clearly – I was slightly too short to be able to see above the heads of the many Coppers before me – but as soon as he left the crowd, I recognized him as Matteo. Sadie's guy, even though she denied it.

Well, her man was the very first person to make his choice known, and it might be the thing we needed to spur other people to make their move too.

A few seconds passed by with no movement, and the hope that had risen as Matteo had moved was quickly deflating. Until someone else walked to Matteo.

Liam.

Followed by the girl that had been there with the leaders of the Refuge and Matteo when we'd arrived at the Refuge – Sarah, maybe?

Once the plug had been removed, a flow of Coppers left the center of the mess hall and went to stand next to Matteo. After a couple of minutes, two thirds of the inhabitants of the Refuge were openly saying that they were willing to fight for their freedom.

It was inspiring, really. I had chills on my arms, and my heart was full of so much joy and pride at the determination that shone in all of these Coppers' eyes.

These people were willing to fight with us, and their trust in our plans was humbling. We couldn't afford to mess up. I wouldn't forgive myself if I led all of these people to Olympus just for them to end up being the contestants for the next edition of the Tournament.

"Great, thank you all for making your decision. We will spend the next few weeks ironing out all of the kinks in our plans and preparing everyone that is willing to fight. Some of our guests are willing to teach us how to use our magical powers more efficiently," Ken announced with a nod in our direction. I wouldn't be much help on the magical side of things, but my friends would.

And in the next few weeks, we would make sure that all of these Coppers were as ready as possible to support our demand that the Tournament be dismantled.

This was why, a few hours later, I was leaving the Refuge with Bella and Liam in tow.

"I can't believe you and Sadie met in the Tournament!" Bella exclaimed, her British accent adding a posh twist to the competition name. "Your mate is bloody strong and impressive, I wouldn't be against some tea, there. Make her feel more human, you know?" She laughed before giving me a conspiratorial look. "So, if you have some funny stories about Sadie, don't hesitate to share them."

Liam rolled his eyes at his girlfriend's antics but didn't reprimand her for asking for tea on Sadie. Gods, it was weird to hear people using today's slang again. After living surrounded by people who had lived on Olympus for years, and thus watched decades pass by on Earth without them, I had gotten used to hearing idioms from forty years ago. Listening to Bella was like diving back into my old life.

"I might have a few stories, but I don't know that they'll make you see Sadie as any less of a badass woman," I added with amusement.

"Yeah," Bella sighed. "I don't think there's any way to push Sadie off of her pedestal of greatness. Although, the way she blushes every time Matteo smolders her way…"

She snickered at her last words and I couldn't help but giggle too. It was true that Sadie got flustered when it came to Matteo, and it was really funny to witness – especially when she had enjoyed making fun of me when Archer and I had been getting closer to each other.

"Aren't we supposed to do something productive, here?" Liam asked with a seemingly serious tone, but his eyes sparkled with mischief.

The reminder of the purpose for our excursion was sobering. Now that we had started making arrangements with the inhabitants of the Refuge and were in the process of discussing our plans with two other pockets of rebellion in North America and Latin America, we needed answers regarding potential help from other magic-users.

That required me to call my grandparents.

I'd called them right before entering the Refuge and explained the whole situation to them. Seeing as we had been forced to leave their house before I'd been able to tell them about the whole running-from-the-Olympian-gods situation, that had made for an interesting phone call. By now, my grandparents were probably hoping that I would finally stop springing surprises on them – especially when those surprises came in the shape of vengeful gods.

All of that to say that I didn't particularly want to face my grandparents again, especially after the huge favor I had asked of them a couple of days ago.

But I needed to suck it up and call them back. Since there wasn't any phone service in the Refuge, I needed to go out in the open. Bella was there to keep any of my powers under wraps, and Liam was there to protect us – but especially Bella – in case of an ambush. Not that anyone with powers had been observed or felt by Bella anywhere close to the Refuge since we'd arrived, so we should be safe enough.

With a shaky breath and a mental push, I turned the phone on and dialed my grandfather's number.

As the tone sounded, my heart pounded in my ears. I really hoped that my grandparents had managed to recruit people that would be willing to help us out, but selfishly, I also hoped that they were still willing to deal with the laundry list of problems I was carrying around. It had taken me twenty-one years to find them and I didn't want to lose them only a week after meeting them.

Bella and Liam turned away from me, pretending like I had privacy in the middle of the forest, just close enough to the road that I had phone service. And I appreciated having the illusion of being alone for this call.

If only my grandfather could answer and if only my heartbeat would calm down, it would be—

"Kalani?"

"Hi, grandpa!"

"I am glad you called, honey. Are you doing okay?"

The concern in my grandfather's voice was a relief. My grandparents might be uncomfortable with the situation I had brought them into – which was understandable – but at least they still cared about me. That was a win, right?

"I'm good. We are safe here, so don't worry about me, okay?"

"We'll always worry about you, kid. You are our Keanu's daughter, which makes you blood. And we care about our family." This time it was my grandmother speaking, her words gentle and warm. Much more loving than they'd been the day before, when I had told them that we were trying to go to war with the Greek gods.

"I appreciate that. And I am sorry again for not telling you guys everything right away."

My grandmother hummed in the way she always did when I asked her a question about our powers, and she wanted me to think on it myself. David was a lot more talkative. "And we understand, Kalani. It was a surprise to learn about what's happening with the Greek gods, but we understand that you had to leave quickly once your friend called. You couldn't explain everything before you left our house."

I appreciated that. Guilt had swarmed through me for the past few days, and I was relieved to know that they didn't hold it against me. I was sure they still wished I had been honest from the start, but knowing they weren't mad was reassuring.

From the corner of my eye, I saw Liam look at his watch nervously before observing our surroundings. I knew both him and Bella didn't want to pressure me into making this a quick phone call, but we were both on a time crunch and way too exposed out in the open like this.

"I am sorry to cut this short, but I can't stay for too long. Were you able to talk to your friends in the magical community?"

I heard movement through the phone, as if my grandfather was giving the phone to his wife. Unsurprisingly, it was my grandmother that answered my question, her voice much closer to the phone now.

"I have been able to contact the rest of our coven, and they have agreed to consider helping you. Most of them seem to be willing to help you ensure this barbaric competition doesn't happen anymore." I didn't miss the *most* in there but decided to let my grandma finish without commenting on it. "I am still discussing with a few groups we have good relationships with, too. The shiver of shark shifters down the road from us doesn't seem to want anything to do with this, but I think I might have convinced a wolf shifter pack from Washington State to help, and maybe a couple of vampires. Most of them want more information regarding your plans and what they would need to do. None of them want to get themselves and their families in a dangerous situation without the assurance that every option has been considered and planned for."

I understood the reservations that everyone had. Deciding to help us take a stand against the gods of Olympus was no trivial matter. We weren't asking them to fight for us, more to bring evidence that the Tournament wasn't needed for the protection of humans. But we also couldn't assure them that there wouldn't be violence involved.

However, knowing that there were people that were willing to help us… well, it meant the world.

"Thank you so much, grandma. This means so much to me, and I can't wait to meet the rest of our coven." I had tears in my eyes at the thought of meeting more of my family, of the people with whom I shared so much history and magic. "And I promise that we will give you some more information tomorrow. Most of the Coppers here have decided to join us, so we are going to go over our plans and I'll share everything as soon as I can."

Next to me, Bella was silently clapping her hands in excitement and Liam was smiling, which was quite an impressive show of joy for him – from what I'd witnessed so far, at least.

"Of course, honey. The coven is your family, too, and we protect each other. No matter what," Kawehi announced, her voice carrying so much determination and faith that it gave me goosebumps.

David agreed, and I felt a smile on my face through the tears. I had a family, and that family was willing to go to war for me. That had never been the case before, not even when I had Mom and Makaio.

Soon enough, it was time to leave. I promised to keep my grandparents updated as soon as I could, and they promised to continue to gather people who would be willing to prove to the gods and Goldens on Olympus that the Tournament wasn't necessary to protect the humans.

And as I walked back to the Refuge with Bella and Liam, I couldn't get my grandmother's last words out of my mind.

Family fights for family, Kalani. We'll be there to support you, to stand with you. Always.

Chapter Thirty-Six

Sadie

The next three weeks were a whirlwind of training, strategizing, and trying to enjoy the few moments of fun we could find here and there.

I started teaching self-defenses classes again, still assisted by Liam, while my twin, Nafula, and Archer taught the Coppers who wanted to fight how to control and wield their powers. Since our time frame was so short, none of us were able to go in-depth in our teachings, but we were doing our best to prepare these Coppers for what was to come.

Things had been slightly awkward at first between me and the rest of the inhabitants of the Refuge, what with me having lied to them for weeks about being one of them. Thankfully, the awkwardness died down after a couple of days, and I was soon interacting with them like nothing had happened.

Except a lot had happened. And the knowledge that we were getting close to moving against the gods of Olympus was weighing on everyone's minds.

From where I stood as their teacher and one of the leaders of this rebellion, I could tell that most of the Coppers felt a mix of fear and excitement. Fear that they were going to willingly go to the place they had run away from for years. Terror that our plan wouldn't work out, and they would end up in the Tournament, forced to kill each other for survival. But there was also the half-hidden, almost shameful excitement of seeing Mount Olympus, this mystical place they'd dreamed about, for the very first time.

It reminded me of the first time I had set foot on Mount Olympus. I had been terrified, though not nearly as much as Coppers were when doing the same trip. But I still remembered how scared and sad I had been. And even through all of those emotions, the beauty of Mount Olympus had been life changing. The mountain of the gods was the most beautiful place I had ever seen – maybe the most beautiful place in the whole universe.

I could understand why these Coppers wanted to see it. Even though they didn't *want* to desire to witness Olympus for themselves, the place was magical enough to cause them to dream. And we all pretended like we couldn't see the excitement shining in their eyes every so often.

Every day ended with hours upon hours of discussing our plans and how to best approach the situation. What looked like a war council formed, with representatives from the Refuge – namely Ken, Thomas, Bella, and Liam – and my friends and me. After a couple of days, we figured out a way to establish secured communications between our Refuge and the leaders of two other pockets of Copper resistance located in Peru and Canada, as well as with the leader of Kalani's coven.

To say that some of our meetings ended in heated arguments was an understatement.

But we made it work. We debated our options, analyzed every outcome we could think of, and made the best adjustments for every succession of event until everyone was content. Or as content as possible, seeing as everyone had different expectations and willingness to risk themselves and their people.

Three weeks after our arrival in the Refuge, we were finally ready to go.

Or, as ready as we could afford to be, seeing as the Hunters had lost one of their own — dear Sergio I had taken prisoner almost a month ago — and would start looking for him with more intent soon enough. I was even surprised that there hadn't been more of a search party for him — or for me, for that matter — since he'd dropped from the face of the Earth.

More than that, Ken and Thomas had received information through the internet that a surprisingly high number of Hunters and Huntresses had been spotted around all corners of the Earth. That could mean one of two things. One, the gods were using all of their resources to hunt my friends and I out. Two, the gods wanted to hurry the Copper recruitment process in the hopes that a new Tournament would provide the entertainment that the people of Olympus needed to forget about the human rebellion — or the fact that a human had won the last edition.

Either way, it wasn't good for us. Every day we spent here, training and prepping was one more day we could get discovered. We couldn't risk losing the advantage of surprise. And we needed to act before another round of Coppers were forced to fight to the death in the Pit.

Today was the day.

We weren't nearly prepared enough, but we couldn't afford to wait anymore. And, to be fair, it would take years of training for me to feel confident that the Coppers were fully prepared to take on Olympus. We just didn't have that kind of time.

I should be terrified. Stars, everyone around me was hiding their shaking hands. Standing next to me, Kalani was looking a little too wide-eyed and kept on wetting her dry lips. On my other side, Matteo was fidgeting and moving from one foot to the other, clearly uncomfortable.

But me? I was like Søren and Archer a few paces in front of me: ready for battle. I wasn't sure if it was the extra ichor in our blood or because we had been raised since our teenage years on Mount Olympus, surrounded by bloodthirsty deities, but we craved this kind of adrenaline rush.

In my defense, Søren was a lot more excited than I was. He had a huge grin on and was seconds away from sauntering all over the mess hall, acting like an overexcited puppy. That man really needed to learn to keep his emotions in check, but that was also his charm, I guessed.

However, I couldn't deny that Archer and I were also much more eager to start this fight than anyone else here. We had been trained to fight for years, so waiting around and not doing anything was against our very nature.

"Am I the only one who's sweating? Should I change into something more lightweight, maybe?" Matteo murmured, clearing his throat nervously.

"Nope, I'm sweating, too," Kalani answered with a tight giggle. "But you should probably keep your jeans on, they are better than shorts in case you need to protect yourself."

She was right. Matteo's faux-leather jacket and thick jeans weren't exactly armor. But we had instructed everyone to wear the thickest clothes they had that still allowed them to have a good range of motion.

"You'll be fine," I told Matteo with a reassuring smile. "The nerves will pass once we get there. And everyone's stressed, so don't feel weird about it."

"You're not," Kalani retorted with a raised eyebrow, calling me out on my bullshit. "Miss I'm-Excited-to-Fight-Zeus."

"Why are we talking about *him*?" Archer asked as he joined our little group. He winced at the mention of his dad, but I probably wouldn't have noticed his reaction if I hadn't been looking for it. I really hoped my friend managed to keep his cool when we came face-to-face with his dad.

"Just teasing Sadie on her love for action. She's not as crazy in love with danger as Søren is, but it's still pretty worrying," Kalani said with mock concern.

Archer snickered at me and I rolled my eyes at his amusement. The man was just as impatient as I was. But I didn't argue with Kalani, not when Matteo was still looking at the entrance of the Refuge with wide eyes and poorly hidden concern.

I caught his eye and gave him a gentle smile. His eyes softened but his jaw remained clenched. I wished I was able to talk to him in private and reassure him, but there was no time. There hadn't been any time in the past three weeks, actually. Every waking second had been spent preparing for this very moment, and I wished I had been able to spend more time with Matteo.

If the events of today were slightly overwhelming for me, then I couldn't even imagine how terrified Matteo and the other Coppers were.

Next to us, Archer and Kalani started whispering — probably professing their love to each other like the two lovebirds they were. They were disgustingly sweet.

Ignoring them, I reached into my pocket and removed the small packet of candy I had snagged from the kitchen earlier that morning. Matteo had a raging sweet tooth and I hoped some of his favorite candy would help him relax a little.

"Is that for me?" Matteo asked with a blooming smile.

"Who else around here eats candy like diabetes doesn't exist?"

A warm laugh left Matteo's chest as I gave him the packet. A second later, he had the plastic bag open and was popping one candy in his mouth.

"Thanks, Zombie girl." He looked straight into my eyes, his gaze burning through me. I felt my cheeks heat and had to look away as he popped another candy between his lips.

Stars! Get a grip, Sadie!

Before I could try to formulate a sensical answer, Ken walked to the entrance of the Refuge and started opening the door.

They were here.

Silence fell upon the room, accompanied with a wave of tense anticipation, as the rocky door fully opened.

The first person to appear on the other side of the door was an older woman with long hair that had once been black but was now closer to grey, and an aura of wisdom that impressed even me.

"Grandma," Kalani whispered next to me, frozen in place for a second. Then, as the woman took a step forward, Kalani bolted from her spot and ran to the entrance.

A few seconds later, the two women were embracing each other, and my chest constricted, tears prickling my eyes. It was so good to see my friend with her grandmother, especially after witnessing how hard it had been on her to lose touch with her little brother. Her grandma would never replace Makaio, but forming this relationships with her grandparents would help her deal with the loss a little better.

After a few moments, Kalani and her grandmother stepped apart, letting a group of people enter the Refuge behind them.

The witches and shifters had arrived.

I couldn't tell who everyone was from where I stood, but I knew there were eight witches coming, as well as ten shifters, and two vampires. Twenty magic-users were here and none of them had a drop of ichor in their blood. And they were here to support us.

It was incredible, really. Mere weeks ago, I never would have believed magic outside of the Olympians to be possible, but here we were, undeniable proof that magic was not reserved to the Greek gods.

"I can't believe they just flew right to us," Matteo remarked. "This is so anticlimactic for a super-secret mission."

He wasn't wrong. The magic-users had taken flights to Geneva, and then rented a minivan to drive all the way here. It wasn't exactly what any of us had initially imagined when thinking of a rebellion against the gods of Mount Olympus. But we hadn't been able to do dozens of roundtrips between here and the homes of these people with our two translocators, not when so many trips could have alerted the Order of Hunters. So, the magic users had needed to find another way to come here. Somehow, Kalani's grandma had managed to convince the other leaders of her coven to pay for everyone's plane tickets – a loan that Archer had promised he would pay back once he could safely get the endless piles of money he had on Olympus.

The money was one of the perks of being the son of the most powerful Greek god and one of the smartest women on Olympus.

Thankfully, we wouldn't need to book fifty plane tickets to Olympus to go and confront the gods.

Turned out, the Refuge had a Copper that could control energy. The Copper in question was a Spanish kid, Juan, who was barely older than seventeen and looked as dangerous as a kitten. But when it came to his magic, he could probably power up a skyscraper's worth of lights. He was a real powerhouse, and after weeks of trial and error, he had been able to charge one of our translocators.

That meant we had a way to recharge our translocators without having to let them sit there for hours. And, more than that, we were now able to transport three times as many people as before in one run.

Really, having Juan was a blessing.

However, getting Juan to a point where he could control his powers well enough to charge the translocators without frying them or completely depleting his reserves of magic had been challenging. We had needed every hour of practice we could get, and we hadn't wanted to overwhelm the kid with translocating twenty people hours before the real deal even started.

As the twenty magic-users entered the mess hall and clustered in a small huddle, I decided to go and join Kalani as she welcomed them. Bella, Thomas, and Ken did the same thing, and soon enough all five of us were gathered in front of our guests.

"Thank you so much for making the trip here and for being willing to support our fight," Kalani thanked everyone with an especially long, grateful look in the direction of her grandmother.

I caught Thomas giving a nasty look in Kalani's direction, probably annoyed that she was thanking our guests instead of him. Thankfully, he didn't make a scene about it.

"Yes, we are very grateful to have you here," Bella added with a bright smile, her cheeks pink with excitement.

Kalani's grandmother nodded before responding, "Of course, we are happy to be here. My name is Kawehi Hale and I am acting as the head of the Hawaiian coven for today." She then proceeded to introduce all of her coven mates, most of which were women and men in their late twenties to early thirties. I promptly forgot everyone's names – too many introductions, too quickly – but I tried to pay special attention to the leaders of the shifter pack and the two vampires.

The shifter pack was being led by a middle-aged man called Jared who looked like he could star in a commercial for a deodorant with a savage name and a mountainous backdrop. He was intense, bulky, and I was relieved that we were on the same team.

To be fair, the rest of his packmates weren't anything to laugh at, either. Most of them were younger than their alpha, closer to our ages, but they had this aura of danger about them. All of them had muscles upon muscles and looked like apex predators even in their human forms.

Once I focused on the vampires, though, my whole body reacted to the danger that emanated from them. There was a different type of power to their presence – not quite the showy, strong type of danger, but something that made my heart pound for no obvious reason. After all, the two vampires looked like a cute couple that lived in a quiet neighborhood, with a golden retriever and two children – one boy and one girl. But when you looked a little closer, there was something about the two young vampires that made you shiver and feel uncomfortable, like there was a danger you couldn't see but *feel* was there, close to you.

And when they smiled... those pointed canines were deeply unsettling.

There would be no denying that these two were vampires, and that would work in our favor.

Ken offered the magic-users to show them rooms if they needed to drop their things or wash up after traveling. All of them seemed grateful for the opportunity to get ready before we were due to depart in less than an hour, and they followed Ken out of the mess hall.

Once all of them were gone, excited chatter started among the Coppers that were gathered in the mess hall. I could tell from the wide eyes that this was becoming real for many of them. Being told that they weren't the only people with magic in the world had been surprising, but actually seeing some of these other magic-users in real-life? It was life changing.

"I can't believe they're here," Kalani murmured next to me. Her tone was excited, but I knew her well enough to spot her shaking hands and the way she shifted from one foot to the other without break.

"Are you doing alright, K?" I asked quietly so that she was the only one hearing my words. "We won't let them get to you. You know that, right?"

Kalani swallowed roughly and nodded, but the half-smile she gave me didn't reach her eyes. "I know."

I wanted to reassure her that all of us would fight for her and that we wouldn't let Artemis or anyone else make an example out of her. But before I could add anything else, Bella rushed over and grabbed Kalani, leading her out of the mess hall while chatting excitedly.

"She's worried. She won't admit it, but she's scared that the gods will take her and execute her to squash the human rebellion." Archer, who I hadn't seen walk over, stepped next to me and stared after his girlfriend.

From the corner of my eyes, I saw his jaw clench in frustration, and I knew it killed him that he couldn't keep her safe from the danger. There would never be a way for him to ensure that Kalani remained a hundred percent safe, not when we were all coming back to Olympus to face the gods.

Anything could happen once we stepped foot back on the mountain. And there was no denying that Kalani already had a target on her back.

"We'll keep her alive. No matter what." I tried to instill determination and certainty into my words, but we both knew there was no way to know that we would be enough.

There was no time to dwell on everything that could go wrong, though, because we needed to finish getting everything ready.

For over forty minutes, I checked that every Copper leaving with us had appropriate attire, made sure everyone had a weapon they somewhat knew how to use, and pumped Juan up so he would be able to charge our translocators without throwing up all over the place. By the time the witches, shifters, and vampires came back from their rooms, we were as ready as we would ever be.

"Alright, listen up everyone!" Ken hollered from the top of a table. Silence fell over the room. "We are about to leave. If any of you have changed your mind, this is your time to say so and walk out. For everyone else, please move into your assigned travel groups and wait for the translocator teams to reach you. Any questions?"

He surveyed the room with his icy blue eyes, but no one came forward to ask a question.

We'd prepared, we'd explained our plan so many times that these people knew it almost by heart.

There wasn't any room for error, but we had prepared for every possible avenue. Or, at least, I hoped so.

Two minutes later, two Coppers had decided to stay and everyone else had separated into four groups of ten. There was a heavy slab of tension weighing over the whole room, especially as some of the Coppers who were staying in the Refuge gathered by the back wall, anxiousness written all over their faces.

Archer, Juan, and I were the three people on translocator duty. Archer and I because we knew how to work with the magical objects the best, and Juan because he was our human-sized battery.

Being responsible for translocating everyone to Mount Olympus and then back here was stressful. We couldn't mess up the drop-off location or the timing of it, or even how we were directing Juan in his efforts to charge up the translocators. Everything would require precision and efficiency.

And because we'd be carrying people across realms, we would be forced to leave part of our friends and allies on Olympus while we went back to Earth.

I looked around at the different groups that had formed and tried to calm my anxiousness. Kalani, Søren, Bella, Liam, and Matteo would be okay. They would have to be okay. And we would only be leaving them on Olympus for a few minutes, just long enough for us to finish bringing everyone from the Refuge and to get to Peru where we would pick up another fourteen Coppers.

We wouldn't be gone long enough for anything bad to happen. *Right?*

Each group had been assigned so that there was a mix of Coppers and other magic-users, as well as an even distribution of leaders across the groups. In the end, it shouldn't matter, especially if, as we had planned, we were able to bring everyone to Mount Olympus quickly enough that none of the gods would attack the groups waiting for us to finish the rounds.

My heart couldn't stop worrying, though, especially not when I met Matteo's eyes.

I wasn't in charge of his group. Instead, I was in charge of a group that was composed mostly of Coppers, as well as a few shifters, and led by Ken and Liam. But I couldn't stop myself from looking at Matteo as he stood among the members of group three, which would be translocated by Archer.

We stared at each other for a few long seconds, every sound dampening around us, and I had the utmost desire to run across the room and—

I took a deep breath to calm my pounding heart.

I wasn't sure what I wanted to do exactly, but I knew that I didn't want to go through this plan without hugging him. That was crazy, wasn't it? I was supposed to be focused on my job, not on a guy with kind brown eyes and a gentle soul who I had met a month ago. I really needed to get a grip on myself and focus.

So, I forced myself to remain where I stood and mouthed, "Be safe, okay?" Matteo bent his head to the side, his eyes crinkling at the sides. One corner of his mouth tugged up and he mouthed back, "I'll see you after, Zombie girl."

A second later, I dropped Matteo's eyes and was forced to focus on what I needed to do. Juan powered up our transporters. Archer and I took a synchronized deep breath as every member of our respective groups linked hands and one member reached out to touch our forearm.

This was it. No turning back.

Another deep breath. I closed my eyes.

And I activated the translocator.

Chapter Thirty-Seven

Kalani

The air of Mount Olympus smelled different, like flowers and warmth and power. I couldn't quite explain how power smelled, but it was there, in every breeze and every scent.

It was disarming, though, to step foot on the magical mountain again after everything that had happened since I had left. When I had fled from Olympus with Archer, I didn't know that I was anything other than human – I had suspicions, but I didn't have any answers yet.

Now, I knew that I came from a long line of witches who could communicate with the spirits of Nature. And as I stood there, on Mount Olympus, I was acutely aware of how far away the Nature spirits I had gotten used to feeling were from me. Nature was still present on Olympus, but it felt different from the one I'd gotten familiar with on Earth. The spirits felt more subdued maybe, like the magic that permeated the air had turned them into shadows of what they were on Earth.

And it made me deeply uncomfortable.

No quite as uncomfortable as being back in the Pit was, though.

When it had come to deciding where we wanted to bring the confrontation to the gods, choosing the Pit had been the most logical choice. Our goal was to make a stand and to attract a lot of spectators. If it was just us against the gods, they would kill all of us just to make a point and keep our knowledge secret. But if there were dozens or hundreds of Goldens there, learning the truth from us, the gods wouldn't be able to keep things quiet.

Now, we just had to make sure enough Goldens showed up, but not before we were ready for them.

Søren, who stood next to me, had his face shuttered in focus and determination. "I hate being back here," he murmured, just loud enough that I could hear him.

I hated it too. The Pit did not bring happy memories. The last time both of us had been here, Søren's girlfriend had lost the fourth trial and I had almost died from Elena attacking me after I'd won the Tournament. Before that, the Pit had brough us plenty of pain and tears too.

I hated this place, and I hated everything it represented. But it was a necessary evil because the Pit was the setting of the Tournament.

And we were going to destroy the Tournament forever if that was the last thing we did.

"This is for her." I gave Søren an insistent look, telling him through my eyes that I was dead serious. "She's here, with us, and no one else will have to go through what she went through."

Søren's jaw clenched and he nodded sharply. Then the pain was gone from his face and he was back to business.

Right on time for our first guest to arrive.

"Well, you guys have guts coming here!" Hermes hollered from where he was sitting in the front row of seats, manspreading with an arm around the back of the seat next to his. He looked amused and curious, just like the last time I'd seen him.

Behind me, the first two groups of Coppers and other magic-users quieted down instantly, tension crackling through the air. This was the first god they'd ever seen, and it made everything we were doing seem more real. More dangerous.

I heard Ken and Liam ask people to let them through, but I didn't turn to see them coming to stand next to Søren and me. My eyes weren't going to leave the god until there was an even bigger threat to focus on.

"Nice to see you, Hermes," I shouted back, forcing myself to remain relaxed. I wasn't about to give him the satisfaction of seeing me worried.

"Kalani. Søren. Where's my brother? I don't imagine he allowed his dear little lover to come back to us without protection. Am I wrong?"

He would see Archer soon enough when he and Sadie translocated the two other groups from the Refuge. But I wasn't about to let the god direct the conversation, not when we didn't know whose loyalties Hermes held.

Søren seemed to agree with me because he took a step forward, asking, "So what's new, bro? It's been a while, hasn't it?" Then, with a chuckle, "Are you here as a friend? Or are you just at the head of a horde of angry deities?"

"Shouldn't I be the one asking that, seeing as you brought a sports team worth of Coppers with you? Are you trying to take over the job of every single Hunter we have on payroll?"

Ken shifted, as if to take a stand, but he was stopped by the arrival of twenty more of our allies. They appeared from thin air, slightly to the side of where we had been dropped off.

"There he is! Archie, my man!" Hermes exclaimed with a big hand wave.

From the corner of my eye, I saw Archer stiffen at Hermes' words. We had hoped that we would be able to bring everyone safely to the Pit before any god arrived. Unfortunately, the god of Travel and Messages found us quickly – quicker than was ideal. But we'd prepped for that scenario, too.

With one look between Archer and Sadie, they moved from plan A to plan B. A second later, Juan was powering up Sadie's translocator and they were both gone.

"Hermes, nice to see you!" Archer called as he walked toward us.

"I wasn't expecting you or your friends anytime soon, so color me surprised when I felt all of you guys translocating in the Pit." Hermes raised an eyebrow in curiosity, looking like a cat playing with a mouse. He was reminding us how powerful he was and how easily he could send a message to every one of the other deities.

"We're here for a show," Søren said with a taunting smile.

Hermes knew it was a bait, but he still decided to take it. "What show, exactly?"

"I guess you'll have to wait and see, don't you think?"

Søren continued to occupy Hermes for a few seconds, just long enough for Archer to use his powers to contact his mother. I still didn't like when he used his powers on me, but I could admit that they were more than useful when we needed to contact someone discreetly.

While Søren was still trying to keep Hermes' attention off of Archer, Ken shifted closer to me and whispered to my ear, "Is he a friend or not? I can't tell."

"He's as close to a friend as we have among the gods, which doesn't mean much," I murmured back, hoping the god in question wasn't using his powers to listen in to our whispered conversation. "But he hasn't called the cavalry yet, so he's not quite in the enemy category. For now."

Ken hummed along but didn't seem convinced. There was nothing we could do about the god of Messages, though. He was here and all we could hope for was that Sadie would come back and Priya would come through before the other deities decided to come investigate what was happening in the Pit.

Our presence must have been felt or heard because a small group of wide-eyed Coppers emerged from the door that led to the inside of the training compound. These were the first few Coppers that had been brought here to compete in the next edition of the Tournament.

Behind me, the Coppers from the Refuge had moved into a tight group, looking around the Pit with a mix of wariness and awe.

"Did your twin decide to abandon your little group, *again*?" Hermes taunted Søren, clearly trying to get more information out of him.

Søren must have known this was a poorly hidden trap, but he winced at the way Hermes referenced his sister fleeing from Olympus – from *him*.

"Look, Hermes, why are you here?" I finally asked, moving the god's focus from Søren to me. "You know very well that we are fugitives, so are you here as a friend or as a foe? Because this little chase is getting tiring."

Hermes narrowed his eyes at me, but the glare only lasted a second before he had his usual amused smile on. The guy enjoyed this way too much for my liking. Before he could answer, though, Archer stepped in with swagger and confidence that told me his mental conversation with Priya had been successful.

"Hermes, I'm glad you're here. Let's stop playing games, shall we?" He took a few steps forward and crossed his arms, his posture screaming confidence. "If you want to call our dear old dad, you should probably do it soon, because the rest of our guests are about to arrive."

The god's eyes glinted with hunger for information at Archer's words. Hermes was clearly a sucker for gossip and surprises, and we were offering him the drama of the decade. And, still, no Zeus or Artemis in sight. Was Hermes scared of going against the king of the gods but also purposefully waiting for as long as possible before ringing the alarm?

Right then, Sadie appeared with the group of Coppers from Peru. Since Archer hadn't gone with her, she probably hadn't been able to transport all fourteen of the Coppers who had volunteered to help, but any was still better than none.

Now that Sadie was with us, I felt a little better. I hated being separated from my friends, especially after everything we'd all gone through on our own the past few weeks. And I wasn't the only one who was relieved at seeing the blonde Golden's arrival, as seen on Liam, Bella, and Matteo's faces behind me.

We weren't out of danger, though. This was just the beginning of our plan.

Now we needed—

A cloud of blue-purple glittery smoke appeared next to Hermes, and a second later, Hecate stood there. She wore her kickass black heeled boots and another of her red minidresses, looking like she was on the way to the club. "Well, well, well, if it isn't my favorite human!" she exclaimed with sultry voice. "And who are all of these people? Coppers, many Coppers, and…" She stopped, her eyes widening ever so slightly. And then a huge grin spread on her face. "Oh, I am so glad I came, this is going to be interesting!"

With a wide smile, she magicked a cocktail glass into her hand and sat on one of the seats, as if she were getting ready to watch a Broadway show.

Hermes frowned, annoyed that he wasn't in the know. But I was certainly glad that Hecate had decided to keep quiet on the identity of the magic-users we'd brought with us. Now wasn't the time for the grand reveal, not when we didn't have our crowd present yet.

Unfortunately, if Hecate had sensed our arrival, it meant that—

Thunder boomed through the air and lightning shattered the sky in a million pieces. Behind me, I heard more than one cry of fear, but I couldn't take the time to reassure our friends and allies. Not when Zeus was making his grand entrance.

As expected, the king of the gods appeared in the same box he had sat in during the Tournament, his lightning scepter in hand. If I hadn't been more intimidated by Artemis on a good day, I would have probably started shaking in fear at the view of the god of the skies, his eyes alight with power and fury.

As a flurry of other gods started appearing next to their leader, lightning continued to illuminate the increasingly darkening sky, thunder sounding closer and closer to us.

But Zeus wasn't going to use his powers to fry us alive. No, he needed to show that he had control over the situation. Killing over fifty people without trial or even demanding an explanation would be considered a loss of control over his power – both as deity and as leader.

Especially when a group of a dozen Goldens led by Priya Vasilias walked into the stands from one of the doorways. *There they were*, I thought with relief. And hopefully this group was just the beginning. We needed these stands filled with Goldens, especially Goldens that had children.

"Have you come to surrender, traitors of Mount Olympus?" Zeus' voice boomed, rattling my bones. "And have you brought us the next round of Tournament competitors in the hope that I would forgive your offenses against the Olympians' rule?"

Even though I kept on telling myself that we would be okay, that everything was going according to our plans, I couldn't stop my heartbeat from quickening and my palms from sweating. I would be damned if I let the fear show on my face, though. I might be labelled as a traitor for refusing to help destroy the human rebellion on Mount Olympus and knew I was risking my life coming back here, but this was so much bigger than me. We were fighting for the survival of hundreds of Coppers, of children who were being trialed to the death just because they were alive.

So, while the fear was present, my heart was full of so much determination and hope that it drowned the terror.

That was the only reason I had the courage to step forward in the direction of Zeus, ready to defend my values and the dozens of young people behind me who just wanted to live their lives peacefully.

"We did not come to surrender, nor did we bring these Coppers to participate in the Tournament." Somehow, my voice echoed in the Pit, louder than it should have been – as if the spirits of the Wind wanted to help me carry my words to the ends of the world.

From where I stood, I saw the faces of the gods surrounding Zeus – including Artemis, who had just arrived – shift in surprise at my words.

But none of them showed the amount of rage that the king of gods demonstrated as my words reached him. "How dare you address the King of the Gods this way? You are an insignificant—"

"I would stop right there if I were you, Father," Archer interrupted Zeus, his voice cold as ice and slicing the air with deadly precision.

"And why would I? You have taken your human puppet away, directly going against my ruling that she was to be eliminated for her role in the servant strike. Two of your friends have deserted Olympus to go and help your fugitive of a lover. And to top it off, the second Aska twin took it upon herself to desert her job as a Huntress. And now, you have returned with a ridiculously small army with you. Really, it would be well within my rights to execute all five of you. Right now."

Artemis whispered something to Zeus, probably trying to convince him to take action right then. After all, I doubted she had changed her stance on humans being beneath her since the last time we'd seen each other.

From the corner of my eye, I saw more and more Goldens arriving in the Pit. I didn't have the time to count, but I guessed there were at least fifty of them there already. That was good. Now, we just needed to direct the conversation to our demands.

"I think the most important question is why are you here, putting on a show for us," Athena intervened before Zeus could speak again. "Tell me, who are these people with you?"

I wasn't surprised that Athena was the one who was asking the right questions. As the goddess of wisdom and war strategy, I expected her to look at the situation with a cool temper and calculating eyes.

Ken stepped forward and cleared his throat, managing to hide his nervousness pretty well for a first time in front of the gods. "My name is Ken White, and I am the leader of this group of Coppers."

"And are you here to compete in the Tournament?" Poseidon asked, one hand around his trident and the other playing with his long dark beard.

"No, we will not compete in the Tournament," Ken announced, straightening his back under the scrutiny of the crowd. "We are here to support our allies' demand that the Tournament be dismantled."

For a second, everything was quiet in the Pit. All deities and Goldens were shocked at Ken's words. Then Zeus' laugh thundered through the space, quickly followed by all of the gods laughing along too.

The only person who wasn't laughing was Hecate who still had a wicked gleam in her eyes. She knew about our secret weapon, but she thankfully didn't seem to want to share it with the rest of the deities.

"We are not joking," Archer called out, fists clenched tightly. "There is no reason for the Tournament to exist. It is a cruel, antiquated practice that needs to stop. *Now.*"

There was power in that last word, so much so that the laughs came to an abrupt stop.

I couldn't see Archer's eyes from where he stood in front of me, but I knew that they glowed with his powers. This was more than just fighting for what was right for him, it was personal. His father had forced him to compete twice in the Tournament – the first time when he was barely thirteen. The trauma tied to the competition and to this very Pit was anchored deep into his soul.

"The Tournament is a necessary way to ensure that the strongest Coppers are offered the limited spots to live on Mount Olympus. All of you know that. There is no other way to—"

"We both know that isn't true," Archer spat at his father. "And we have proof. Proof that the Tournament is not necessary at all for us to remain hidden from the humans."

I might have imagined it, but I could swear that there was a gleam of fear in the gods' eyes as Archer mentioned proof. And Hecate's snicker was evidence that the deities were starting to worry.

"I am the King of Olympus," Zeus exclaimed, his thunder like an exclamation point after his words. "I do not bend to the whims of Coppers or *humans*, especially not for my traitor of a son. So, I will give you twenty seconds to abandon all weapons and surrender to my rule. The Coppers you have been nice enough to bring us will be escorted to the training compound where they will stay until the beginning of the Tournament. And the rest of you will be detained until your trial—"

"No, we will not surrender!"

The words left my chest before I could realize it. But it did the trick of stopping Zeus in his tracks.

"You can try to intimidate us all you want, but we will not leave or abandon until the Tournament is abolished," Archer added.

This time, there was no mistaking the fury in Zeus' eyes, nor the pure disdain in Artemis'.

"If you do not surrender in the next ten seconds, I will be forced to use my powers to take you to your knees."

The threat coming from the king of the gods wasn't anything to laugh at. But we were determined, even through the fear. And I was glad to see that none of the Coppers from the Refuge or from Peru abandoned us, standing proudly next to the witches, shifters, and vampires.

"If I were you, I wouldn't underestimate the power of a group of Goldens and Coppers fighting for their lives," Sadie spoke, eyes glowing with anger.

"As if any of you are a threat against us," Artemis laughed darkly, her bow in one hand as if ready to start hunting us down.

"None of you will ever come close to our powers. And nothing you can do will bring the Tournament down."

Sadie had never been one to back down from a challenge, even before she'd been backed into a corner and had so many of the people she loved and cared for to protect. So, I wasn't surprised when she decided to shut Artemis and Zeus up, once and for all.

She raised her hands at her sides, palms glowing a dark red. "Oh, really? Do you want to bet on that?"

And then she raised the dead.

Chapter Thirty-Eight

Sadie

There were hundreds of bones under our feet. Hundreds of dead bodies that had been buried under the sand and the rocks. These Coppers might have fallen into the magically opened pits filled with Hell fire or half-frozen water or deadly beasts, and no one had bothered to remove their bodies at the end of the trials before the holes had been magically filled in.

There were hundreds of bodies under our feet, some half-decomposed and others only bones. And I had dug every single of them up.

And now there were hundreds of skeletons and dead bodies surrounding our group of misfits and fugitives. Ready to fight for us. Ready to kill and destroy whatever or whoever stood in our path.

"These are the bones of the children you have killed," I yelled, molten rage in my chest. "This Pit has been the theater of Death for decades, and it will see blood no more!"

There were screams behind me, but I barely heard them. My whole focus was on the stand where the gods and the Goldens were staring at us – at my work – with horror on their faces.

It wasn't fun to be faced with the consequences of their decisions, was it? They had tricked everyone into thinking that the Tournament was a necessary evil, that it wasn't *that bad*, but here they were, faced with the bones of all of those kids they had killed and tortured.

There was no denying the horror of the Tournament anymore. No more burying their heads in the sand, pretending like they were working for the greater good.

None of this – the Tournament, the horrors that had happened in the Pit for so many years – was warranted or easily forgivable.

And I would make them remember.

"These are your children!" I stared down the large group of Goldens who were acting like they had never realized what had happened in this place. Like this was all a surprise. "You let your children walk onto this very sand, forced to fight for a decision *you* made. And now they're done paying for your mistakes and your cowardice."

I could tell that my words were meeting their mark. Or maybe it was the sight of the skeletons and partially decomposed bodies that represented the children they'd abandoned.

"How dare you spew such blasphemy?" Zeus asked with the promise of death in his voice. Good thing I had grown up around ghosts and the remains of dead people – Death didn't scare me, not when my loving dad was its god.

"And how dare *you* pretend like the only way to protect us as a society is to force children to fight to the death? How dare you pretend like there aren't thousands and thousands of magic-users on Earth that live among humans without issue?"

There it was. The nuclear bomb. If I wasn't so full of pent up rage, I would have laughed at the way Zeus sputtered, words failing him for what was probably the first time in his life.

"Are you relying on lies, now? None of us believe this crazy story you are spinning here, *Golden*," Artemis sneered, disdain dripping from her last word.

"Actually," Archer intervened, "we both know we aren't the liars. Especially when we have proof that there are many people on Earth who have powers and don't have a single drop of ichor in their blood."

There were two opposing reactions going on at that moment: while the gods bathed in a mix of anxiousness and righteous fury, the Goldens were shocked at our revelations.

Who would have thought that one sentence could bring such worry to the Olympians? Not me, that was for sure. But being able to see fear in Zeus' eyes was worth every second of pain I had experienced in the Tournament. It was almost as great as seeing Hera, usually so full of disdain and cruel judgment, try to rein in the situation with a few words that were abruptly stopped by Priya. Archer's mom, as assertive and direct as usual, exclaimed, "Let's stop playing those childish games. I think all of us want to know what our *children* mean, don't we?"

A wave of nods went through the ever-growing group of Goldens. Right then, I knew we had just won our first battle.

As Archer started explaining what we had discovered, he knew we were closer to victory too. He wasn't speaking to the gods but the Goldens, knowing full well that they were our opening. We had a sizable group of Coppers with us, and together we were powerful enough to make some damage to Olympus. But if the Goldens joined our cause? Oh, stars knew we would become unstoppable.

The gods were powerful, but they wouldn't be able to defeat hundreds if not thousands of their descendants.

We just needed to make sure the Goldens understood they had been played for fools for centuries.

All of us, with ichor in our blood, we had pride. More than we should, more often than not. And we all hated to be lied to.

"…magic-users do not have a single drop of ichor in their blood. They are not descendants of the Greek gods, and they have no connection whatsoever to Mount Olympus. But they still have magical powers that rival ours. They are able to control the elements, shapeshift, controls minds, or have incredible strength and speed." Archer stopped for a second, building tension. And the Pit was silent in that moment, everyone hanging on to Archer's every word.

Zeus took this time as an opportunity to regain control of the situation with yet another threat. "Son, if you speak one more word, I will have to resort to strength to stop this nonsense."

The god punctuated his threat with another lightning strike – showoff – hoping that it would dissuade us from continuing to fight.

But if he wanted to go into a magic fight, I was waiting for him. I wasn't in the habit of using my magic very often – not when it relied on dead bodies. All that excess power I had let built up over the years was now overflowing, ready to be used to defend all of my friends.

"Try it, Zeus," I taunted with what I knew was a too-wide smile. "We're ready for you." And I punctuated that with a surge of my power, a dozen more skeletons emerging from the ground, dead bodies moving to form a ring of protection against my friends and allies.

Behind me, Søren laughed, "Hell yeah, bring it on, old man!" Then, I felt the tell-tale heat of my brother's Hell fire behind me.

I knew from experience that the two of us were a good team together, a terrifying team for our enemies. Him with the only fire that could burn even a god, and me able to control immortal, undead fighters.

And if Zeus or any other god continued to try to quiet us, the Aska twins would bring the full force of our powers onto this Pit and Mount Olympus.

We wouldn't be the only ones to fight either. Around me, human-sized carnivorous flowers and plants grew, ready to attack. My heart warmed at the sight of Matteo's power. From the man who had hated to use his powers, resenting the deadliness of his magic, it meant a lot for him to use his powers right then.

And he wasn't the only one to take stand either. The air around us seemed to quiver in anticipation, probably the work of Kalani and the other witches. And behind me, I could hear the hum of magic coming from dozens of people. Everyone was getting ready to defend ourselves and our values.

"Now, now, Father. I know you want to hear the rest of what we have to say," Archer continued with a raised eyebrow and a smug smile.

"I sure do," Hecate snickered from where she was lounging on the lowest bleachers, sipping her drink with glee.

Archer ignored the Titan and continued his spiel, preparing to deliver the killing blow to the gods' rule.

"I know this seems crazy. We were surprised too, when we learned of this. But we have proof for you all. Proof that there are other people with magic out there. And proof that it is possible for us to live among humans safely."

The next second of silence was deafening, everyone holding their breath, waiting for the proof to be revealed.

And then footsteps sounded as someone walked out of the tight group the Coppers had formed. I didn't dare turn to watch – not when there were so many threats in front of me – but I knew this was the next part of our plan.

"My name is Kawehi Hale and I am a witch. My coven and I honor our ancestors by communicating with the spirits of Nature. Our respect and love for Nature gives us the opportunity to ask of the spirits to act in our favor." As soon as she her last words echoed in the Pit, Kawehi raised the wind spirits, creating a small tornado that raced around the edge of the Pit, gathering sand in its path before trickling out.

Before any of the gods could protest, the other witches introduced themselves one after the other, showing the crowd how they could interact with the spirits of Nature. The demonstrations were short, but they were effective.

And through it all, the Goldens standing in the stands kept on staring, their mouths half open in confusion.

Soon enough, it was time for the shifters to announce themselves.

"My name is Jared, and I am the alpha of the Whiteclaw Pack." A second later, all of Jared's packmates shifted into their wolf form.

They were majestic, prowling forward to stand next to me in front of our group. It took all of my willpower to remain focused on the threat of the Olympians and not stare at the giant wolves that stood next to me, teeth bared at the gods in their special viewing box.

The murmurs that ran through the Goldens were proof enough that they were shocked at the sight before them. While there were shapeshifters in the Greek gods' descendants, none of them looked like the wolf shifters here. A few of Ares' and Pan's children and grandchildren could transform into animals using their magic, but the wolf shifters had their wolves ingrained in their DNA. When they shifted, there was no magic, no glow in their eyes or on their skin – it was bones breaking and their whole body changing into an animal's.

Finally, it was time for the two vampire lovebirds to introduce themselves. "Hi everyone! My name is Jenny, and this is Eric. We are both vampires. By birth, not transformation," the lady vampire specified, as if it meant anything to any of us. "And our powers aren't as showy as our witch and shifter friends here, especially since we don't want to bleed any of you out," Jenny giggled as if this was a fun afternoon conversation. "But I guess we'll try to show you guys how fast we can run. Right, Eric?"

"Let's do it, baby," Eric answered.

And then the two of them were gone, running around the Pit so fast that they were blur.

No one on Olympus could run this fast, not even Hermes with his powers over travel.

Once they were all done, silence settled over the Pit once more. The Goldens seemed slightly overwhelmed by everything they'd been shown, and the gods appeared to be looking for any way to get out of this mess.

Artemis was either grasping at straws or deeply dishonest – probably both, let's be honest there – because she shrugged like none of this was important. "Nice tricks, kids. But this does not prove anything. These people could have diluted ichor in their blood, to the point that they have powers but not the blood color distinctive of Coppers."

I saw the doubt in the Goldens' eyes right then. Artemis' explanation filled the holes that our arguments had torn into their perception of reality. It was easier to believe that there was a logical explanation to all of this than to admit to themselves that they'd been too blind and trusting to question the gods on the necessity of the Tournament.

Thankfully, Hecate seemed to believe this was the perfect opportunity to take her revenge on the Olympians that had taken her, one of the last Titans, as a glorified servant.

"Well, I can swear on Lethe that none of these witches or shifters or vampires are descended from Olympus," the Titan intervened with glee, raising her glass as if to toast. "They don't have any ichor in their blood, not even at a level so diluted that we can't see it visually. All of this is legitimate!"

Artemis' face turned a shade of red I'd never seen before, proof of her rage, and Zeus' control over his power slipped slightly, causing the sky to shatter in a million of dark pieces again.

"None of this is real, this is all ridiculous and—" Zeus' voice cut short, broken by what I guessed was some of the witches using their connection to the wind spirits to stop his voice from traveling to us.

"We are not lying," Archer declared with strength in his tone. "These witnesses here are magic-users and they live on Earth, among humans, for their whole lives. None of them have to fight to the death to come and live in another realm like we've forced Coppers to do."

"There is no reason why any of us should have to compete in this Tournament, not when we could be trained to control our powers so that we can remain on Earth, with our human families." From the corner of my eye, I saw Ken straighten and close his fists in determination. "None of us will compete anymore. We refuse to be forced to fight and die for something none of us have asked for. And we ask that you, our parents, support us in finding a new, sustainable way to train us to remain safe with our magic in the human world. Just like the other magic-users have been doing for millennia."

Still blocked by whatever wind shield had been created around them, we couldn't hear the complaints and threats that the gods were spewing in response to Ken's revendications. Thank the stars for that, because I had no desire to listen to their ridiculous behavior. It was clear now that they had been found out – continuing to deny that they had lied and concealed important information was childish behavior.

Unfortunately, I couldn't quite catch what the Goldens were murmuring between themselves. There was a lot of agitation within their ranks, with hands being thrown in the air and teary eyes.

All of us were waiting with bated breath to know if our plan had worked. If the Goldens didn't want to support our demands that the Tournament should be burned to the ground, then we'd have to fight our way out of Olympus. Things would get bloody and dangerous, but we had known this was a possibility. I just hoped Juan had it in him to continue to charge our transporters for the travel back to Earth.

If I unleashed my skeletons, they would provide us with a few precious seconds – maybe even minutes – of time to escape. And I knew Søren, Nafula, Archer, and Kalani would also fight to save our allies. We had been the ones to bring up the idea of dismantling the Tournament in the first place, so we would take responsibility for anything that might come.

"You are right," Priya declared strongly, her eyes shining with pride as she looked at her son. "As Goldens, we have let the Tournament go on for too long. We will stand with you, Coppers, in your fight."

Ensued a few seconds during which many of the Goldens around Priya voiced their agreement, some of them crying as they looked at the Coppers behind me. Some of these kids might have been theirs that they hadn't been allowed to see in years. The rule of the gods had not only been cruel to the Coppers but also to their Golden parents who weren't allowed to go back to Earth to bound with their children.

But it was about to change.

We had won the Goldens' support. Our forces had multiplied in numbers and strength. And there was little that the gods would dare to do when everyone on Olympus was protesting against them.

At least I hoped so. I didn't think the gods would be foolish enough to believe that they could afford to imprison or kill so many of their Goldens, especially when they had already lost the support of every single human servant on Olympus.

The news that there was something to see in the Pit must have spread through Olympus because there was a steady stream of Goldens joining the group of their peers and getting brought up to speed.

And the crowd of almost two hundred Goldens was getting angry. Enraged that they had been forced to watch their children die for something that could have been avoided. Frustrated that they had been played for fools.

Based on the way the gods looked at the Goldens with wariness, they could feel how dangerous this situation had become for them.

"Why was this information never disclosed to any of us?" A male Golden I'd seen around but never interacted with, exclaimed with palpable anger directed at the gods. "Were you all aware that there were people with powers living on Earth that weren't Coppers or Goldens?"

Many of the gods had a decent poker face, but Zeus was strangely easy to read – especially for a guy whose whole job was to be a mysterious, powerful leader. And the way he winced was as good as a confession.

The Goldens came to the same conclusion that we had – namely, that the gods had known about these other magic-users for millennia but had chosen to keep their existence secret from their descendants – and it spurred an even stronger wave of anger to go through their ranks.

Tensions heightened as many of the Goldens' hands started glowing, their powers coming to the surface. And the gods' tempers were also heightening, probably because they hated to be put in this situation and forced to admit their failures.

And then the tension exploded.

It started from Zeus who decided he'd had enough of hits to his pride and needed to assert his leadership again. He roared and five lightning bolts stroke the Pit all around us, causing part of the stands to crumble and burn. "You are all committing blasphemy. The hubris of your actions must be punished!"

And then a deluge of lightning fell on us, triggering screams and panic behind me. Thankfully, the witches came through and created a dome of *something* that stopped Zeus' magic before it could reach us. Still, even I was slightly worried about the turn of events. If the gods decided to actually fight their way through this… not all of us would make it out alive.

Zeus hadn't just decided to attack us, standing in the middle of the arena. He had also decided to take a stand against the Goldens who were in the stands in a distinct group from the deities.

And they reacted poorly to being attacked.

Suddenly, there was a full-fledged battle going on before us. The Goldens replicated with the full force of their magic, attacking not only Zeus but every god standing with him.

Fire, ice, huge rocks, shadows, and so much more flew at the gods with one goal – causing as much damage as possible.

And I knew for a fact that the gods hadn't been attacked as a group in a long, long time.

It took them a second to go over the shock of being attacked before answering. But then it was like a scene from a history book – deities and their children fighting like nothing else mattered.

I was more than thankful that my dad and the few gods I actually liked – such as Hades and Persephone – weren't among the group of Zeus' followers but standing all the way on the other side of the Pit, observing the situation.

Soon enough, the gods and Goldens had mostly forgotten that we were there, and they were going at each other with the violence and desire to hurt that had accumulated over centuries.

And we weren't going to go anywhere. Our goal was to destroy the institution of the Tournament, not to have a front-row seat to a deadly battle.

Archer must have agreed with me because he came to stand right next to me and sighed. "I was hoping for more civil conversation about how to dismantle the Tournament, not… whatever this is."

I nodded my agreement, trying to rein in my powers. All of that magic being used and thrown about around me was tugging onto my own powers, and the tingles in my hands were a tell-tale sign that I needed to focus to control my magic.

"What now?" I asked, clenching my jaw at the need I had to unleash my power and let my skeletons attack the gods. It was tempting, but it would be counterproductive to add to the magical battle going on before us.

Before Archer could answer, an arrow whizzed by our heads, aiming for someone behind us. The first thing I saw was Artemis, her bow in hand, looking like a true warrior.

And based on her ruthless smile, the arrow she'd drawn had hit her target.

Chapter Thirty-Nine

Kalani

I hadn't been paying attention to Artemis when the battle started. There was so much happening, so many deadly things to pay attention to, that I had forgotten where the true threat lied.

Then, two things happened at once. Bella pushed me so forcefully that I fell on the ground roughly. And something hit me straight in the shoulder.

The pain didn't come right away. First was the shock – what was happening? Had I hurt myself during the fall?

Then I registered that there was an arrow protruding from my shoulder. And the pain hit like a bomb had exploded in my chest.

Instantly, I knew this was courtesy of Artemis. She'd been looking for an excuse to get rid of me and everything I represented for months, so I wasn't surprised that she'd taken a chance today.

Why were people always so determined to kill me every time I entered the Pit? The last time it was Elena during the fourth trial, and now Artemis taking a coward shot?

Someone shouted my name and I forced my eyes to open to see Bella's worried face.

The world was blurry along the edges, but I could see Bella's panicked eyes very clearly. However, I couldn't quite hear what she was saying through the drumming of my blood in my ears.

This was painful as hell. But after a few seconds, I regained enough clarity of thought to be able to assess the rest of my body.

Apart from the arrow that had pierced my right shoulder, I didn't think I was injured. And I was inclined to believe that if Bella hadn't pushed me out of the way, I probably wouldn't have survived Artemis' shot.

How come the goddess of the hunt hadn't finished me off? Even through the pain and the lightheadedness that was creeping up –from the shock of being hit, the pain, or from the blood loss, I wasn't sure – I knew that there was no way Artemis would give up an opportunity to finish me off.

"Stay down," the British girl admonished me, crouched over me but looking behind her like she was expecting another arrow to come at any moment.

I tried to speak but a cough racked my chest, causing pain to stab me through the chest and abdomen again. Fuck, this was awful. Not quite as bad as the last time I'd been attacked in the Pit, but too close for comfort. And I really didn't want things to turn the same way they had with Elena.

"Artemis—" I stopped and winced from the pain of trying to talk. "I need to— I need—"

I couldn't quite get a full sentence out as sitting up completely took the breath out of my lungs. Thankfully, Bella understood what I meant easily enough.

"She won't fire again. I think your boyfriend is taking care of her."

"What?" I wheezed out, trying to see what was happening behind Bella. It looked like a lot of the Coppers around us were using their magic to fight against the gods, and chaos was everywhere. But where was—

Bella shifted slightly and I was finally able to spot Artemis.

She was writhing in pain on the sand of the Pit, mouth open in silent agony.

And Archer was standing a short distance away, immobile. I could only see his back, but his whole body was tense. There was no denying that he was using his powers to make her pay for shooting an arrow at me, and I shouldn't have felt love or safety at that sight – but I did.

However, I didn't have time to worry about my mental health at that reaction because there was a literal battlefield around me. And I didn't have the luxury to lay on the ground and cry out in pain.

I needed to get back up and protect myself and my friends. We needed to get this whole situation back on track.

"Bloody hell, Kalani!" Bella protested when I used her as a prop to start to stand up. "You have an arrow in your shoulder, you should stay down until we find someone to heal you!"

I breathed through the pain and forced myself to stand up. The last time I'd been in this Pit, I had left on the brink of death. Today wouldn't end the same way, and I wouldn't remain a bystander in this war. If that meant I had to fight through debilitating pain and do what I could with one arm unavailable, then that would be what I would do.

I was done being a lifeboat struggling to float during a storm.

Today was the day to do more than hold on and survive. I was going to swim and fight.

To the bitter end, if it came down to it.

Bella tried to fuss on me again, but I waved her away. Clenching my jaw to stop myself from showing the pain on my face, I closed my eyes for a second to calm the dizziness. *I was fine.* The arrow thankfully must not have hit any major blood vessel because I hadn't lost that much blood, and I was pretty sure it had mostly hit muscles. I had experienced much, much worse before.

I'd be fine.

"This is a shitshow," I sighed at the sight of magic flying to and from the gods and the rest of us. The Pit had turned into a scene from a superhero movie – the ones where the heroes destroy half of the city while trying to defeat the villains.

None of this was taking us closer to dismantling the Tournament. Sure, it was good to have the Goldens' support and to show the gods we were a united front against them. But an all-out fight could only lead to disaster, especially since most of our Copper allies barely knew how to fight. My friends had done their best to teach them how to control their powers and defend themselves for the past week, but that didn't turn the Coppers into great fighters overnight.

Somehow, Bella heard me, and she nodded, her eyes wide like a deer in headlights. The poor girl was terrified and for good reasons – real-life magical battles weren't as fun as the ones she read about in her books.

I tried to reach for the Nature spirits around me, but it was impossible to open my mind to them when pain was so overpowering. Not having access to my powers was so humbling and terrifying, even though I'd only had them for such a short period of time. With these powers gone, I—

Oh, my gods. This was it!

"Bella, how many people can you siphon at once?"

The British girl shrugged, slightly distracted by lightning hitting the ground close enough that the ground below our feet shook slightly. "I don't know, at least as many as the number of people that were in the Refuge. Perhaps fifty people, if I concentrate hard enough?"

Well, that wouldn't be enough for every one of the people standing in the Pit, but it might be enough to stop this senseless battle.

"Okay, I am going to need you to try to siphon every single god out there." I looked straight into her eyes, making sure she was focused only on me and my words. "I know this is going to be tough, but we need this battle to stop. You are the only person who can stop it before there are deaths."

Because there would be. Seeing how ruthlessly the gods and Goldens were exchanging magical blows, there would be heavy damage and deaths before the end of the day if we allowed things to continue. And I worried that most of the deaths would be from the Coppers who would become collateral damage.

"They're *gods*. I don't know if I can—"

"You can. And you will." I gave a meaningful look in the direction of her boyfriend and brother who were fighting side by side against some of Artemis' hounds. "Your family needs you. And all of these people believe in you – they believed in you when you protected them in the Refuge, and they believed in you to lead them in this battle. You just have to believe in yourself, now."

Bella swallowed roughly and stared into my eyes for a couple of seconds. I tried to convey as much confidence as I could through my gaze, hoping she'd find the strength to step up when she was already so overwhelmed and scared.

The seconds passed like small forevers, screams and cries and magic exploding in the background like a movie soundtrack. This was it, the big moment.

And Bella needed to become the hero in our story.

The moment she closed her eyes, I knew the girl was going to do it, or at least give it her all trying.

I held my breath as time seemed to slow down to a crawl. A look told me that Archer was now standing over Artemis who was still writhing on the ground in agony. Sadie was busy directing her skeletons to climb onto the stands and attack the gods, just as Søren sent fireballs to any deity that dared to attack our group. Nafula was protecting a group of Coppers from Poseidon's water attack. And my grandma was with her coven, manipulating the air around us to protect the group from most of Zeus' lightning bolts.

My friends were fine. My family was fine. We were all fine. *For now.*

As I raked my gaze over the Pit, I met Liam's eyes. I could tell right away that he was worried seeing his girlfriend motionless, next to me. With my healthy arm, I made a thumbs up and gave him what I hoped was a reassuring smile. He didn't seem convinced, but he didn't have the luxury to mouth anything my way because another hound ran at him.

Another few seconds passed, and I started worrying that Bella wasn't going to make it work. Maybe this was too much for her. Perhaps the gods were too strong for her to siphon their powers away. Or maybe—

Bella opened her eyes and they were glowing bright blue. "Let's turn the switch off, shall we?"

And then she siphoned the magic of not only all of the gods, but most of the Goldens too.

Everything stopped. The fighting, the screams, the explosions of magic. It felt like even time stopped as Bella single-handedly put everyone in magic-jail. Should I mention she did all of it with an ease that was unsettling – a slight tremor in her hands and arms were the only signs of her exertion at the massive use of her magic.

Gods, this girl was impressive.

And she might very well be our salvation, if we could convince the gods that talking things through would be more beneficial than killing everyone on Olympus and starting over from scratch.

"Can we speak like adults, now? I called out as loudly as I could with my chest still constricted from the pain.

I felt the gaze of every single god and Golden fall upon me, with accusation and mistrust clear in the air. Now that none of them had powers, maybe they'd start thinking of how different their lives could have been if they'd been human. And maybe they'd start listening and talking like grown-ups instead of fighting things out like kids with deadly toys.

"Who among you dared to touch the power of the gods?" Zeus' voice thundered through the Pit. I could see his body shaking from rage from where I stood.

"It doesn't matter," Archer snapped back from where he was standing over an Artemis who looked too exhausted from the torture session she'd experienced to even move. "All of you will regain access to your powers soon enough. Once we have all come to an agreement for how to go forward without the Tournament, *of course*."

Zeus and Archer stared at each other for a few tense moments during which I couldn't help but worry for him – his father might not have access to his powers for the time being, but he remained a serious threat to us and to his son.

For a second, I really thought we had managed to convince Zeus and the gods that followed him that conversation was the best option to get out of this situation. I saw Poseidon drop his trident-yielding arm down his side, which was a clear sign that the god of the ocean wasn't in fighting mode anymore. And he wasn't the only one – all of the gods standing behind Zeus seemed to be utterly confused by the loss of their powers.

For that tiny second, hope sparked in my chest.

And then all hell broke loose.

Somehow, in the middle of the chaos that had been the last ten minutes, a Golden has managed to get to the back of the VIP section of the stands, where the gods were standing. I wasn't sure how the Golden had managed to walk in the middle of the gods so easily, but here he was, standing right behind Zeus.

And the man must have wanted to ignite an all-out war because he tapped on Zeus' shoulder, waited a second until the god shifted around, and punched Zeus straight in the jaw.

Damn. I would have been lying if I'd said it wasn't satisfying to see the shock and pain in Zeus' eyes as he cradled his jaw with one hand. I doubted the god had ever been punched in his life. And gods knew he deserved it after all of the pain he'd put Archer through over the years.

Sadly, the gleeful satisfaction I felt was short-lived. Even from where I stood, half of the arena away from him, I saw the rage fill Zeus' eyes.

Half a second later, Bella whimpered next to me and Zeus' power exploded out of him. Lightning struck the sand of the arena in quick successions, making the ground shake under my feet. Behind me, the witches screamed something I couldn't understand over the deafening thunder. It must have been a call to action, though, because a new air barrier appeared over our heads, protecting most of our group from the magical attack.

Next to me, Bella was shaking under the strain of her magic. She wouldn't be able to keep her hold onto the powers of the other gods for much longer, and she sure wouldn't be able to siphon Zeus' powers again.

We were in serious trouble, but hopefully the air barrier would protect—

My eye caught on Sadie who was standing the farthest away from the rest of our group of Coppers. She still had her skeletons around her, and she was unleashing them toward the gods. She looked like goddess, with her hair flowing in the breeze and her eyes glowing. She was a warrior who stood her ground even as lightning struck the sand mere yards away from her.

She wasn't under the protective dome that the witches had created. There was nothing protecting her from Zeus' attacks.

"Sadie!" I screamed for her, but my voice got lost in the chaos of the battle.

I looked up for a half second and saw Zeus' eyes narrow as he realized that Sadie wasn't under the protective dome. And right then, I knew that he was going to take advantage of that.

Even if I'd been able to run – which I couldn't do with my whole chest in pain from the arrow – I never would have been able to reach Sadie in time. She was too far from me, from safety. And there was nothing I could do as Zeus' lightning hit her.

Chapter Forty

Kalani

I watched Sadie fall to the ground in slow motion. A scream caught in my throat, quickly followed by a sob.

She wasn't moving.

Maybe I was too far away from her to be able to tell if she was breathing. Yes, that had to be it. I was too far to be able to see her chest rise and fall, but she was breathing. She had to be breathing.

Right?

Sadie wasn't going to die here, in the Pit. She wouldn't abandon us. This wasn't how her story ended.

But even as I tried to reassure myself that Sadie was fine, panic was overwhelming me.

I watched as Søren ran to his sister and my heart thundered faster as the thought that he might get hit too, now. Would we lose both Aska twins today? Perhaps we never should have gone on this fool's errand. The Tournament had been in place for decades, so why did we believe that we could change the system?

Just as Søren reached Sadie and knelt by her side, the temperature of the air around us dropped suddenly. It was cold enough that I could see my breath in the air, and I started shivering.

"If you dare to harm a single hair on my children's heads, I will end you, Zeus."

The voice was coming from behind us. Thanatos, god of Death, had thinned the veil between the living and the dead. And he was angry.

I wasn't sure when Thanatos and a small group of other deities had arrived, but they were far enough away from the fight that they had gone unnoticed by all of us, including Bella when she'd siphoned everyone's powers.

The chill in my bones had nothing to do with the cold — it was a reflection of the fear that captured my heart as I felt Death all around me.

Everyone was silent now, waiting with bated breath as the chill of the Underworld covered the Pit. Except for Zeus, of course.

"This is not your place, Thanatos. They are traitors to Olympus, and they deserve to pay for they hubris."

The god of Death didn't back down, though. As I shifted to look at him, I saw more than a few gods standing beside him, clearly in opposition to Zeus' rule.

"I disagree, Zeus." Thanatos' voice was powerful in a cold, hypnotic way. "All of us have obeyed you for centuries, including your order to keep the existence of other magical users on Earth a secret from our children and grandchildren. The time has come for all of us to face the truth and the consequences of our actions."

If we had needed further evidence that all of the gods had known about the existence of magical beings without ichor in their veins and had kept it as a dirty little secret, we had it now.

The clouds above our heads became darker as Zeus' temper rose again. But this time it wasn't Coppers or Goldens attacking him – it was fellow deities. Unsurprisingly, Zeus seemed more hesitant to use force, now.

"Are you defying me, Thanatos?" Zeus hollered, rage pouring from each word.

I gave a quick look in the twins' direction, just long enough to see Søren trying to carry his sister to safety. I wished I could go and help, but he had things in hand, and there were a lot of moving pieces around us.

"I am refusing to go along with this madness. The children are right. The Tournament is not necessary for our survival. It's high time that we do what is right, and forcing children to fight and die is wrong."

Behind Thanatos, a god with a dark crown resting on onyx hair stepped up and put a hand on the god of Death's shoulder. This was a clear sign of support from who I was pretty sure was Hades, king of the Underworld.

"Brother, it might be time to advance with our time, don't you think?" Hades asked Zeus with a raised eyebrow. "The Underworld is becoming quite crowded with the souls of young Coppers and I'd like to have a few decades of rest."

Silence fell upon the Pit. All of us were holding our breaths, wondering whether the support of a few of the gods would turn the tide in our favor or not.

Zeus swiped his gaze over the crowd of Goldens in the stands, then over the group of Coppers in the middle of the Pit, and finally over the smaller group of deities who were on our side.

As he assessed the situation, his jaw clenched, and he frowned in the same way his son did when he was coming to terms with a difficult realization.

There was some muttering behind him, coming from some of the gods who were probably irked that their powers were out of reach or that they were being backed against a metaphorical wall by their descendants. However, Zeus stopped all complaints with a single hand raised up.

My breath caught in my chest as I waited for his decision. If he decided that negotiating was still below him, then we would be forced to—

"Fine. I do understand that times have changed, and now that new information has been revealed to us," he insisted on the 'new' as if to pretend like this was all in good faith and he hadn't know about the existence of other magic-users, "I am willing to listen to my subjects' wishes. I promise to discuss and seriously consider the option of providing a new, safer way for Coppers to be trained while remaining on Earth with some Goldens, Coppers, and other magic-user representatives."

A few deities around Zeus started arguing, but he stopped them again with a simple finger held in the air.

"Until a decision is reached, I promise that every Copper and magic user present illegally on Mount Olympus right now will be granted temporary residency on Olympus. No harm will come to you unless you actively break any of this land's rules."

There were a few tentative sighs of relief behind me from some of the Coppers. All of us could feel how close we were to success, but things still felt very unsure.

"How can we be sure that you and the other gods will seriously consider our demands and work with us to reach a decision that will satisfy everyone?" Archer called out.

Zeus inhaled in a way that told me that he didn't appreciate being questioned, but he remained calmer than usual.

"I also promise on Lethe that I, and the other Olympians I invite to participate in the discussions, will do our best to accommodate your demands and enable Coppers to remain on Earth, so that they do not have to fight for their survival. Does that calm your worries, Archer?"

Zeus' tone was slicing, and the way he pronounced his son's name – with resentment and frozen anger – gave me chills.

The god of Death must have liked the direction that Zeus had taken because the temperature of the Pit increased by a few degrees. It was still cold, but nowhere near frostbite-cold anymore.

Zeus ignored Thanathos' show of power and kept his eyes firmly on us.

Archer shifted to look at each of us – me, his mom, Søren, Nafula, Ken, Thomas, Bella, Kawehi, Jared, and finally the vampires. All of us nodded.

"Good. We'll accept. Let's discuss."

Relief washed over me like a strong wave, but I couldn't shake the worry I had for Sadie.

Around me, Coppers and magic users congratulated each other with tears of relief in their eyes while still keeping a worried eye on the gods. None of us would truly feel safe here until Zeus' words were followed by action. However, I couldn't appreciate the win, and before anyone could congratulate me, I was limping toward Søren who was still bend over a motionless Sadie.

Each step was a battle against the pain that was radiating from my shoulder, the world spinning around me, but I still made it to the Aska twins.

"Søren," I whispered through a half-clenched jaw. "Is she…"

I couldn't get myself to say it. I couldn't say the words 'alive' or 'dead', or even 'breathing'. Sadie couldn't be anything but okay. I refused to even put those words out in the world – gods knew I wasn't about to tempt the Fates that way.

Søren looked up slowly, silent tears streaking his face. For a second, I felt the world stop moving and a ringing started echoing in my head. *No. No, she couldn't be—*

The blond Golden nodded slowly and a shuddering breath left both of our chests. The relief was so potent that I felt my whole body shut down. We were alright. We had made it – at least, we had managed to get one step closer to freedom for all Coppers. And we were all going to leave the Pit alive, this time. At least, I hoped so, I thought as I felt myself fall to the ground.

Before I could crash on the sand, strong arms caught me and then I was airborne. Fighting to keep my eyes open, I met Archer's worried gaze.

"What did I tell you, Mayfield? You need to stop getting hurt. It's upsetting me."

I wanted to laugh at Archer's poor attempt at humor, but my chest was constricting so much that I could barely breathe.

"It's not like I'm actively seeking out danger or asking for people to shoot me," I choked out.

"I know, Mayfield." He dropped his forehead to mine, his eyes burning with something that looked like a mix of anger, pride, and love. "But every time you find yourself in danger, I'll be there to destroy your enemies and catch you when you fall."

The pain was too much then, and I felt myself drift to a dreamless sleep. Right before everything went dark, I felt Archer's arms tighten, bringing my body closer to his chest.

"Us against the world, Mayfield. You'll fight for your dreams and I'll make sure no one hurts you again. I promise."

Somehow, I survived Artemis' arrow to the shoulder and Sadie survived a direct hit of Zeus' powers. How we'd taken the Greek gods by storm and survived, I didn't know.

But we had. We had managed to make the gods listen and bend their rules. Now, we just needed to finish the job and ensure the Tournament never happened again.

So, as soon as the both of us could stand without debilitating pain and hold a conversation, Sadie and I joined the negotiations. Zeus had promised that there would be opportunities for us to plead our cases and discuss options for the management of Coppers, and he thankfully didn't go back on his word.

For almost three weeks, we met in one of Zeus' palace meeting rooms and discussed how we could make things work for everyone. Zeus, Athena, Hermes, Poseidon, and Hades were representing Olympus' interests. Ken, Bella, Thomas, and Liam were there as the Coppers' spokespeople. Priya and two others Goldens whose names I couldn't for the life of me remember were there to represent the Goldens of Olympus. My grandma, Jared, and both vampires were there to add explanations on how so many magic-users lived on Earth safely, controlling their magic so well that no one ever wondered if magic was possible.

And then the Aska twins, Nafula, Archer, and I were there as moral support and as a link between the people of Olympus and the people of Earth. We were also the only ones who had experienced the cruelty and horrors of the Tournament first-hand, so we were in a great position to fight for its dismantlement.

However, coming to an agreement when there were over twenty people in a room, all with strong personalities and the conviction that they were fighting for their survival and values wasn't easy. Far from it, actually.

We argued, we bickered, we pleaded, and we came close to all-out fights more times than I could count. Getting rid of the institution of the Tournament meant changing the ways the gods had dealt with their numerous progeny – and their progeny's children – for centuries. The Tournament reflected not only a law that solved the overpopulation problem on Olympus, but also how Olympians had dealt with conflict for millennia – with violence and power hierarchies.

Many times, I worried that we would never get to any kind of agreement that would help the Coppers. When heated arguments exploded in the meeting room, I worried that everything we had done and fought for would explode in our faces. When emotions ran high, I worried that we had brought the Coppers here to be used and abused by the gods in a pride war.

Still, we fought and argued and compromised. We did our best to convey to the gods that the Tournament was outdated and unnecessary. We brainstormed solutions and negotiated for every bit of change. And all of it was worth it, because when we went back to the Copper training compound every night, the hope shining in the Coppers' eyes was priceless.

Chapter Forty-One

Sadie

The moment Athena announced that we had reached an agreement, that the laws of Olympus were officially changed to protect all Coppers, now and still to come, my breath left my chest in relief.

We had done it.

We had won.

We had fought. We had bled and cried. We had hoped and lost so much. Much more than we should have ever been forced to lose.

But we had done it.

We had won.

No one would ever need to fight in the Tournament ever again. No one would ever walk in the Pit, knowing that they were going to die in front of thousands of people. And no one would ever come out of the Pit with the blood of their peers on their hands.

I wished this moment could erase everything that had happened to me – to us, my friends and I – a few months ago. But it couldn't. Destroying the Tournament was the best thing we had ever done, but it would never bring Mei back, nor would it ever make us forget that we'd killed in there.

But we had survived. And no one would ever die like Mei had.

The blood of Coppers would never stain the sand of the Pit ever again.

I couldn't quite believe it. Seeing this new law in writing, witnessing Zeus sign it in front of me, was surreal.

When I brushed my fingers over my cheeks, they were met with tears. So many tears. And I wasn't sure if they were tears of joy or sadness. They felt like a bit of both, like the relief of having managed the feat of destroying the Tournament had brought to the forefront of my mind everything I'd endured in the past few months.

"It's over," Kalani murmured with awe, her left hand that wasn't in a sling reaching for mine and holding on tight.

It was over. The fighting, the constant worry of losing another one of my friends, the unending guilt in my chest, it was all over. Although, that last part would take some time to heal.

"It's over," I repeated, my brain still trying to process everything and catch up to my emotions.

On my other side, Søren doubled over, his shoulders shaking with quiet tears. At that sight, my heart broke for him. My twin had never been the kind to show vulnerability – he preferred to laugh things off and pretend like life was a joke. He hadn't cried in the aftermath of Mei's death, or at least not that any of us had seen. But now that we had officially ensured that our edition of the Tournament had been the last, that no one would die the way Mei had… well, emotions were finally spilling over for Søren.

Things were better between us since we had found each other again on Earth, but I still wasn't sure if he would want me to comfort him. After all, Mei had died so that I could live. It made things complicated.

Dropping Kalani's hand so she could go to Archer, I rested a gentle palm against my brother's trembling shoulder. For a second, he stilled, and I worried that he would reject me. I would understand if he did – grief was a complex thing, and I could understand that he loved me but that my presence reminded him of some of his worst memories.

But instead of flinching away, Søren put a hand over mine, holding it against his shoulder. And then he turned around, wrapping his arms around me, his tears wetting my neck.

"Do you think she would be proud?" he whispered, so low that only I could hear.

My heart clenched at the pain in his voice, and I held him tighter. "Of course, she would be proud."

We remained this way for long moments, relying on each other the way we hadn't done in months. And while our relationship had forever changed after the Tournament ended, I could tell that things were getting back to a good place.

"I needed that," Søren murmured as he finally stepped away from me, a sad smile on his face.

I nodded at him, hoping he could see on my face all of the things I wanted to tell him but couldn't when there were so many people around. And then, as Søren started walking to Archer, I felt it – the need to leave that had been building in my chest since the moment Athena had announced that we had come to an agreement.

I needed to announce it to Matteo. *Now.*

This thought should have scared me. I should have wanted to celebrate with my friends that had been with me throughout all of this fight. I should have wanted to fall into Kalani's arms, continue to comfort Søren, congratulate Nafula, and hug Archer.

But all I wanted was to tell Matteo that he was safe.

So, I left the room. Everyone was still congratulating each other, but I couldn't stay. I needed to go and find him. Tell him that he didn't need to fight anymore, that he wouldn't ever be hunted down and forced to flee his home.

Before I could even realize it, I was running. Sprinting out of the palace and down the mountain in the direction of the Copper training compound. I wasn't sure I had ever run so fast – not even during the third trial of the Tournament, when I'd been chased by a hellhound hybrid down the Pit.

The run was a bit of a blur. By the time the cool air of the inside of the compound brushed my flushed cheeks, I was breathless, but I didn't stop running. I sprinted by Coppers who looked at me with surprise. Hallway after hallway, I searched for dark curls and the olive skin of the man who had unknowingly helped me find myself again.

As the seconds and minutes passed without sight of Matteo, my heart pounded louder and louder from anxiousness. Where was he? Had something happened to him? Had one of the deities decided to go against Zeus' rules that no one could harm the Coppers until a decision had been taken by the groups of representatives?

Where in the stars was that man?

My hands were shaking as I entered the cafeteria and looked around for Matteo. There were two groups of Coppers sitting at the tables and he wasn't—

"Sadie?" a low voice I knew by heart asked from behind me.

I spun and there he was, his brows frowned in worry. With one assessing look, I hunted for any wound he might have and found none. He was fine. We were both fine.

"Are you okay? Did you guys finish your meetings earlier than usual, today?" he wondered, taking a step closer to me.

I opened my mouth to answer but no sounds came out. My throat was so tight with emotions that I couldn't speak, not when Matteo was staring at me with so much concern in his dark eyes.

So, instead of explaining everything that had happened, I rushed forward and wrapped my arms around him, hugging him tight.

Startled, he stood still for a second before closing his arms over me and hugging me back with the perfect combination of strength and gentleness. The way my body melted into his should have been illegal. And I wasn't too proud to admit that my heartbeat slowed, and my chest became lighter as I felt Matteo there, in my arms.

"I am not complaining at all, because I love a good hug, especially from you," Matteo murmured in my hair. "But what is this for?"

Taking a deep breath of Matteo's earthy scent, I took a small step back and looked up into his warm eyes. I didn't want to miss a single micro expression on his face as he learned that his fight was over.

"It's over. We won." My eyes watered through a growing smile as Matteo's eyebrows raised in surprise. "There will never be a Tournament again. Ever."

Watching Matteo's face as he processed the information was a beautiful experience. I saw the shock in his eyes, followed by a mix of joy, sorrow, and hope. So much hope.

A laugh trickled out of his chest as he wrapped his arms around me and spun me in the air, and then I was laughing, too. "We did it! *You* did it," Matteo exclaimed with so much awe that it made my heart swell.

And then his lips were on mine.

It was like a surge of electricity running through my whole body. For a second, I was surprised by the kiss – Matteo had been taunting me with the promise of a kiss for weeks, now, and I couldn't quite believe it was happening.

But then, Matteo's soft lips on mine, his hands on my hip and neck, and the desperation in his body language were enough to completely wipe my mind of everything except *him*.

Then everything was a blur of Matteo, and my hands were in his hair, trying to bring him closer, so close that nothing was separating us.

Stars, I wished this moment could have lasted forever. Unfortunately, my lungs weren't superhuman, and they started burning from a need for air.

Moving apart just enough to take a breath, I murmured with tingling lips, "Is that a thank-you kiss?"

The laugh that rumbled through Matteo's chest gave me shivers down my back. "No, this is a happy kiss. And a my-girl-is-incredible kiss."

"Your girl?" I breathed, unsure how a simple word could make me feel so happy inside.

Matteo put a finger beneath my chin and brought my face higher until our eyes met. "You've been mine for a while now, Zombie girl. Just like I've been yours since the moment you've let me see who you are. The real Sadie, who fights for the people she loves, ugly moves and everything. And I love that person, the one who's not afraid to be both dark and full of light." His finger slipped down my neck like a sweet caress. "Is that okay with you, sweetheart?"

The challenge in Matteo's husky voice made my spine tingle. I wasn't aware of anything around me except for the man in front of me. And my eyes were caught in the snare of the Copper's dark brown gaze.

My whole universe had narrowed until the only people left were the two of us.

"I guess that's acceptable," I teased him with smirk.

"*Just* acceptable?" he laughed softly, amused.

I knew the blush that had appeared on my cheeks and the way I still hadn't caught my breath were dead giveaways that Matteo's words were much more than acceptable.

Then we were embracing again, relishing in the happiness we felt at finally being free to be together without fear of the future.

And then we were kissing, and laughing, and I couldn't remember the last time I'd been so happy. Stars knew things had been rough for a while, and the butterflies in my stomach were a stark contrast to the constant worry I had felt for months. Years.

But as I celebrated with Matteo, as the rest of my chosen family joined us and we laughed and cried and hoped together, I knew everything would be fine.

There were still a lot of things to do. We had to create schools for Coppers on Earth, and safe ways for Coppers to train and become responsible magic users. We knew there would be pushback from the deities and some of the Goldens who had particularly enjoyed the Tournament. And our negotiations over the past couple of weeks had allowed us to help push for the human servants of Olympus to have more rights and freedom – but things weren't great yet. And organizing everything, making sure everyone was on the same page…

We had a lot of things left to do. So much to worry about. So many people to train and lead.

But I knew I'd be fine, because I had my family with me. My friends who had been with me for years and the new ones who already had such as big place in my heart. And now with Matteo's hand in mine, I felt happier than I had in a long, *long* time.

Epilogue

Kalani

One year later

As I walked out of the Refuge, the scents and sounds of spring assaulted my senses. Flowers, bright green grass, and chirping birds in the trees surrounded me, bringing a smile to my face.

I loved the spring. And though I missed the ocean, I loved seeing the mountains and their four seasons.

We had spent the past year turning the Refuge into a school for Coppers. The purpose of the place was the same at its core – a safe place for Coppers. But instead of hiding away from the gods of Olympus, the Coppers within the Refuge were learning how to use their magic safely.

To say it had been a challenge would be an understatement. Getting young Coppers to trust us and want to come to our school was more complicated than it should have been. First of all, we had needed the Goldens to give us a list of their children – and unsurprisingly, quite of few hadn't been able to give us an exhaustive list. Then, reaching out to Coppers who often didn't have any idea about their upbringing and powers had led to awkward and difficult conversations.

Moreover, dismantling the Tournament hadn't been a unanimous decision on Olympus. Most Goldens and many of the gods had been satisfied at the change of laws. But the Tournament had been a big event for gambling and a demonstration of political power that some of the Goldens and deities loved. There had been – and still were – quite a few arguments and protests on Olympus demanding that the Tournament be reinstated.

And that was without even mentioning the issues that were still ongoing with the human servants still living on Olympus. They had been given more rights – such as better work conditions, higher wages, and the ability to change jobs if they wanted to – but things were still icy and complicated, especially because many of the humans wanted to be able to go back to Earth without quite realizing that all of their families were long gone.

The past year hadn't been easy, far from it. We had struggled and troubleshooted our plans. We had argued between ourselves about what to do. And we had fought and screamed at each other quite a few times while building the Refuge into something new.

Something better.

Something that will change the future of hundreds of kids.

And we were getting there. Slowly but surely, we were building a school that would teach young, teenage Coppers how to use their powers and what their people's history was.

I loved it. I loved living with my best friends and teaching young kids how to love themselves for who they were, powers and all. It felt like a full circle moment. I used to teach young kids how to do gymnastics, and now I was a teacher again, but for magic and random science classes – kids still needed normal, human education, after all.

All of us had decided to live in the Refuge for the past year – Sadie, Søren, Nafula, Archer, and I. Staying on Olympus hadn't even been a choice, not when we could make a significant change by helping the Coppers out there. And the past year had been hard but fulfilling.

If someone had told me, two years ago, that I would end up living in the Alps, building a magical community with the grandchildren of the Greek gods, I would have thought they were crazy. But here I was, teaching young teenagers about their magic, learning about my own magic from my grandmother, and building a new family with my best friends and partner.

I wasn't sure I would do it all over again if I could, not when I had lost my little brother and been forced to fight in a traumatic, deadly Tournament. I still had nightmares about the trials, about Mei and Charlie. But among all of the pain and horrors all of us had gone through, we had found happiness and peace.

Mostly.

"Hurry, we're going to miss it," Sadie whispered with excitement, tugging on Matteo's hand as we trekked through the forest.

The both of them were annoyingly in love, living on a cloud of happiness and cuddles since we had moved back in the Refuge. I often teased Sadie about it, but it was good to see her so happy. My friend deserved the sweetheart that was Matteo, and he was good for her soul. Sometimes, I still saw the pain and shadows of her past in her eyes, but they were fleeting, now.

"I can't believe he's going for it," Archer snickered as he bent his head to avoid a low tree branch.

"Why, is it so crazy to want to spend the rest of your life with the person you love?" I asked with a raised eyebrow in the direction of my boyfriend.

The man wasn't dumb – he knew right away that he had stepped into hot waters. "Come on, Mayfield, you know what I mean," he tried to butter me up with a sexy smile.

I rolled my eyes at his poor attempt at trying to backpedal, while Søren was wheezing, tears of laughter in his eyes. "Oh, man, you chose your moment," he laughed.

Nafula shushed him with a tap to his chest. "Can you guys be any louder? We're supposed to be discreet, not announce our presence to the whole world."

The two of them had become unlikely friends. They mostly bickered like old people, but they loved it. And I enjoyed seeing Søren rebuild himself after everything that had happened.

As Søren finally managed to get his laughter under control, Archer rested a hand on my low back, an uncomfortable wince on his face. "You know I want to spend the rest of my days with you, Mayfield, right?" he murmured just loud enough for me to hear.

"I know, Sunshine." And I did. We might not be the ones having a special day today, but I knew that we were *it*. We were forever.

Sadie, who was still at the head of our group with Matteo, stopped and hid behind a bush. "They're here!" she whispered with an excited tone.

I couldn't lie and say I didn't feel a little emotional as I hid behind another bush and peeked at the clearing in front of us.

It was beautiful out there, with wildflowers all over the ground. Directly across from us was a wooden arch with string lights and flower bouquets all over it. And right under the arch were Liam and Bella.

Liam had spent hours building the arch and choosing the best flowers to decorate it with. The guys had teased him for days about it, but they had also helped him with the construction.

To say Liam had taken a deep dive into Bella's romance books was an understatement. But the Copper had decided that he wouldn't do this without knowing exactly what the main characters in Bella's stories liked when it came to romantic gestures. Somehow, all of us had been recruited in the endeavor – I had never read so many rom-coms before.

I couldn't lie, though, many of these books had been awesome and I'd taken a few notes for what I hoped Archer and I could reenact.

The end product was almost perfect. The flowers, the beautiful clearing, the romantic arch, the setting sun turning the sky pink and orange... it was beautiful.

Now, Bella just had to say yes.

With a shaky breath we could see from where we were hiding, Liam gently let Bella's hands fall down from his and dropped to one knee. Bella gasped and her hands flew to her mouth as she watched Liam remove a small box from the pocket of his dark jeans.

We couldn't quite hear what was said from where we stood, but we all saw the emotion on Liam's face and the tears that ran down Bella's cheeks as she frantically nodded. A second later, she jumped into Liam's arms, almost tackling him to the ground.

Then there were tears of joy in my eyes as I jumped up and hugged Archer. And then we were all running, cheering, and entering the clearing to congratulate the newly engaged couple.

We laughed, and we jumped in excitement, and we cried together.

It was beautiful. It was friendship. And love. And a family that I had built all on my own.

That moment was more than just a proposal from one of my friends to another. It was a symbol of our win. A symbol of life and freedom.

The past few months had been filled with pain, loss, and grief. We had fought for our survival. We had bled for our freedom. And we had lost so many people along the way.

Nothing would ever fill the hole that losing Makaio had created in my heart. Nothing would patch up the scars that the deaths of Mei and Charlie had carved on my soul. Nothing would erase the terrors that still haunted my dreams every so often.

But that was okay. This life hadn't been easy – it had been downright awful at times – but it had brought me these people. They were lights in the darkness that surrounded me and made the world brighter. Better.

Against all odds, we were here, thriving.

And we would continue to thrive. We would continue to look for the light in the dark, for hope in a sea of despair, for love in a world that had done its best to crush us.

As I intertwined my fingers with Archer's and watched my friends celebrate around me, I had the ultimate conviction that we would be fine.

All of the shadows of pain behind us had made us stronger. They were links between our souls that reminded us of everything we had overcome together. They made us into a team. A family.

I looked around at my friends and my heart filled with so much love. None of the hardships we'd overcome had managed to dim the hope in our souls. The light in our eyes was still there. Still so bright that it lit up the dark around us.

We were alive. We were free. We were survivors.

So, I had no doubt that we would be fine. We had a Refuge full of kids who wanted to learn. We had a world ready for us to explore and enjoy life.

And, most importantly, we had each other.

THE END

Acknowledgments

Writing this second book was infinitely harder than it had been for my debut book, *All the Gold Between Us*. The doubts and impostor syndrome were very present throughout the whole process, and I am incredibly proud to have persevered and published *All the Secrets Within Us*. But this book wouldn't be what it is today without the help and support of so many incredible people.

First, thank you to my family for their constant support and love. Mom, Dad, and Noah (and Tampa, the sweetest puppy ever), thank you for always supporting me in my crazy adventures.

Thank you to my friends for always being there for me. Elsa, thank you for reading the very first drafts of the first few chapters and helping me figure out where I was going with this story. Kaylie, thank you for being my biggest cheerleader and for always checking in on me. And thank you to Laura for reminding me to be gentle to myself when writing was tough.

Thank you to my amazing beta readers: Emma, Anneke, and Cristina. Your feedback was incredibly helpful, and you helped make this story so much better.

Of course, I have to thank Alice Power for the incredible cover art (how do you always make these illustrations so amazing?) and Beck Michaels for the design of the final cover. You have both brought Kalani and Sadie to life!

Finally, thank you to all of you, dear readers, for giving my books a chance. I hope you have loved Kalani's story as much as I did over these past two books!

Author's Note

Thank you for reading *All the Secrets Within Us*, the second book in the *Claiming Olympus* duology. Writing this duology has been the adventure of a lifetime and I am so glad my books have found their way to your bookshelves/e-readers.

If you have enjoyed Kalani and Sadie's story, I would be very grateful if you could leave a review for this book on Amazon and Goodreads. Reviews are extremely important for us authors to reach out audience.

If you would like to be informed about new releases, translations, or other fun things, please consider signing up for my newsletter at jadelebrisauthor.com and following me on Instagram and TikTok (@jadelebrisauthor).

About the Author

Jade Le Bris is a fantasy author writing novels inspired by Greek mythology. *All the Secrets Within Us* is the second book in her debut duology, *Claiming Olympus*. During the day, she is a Doctor of Osteopathic Medicine and Microbiology PhD dual degree student at Michigan State University. Growing up in France, Jade spent twelve years writing stories before finally publishing her first book. In her free time, she enjoys reading fantasy and romance novels and watching shows with a pink drink in hand.

www.ingramcontent.com/pod-product-compliance
Lightning Source LLC
Chambersburg PA
CBHW031825310726
48972CB00005B/1168